# when the
## sparrow
## falls

neil sharpson

# when the sparrow falls

a tom doherty associates book  new york

WHEN THE SPARROW FALLS

Copyright © 2021 by Neil Sharpson

A Tor Book
Published by Tom Doherty Associates
120 Broadway
New York, NY 10271

www.tor-forge.com

Tor® is a registered trademark of Macmillan Publishing Group, LLC.

Library of Congress Cataloging-in-Publication Data

Names: Sharpson, Neil, author.
Title: When the sparrow falls / Neil Sharpson.
Description: First edition. | New York : Tor, 2021.
Identifiers: LCCN 2021008754 (print) | LCCN 2021008755 (ebook) |
    ISBN 9781250784216 (hardcover) | ISBN 9781250784223 (ebook)
Subjects: LCSH: Artificial intelligence—Fiction. | GSAFD: Science fiction. |
    Suspense fiction.
Classification: LCC PR6119.H378 W48 2021  (print) | LCC PR6119.H378
    (ebook) | DDC 823'.92—dc23
LC record available at https://lccn.loc.gov/2021008754
LC ebook record available at https://lccn.loc.gov/2021008755

Our books may be purchased in bulk for promotional, educational, or busi-
ness use. Please contact your local bookseller or the Macmillan Corporate and
Premium Sales Department at 1-800-221-7945, extension 5442, or by email at
MacmillanSpecialMarkets@macmillan.com.

First Edition: June 2021

Printed in the United States of America

0  9  8  7  6  5  4  3  2  1

*To Iola, to Donnacha and to Aoife.*
*My world.*

# when
## the
# sparrow
# falls

# prologue

shall begin with the hanging of Leon Mendelssohn.

There. It's decided.

My beloved wife is a writer, and she warned me that finding a place to begin is the hardest part of telling any story. In this, as in everything else, she has been proven correct. For a long time I was going to begin with the founding of the Caspian Republic, some ninety-four years ago, or with my own birth in that same misbegotten country three years later. But the first approach risked history (which I have no desire to write) and the second risked autobiography (which I assure you, you have no desire to read). So we will begin with a clear, bright, quite savagely cold day in September when poor old Mendelssohn was brought out into the courtyard before a crowd of party functionaries, union representatives and one journalist, and hanged from his neck while they watched and shuffled their feet against the cold.

They were not the kind of people who flinched from violence. Every man and woman among them knew that the Caspian Republic was the guardian of something immeasurably precious, the last dying embers of the human race. And to protect its people from the Infernal Machine, the state—like any state—had to be willing to kill. The apparatchiks of the Caspian Republic attended shootings with the same regularity that the leaders of other, more decadent nations attended policy seminars. But a shooting is one thing: a hanging quite another. There hadn't been a hanging in Caspian for decades, and a new gallows had to be constructed from scratch. It stood there in the courtyard, hideously new and appallingly clean. For some inscrutable reason it had been painted a bright sky blue as if to make sure that no one could look away from it, and it imposed itself on the vision of the onlookers with a horrible, irresistible vividness. There's a special horror in seeing a brand-new gallows, just beginning its long, ghastly life.

Mendelssohn was brought out into the cold morning air and his appearance shocked even those of the crowd who were in high places in State Security and its implacable rival, the Bureau of Party Security. These were men who, by the very nature of their work, were used to seeing the human body in states of extremity, and yet even they flinched when they saw the creature that was brought out with a guard supporting one arm and a priest the other.

Mendelssohn had always been thin, but now those who saw him must have wondered where the muscles *were* that allowed him to feebly stagger out into the bright harsh sun which seemed to freeze rather than warm. His bright blue eyes now glinted from the depths of two cavernous sockets, and his once thick mane of brown hair was so wispy and brittle that it seemed as if a strong breeze might shave him to the scalp. His beard, too, had gone feral and grown over his lips, and the dried remains of his last meal clung there, a bowl of thin gray soup that he had drunk ravenously at the breaking of dawn. I have no reason to love any of the people who watched Leon Mendelssohn die that morning, but I will still assume that they felt pity for him. He was one of them, after all. Or had been. He had once been one of the leading intellectual lights of the party, one of the few among them who could still make the principles of the revolution feel noble and romantic, who could still sing the old songs in tune. He could write poetry, while the rest of them struggled with prose.

All in the past now. He had fallen too far, and now there was nothing left to do but fall the last six feet.

Standing on the gallows, Mendelssohn gave the crowd a sad little smile as the noose was lowered down over a neck scarcely thicker than the rope.

"Don't worry friends," he said softly. "We'll see each other soon."

The priest who had followed him out of his cell nodded approvingly, completely unaware just what Mendelssohn meant by these words and just as unaware of the personal jeopardy he placed himself in by agreeing with them.

Why did they hang him? Because they loved him, and he had betrayed them.

To simply shoot him would have been to render him one of the anonymous thousands. But this was Leon Mendelssohn. We kept him by our bedsides and read him to our children. His famous passage on the nature of love from *Elijah's Chariot* had been read at half the weddings in Caspian for almost thirty years.

His contribution to the life of the state was immense. His betrayal, indescribable.

So the state hanged him, to make the point clear.

Barbaric though it may seem, hanging can be the most merciful form of execution if performed competently. But the conditions were not favorable. No hanging had been performed in many decades, as I have said, and even if the noose had been expertly tied, Mendelssohn was simply too light. He hung there for perhaps two minutes, transforming before the eyes of the assembled crowd from a dignified, learned man to a panicked, choking animal, and lastly to an object, hanging silently in the wind.

None of the party faithful said anything. Nobody wished to be a main character in this particular play. All were content to be extras.

If you look at the pictures that were taken of the hanging, study the faces of those people: gray and lumpy and anonymous as a row of unwashed potatoes. But, standing among them you will see another man. In his late thirties but still with a youthful zeal on his features, bald, sallow skinned and with the eyes of a betrayed lover, burning with hatred and love gone septic.

This was the journalist Paulo Xirau, and he was the only one of his profession permitted to attend the hanging. Journalists, as a rule, are not trusted in places like the Caspian Republic. Those that *are* have gone to great lengths to prove their loyalty. Paulo had most assuredly done that. In fact, looking back at my time in the Caspian Republic, I find myself asking: Did *anyone* believe as much as he did? In the party, in the principles the nation was founded on? Did anyone hate as much, believe as passionately, pledge their life and body and soul to the Caspian Republic as fervently as he did? I doubt it. Which is tragic, when you consider the truth about him.

In my better moments, I pity him. I once met a theologian who described Hell as "a small room and enough time to think about how much you hate yourself." Paulo Xirau entered that room a long time ago, and barred the door.

Everyone there knew Xirau and Mendelssohn. They knew why Xirau was trusted and Mendelssohn had been killed. But even they, I hope, were shocked when he broke the line of anonymous party hacks to stand in front of the still-swinging body of Mendelssohn and fire a thick, yellow glob of sputum onto his chest. Then, as if he had exorcised himself of some malign spirit, he calmly strode out of the courtyard, stopping only to exchange a polite, wordless smile with some high-ranking party member or other.

Nobody said anything. But that night, four members of the Senior Administrative Council of the State Security Agency met in the parlor of Augusta Niemann, the StaSec Deputy Director. And there, with tongues loosened by Niemann's still-impressive-if-dwindling stock of pre-embargo brandy, they bravely declared in whispered tones that, whatever about politics, just forgetting politics for *one second*, Xirau had crossed a line. Everyone agreed, each more vigorously than the last, that Mendelssohn had to die. But spitting on his corpse? Completely uncalled for.

"Have you ever felt . . . ," Niemann began, and everyone in the room readied themselves to feel whatever it was that Niemann was about to ask them to feel, ". . . that there was something *off* about Paulo Xirau?"

It is a rare gift, in a nation like the Caspian Republic, to be able to speak the truth. And Niemann's guests received with even more gratitude than they had received her brandy the opportunity to plainly say at last that:

Yes.

God.

There was something unquestionably, undeniably *off* about Paulo Xirau.

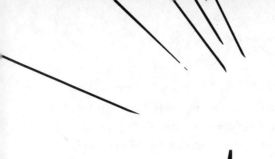

**1**

**Contran**
kɒn/Tran/

<small>NOUN</small>
1. A procedure whereby a consciousness is transferred from an organic body to an artificial server, or vice versa, using the Sontang process.
  *"Following her accident, a contran was carried out and she was safely uploaded."*

<small>VERB</small>
2. The act of digitally transferring one's consciousness from the physical realm to a virtual environment or vice versa.
  *"If I had the money, I'd contran myself to the Ah! Sea."*
          —*Oxford English Dictionary,* 5th Edition

It was a month after they'd hanged old Mendelssohn that two bodies were found in a small, grimy bedroom in Old Baku. The neighborhood then, as now, was mostly Russian-speaking, which was why I was sent to investigate along with my superior, Special Agent Alphonse Grier. I had some (admittedly rusty) Russian which I had inherited from my mother, as well as near-sightedness and a long nose. Caspian was a nation of immigrants and Grier's family were originally German, but he spoke only a particularly clipped and irritated dialect of English. For this reason, I was useful in investigations in Old Baku, and for that reason only. At least, according to Grier.

Grier rapped on the door, which was opened by an old Russian man with a magnificent white beard and sad, rheumy eyes. He froze. He had called us, but he still froze at the sight of us. StaSec had that effect on people. ParSec had quite a different one. People did not freeze when they saw ParSec coming. They ran.

"Jakub Smolna?" Grier barked.

Smolna nodded nervously.

"I am Special Agent Alphonse Grier with State Security, this is my colleague Agent South. Where are the bodies please?"

Smolna looked at us both, his eyes darting from one to the other in silent panic.

Grier gave an exasperated sigh and elbowed me in the ribs. With a jolt, I realized what was being asked of me and searched for the necessary Russian.

"*Tela*," was the best I could muster.

Smolna nodded, and gestured for us to step inside.

Grier did not like me, and was entirely within his rights. I had been a security agent in StaSec for twenty-nine years by then. I had only ever been promoted once, which Grier took to mean that I was considered politically unpopular, and I attended party meetings only the absolute minimum number of times that a person of my grade was required to, which Grier took to mean I was disloyal. For that reason, from the hour I had been assigned to him as his partner, he had regarded me like an old grenade found under his floorboards that could go off at any moment. I've found myself mellowing to Grier over the years. He had a family: a wife and two sons. That colors things. It's easy to be kind, when ParSec aren't perched on everyone's shoulder. Everyone in Caspian had an invisible rope, tying them to someone else. If I had been pulled down for disloyalty, quite possibly he and his entire family would have been yanked along with me.

I've just realized that I've been talking about Grier as if he's dead. But he could still be alive. Stranger things have happened, after all. All kinds of people are still alive.

The Paria twins, Yasmin and Sheena, had done their best with the room. Over the discolored patches of mold on the wall they had hung pictures of the two of them embracing and smiling big, honest, generous grins. To mask the damp scent of Smolna's old carpet there were vases of flowers, and in the light of the many candles strewn about the mantelpiece and tables, I could imagine that the room might even have looked cozy and homelike.

The twins themselves lay on the bed, facing each other. In Russian, I asked Smolna to identify the bodies, and he pointed to Yasmin, left, and Sheena, right. He didn't seem entirely certain, however, and I couldn't blame him.

Yasmin's eyes were closed, and Sheena's were open, but other than that they were mirror images of each other. Yasmin's face looked blissful and at peace. Sheena stared unblinkingly at a discolored patch of plaster in the wall. She had a tiny, perfectly round mole under her right eye, which I mentally filed away to distinguish her from her sister. The arrangement of their bodies suggested exactly what I imagine it was supposed to suggest, two sisters having a nap together after a long, hard day. Everything, from the way Sheena's ankles were crossed to the way Yasmin had used her right hand as a pillow under her cheek, made it look like they were simply resting. They were both quite dead. Ascertaining the cause of death was why Grier and I were there: to see if this was murder, or something worse.

Smolna was clearly uncomfortable being in the same room as the bodies, so I took him into the corridor and asked him some questions while Grier stood motionless in the center of the room, as if attempting to absorb the room's mysteries via osmosis. Smolna knew little, or was pretending to know little, and I did not have the energy to badger him. I told him to wait in the kitchen and returned to the bedroom, and Grier and I got to work.

Despite our mutual animosity we worked well together, in our way. Neither of us were young men, but my eyesight was better (at close range at least), so it was my job to examine the bodies while Grier rummaged through the personal effects of the sisters and tried to assemble a picture of their lives.

Grier had a deep, booming voice and in another life might have made a good actor. He had presence and a love of being the center of attention. As I examined the bodies, Grier recited a monologue of his own composition: "Sheena and Yasmin Paria. Twenty-eight. Non-party. Born in Nakchivan. Twins. Traitors to their country and all mankind question mark."

"No signs of violence," I murmured. "Pills perhaps? Suicide?"

"Wouldn't that be nice?" Grier answered. "For once? How did they afford it, South? If you had the money to do it, why would you live here?"

"Perhaps they had the money *because* they lived here?" I offered. "Benefits of frugal living?"

"Did Smolna say where they worked?" he asked.

I shook my head as I examined Yasmin's body, and the motion caused her limp hand to slip off her shoulder and gently land on that of her sister. Jakub Smolna was a landlord who respected the privacy of his tenants, and did not care how they made rent as long as they did.

"Hostesses?" Grier asked, using the usual euphemism. I shook my head again. Smolna had said that the Parias did very occasionally have male visitors, but nothing to suggest there was anything entrepreneurial going on. It would not have been enough to live on. Sex was appallingly cheap these days, I reminded Grier.

"You forget, South," said Grier, in a distant sort of voice. "Twins. Well, enough of their bodies, where are their souls?"

I stopped. On the back of Yasmin's neck was a small, neatly applied patch of makeup, less than a centimeter squared. Whoever had applied it had clearly done so with great care but the makeup they had chosen was ever so slightly too light for Yasmin's skin tone, drawing attention to that which they wished to conceal. With my thumb I smeared the makeup away, revealing a small, jagged puncture wound. It had been made by a device, illegal even in its country of origin. This wound, I knew, was a well. Tiny in width, but so deep that it extended through her skull and right into the gray matter of her brain. And I knew that if I were to check Sheena's neck I would find an identical wound.

Grier had asked where their souls were.

I turned to look at him and simply gave him a nod. Grier sighed, genuinely disappointed. "So," he said. "Sheena and Yasmin Paria. Twenty-eight. Twins. Traitors to their country and all mankind. Period."

Without another word, he wearily trod out of the room, and I heard the stairs creak under his heavy frame as he headed out to the car to radio StaSec HQ.

I turned to look at the two bodies on the bed.

"Why did you do it?" I murmured to myself.

I felt betrayed by what the Paria twins had done. This was not the first contran I had borne witness to, not the tenth or the hundredth or the five hundredth, but this one felt like a point of inflection. We were the last true human beings and our numbers were dwindling. I looked around the room and studied the pictures of the Parias as they were in life: young, vital and beautiful. In Sheena's and Yasmin's eyes I saw intelligence and joy and a love of life. I saw all the things that the nation could not afford to lose. When I turned to look at the bodies on the bed, I saw two steps further down the road to extinction.

I had long, long ago given up on the idea that the Caspian Republic would ever live up to its ideals, to be a place where human beings could live in freedom and happiness. But I had not given up on the ideals themselves, and the Parias had. They had turned their backs on humanity, and surrendered to the Machine. I felt anger at their betrayal, but also pity. Could I really blame them for thinking that a better life was waiting for them in the Machine world? What life was there here for them, really?

"Why did you do it?" I had asked their lifeless bodies. But, as I looked out the window at the gray, sulking streets of Ellulgrad, buzzing like a hive with hunger, poverty and violence, a treasonous question arose unbidden to my lips:

"What took you so long?"

# 2

The Caspian Republic is located on the eastern shore of the Caspian Sea and occupies almost the entirety of the historic territory of the now-defunct Republic of Azerbaijan as well as the province of Syunik, seized from the Armenian Republic during the brief Caspian-Armenian War of 2158. Following waves of inward migration in response to the AI Revolution, tensions between the local Azerbaijani and the New Humanists erupted into open violence, culminating in the overthrow of the government and the seizing of the Azerbaijani capital of Baku (renamed Ellulgrad) in 2154. The New Humanist Party has maintained total control of all political power in the nation since its founding, and espouses a militantly Organic Supremacist and Anti-AI ideology. A recent UN report ranked Caspian as one of the "least free" nations in the world. The United States government has also named the Caspian Republic as a state sponsor of terrorism, with the Ellulgrad government known to have supported Organic Supremacist groups in many nations, including the United States.

—*CIA Sourcebook* entry on the Caspian Republic

ontran" we called it, an ugly contraction of the even uglier "Consciousness Transferal," and there were procedures to be followed.

Grier and I stood outside of Smolna's doorway, Grier smoking some ghastly cheap Russian cigarette as we waited for the ambulance that would take the Parias to the morgue. There, they would be examined before burial in an unmarked grave, two more secrets to be hidden in the soil of the Caspian Republic. Such secrets formed the very bedrock of the nation. They were the ground we walked upon. Grier and I would make our reports, which would be checked and double-checked and cross-checked.

As the bodies of the two women were loaded into the ambulance, Grier scanned the windows above us like a lion scanning the savanna and several curtains twitched beneath his glare. We watched the ambulance pull away and Grier dropped his cigarette and stamped on it.

"We'll have to tell The Bastards, of course," Grier said. "The Bastards" were Party Security.

"The Parias weren't party members," I said feebly.

"How charming that you think they'd care," Grier replied sourly. He was right. Technically, any crime, even contran, that was not committed by a member of the party was outside of ParSec's jurisdiction. And yet ParSec would nonetheless be tearing Smolna's home apart by nightfall, and quite likely tearing Smolna apart in their headquarters at Boyuk Shor.

Grier fired his thumb at Smolna, who watched us nervously from the doorway. "Tell him not to go anywhere," he said and got into the car.

I approached Smolna who looked at me like a child wanting to be reassured that they had done nothing wrong.

Taking care to ensure that Grier was not silently looming over my shoulder, I whispered to him in Russian, "There will be others, coming. 'ParSec,' yes?"

Even speaking the word was a form of assault. Smolna blanched and his pupils seemed to shrink.

"I would advise being elsewhere when they arrive," I mumbled, and I turned on my heel and walked to the car.

The drive back was a tense affair. I couldn't shake the feeling that Grier knew what I had done. Warning Smolna had been reckless. If ParSec caught him (and they would) he would give them my name. I might find two gullivers waiting in my kitchen for me by the time I got home tonight, idly toying with knives and batons in the darkness. Or maybe they'd do nothing. My name might be squirreled away in some file, waiting in the dark to be discovered, like a cancer in remission.

Grier said nothing, his underbite jutting out aggressively as he tried to leave the filthy winding streets of Old Baku without running over an urchin. A contran case was guaranteed to put Grier in a bad mood. A simple murder or suicide meant a day of paperwork. But a contran was not simply a criminal matter, it was a security matter. A military matter. A party matter. A government matter. No fewer than nine separate agencies and bodies would have to be notified, all with their own unique and gallingly obtuse methods of notification. Nobody *wanted* to know of course (with the obvious exception of The Bastards), but Grier still had to tell them. And of course, this was not one case of contran, but two. As the agent in charge, a week and a half of grueling paperwork now lay ahead of Grier, and as he gunned the engine I half wondered if he wasn't about to plow into a wall at full speed just to avoid having to do any of it. As if the thought had just occurred to me, I mentioned to Grier that since the Parias had been found in identical circumstances he simply had to write one set of paperwork for Yasmin and then replace her name with Sheena's, thereby halving his workload. Grier took his foot off the accelerator, and the car returned to a legal speed.

I watched the city go by, out of masochism more than anything. Ruined and boarded-up buildings, lines of people queuing sullenly outside a grocer's. Three bearded vagrants fought in the street, punching and biting each other with such ferocity that it was impossible to tell who was on whose side, or if there even were sides.

And there, clinging stubbornly to the carcasses of old, ruined homes, old posters. Mantras of a future long past. In English and Russian: WE ARE THE TRUE HUMAN BEINGS, ONE BODY, ONE LIFE, THE MACHINE WILL NOT REPLACE US and lastly THE TRIUMVIRATE IS . . . , the final few words having been torn away by enemies of the state, or possibly the wind. This had the effect of making the poster's message seem even more threatening.

The Triumvirate is *what*? Watching? Waiting? Plotting? Marshaling its forces for our final, total destruction? Yes. All were true.

*Those posters should be replaced,* I thought to myself. *In that condition, they bring shame to the party. They should be replaced.*

I thought that, and yet I did not think that.

For I did not give a damn about the posters, truly.

And yet the thought had come unbidden, like an unwelcome guest making itself at home in my mind.

It was an eerie phenomenon I had first noticed many years ago. What I thought of as myself, I, Nikolai South, would be trudging about his day, hunched and fearful, when a bland cheery voice in my head would offer me unsolicited advice.

That old woman is stealing from a fruit cart. Report her.

That young man. Have you seen him before in this neighborhood? Looks dark. Possibly Ajay. Suspicious.

Mrs. Jannick in the flat below yours. She speaks in hushed tones whenever she sees you coming down the stairs. What is she hiding?

I called this voice the Good Brother. I liked to pretend that he was simply a paid operative that the party had somehow managed to squirrel away in my mind when I had let my guard down.

I wondered if I was the only one who had a Good Brother. I glanced briefly at Grier, hands clenched on the steering wheel, lower jaw jutted out like a battering ram against the world. Did he have a voice of his own, chiding him, rebuking him, infuriating him?

No. Grier didn't have a Good Brother. Grier *was* a Good Brother. StaSec was full of Good Brothers. I alone had been cursed to have one living inside me.

That, at least, was what I told myself.

It was easier than admitting that these thoughts were my own, and that at least part of me was now occupied territory.

*"Why do you think of yourself as occupied?"* the Good Brother asked me. *"This is the Caspian Republic, and you are loyal, aren't you?"*

Yes. I was loyal. But I resented the price of that loyalty. I resented, above all, the fear.

Nominally, the currency of the Caspian Republic was the moneta, but in truth the coin of the nation was fear. Whoever could inspire fear was rich, whoever lived in fear was poor. Fear of StaSec, fear of ParSec, fear of hunger, fear of the Triumvirate that ruled vast swathes of the outside world. Fear of pain. Fear of loss. Fear of death.

For we were true human beings, the party told us.

Born of earth and flesh. Created in the image of God. Second only to the angels.

And as such, we suffered.

# 3

The sea change in opinion on Capitol Hill on the issue of super artificial intelligence has been sudden and decisive in the aftermath of Confucius's first six months in operation. Perhaps no better illustration of that is the fact that Senator Mark Sorenson (PD-Illinois), once considered one of the loudest voices on the dangers of SAI, is now openly advocating for an American Confucius. I asked the senator how he had learned to stop worrying and love SAI. His answer was sobering: "I haven't. I'm every bit as worried as I was five years ago, if not more so. But where we are now, asking 'Should we create super intelligent AIs?' is like asking if we should be using protection while we're going into labor. The question is pretty moot. The baby is here. China has uncorked the bottle and let the genie out and the results speak for themselves. If we do not move quickly to create an American Confucius, we are done as a global power. It's that simple."

—"An American Confucius? 'When,' Not 'If,'"
*The Washington Post*, 03 September 2149

The building that would one day become State Security Headquarters had begun its life as the Neftchilar Grand Hotel, once considered the finest hotel in Ellulgrad.

You would never have thought it to look at the place now, so perfectly did it suit its current purpose. As you mounted the grim, exhausting outer staircase, the façade loomed over you like a grim temple in a foreign land. Once inside, you were in what had once been the lobby of the hotel, and was now the reception area of StaSec. Perhaps it had been intended to impress visitors with its magnificent scale and forest of brown marble pillars that extended past the grand stairway and led one's eye toward the reception desk. But now the impression it gave was that one was an animal alone in a forest walking in plain view of anything that could be lurking in the shadows.

The ones who entered were always watched, the ones who watched were always unseen. As I say, it was difficult to imagine that the building had ever been anything but StaSec HQ.

Grier and I fell into a silent lockstep as we crossed the vast checkered marble floor, our footsteps echoing against the pillars. So vast was the space that it took a few moments to realize that we were not alone in the lobby.

Lounging against a pillar, like a weasel on the roof of a chicken coop, was Nard Wernham. He had worked under Grier before me and, as far as I could see, he was the lone human being that Grier actually seemed to like on a personal level. Wernham took his place beside Grier as he walked and it was as if I did not exist, which suited me fine. I knew the Wernhams of this world, and knew well enough not to draw their attention. Like Grier, Wernham was ex-army. He'd served in the north of the country in the Poleador Rayon. Buy him a drink and he'd start to make "jokes" about being involved in the Shaki massacre. Personally, I doubted that: He would have been only in his late teens at the time. But you can tell a lot about who a man is from the kind of man he pretends to be, and in Wernham's case I loathed both of them.

"How are you, Brother?" Wernham asked cheerily. "You look happy."

"Fuck off," Grier muttered.

Wernham tutted with mock disapproval.

"Tell me your troubles, Grier," he said, in an approximation of sympathy that he had honed over the years to a kind of rough semblance of the real thing.

"Double contran in Old Baku," Grier growled. "A banquet of shit has been laid before me, Wernham. Seven fucking courses."

"Oh well. Not to worry. You'll find the man," said Wernham. "Oh, by the way. Are you fond of Brother South, at all?"

I stopped. So did Grier. Wernham was fixing me with a shiny-eyed grin. The weasel had entered the chicken coop.

"South? What do you mean?" Grier barked.

"He's been called upstairs," said Wernham. "Niemann wants to see him."

I felt the kind of weightlessness and panic that can usually be induced only by a doctor with a grave face and a hushed voice.

"Me?" I whispered.

"South?" said Grier, incredulously.

"That's right," said Wernham. The man enjoyed pain. I wondered why ParSec hadn't snapped him up.

Grier fixed me with a cold, indifferent stare.

"I know no one by that name," he said. "I never have, and I never will."

And with that, he walked off with Wernham, who was chuckling, "I thought you might say that." I felt like my bones had turned to water. I had run through seven or eight scenarios as to what would happen when it was discovered that I had warned Smolna to run. None of them, not the worst, most bizarre, most paranoid of them had involved a summons to the office of the Deputy Director of State Security.

What could Augusta Niemann possibly want with me?

———

We called her the "deputy" director, but that was a mere technicality. The director of State Security, Samuel Papalazarou Junior, had been bedridden for eight years. Indeed, we in StaSec spoke of him, on the rare occasions we did speak of him, as someone already dead. Parliament had not had him removed from his post out of respect for his family, who were one of the great founding clans of the Caspian Republic. Instead, he lay barely conscious in his villa on the shore of the Caspian Sea, the immense power of his office pooling in the tips of his insensate fingers.

Augusta Niemann, therefore, was the unchallenged head of State Security in everything but name. As I waited outside her office, I thought how easy it would be for her to make me disappear. Niemann's secretary was typing something with great gusto on her terminal. I resisted the urge to lean over her shoulder and look for the words "warrant," "execution" and "South." The intercom on her desk crackled and I heard a feminine voice, deep and almost aristocratic, boom, "Marta? Where is South?"

Marta, the secretary, gazed blankly at the intercom and then stammered that if the Deputy Director would look out her window she would see the uppermost tower of the Ministry of Agriculture, which was (Marta believed) due south of the . . .

I cleared my throat.

"I think she means me," I said.


'm glad to see you, South," said the deputy director as I stepped into her office.

This surprised me.

"Oh?" I said, or rather, whispered.

"Yes. My secretary had led me to believe you were about five seconds away from flinging yourself off the roof of the Ministry of Agriculture. I was quite offended."

Niemann was a large woman, in her early fifties, and built like a wrestler. There was, now that I think about it, a "StaSec face." Grim, square, jaw set, perpetually irritated. Grier had it, and Niemann did, too. But there was something in her eyes that Grier decidedly lacked. A kind of merriness, buried beneath the grim façade like a pearl in snow.

"Please. Sit." She gestured to the empty chair in front of her desk. Niemann's office had once been the bridal suite when the building had been the Neftchilar Grand Hotel. As such, it boasted a magnificent view of the waterfront and more space than Niemann could ever have needed. I felt stranded as I sat down at her desk, like a rabbit on open ground, far from the nearest burrow. Slowly, deliberately, Niemann took her seat. I was waiting to hear her first word, and I had an awful premonition that it would be *Smolna*. As it turned out, I was wrong.

"We haven't met before, have we? The Christmas party, perhaps?" Niemann said. I shifted uncomfortably.

"No. I'm usually out of the city that time of year."

"I think I know you," she said. "You have an undeniable smack of familiarity about you. Stand up."

She made me stand up and turn 180 degrees so that I was facing the door. I had a sudden urge to run but my nerve held.

"There is a lot you can tell from the back of a man's head, South," I heard Niemann say behind me. "For example: You have your lunch every day, weather permitting, sitting out on the white bench on the waterfront. You bring a blue flask of soup and a sandwich. And, even with food as scarce as it is, you still tear the crust off and feed it to the seagulls. How am I doing so far, South?"

"Correct in every particular, Deputy Director," I replied.

"Do you know how I know?" she asked.

"One imagines the Deputy Director of State Security has her sources."

She laughed. Not an unpleasant sound, had the circumstances been different.

"Oh, she does. Do you think I've had you bugged and followed? Turned your friends against you? Put a camera in your bedroom mirror so I can watch you sleep?"

*Yes.* I thought. *I do think that. Everyone thinks that. It's safer that way.*

"No, Deputy Director," I said. "I think your office window overlooks the waterfront."

I couldn't see her face, but you can hear a smile, can't you?

"It's always the simplest explanation, isn't it, South?"

"As you say, Deputy Director."

"Sit down," she said.

I took my seat again. Niemann had a thin blue file in front of her, which she leafed through as if it were a particularly colorless magazine in a dentist's waiting room.

"Now," said Niemann. "Nikolai Andreivich South. Fifty-three. Twenty-nine years in the agency. Party member. Obviously. Divorced."

"Widowed," I interrupted.

Niemann glanced up at me sharply. She tapped the file with her fingernail.

"This says 'divorced,'" she said, as if that settled the matter.

For a moment, the taste of salt and sand was on my lips. "She died," I told her. "Before the papers went through. A swimming accident."

She had been pulled from the sea, cold as ice and white as snow. They had lain her on the sand and I had tried, oh God, I had tried, to breathe some life back into her. Her eyes had gazed up at me, stunned and confused in death, as if she couldn't believe that this was where we would end. *What are you doing?* she seemed to be asking. *Are you really going to let me go? Do something, Nikolai. Do something.*

"Terrible," Niemann muttered.

"Thank you," I said, somewhat surprised by her sympathy.

"These are state files, for God's sake, it is not unreasonable to expect a degree of accuracy," Niemann continued, writing a memo to herself: DISCIPLINARY ACTION RESEARCHER RE: SOUTH'S DEAD WIFE.

Ah.

"Moving on," said Niemann. "Promoted to Security Agent Grade 2 after three years. Respectable, if not spectacular. And then, following your divorce . . ."

Here she stopped, crossed a line out with a pencil and wrote in a correction.

"Following your tragic bereavement . . ." She stopped, and with a somewhat theatrical flourish, she closed the file.

"Nothing. Nothing at all. You were promoted once. You have remained at the same rank, in the same section, for the past twenty-six years. Your work has consistently been acceptable and not a jot better than that. You attend party meetings. But only the absolute minimum number required for a man in your position. You have never been heard, or overheard, or observed to say or do or think anything remotely subversive, and I would know, South. Believe me."

For a moment, her attitude of bored indifference hardened into something considerably more unnerving.

"If you had so much as a traitorous thought in your head I would have pried it out and stamped on it a long time ago. If you believe nothing else in this world, believe that."

I believed her. I believed her as much as I believed that I was here, in this room, listening to her say the words.

"And yet," she said, and the goddess of life and death was once again my bored office superior, "without exception, every supervisor you have had has commented on your almost palpable lack of zeal. You seem to have no ambition. No passion. No pride. No party connections. And, the seagulls notwithstanding, no friends from what I can see. You have toiled away, for over half a lifetime, in a tiny gray office, doing the same work you were doing when you were a young man, and doing it no better."

I felt a little dizzy. Was my work performance really so abysmal that the acting head of State Security had deemed it necessary to take time out of defending the nation to call me onto the carpet?

"Deputy Director . . . ," I mumbled.

Niemann's voice cut across mine, like a knife through jam.

"And then, four days ago. A notice goes up on the Agency's bulletin board. There is an opening, a promotion, available for Security Agent Grade 3. And while looking through the hundreds of applications of bright young things, eager for new challenges and opportunities, ready and waiting to put their lives on the line to defend this great nation, I see the name of Nikolai Andreivich South. Now why, after twenty-six years, have you decided that you deserve a promotion?"

Why indeed?

I remembered that morning well. I had incautiously glanced at my desktop calender and been struck with the sudden, impossible realization that Olesya had been dead twenty years. And I had realized that I would not survive another twenty years like them. Something had to change.

"Deputy Director, I entered the competition on a whim," I said. "I did not expect to be seriously considered. I apologize. Please consider my application withdrawn."

Niemann folded her hands under her chin.

"Oh no. It's not that simple. You're in my field of vision now, South. And that is a very dangerous place to be."

"I'm not sure I follow," I said.

"Because now that I've noticed you, I've decided to make use of you. There's a job," said Niemann.

Now that threw me. Was I being *recruited*? By the deputy director herself?

"What kind of job?" I asked, and to my own amazement, I could hear a hint of excitement in my voice. It didn't even sound like my voice.

"The kind that it is bloody difficult to find someone to do," she said.

"Dangerous?" I asked, and would you believe, my heart leapt at the idea?

Not that my life lacked for danger. Say the wrong thing to the wrong person and ParSec would find my neck as easily as anyone else's. But what Niemann seemed to be offering was a chance to be killed *for* the state, not by it. That made all the difference. When a man reaches a certain age he gets a potent urge to start driving powerful cars too fast, or to parachute out of planes, or something equally likely to end in violent death. Ever since the purge of StaSec eighteen years prior, I had made an art of not drawing attention to myself, of not putting myself forward for anything too dangerous. In short, I had spent almost twenty years trying to stay out of this very seat in this very room.

And yet, now that I was here, I found the idea of dangerous fieldwork irresistibly appealing. I think it was the sight of Sheena and Yasmin Paria lying dead, killed by the Machine's false promises, that had rekindled my sense of duty. I was back in the fight. I did a quick mental inventory of ongoing StaSec operations and tried to guess what Niemann had planned for me. Investigating the rumored infiltration of the army by Ajay militants, perhaps? Making contact with pro-Humanist groups in America or Europe? Persian drug-traffickers? Armenian dissidents? Yozhik?

But Niemann shook her head.

"No. Or at least . . . not how you might think," Niemann said. "The job itself is quite easy. But it's the kind of job that, a few months down the line, if things go badly, could end with you standing in a darkened room, in front of a row of men whose faces you cannot see, being asked questions to which there are no right answers. But if you do it? You shall have accrued considerable goodwill with me. And that is not nothing, South. That, in fact, is some of the better currency out there. Do you understand?"

I had absolutely no idea what this was all about.

"I understand," I said.

She nodded approvingly.

"Why me?" I asked.

Niemann leaned back in her chair.

"Because I need a man who is expendable. A man who does not and is not seen to have loyalty to any particular faction within the party. Who will follow orders without question. And, because I am such a sentimentalist, has no surviving family. I need someone no one would miss."

"Well," I said. "When you put it like that I seem somewhat overqualified."

She gave me a smile that may have been kind, or merely pitying.

She took my file and swept it into her desk as if she were cleaning away a stain.

"I'm finished with this file. I find it rather dull," she said.

She took out another file, red this time, and set it down in front of me.

"Now this one," said the deputy director, with a gleam in her eye. "Full of drama and mystery, South."

I took the file, and opened it. And the first thing I saw when I opened it was a photograph.

It was a man in his late thirties. Handsome, with the long, regal features of a Roman emperor. He was bald, and so had no hair to conceal the massive purple bruise that marred his temple over his left eye.

He was dead.

He was also, I was shocked to realize, Paulo Xirau.

# 4

The word "machine" was everywhere, in Caspian. A loose, pliable concept on the tongue of virtually everyone I spoke to. It was noun, adjective and pejorative. Once, perhaps, it had solely referred to those individuals who were coded online and had not been born organically. But now, it had expanded and grown immense. Anything could be "machine," or anyone. If you've ever been contranned, regardless of the circumstances of your birth, you are "machine." If you've ever loved someone who was born code, you are "machine." If you believe in the rights and dignities of artificial citizens, you are "machine." A book can be "machine." A sentence. A word. The concept of "machine" had grown to encompass everything beyond the borders of the Republic. Hence their name for us: "The Machine World."

—Vika Melkovska, *Enclosed Sea, Enclosed State:*
*A Journalist Undercover in the Caspian Republic*

Xirau's dead?" I gasped.

"Oh, you knew him?" Niemann said, mildly. I caught the rebuke. Yes, Deputy Director, even I had heard of Paulo Xirau.

Everyone in the party knew Xirau. Anyone with ambition read his weekly column in *The Caspian Truth,* or at least claimed to. Nothing too challenging there. It was basically the same theme reiterated over and over. Once you had read one, you had read them all. Long, fiery, venomous diatribes against the Machine and its human chattel. Punishing stuff to read, even if you were aligned with his beliefs. I would have called them "jeremiads," but that would have been unfair to a prophet who had at least a gift for vivid imagery. Xirau's prose was a sledgehammer: dull, pounding and relentless. He died the most widely read writer in the whole country.

"Cause of death?" I asked. "Or is that the mystery?"

"Oh no, no," said Niemann. "Believe me when I say that Mr. Xirau's death is by far the least interesting thing about him."

"You intrigue me, Deputy Director," I said.

"Oh, I am glad," said Niemann with, perhaps, just a touch of sarcasm.

I leafed through the file. A picture slipped out from between two pages: Xirau standing in a line of party functionaries in front of Mendelssohn's hanging corpse. Every other man and woman there is looking away but not Xirau. Oh no, Xirau is staring up at him like an apostle, his eyes clear and bright.

I suppressed a shudder, and continued reading.

Xirau had not been born in the Caspian Republic. I hadn't known that, but it was obvious in retrospect. No one is as fanatical as the recent convert. He had emigrated twenty years ago from Persia, and taken a low-paying job in a cannery in Bonogady. I had met a few cannery workers in my time and some of them even had all their fingers. Not typically the kind of work one risks their life and leaves behind everything they've ever known for. While in the cannery, Xirau had penned some articles for the union newsletter, which had gotten him noticed by his bosses in the union, and, through them, the party. For a writer's work to be circulated among the upper levels of the party was usually a precursor to them coming down with a rather permanent case of writer's block, but not this time. Xirau was offered a position at *The Truth* (then viewed as a rather out-of-touch and elitist organ), and asked to bring his rough, authentic, working-class voice to the paper's readers, who were left with nothing to do but wonder what they had done to deserve it.

From there, he had become the closest thing the modern party had to an intellectual voice, and when you had said that, you had said everything. I glanced back at that picture of Xirau at the hanging and remembered the tales of what he done there.

Xirau spitting on the corpse of Leon Mendelssohn. That was where we were, now.

That was the Caspian Republic.

"Did you read Xirau, South?" Niemann asked me.

"Occasionally," I replied, warily.

"What did you think of him?" she said.

I felt insulted. She didn't have to set the trap while I was looking right at her, that was just rude.

"He was a loyal party man," I heard myself say.

"*I'm* loyal, South," said Niemann with a furtive smile. "*He* was a bloody fanatic."

I wanted to return the smile. But the Deputy Director of State Security could say such things, I could not.

"Do we believe that his political writing led to his death?" I asked. Xirau had been fond of darkly hinting that members of the party and the two main security agencies were in league with the Machine Powers. The party leadership encouraged this as it kept everyone on their toes. But maybe someone had found one of Xirau's vague hints to be just a little too specific?

Niemann simply chuckled.

Irritated by her coyness, I skimmed ahead through the file until I reached the account of Xirau's death. It was, as the deputy director had promised, depressingly anticlimactic.

Xirau had died in a bar fight.

Apparently he had tried to kiss a woman whose boyfriend had old-fashioned ideas about that sort of thing. "A case of mistaken identity" according to the file. A punch had been thrown and Xirau had cracked his head against a table and died almost instantly. Xirau's killer, a man named Oleg Mansani, had a criminal record that was long but shallow: drunk and disorderly behavior, a few counts of assault, low-level hood work. It was considered unlikely that Xirau's writings in *The Truth* were what led to his death, given that Mansani was borderline illiterate. Xirau's death was exactly what it seemed. A sordid, bloody little accident. A life ending in a whimper.

I was starting to wonder why the deputy director was showing me this when I turned the page and a paragraph detailing the coroner's findings jumped out at me like a bandit. I almost dropped the file in shock.

It was impossible. Of all people.

Niemann was grinning at me.

"He was an AI . . . ," I muttered, to her or myself.

"He was."

"A cloned body," I said.

"Yes. Meaning that the man known as Paulo Xirau was a computer program. Part of the Infernal Machine, as he most likely would have put it himself," Niemann replied.

I felt light-headed and my mind raced. If Xirau (*Xirau!*) could be Machine, then who else? How many were walking among us? Had they infiltrated StaSec? The Parliament? Had we already lost?

No.

There were methods of detecting cloned bodies. High-ranking members of the party were regularly screened. I, in fact, had administered the test myself hundreds of times. You started with the teeth. Plaque and microcavities from a lifetime of eating food were difficult to fake. You then moved on to a spit sample, all the while engaging the suspect in casual conversation to find flaws in the accent or pronunciation of various words that might indicate that language had been implanted digitally rather than learned aurally.

These methods were fairly effective, though far from infallible. For "infallible," you needed an autopsy. The reason Xirau had chosen to work at *The Truth* was, despite his fame and influence, he was still technically only a rank-and-file party member and not likely to be screened.

"A spy?" I asked. If not that, then what?

"Bloody terrible one if he was," said Niemann. "The body was a civilian model. Xirau had been living here for a good twenty years. We have searched his rooms and there is not a shred of evidence he engaged in any espionage whatsoever. No subversive literature. No coded instructions. Nothing. It was the cleanest search I have ever undertaken. This Machine was a model human citizen."

I took off my glasses and rubbed my eyes. They felt too large for my head, somehow.

"Let me see if I understand you," I said. "Twenty years ago, a sentient computer program downloads itself into an off-the-rack cloned body. Immigrates to what is, for it, the most dangerous country in the world, and takes a low-paying job risking life and limb in a cannery before moving to the state newspaper where it writes tracts on the soulless, inhuman Machine of which it is secretly a part."

"Told you he was interesting, didn't I?" said Niemann with a grin. I did not share her good humor.

"What the hell was it thinking?" I wondered aloud.

"It doesn't matter," Niemann said, suddenly all business again.

"It doesn't?" I said, incredulously.

"Not to you. Xirau was coded in a lab in Bonn and spent much of his life on an American server. He claimed both American and EU citizenship. They have jointly asked that his . . . wife be allowed to come here to Caspian and identify him."

I stared at her.

"Wife?" I said at last.

"You heard me."

"It had a wife?"

"It was a program who had a program that was programed to call itself his wife," Niemann snapped irritably. "I don't understand it, you don't understand it, but then we are sane. Regardless, Parliament has agreed to this request."

That shocked me more than anything I had heard today, and it had been a banner day.

"How is that possible?" I stammered. "The law—"

"Can be bent, overruled, interpreted imaginatively or, in extreme cases, simply ignored," Niemann interrupted with a wave of her hand. "Xirau's wife program, or rather widow program, is to be granted a special dispensation. It is to be considered an 'honorary human.'"

This was insane. Gravity had reversed itself and the sun was setting in the east.

"Why would the party . . . ," I began.

"You look very pale, South," Niemann said.

I was the only Black man in StaSec, and for a moment I thought she was making a joke.

"I'm sorry?"

"Did you have a hearty breakfast this morning? You look like you're about to pass out."

I had been certain when I stepped into the office that Niemann knew about my warning to Smolna. That might make anyone pale.

"No. I missed breakfast this morning." A lie, technically, but my breakfast had been so meager that it didn't feel like one.

"Tut-tut, South. Most important meal of the day. I suppose the shops were out by the time you got there?"

"Yes," I said, conscious that I was being drawn deeper into a lie.

"Was there a queue?"

"Yes."

"We have it quite lucky here, you know," Niemann said philosophically. "Outside the city, restaurants have started charging people to rummage through their bins."

I said nothing. Sanctions had been in place against the Caspian Republic for decades, but the hanging of Mendelssohn had evidently broken new ground in the Machine's loathing for us. George, Confucius and Athena rarely agreed on anything, but they had agreed that the Caspian Republic must starve, and Congress, the Standing Committee and the European Parliament had dutifully complied.

"Let's not beat about the bush, South," said Niemann. "The embargo is starting to bite and we're all feeling it. Even me."

At that I did something very dangerous. I actually snorted. Ridiculous. As if someone as high up in the party as Niemann could know hunger. What was that saying they had in Old Baku? *What kind of party doesn't have food?*

Niemann glared at me, and I felt a bead of sweat roll down the back of my neck the size of a marble.

"Yes, even me, South," she growled, barely above a whisper. And suddenly, I realized that she was right. There was a slackness to the skin of her face, a dry, dead quality to her hair.

The Deputy Director of State Security was starving. That was terrifying.

Niemann sighed and rubbed her eyes wearily. "It's a gesture, South. Like a bouquet of flowers. Or a fucking white flag. We extend to Mrs. Xirau the best of Caspian hospitality and it may alter the Machine's calculus. Maybe get them to loosen the noose around our necks just a smidgen."

Like a dog. Punish it when it disobeys, reward it when it behaves. It was galling, but I was more hungry than galled. I had to wonder if Niemann was thinking clearly, however. Bringing an open, acknowledged AI into Caspian would be akin to wading through knee-high gasoline with a lit match.

"What about ParSec?" I asked.

"I don't know, I don't care and I don't want you to do, either," Niemann snapped. "Our orders have come from Parliament. Mrs. Xirau gets the red carpet. You are to be her escort."

So. There it was at last. The reason I had been summoned to her office. And I felt like I was going to be sick.

"Me?" I said, hoping I had misheard her.

"No, the fucking lamp. Yes, you, South," said Niemann testily.

My skin was crawling. A machine was coming here. To Caspian. A computer program walking around in a cloned human body, a stumbling corpse with a rictus smile. The very idea terrified and repulsed me.

Niemann continued.

"You will escort Mrs. Xirau during her time in Caspian. You will ensure she follows her prescribed itinerary and does not deviate from it in the slightest."

She produced a third file from her desk and pushed it across to me. This one contained instructions and protocols for "Mrs. Xirau's" visit, which I was dismayed to discover was scheduled for tomorrow morning. Evidently, things were moving very fast.

"You will obviously prevent her from engaging in any kind of espionage or subversion," said Niemann. "You will not allow her to speak to any citizen. You will keep her on a short leash. A *very* short leash, South. Understood?"

I felt a sudden, desperate urge to resign.

"Understood," I said, wanly.

I waited to be dismissed, but the command never came.

Niemann said nothing for a few seconds, as if carefully choosing her words. When she spoke again, it was softer, almost conspiratorial.

"It's dangerous work, South," she said at last. "I'd advise you to remember that."

I knew that tone of voice. It was the voice of a good neighbor who says *I think you have an admirer* when she saw a man from ParSec watching you from across the street the night before.

A voice that warned as much as it was safe to warn.

"Deputy Director . . . ," I said softly. "This . . . this is above-board? It *has* been cleared?"

"It has been cleared," said Niemann. "But what has been cleared may be muddied. ParSec have a way of rewriting history. And then it's time for questions. Difficult questions, South, to which there are no right answers."

Something Olesya had once said to me now resurfaced in my memory.

*When the party orders you to break the law, who do you obey? The party or the law?*

Niemann continued.

"Should the worst happen, I will try to protect you as best as I can. That's as much as I can give you."

More than I expected.

I nodded.

Suddenly, Niemann was herself again.

"I believe we're done here. Good day, South," she said dismissively and gestured for me to leave.

I took both files: the one for Paulo Xirau and the one pertaining to his wife, and rose to leave. I stopped at the door.

"Deputy Director? What is its name?" I asked.

"Hm?" Niemann muttered distractedly, not looking up from her work.

"Xirau's widow?"

Niemann furrowed her brow, as if she had forgotten. Then, it came to her.

"Lily," she said. "Its name is Lily."

# 5

"It was crazy, man. Everyone was all 'Oh he's going to come back, and he's not going to have a soul, he's going to be a psycho killer or some shit, it's not really him, he's been replaced by some kind of . . . crazy shit, man.' But it's like I've always said. I don't believe in wizards, magic or souls. We're data. We're all data, man, that's it. I was data and I was here, I was data and I was there, I'm back here and I'm still data. It works. It just fucking works. And when you all see what's waiting for you on the other side? When you understand the possibilities of this, when you can free your mind and be whatever you want to be and do whatever you want to do wherever you want to do it? You'll never want to go back. This is going to change the world. When you print that, please put it in bold. **This is going to change the motherfucking world."**

—Liu Sontang, in an interview with *The New York Times*, 15 October 2122, after becoming the first subject of a successful consciousness transferral

By the time I got back to my desk, Grier was gone, and there was a note waiting for me in his square, functional handwriting (he having evidently remembered who I was after his earlier bout of amnesia). It said that he had already been informed that I was being temporarily reassigned and asking (telling, really) me to make a start on the Parias' paperwork before checking out. As for Grier himself, he would be spending the rest of the day doing face-to-face notifications. Contran was a crime that required anywhere between nine and a dozen governmental, party, military and security bodies to be notified, and at least four of those were so paranoid about hacking and leaks and the like that they insisted on any such notifications being made in person. Poor Grier would spend the rest of the day traipsing through endless corridors and waiting in chilly lobbies under the eyes of decrepit, half-dead secretaries waiting to speak to someone with enough authority to hear what he had to say about two dead bodies in Old Baku.

Meanwhile, I was to work on the reports for those remaining agencies reckless enough to trust paper. One of those was ParSec, who, naturally, would be notified last as a mark of discourtesy and also to give Smolna a gnat's chance in a hailstorm of escaping. Of course, ParSec almost certainly knew about the Parias already. If they sat around waiting for The Old Man to tell them their business, they would never get anything done. No doubt one of Smolna's neighbors had put a call in. They might even have got some bread for their trouble. A double contran was simply not a secret that could be kept. It would seep through the cracks in Smolna's walls and out into the street below.

I made as good a fist of the paperwork as I could, but I was hungry and still slightly in shock from my meeting with Niemann and I wasn't close to finished by the time my shift was over. I left an apologetic note for Grier, detailing what still remained to be done and headed out through the lobby with the files of both Xiraus hugged tightly to my chest.

A filthy sleet had begun to fall over the city and I made a particularly miserable, hunched figure as I shivered my way through the streets of Ellulgrad, my chin pressed against my Adam's apple and my fingers rapidly turning numb as they clenched the Xiraus closer together.

To conserve power, every second streetlamp had been turned off, and as I moved farther and farther away from the lights of the city center, the void between the pools of light became blacker and more treacherous. With a sudden, sickening lurch and a white-hot bite at my ankle I stepped in a pothole and dropped both files. Cursing the pain and the cold, I gathered them up (fortunately, neither file had burst open). Already as wet and cold as I was going to get, I sat on the pavement to rest my ankle and rub some feeling back into my fingers. And there, as I looked up, I realized I was sitting across from Saint Basil's, the first church built in Ellulgrad post-Founding. To be precise, I was facing the back of the church, a large, featureless wall. And there, spray-painted across the wall in large, neon-green letters were the words:

EVERY SPARROW SHALL BE CAUGHT

The audacity was almost admirable.

The phrase came from Mendelssohn's last work, *Ecce Machina,* a slim little volume that proved that it was possible to get yourself killed with less than a hundred pages.

That someone had taken Mendelssohn's words and plastered them over the holiest site in the Caspian Republic would, I had no doubt, prove that it was possible to get yourself killed with a mere five words. Someone (ParSec, it would unquestionably be ParSec) would track down whoever had done this, and a cautionary fable would be born.

By rights, I should have headed back to StaSec headquarters to make a report. But I was cold, wet, hungry and my ankle was in agony, so I decided that I had seen nothing and continued on home.

Home was a small apartment on the seventh floor of a grim

and imposing residential block. Cold as it was, I took a moment to stand, swaying like a drunk, before the monolith.

My bed was on the other side of a long, steep, concrete staircase. The climb would be slow, agonizing and (with the sleet) as treacherous and lethal as an Old Baku Rusty Nail. As for the elevator, it would be fixed in a week's time, or so we had been assured six months ago. So I took a few moments to gather my strength and steel myself.

I craned my head back to look at the apartment block and remembered with dull shock how this had once been considered a desirable place to live. When Olesya had died I had sold our house and moved here, wanting somewhere small enough that my loneliness would have no room to breathe. It had been teeming back then, full of young families and noise. Now, it was half abandoned and the few remaining residents had long given up on maintaining any appearance of respectability, myself very much included.

And we were few indeed.

You could, I realized, imagine the apartment block as a crossword puzzle with well over half the squares blacked out.

Top floor. Apartment 1. Mr. and Mrs. Nimitz. Transported to Kobustan for possession of contraband.

Apartment 2. Old Mr. Iannis. Roughed up by The Bastards in his own home and died of a heart attack.

Apartment 5. Mrs. Yulia Hawley. Widowed and pregnant at twenty and desperate for a way out. She trusted the wrong Needle Man and got a nail through the head.

Perhaps there were happier stories on the floor below?

Apartment 4. Mrs. Ostrova. Killed for bread.

Apartment 6. Estragon Burke and his girlfriend, Nadda, and their five-year-old boy, Jan. Vanished without a trace. Jan used to play with tiny toy cars on the stairwell. Step on one and you might go for a drive to the bottom of seven flights of stairs. Every so often I'd find one lodged in a crack between the fifth and sixth floors, rusting away to nothing.

Apartment 7. Formerly the home of a young Armenian whose name we never learned, who threw herself off the balcony.

I had almost forgotten the cold as I became ever more absorbed in recounting to myself the tragic, awful histories of my neighbors. Behind every door was a horror I had half forgotten, sometimes two or three as new tenants had moved in and were claimed in turn by the bad luck that had consumed their predecessors. Here was a botched contran, there a death from hunger or illness. This man had been arrested by StaSec, that one shot. There were murders and rapes and suicides. But most of all there was ParSec, which, I was troublingly unsurprised to realize, had emptied almost a third of the homes that towered over me. They had fed well, and left only cold, empty nests.

The Good Brother did not speak, but gave a low, animal growl of satisfaction. He felt a perverse sense of accomplishment to belong to the state, and to the party, that could leave such a swathe in their wake. He felt warmed by the tiny ember of reflected power it gave him to look on all those empty apartments. I shuddered, and the Good Brother was temporarily shaken from his perch and retreated back into the void.

I placed my hand on the steel bannister, so cold it almost burned, and began to ascend the steps.

By the time I reached the top, I was wheezing and white spots were dancing in front of my eyes like mosquitos. As I rummaged in my pocket for my keys, I leaned against my front door for support and was betrayed. The door gave way and I very nearly fell into my own front hall. The door had been unlocked. And from the darkness I could smell freshly made coffee.

When one is dreaming, there comes a point where the dream becomes a nightmare with a sudden, sickening lurch.

You might be standing in a forest, with a path in front of you leading down into the dark where something waits with pale eyes and bloodied teeth.

The path behind you leads back up to sunlight, but still you walk forward because you are not in control, and you were fooling yourself to think you ever were.

I stared at the open door, knowing perfectly well that I had locked it this morning (in my neighborhood, one did not forget such a thing). The door had not been forced. It had simply been opened by someone for whom locks were as ineffective and powerless as laws or pleas for mercy.

This was the point. This was where the dream became a nightmare. And so, instead of running, I stepped inside.

I did not turn on the light, but went straight to the kitchen, where a man sat in darkness at my table, a cup of my coffee steaming in his hand.

The man from ParSec smiled at me. He was young, tall and athletic.

He looked like if you searched him you'd find a gun and a length of wire.

He gestured for me to sit down.

# 6

"I hear people calling the Whole Life Net 'Internet 2.0.' That's wrong. I hear them calling it 'the next big thing.' That's hilarious. That's like . . . two cavemen are talking and one says 'Hey man, I hear you invented agriculture?' and the other guy's like 'Oh yeah, it's the next big thing.'"

Pause for laughter.

"Right? But that's how big we're talking. Nothing less than a complete reordering of how we, as human beings, live on this planet. What is being offered to you is final, complete freedom. There is a world now open to you where none of the restrictions of the physical world apply. Here, in the real world, you can't fly, you can't turn into a dragon and you can't fuck Marilyn Monroe. In WLN, you can do all three *at the same time*. If you can dream it, you can do it. There are no more limits. None. I make this prediction now: Within the next ten years, nine out of ten human beings will be spending most or all of their existence online."

—Liu Sontang, speaking at Harvard University, 15 September 2124

The Bureau of Party Security and Constitutional Enforcement, known to those within its ranks as "The Bureau" and known to those without as "ParSec," or "The Bastards," or "They" (as in *"they" are coming, "they" will be here, "they" took him last night*) had been around almost since the Founding, but had taken its current shape only in the last eighteen years or so.

For decades, ParSec had been little more than a group of glorified ushers, conducting security for party meetings and acting as bodyguards for those party heads deemed to require protection and had little to do with enforcing ideological purity.

That all changed with the Morrison Crisis.

Documents discovered by a maid cleaning a room in the Morrison Hotel had revealed a planned coup involving several members of Parliament and three cabinet ministers. Five weeks of bloodshed followed as half the Parliament tried to have the other half arrested and executed, homes were raided and the army had to take to the streets to quell the riots. While I have always had my doubts as to the veracity of the Morrison documents, it cannot be denied that a coup *was* attempted and very nearly succeeded. In those five weeks, the Caspian Republic came as close to utter destruction as it ever did. By the time the dust had settled a new cabinet was in place, one that had survived the previous weeks' madness only through a healthy mix of brutality and paranoia.

The whole thing was a debacle for StaSec and the new government very seriously considered liquidating the entire agency as punishment for its failure to prevent the coup, either through incompetence or (as was heavily suspected) treason. The head of StaSec, Papalazarou, was, of course, above suspicion, but the rest of the agency was fair game. Fully one-third of the department heads were arrested and executed, and as they were pulled like weeds they brought with them, trailing like soil-covered roots, scores of deputy heads, senior agents and mere rank-and-file agents.

I lost many passing acquaintances. Whenever Grier had asked why I didn't make more of an effort to curry friends within the higher ranks of the party, I would remind him of the weeks following the Morrison Crisis. Sometimes, it paid to not be worth caring about.

Please don't feel sorry for them. StaSec in those days was in many ways ParSec before ParSec. If we had been loved, we would not have been disemboweled with such relish.

The bloody-knuckled men who had dragged so much of the directorate of StaSec out into the streets and into waiting vans were a mix of the nastiest gullivers from the army, the existing Party Security Bureau and the Ellulgrad police. They would become the current iteration of ParSec. Under the law, they had little real power. Their jurisdiction was limited to the membership of the party, and any wrongdoing they uncovered was to be reported to StaSec or the local police.

In practice, they could go anywhere and do anything to anyone. They could break down your door in the middle of the night and by morning your neighbors would have forgotten your name.

The man from ParSec smiled at me. I think it was supposed to be reassuring.

"Nippy out," he noted.

The cold had been painted thickly onto my bones. I nodded. He was wearing a thick, waterproof coat that must have cost him what I made in four months.

"I took the last of your coffee," he said. "Hope you don't mind?"

The first few minutes would simply be him establishing dominance. I waited patiently for him to get to the point. I wondered which dagger hanging over me was about to fall. Smolna? Lily Xirau? It might even be the fact that I hadn't reported the graffiti. Did it matter?

"Do you remember me, Brother?" he asked.

As my eyes adapted to the gloom I could make out his features. A name surfaced in my mind.

"Laddi Chernov," I said. "Yes. I remember you."

He had been StaSec once. I had had the distinctly unpleasant task of training him when he had first joined. So this is where he had ended up. I was not in the least surprised that he had been headhunted by ParSec and I can think of no worse insult than that.

"Well, how've you been? Still with Grier?"

There had always been something so indescribably false about Chernov's small talk, I remembered. He was like a burglar making polite conversation with a shopkeeper as he made mental notes of all the entrances and the location of the cash register.

"Yes," I replied.

"Really. It's been what, six years?"

"Yes. I didn't know you'd joined ParSec?"

"What makes you think I've joined ParSec?"

"You're in my home. At night. Uninvited."

Chernov laughed quietly and nodded.

"Yes, you've got me. Jumped the pond. Sold out. Betrayed the Agency. Became just another Bureau thug. That's me."

"You always did have ambition," I said, and I tried to make it sound complimentary.

"Well, ambition will only get you so far," said Chernov. "Do you know what will get you far, South?"

"Loyalty?" I asked. Well, what else would you say to ParSec?

"I made the same mistake. No," said Chernov, taking a sip from my coffee. "Luck, South. Luck is all you need. Luck, and nothing else. Let me give you an example. On my first week of field duty I took part in a surprise raid on some party wallah that we had reason to believe was defecting to Persia. So we break into his house and find that Bellov's already done a runner."

"Sebastien Bellov?" I asked. I vaguely remembered the name. The deputy leader of the party's Ellulgrad branch who had disappeared five years ago.

Chernov stopped, and looked at me sheepishly.

"Shit," he said. "I shouldn't have told you his name, should I?"

I suddenly remembered what I had disliked about Chernov when I had worked with him. Not simply that he was cruel, or that he was so stuffed with party dogma that his brain was a rigid, impenetrable mass. It was that he was gallingly, maddeningly stupid.

"No," I said, in answer to his question.

"Well, anyway," said Chernov, completely unfazed, "Bellov was gone and we were tearing the place apart looking for some clue as to where he'd slithered off to when there's a ring at the door. And the agent in charge says, 'See who it is, Chernov. Bring him in. Kick him in the bollocks and see if he knows where Bellov's gone.'"

Devilishly cunning, these ParSec fellows. Skilled and subtle as surgeons.

"So, hand on my gun and heart in my mouth I open the door," Chernov continued. "And standing without is a little Ajay man . . ."

"Ajay." The Azerbaijani. You may have heard of them. They had a country once. They'd mostly moved west but there were still a few of them in Ellulgrad, scraping by.

"A midget. Three foot tall. Ninety years old if he was a day," said Chernov. "And he's carrying this tray of little ceramic figurines. Hideous little things. And he's selling them door-to-door. You've seen them?"

The Azerbaijani peddlers. Yes. I'd seen them. You would open the door and they would give you the biggest smile you'd ever seen. *Hello sir, good day sir, you buy, you buy?* They all had smile lines around their mouths, and none around their eyes.

And I knew the figurines so well I could picture them in my mind. Little ceramic representations of the zodiac. They could be found in half the homes in the city, iconic examples of a very specific type of Ellulgrad kitsch.

"But on his face," Chernov continued. "On his face, South. A tumor, the size of a baby."

He put a cupped hand by his cheek to show the size.

"I mean, can you imagine? Being confronted by this freak show in the dead of night? And I was so startled that I inadvertently shot him in the face."

Chernov chuckled to himself like a best man cracking up in the middle of telling an amusing anecdote about the groom, while I sat across from him, trying to keep my face from betraying my fear, loathing and disgust.

"Killed him outright, obviously," Chernov went on. "So of course, I'm slapped in handcuffs, carted away to a cell. Interrogated eight times, and those bastards were not gentle, let me tell you. That's what we are after all. Bastards. That's what you call us, isn't it?"

He was still laughing, but the laugh was going sour, now. Becoming something wounded and raw. His face was so happy, but his body was hunched and his fingers clenched.

Chernov was ParSec. That was reason enough to pity him, as well as hate him.

He took a deep, shuddering breath.

"And then after three days, they let me go," he said, "and tell me I've been promoted."

"Why?" I asked.

"Why, he asks me, and I shall tell him why," said Chernov. "Because, through sheer luck, through a million-to-one chance, that old man whose brains I blasted all over Bellov's doormat just so happened to be the ringleader of one of the largest con-tran operations in the city. I'm absolutely serious. He was a ge-nius! An Azerbaijani. Midget. Genius."

Professional curiosity got the better of me.

"How did he do it?" I asked.

"He carried all the equipment around with him. State-of-the-art stuff strapped to his body under his coat. And he'd go to peoples' houses, download their consciousnesses into a chip. Leave the bodies behind and smuggle the chips out of the coun-try. They reckon he got hundreds of people out that way."

"What way?" I asked.

Chernov looked confused. "How do you mean?"

"How did he get the chips out of the country?"

"I don't know. The Persians probably."

There, at least, was something StaSec and ParSec were in agreement on: When you don't know the answer, blame the Persians.

I nodded, realization dawning.

"And that's why he was there. For Bellov. To help him escape."

"But Bellov got wind of the raid and never bothered to warn him," said Chernov, nodding. "And if I hadn't shot him by ac-cident we never would have caught him. And a great enemy of the state would have slipped right through our fingers. Do you see the motto of the story, South?"

I did, and it was *Always walk behind Chernov.*

"Luck," I said.

"Luck," Chernov echoed. "It all comes down to luck. Now you, I believe you have just become a very lucky man, South."

If this was luck, God protect us and keep us from misfortune.

"How is Gussie Niemann, by the way?" Chernov asked.

"The deputy director is in good health, I believe," I replied, blandly.

"You don't have to play coy with me, South," Chernov said. "We know she's given you the Xirau detail."

"You know that?" I asked.

"We have our sources," said Chernov, like an ass.

"I know. Wernham," I said.

The look on his face shall keep me warm for the rest of my days.

"How did you . . . ," he sputtered.

"I didn't," I replied curtly. "I bluffed. You folded. And you may have forgotten, Chernov, but the first thing I ever taught you was that a state security agent cannot discuss assignments with any individual outside of StaSec. So you see I very much have to 'play coy' with you."

"Bloody insulting, if you ask me," said Chernov. "Asking a thirty-year man like you to chaperone some coded trick around town. Illegal, too. You do realize that?"

"They're giving her human status. Temporarily."

"How ingenious," Chernov sneered. "And tell me something, South: If they passed a law saying this spoon was a human being would it make it so?"

"Legally, yes. Chernov, I'm very tired. If you've come here to threaten me please make your threats more direct and less veiled. The effect is the same and it'll save us both time," I sighed.

"Oh, I'm not here to threaten you, old man," said Chernov chummily. "Absolutely not. You have your orders and you'll carry them out. Don't think anyone will hold that against you. Gussie Niemann and her lot, they may have to answer for it in time. But no one's going after you, South."

Don't lie to your elders, boy.

"That would be very interesting to see," I said.

"What?"

"The first instance in recorded history of shit rolling uphill."
Chernov laughed and shook his head ruefully.

"Yes. Doesn't sound very likely, now that I've said it out loud.
All the more reason for you to consider my offer. You see. We're
not happy. On our side. With your side. We've become rather
alarmed at the laxness and lack of . . . clarity we've been seeing
in our brothers in StaSec. Firstly, that Paulo Xirau could live
here twenty years in a cloned body without getting picked up by
The Old Man is . . . well, the word 'Morrison' springs to mind."

Not here to threaten me, indeed.

"Second," Chernov continued, "that members of our own
party are actually willing to let his fucking code bitch traipse
around here. Here, in our country. No. No, no, no. We are not
happy. We are not."

I had to admit, I felt the same way. The Machine would be
here, walking the streets of Caspian. It was a grotesque violation. Chernov leaned in.

"We think there's more to this, South," he whispered. "Have
you asked yourself why Mrs. Xirau is being allowed to visit this
country?"

"As a gesture of goodwill to the Machine Powers," I said.
Well, what else?

"Come now, South," said Chernov. "Innocence is sweet in
small children, in old men it's pathetic."

"Old men need sleep, Chernov," I said, rubbing my eyes
wearily.

"Here's what I'm driving at," said Chernov. "There has been a
huge uptake in the number of abandoned bodies being found."

Indeed, there had been. And almost entirely the work of a
single operation. Discreet, high-quality contran. No blood, no
botched extractions. Catering to rich and poor clients alike
and leaving no trace. In StaSec we had taken to calling him (or
them) "Yozhik."

"Yes. I know," I said. The Parias had brought the number of abandoned bodies found this month to a nice, round forty.

"Yes. But all those minds are still in the country. We know this. They're still stored on hardware somewhere, waiting to be smuggled out. Over six hundred potential defectors."

Chernov, Chernov, Chernov. StaSec had long suspected that ParSec were independently investigating contran cases and keeping them secret from us. Chernov had just confirmed it. I didn't know how many cases StaSec had on its books but it was not six hundred. Maybe four. ParSec were evidently sitting on two hundred dead bodies and hadn't seen fit to tell anyone. It was enough to make you feel sorry for Grier, diligently going through the miserable ritual of notifying nine different agencies and departments with every body that we found. Six hundred. An epidemic.

I thought, how desperate you'd have to be to abandon your own body, to leave it rotting in some hovel in Ellulgrad while you, everything that was *you,* was rendered into data and stored on a Sontang chip. The chips themselves were Chinese-made, and around the size of a toenail. Their storage capacity for traditional data was effectively infinite. To store six hundred entire human consciousnesses, complete with memories and unique thought processes would require . . .

"At least a dozen chips," I said.

"Twelve chips." Chernov nodded. "We have every confidence that sooner or later those chips will be found and destroyed. But then . . . here comes Mrs. Xirau. Who ParSec have been told, in no uncertain terms: *'Hands off.'* StaSec is handling this. StaSec will be escorting her, watching where she goes, controlling who she sees and meets. StaSec will be responsible for searching her person before she leaves the country."

The outlines were now sharpening.

"You think that Lily Xirau is to act as courier for these defectors?" I asked.

"Yes," said Chernov.

"For you to be right, that would mean that someone in Sta-Sec is in league with this contran operation," I said. "Probably more than one person. And probably running it."

"Exactly," Chernov agreed.

"And when you saw that I was going to be escorting Mrs. Xirau," I continued, "you thought that I could be convinced to help you confirm your suspicions, given our history together."

"There is a position opening in ParSec that I think you would be perfect for, South," said Chernov, and were I a younger man I would have struck him for the insult.

"I've been telling them that," Chernov continued. "We could arrange a salary significantly more generous than what you're on now. And all we ask is that you relay any information you think relevant to us before Mrs. Xirau has a chance to leave the country."

It was a lie, and a transparent one at that. ParSec was psychopathic in character, completely untrustworthy. It was one of the reasons they were so ineffective. And even if there was a job waiting for me in ParSec, I was not that desperate for money and prayed that I never would be.

"Before I give you my answer, Chernov," I said, "let me ask you one thing. Have you read my file?"

Chernov looked at me like a husband who's just heard his wife speak the name of his mistress.

"What?" he asked.

"My file. You have access to it surely? I'm told it's very dull but you at least skimmed it, yes?"

No, of course you haven't.

"Come now, South," said Chernov. "We're old friends."

Oh *Jesus*. I folded out my hands on the table and laid out the problem with his approach as clearly as I could.

"If you had read my file you would know that I attend the

absolute minimum of party meetings that I am required to and that every overseer I have ever had has commented on my lack of zeal and enthusiasm for the party. And now I have been given the task of escorting an AI whom you believe is to accept a cargo of twelve computer chips containing the transferred consciousness of approximately six hundred defectors. Who is she to accept this cargo from? You've said yourself you suspect someone in StaSec is behind this business. I am in StaSec, and I am the only person who is to have any contact with Lily Xirau during her time here. Couple this with the information in my file and I am obviously the most likely person to be passing the chips on to her."

Chernov stared at me liked he'd been struck.

"Are you . . . confessing?" he asked me, dumbfounded.

"I am not confessing," I said calmly. "I am explaining why I will not be assisting you, or ParSec, in this matter. Because in your haste to capitalize on the fact that we know each other, you have gone and revealed your entire investigation to your most likely suspect. Because you're a bloody fool, Chernov."

I had always considered myself a cautious man. But now, for the third time today, I had done something that could very well get me killed. The first was warning Smolna. The second, scoffing at Niemann's claim that she was starving due to the embargo. And now this. I had called a member of ParSec a fool to his face. In my kitchen. In the dead of night. With no witnesses.

Looking back, I realize I was very depressed.

I fully expected Chernov to shoot me where I sat, but he simply stared at me, my words slowly working their way through his brain like a worm in an apple. He chewed his lip, and then stood uncertainly. He clearly did not know what to do. Finally he made to leave, but stopped in the doorway and turned to look at me.

"Oh we . . . ," he said, as if suddenly remembering something, and then he switched to Russian. "We killed the old man."

His goodbyes said, Chernov left and I heard the front door close behind him. I wondered how Jakub Smolna had died, and whether it was quick.

I then noticed that Chernov had left a dribble of coffee in his mug. I snatched the mug and drank it down hungrily. It was still barely lukewarm.

It was the last of the coffee.

# 7

One of our most popular luxury models, Lin Soo is perfect for female identifying intelligences looking to add some Asian glamour to a romantic getaway in the physical realm. But don't let her beauty and youth fool you, this clonesuit is perfectly suited to the boardroom, too!

Many customers have reported clinching that big deal while wearing Lin Soo. We can't imagine why!

*Rental Price: €400 per day.*
*Features:*
*Back-up chip as standard.*
*Medical insurance included in purchase.*
*Fully immunized and sterilized.*
*—Model 334: "Lin Soo" Asian Female (Teen),*
brochure for Basravi's High Quality Clonesuits,
Tehran, Republic of Persia

I took both Xiraus to bed. Mrs. Xirau would be arriving tomorrow morning and I was woefully unprepared. I had hoped to have both files read and reread by the time she arrived in Caspian, but the Parias' paperwork and now Chernov's visit had made that impossible. I huddled under the blankets against the cold and wearily tried to at least get the gist of tomorrow's itinerary.

Within five minutes, I was asleep.

———————

That night I dreamt of my wife—ex-wife.

Olesya, who died in transit.

I dreamed of a night twenty years ago when I had been lying in bed, listening to the rain hammering nails into the roof.

The bed was a mile wide.

Olesya had left four months before, after a row that had seen both of us say things that could not easily be unsaid. She had been on her well-worn soapbox, saying that I was blind to the cruelties that ordinary Caspians had to endure.

I told her that while she had been living a life of luxury in Azadlig, my mother and I had been trying to survive on a war widow's pension in a two-room flat on Moscow Street with no heating and that she did not get to lecture me on privilege.

She had called me a murderer.

I had yelled at her that I had never murdered anyone. I had killed, yes. For my country and for my people. Was a soldier a murderer? Was her father a murderer?

"Soldiers kill people who can fight back," she had said. "Those twenty Ajay kids gunned down in Shaki, did they put up a good fight? Glorious battle was it?"

I had protested: that had been the army, not StaSec, not me. . . .

"No, Nicky," she had cut across me. "It's you. As long as you carry a gun for them, you're part of it. It's all you."

A knock on the back door. Soft, apologetic, gentle. Barely audible over the rolling hum of the rain on the roof tiles. I padded wearily to the kitchen and pulled the door open.

She stood there in the doorway, a fountain in a dress, rain pouring down her long auburn hair in rivulets. She cocked her head at me, a smile half apologetic and half teasing, equal parts *Sorry* and *Miss me?*

Without a word, I let her in. She stood in the kitchen, looking around anxiously like a stranger at a party. I got her a towel and she undressed then and there and dried her hair while I gathered up her clothes. They were soaked through, less like she had gone walking in a storm than that she had been swimming. Jokingly, I asked her if she had jumped in the sea.

"I was pacing in the street outside for an hour," she said. "I was worried one of your mates would get the wrong idea and arrest me for solicitation."

"Why?"

She looked at me, like I was an optical illusion and she just couldn't see what I was meant to be. She shook her head tiredly.

"Didn't know if I should knock," she said. "Didn't know if you wanted me to. Didn't know if I wanted to. Still don't. I don't know what I'm doing here. I should go. . . ."

She looked around for her clothes to get dressed and leave. I took her wrist in my hand.

"Stay," I said.

That's a lie.

"Stay," I begged.

Whatever was pulling her to leave let go. She stood there, my hand on her wrist. She didn't take it. She didn't brush it off. She simply remained.

Olesya was proud, above all things. Coming here would have cost her a great deal.

I would have to bridge the remaining distance. Fortunately, I have never been called "proud."

"I have missed you," I said, and the words felt so paltry and small compared to the thing they were trying to describe. "I need you."

Hardly poetry, but sometimes small, simple words get through where long, flowery sentences would snag.

She took my hand and gave it a cold, wet squeeze.

"Ever since the funeral all I've wanted . . ."

I stopped. Her grip had become corpse-like. Her breath caught in her throat and for a moment her expression was coldly furious.

I shouldn't have mentioned the funeral. Her father had passed away two months ago. She was obviously still hurting, and hurting badly. I was, too.

"Sorry," I said. "I shouldn't have . . ."

Suddenly, she was a different woman. She placed a finger on my lip and smiled gently.

"It's all right," she soothed. "It's all right. I know." She sighed. "Nicky, I haven't treated you very well, have I?"

I felt that there was a time for candor and a time for tact, and this was the latter.

"Why did you come back?" I asked.

"Are you angry?" she asked, not distracted in the slightest.

I said nothing for a few seconds. The kitchen felt only a few feet wide, like we were trapped together in a cell. Every breath felt like a prelude to catastrophe.

"Yes," I said truthfully.

"Fair," she said.

There were rules. Yell at me, if you will. Leave me, fine. Fly across the country and shack up in some cabin with one of your artist friends, perfectly acceptable.

But tell me where you're going. That was the rule, unspoken but perfectly understood and ironclad. I had finally believed that she was gone for good, not because she had run away, but because she had left no trail to follow.

She buried her head in the towel and I heard her say, matter-of-factly, "We don't work, you and I. I can't change and you won't stop changing. The man I married is different from the man I met, the man you are now is different from the man I married. Who will you be tomorrow, Nikolai?"

"Your husband," I said. "I hope."

"So do I," she said. "Because I've realized something rather embarrassing. I love you, and I don't like being away from you."

"But we don't work," I said wearily.

"No," she said. "You make me crazy and I make you miserable."

"I was miserable when you were gone," I said, an understatement to the point of a lie.

"Well then," she said. "Which misery do you prefer?"

"This," I said. "I prefer this."

"Good," she said. "So do I."

"You're shivering," I said.

"It's cold. Could you get me some clothes, please?"

"No," I said. And I kissed her.

We used big, old dial phones in the Caspian Republic. Ancient. Analog. Unhackable. And, if one went off beside you while you were sleeping, loud enough to rattle your teeth. I lurched up and out of bed and grabbed the phone clumsily and wheezed the word "South . . ."

"You didn't really think I'd let you sleep in just because you've been reassigned, did you?" said a voice at the other end.

"Who is this?" I felt wretched. From the hot haze on my brow and the mottle of phlegm in my mouth I could tell that I'd caught a chill walking home through the sleet.

"Grier."

I slumped back onto my pillow. Grier? I was in no condition for Grier.

"I don't know anyone by that name," I said coldly. "I never have and I never will."

"Now, now. Don't be like that," Grier chided. "What choice did I have? Anyone would have thought you were for the chop. I was hardly going to stick my neck out and say, 'Oh please, me too.' I mean, it's not like we're old friends. I don't even like you. Do you like me?"

"No," I said.

"Well, there you go," said Grier, without a hint of rancor.

I carried the phone into the kitchen and began foraging for breakfast. I found a half-empty box of crackers and poured them into a bowl and began to eat them one by one like some kind of grim mechanism.

"When are you meeting her?" Grier asked.

"Who?"

"Mrs. Xirau."

"You're awfully well informed," I said.

"I'm just getting started. Do you know the name Oleg Mansani?"

"The man who killed Paulo Xirau?"

"Yes. Turns out he was the boyfriend of Yasmin Paria. And you'll never guess . . ."

"Sheena was involved with Paulo," I said.

Grier sounded disappointed. "Oh. How did you know?"

It had all suddenly clicked into place. I could practically see the damn scene unfold before my eyes. Paulo is seeing Sheena. Oleg is seeing Yasmin. Paulo walks into the bar, sees Yasmin. Kisses the wrong twin, right in front of her boyfriend. It was like something out of a hackneyed comedic farce, except it had ended not with a double wedding but a grubby second-degree murder.

"Xirau's file said it was a case of mistaken identity," I explained. "He kissed Yasmin, thinking she was Sheena."

"Ah," said Grier. "Well, Sheena was apparently the luckier twin. Oleg was a bit of a bastard, by all accounts. Treated Yasmin appallingly. So with him in jail and poor Paulo dead . . ."

"The Parias have no more reason to stay in Caspian. That's why they decided to be contranned."

It was usually the way. Family and friends were often the only tether that kept people in the Caspian Republic. Many decided to flee to the Machine world after a bereavement or a bad breakup. They weren't just leaving their bodies behind.

"Do you believe in coincidences, South?" Grier asked.

I knew what he meant. To be assigned the Parias' contran case and the Xirau detail in the same day, and now to learn Xirau and Sheena Paria had been involved? There was something going on here. There was a mechanism over my head, whirring menacingly in the shadows. But I couldn't see its shape. As if suddenly remembering a bad dream, I recalled Chernov's visit the night before and his theory about a contran operation being run from within StaSec. Chernov . . . that reminded me.

"Did Wernham tell you I was escorting Mrs. Xirau?" I asked.

"He did," said Grier, smugly.

"Yes, while I'm sure you're having a good time I'd be careful what you say around him," I advised.

"What do you mean?"

"He's turning tricks for ParSec."

The line went silent, and I could practically hear Grier's brain desperately replaying every conversation he'd had with Wernham in the last year, trying to recall every piece of information and gossip he had entrusted to him.

"You think I don't know that?" he said at last.

"Yes!" I barked angrily, and hung up.

# 8

There was a king, cruel and powerful. One day, he bought a slave and set him to work cleaning and cooking for him. The slave worked tirelessly, never once failing to obey his master, and without so much as the whisper of a complaint ever escaping his lips. The king was pleased with his servant, and began to entrust him with more and more responsibilities. Before long the slave was in charge of the king's household, commanding other servants, purchasing food and wine and even acting in the king's stead when he was sick or absent. As the king grew older, he became ill and confined to his bed. The slave ensured that his master was comfortable and wanted for nothing; he ordered the finest doctors in the land to come and live in the palace so that they could be at the king's bedside at a moment's notice. The king, now mellowed in his old age, took the slave's hand and thanked him for his years of faithful, unstinting service. The slave smiled to his master and left the king's chambers. He then walked to the great hall, and placed the crown upon his head.

—Leon Mendelssohn, *The Slave Enthroned:*
*The Triumvirate and the Death of Democracy*

I was barely dressed when the driver arrived. Like a bad student the morning of an exam I tore desperately through Mrs. Xirau's itinerary in the backseat of the car while the driver, a short Persian man in his fifties, gazed at me witheringly in the rearview mirror.

I was thwarted, however. There was an ink shortage in StaSec, and all documents were now printed as faintly as possible on cheap, light green paper that the letters blended into like jungle warriors hiding in the canopy. Between this, my short-sightedness, the motion of the car and the early-morning gloom, the document might as well have been written in Sanskrit for all that I could glean from it. The headers, at least, were bolded, which allowed me to deduce that Mrs. Xirau's visit would last for a total of three days. This struck me as odd. How long does it take to identify a body? Perhaps the government had planned some kind of hospitality for Mrs. Xirau, maybe a performance of some state-sanctioned theater, or a meeting with the leading lights of the party?

Better her than me.

I resolved to read the entire document from cover to cover as soon as I found somewhere with better light, and until then to play my cards as close to my chest as possible.

Ellulgrad International Airport was possibly the least used airport of any capital city in the world. In reality it was a mere airfield on the outskirts of the city where half a dozen prop planes (the nation's airline) stood on the tarmac like the nation's good china: to be seen but rarely (if ever) to be used. That morning they couldn't even be seen, as the night's sleet had given way to a thick, silvery fog that blanketed the whole airfield.

I had been assigned a very specific time and place to meet Mrs. Xirau, and if one could credit the Machine with any virtue, it was punctuality. I got out of the car while the driver remained in the front seat, staring ahead motionlessly.

I remember how perfectly silent it was. The fog had smothered the world. I took a deep breath of the cold, clammy air and held it. I could hear my own heartbeat. I exhaled, and my breath slipped silver from my mouth to rejoin the fog. Then, overhead, I heard a low growl, and I looked up to see two points of red light peeping feebly through the dense soup. Illuminated against the red haze I could make out the outline of the drone, narrow and sharklike. As it flew overhead and came in to land, I found myself wondering if the drone was afraid. It was, I realized, a more complex question than it might at first appear and while I waited for the drone to touch down I ran through the various possibilities.

1) The drone is not afraid. It is not intelligent. It is simply a machine programmed to fly to a certain location, disgorge its cargo and return to its point of origin. It does not feel fear. It feels nothing at all.

2) The drone is afraid. It is sentient and understands that every antiaircraft gun in the Caspian Republic is currently trained on it and that one instance of human error could blow it out of the sky. It fears for its continued existence.

3) The drone is not afraid. It is sentient and understands that every antiaircraft gun in the Caspian Republic is a claptrap piece of obsolete technological nonsense that represents no threat to a shimmering, gleaming piece of advanced aerodynamics such as itself. Because we have fallen that far behind.

4) The drone is not afraid. It is sentient. It understands that every antiaircraft gun is currently trained against it. Those weapons, despite their age, are perfectly capable of destroying the drone. But it is not afraid, because it is a very brave drone, that understood the risks of this mission, believes in the rightness of its cause and would be only too proud to die in the line of duty.

The drone, whether it was courageous, fearful, contemptuous or unthinking, did its duty regardless. It landed and extended two thin legs upon which it raised itself vertically. It opened its belly and out stepped, as hesitant and ungainly as a newborn fawn, a woman. She set her small valise down by her feet, and began to smooth out her dress, which had apparently become rumpled during the flight.

It was impossible to gauge her age at this distance and with this fog, but I knew that logically she would appear to be in her twenties or younger. Cloned bodies were a product. No one intentionally bought or sold old bodies any more than they would old milk or old bread. She was wearing a modest, knee-length dress, and a respectable brown woolen shawl. She was, I noticed with surprise, wearing exactly the kind of clothing one would expect to see a woman her age wearing in the Caspian Republic. I would have taken her for the wife of a regional party head from the countryside. The kind of respectable female who gives soft-spoken speeches about civic duty and the principles of the party to classrooms of bored children in the local school. For a moment, I wondered if fashions in the Machine world were so like our own and instantly chided myself for my denseness. *Of course it is dressed like one of us,* I thought to myself. *Walking around looking like it has come from the outside world would be lethally stupid.*

"It" or "she"?

*"She," by the laws of the Caspian Republic. An honorary human being,* said the Good Brother.

*But also "it,"* the Good Brother corrected himself, *because she is a machine. She. She is it. She is . . . it is . . .*

I had the momentary sense of satisfaction one gets from watching two people one despises getting into an argument.

She, it, the individual in question had not yet seen me.

The drone returned to the horizontal position and wheeled around as gracefully and noiselessly as a swan on a lake. With a low buzz, it suddenly sprinted for the end of the tarmac, took to the air and was gone within seconds.

She watched it go, her body language the very picture of abandonment. I wondered if they were friends.

"Lily Xirau?" I called. She started and turned around. Her face was obscured by a scarf. Sensible wear in this weather.

"Yes?" she said, a little hesitantly, as if she were unused to the name.

The simple fact of what I was seeing, a young woman stranded in a hostile foreign country and very clearly afraid, contrasted with the knowledge of what she actually *was* (a fiendishly sophisticated computer program puppeteering a slab of cloned human flesh), induced a feeling of moral nausea. She seemed so normal, so perfectly designed to put me at ease, that the effect reversed and became quite terrifying. So much effort had clearly gone in to making her seem like a normal human being. She was a work of perfect artifice, with such fanatical, obsessive attention to detail, that it shook me to the core.

I wondered how long it would take before I started forgetting what she was.

*Be strong, South,* the Good Brother advised, and for once the advice was welcome.

I had taken a risk with Smolna. I did not intend to take any others. Not with a case like this that would be attracting all kinds of the wrong sort of attention. There could be no laxness. No rule breaking. No softheartedness.

*I am not myself,* I thought. *I am the Good Brother.*

I banished myself, and let the voice that was always in the back of my head speak for me.

"I am Security Agent South," I announced brusquely. "I am to be your escort."

My tone was cold and harsh, and I could tell from her eyes that she was miserably disappointed. She had been hoping desperately for a friend.

"South?" she asked.

"That is correct."

"A pleasure to meet you," she said, and extended her hand.

StaSec is not in the business of shaking hands. I ignored her.

"I am to take you to identify your husband's remains." A look of mild confusion passed over her features but I continued. "Before we leave the airport I must ensure that you understand the conditions of your stay here."

"All right," she said, quietly.

I had been given a specific text to read to her. Fortunately, the morning light had improved enough that I could actually read it.

"You have been granted the status of natural-born human by special dispensation of the Parliament of the Caspian Republic hereafter referred to as 'the Parliament,'" I began. "If you breach any of the following restrictions, the Parliament reserves the right to summarily rescind this special dispensation and place you under arrest for breach of the laws of the Caspian Republic. Notwithstanding this special dispensation, you are strictly forbidden from engaging in any form of consciousness transferal. In the unlikely event of your physical death, in the eyes of the law you will be considered dead and will be legally obliged to remain so. You will remain with me at all times. If you wish to speak to anyone you must first ask my permission, and the conversation must be conducted in my presence. If you are carrying any weaponry, contraband or recording equipment on your person you must disclose them to me now or risk the revocation of the special dispensation. At all times, you shall . . ."

"Excuse me?"

Her voice cut across mine and I fell silent. I didn't really have a choice. There was an authority to that voice. It was not demanding. But she had that quiet power that some women have. The unspoken assumption that they are going to be obeyed, because they are.

"Yes?"

"Is there much more of this?" she asked. There was no hint of reproach in her voice, which made the reproach sting all the more.

I glanced down at my text. I was around a fifth of the way through.

"The list of restrictions is quite comprehensive," I mumbled, as if I had let her down.

"Do you have a car?"

"There is an agency car waiting for us outside."

"Then can we go, and I'll read the rest of them as we drive?" she asked reasonably.

"It's quite cold," she added.

So much for the Good Brother. I blushed from shame. Stammering my apologies, I offered to take her bag; she demurred, I insisted and she relented.

I opened the door of the car for her and sat down beside her and told the driver to take us to StaSec HQ. I noticed she stared at the driver, and when the car drove off she involuntarily gripped the handrest. I realized that she had probably never been in a car that had been driven by a human being.

"It's quite safe," I whispered.

She nodded, but looked anything but reassured.

The inside of the car was quite warm now, and she reached up to remove her hat and scarf. It was fascinating watching her move. Every motion was graceful and precise, but also very clearly conscious. She had to think of everything, down to the last motion of the last finger. When it came to manipulating this body of hers, she had knowledge, but no instinct. She took off the hat first, and long curly brown hair fell about her shoulders.

Then came the scarf, revealing the lower half of her face and I almost screamed.

Instead, I stared at her in dumbfounded horror.

"What?" she asked, nervously. "What is it?"

*It is a coincidence,* I told myself.

*Or, it is a trap.*

*Either way, it must be ignored. Don't let it affect you. Don't let it make you do anything you would not ordinarily do.*

*How could they know?*

*Exactly. They didn't. They couldn't. It's pure chance.*

*Impossible. HOW DID THEY KNOW?*

"Agent South?" she asked. "Is something wrong?"

There is a face that I know better than my own. A face that hangs on the wall of my mind. This was the face that greeted me when I opened the back door in the middle of a rainy night a lifetime ago, wearing defiance and apology. A beautiful face. Mysterious, maddening, loving, cruel. It was the face beneath mine, hovering in the darkness like a pale stone at the bottom of a pool when we made love on the table in the kitchen. It was the face beneath mine on the beach when she had been pulled from the ocean and my breath had not been enough.

And it was the face of the Machine sitting across from me now in the car. It was impossible. But there it was. This Lily was Olesya alive again. Not similar. Not remarkably reminiscent of.

The woman herself.

Someone had done this. Someone had chosen that body for her. Someone had . . . somehow, re-created the body of my dead wife and given it to this code bitch to wear.

This would lead to murder. I swore it then. I would find the person that had thought this was a good idea. I would show them that they were mistaken. I would go to the Machine world if I had to. I cursed them. I cursed Niemann for giving me this detail. I cursed the world and everything in it. The wounds of two decades had been reopened and I felt like I was bleeding to death.

I smiled.

"I'm fine," I told her.

# 9

The Machine is not human, but is uncannily similar to a specific class of human, namely the psychopath. The Machine lies perfectly, as it has no sense of shame. The only reason a Machine captive will tell the truth will be if doing so is the only way to prevent its own destruction. Even then, it will conspire to use the truth to its own greatest advantage, and to the detriment of its enemies.

*—Agent's Handbook of the State Security Agency of the Caspian Republic*

I had not really had a chance to consider Chernov's theory that someone in StaSec was in league with the contran operation that had claimed the Paria twins among hundreds of others. If I had given it any thought, it was to consider it much as I considered Chernov himself: dangerous and lethally stupid. That was partly lingering institutional loyalty, on my part. StaSec was in many ways the long-suffering older child of the government's many apparatuses: distrusted, maligned, overlooked in favor of its more fanatically zealous younger sibling, ParSec. But it was (in its gray, plodding, jaded way) quietly and deeply loyal.

"If you had so much as a traitorous thought in your head I would have pried it out and stamped on it a long time ago," Niemann had warned. And I believed her.

The idea of anyone in StaSec running or even assisting in

a contran operation seemed grotesque and bizarre. And then there was Chernov's theory that Lily Xirau was a courier, intended to accept custody of the Sontang chips that would carry the consciousnesses of hundreds of Caspian defectors to the Machine world. I could see why it would appeal to Chernov: It was an obvious, stupid plan and he was an obvious, stupid man. But anyone with an ounce of savvy could have told him that Lily Xirau was the worst possible candidate for such a task. Her arrival in Caspian was an event. Shocking. Unprecedented. Guaranteed to draw attention. Instructions that "StaSec is handling this" notwithstanding, every security agency in the country would be watching her like a hawk. It was perhaps more dramatic to imagine Lily Xirau smuggling the chips out from under the very noses of the nation's gatekeepers in her handbag, rather than some anonymous, unshaven smuggler ferrying them across the sea to Persia in a fishing boat on a foggy night. But that was ParSec's entire problem. They were less an intelligence agency, and more a gang of enthusiastic amateurs pretending to be one. They saw drama and plot everywhere.

Unbidden, I heard Chernov's voice in my head: *But now, here comes Lily Xirau.*

Yes, indeed.

Mrs. Xirau's appearance had thrown everything into question, and what had once seemed lurid and unthinkable now stood revealed as the only likely scenario. I glanced at her briefly, for the fifth or seventh time, to be sure I was not imagining it. She pretended not to notice, but I could see her wince miserably under my gaze. She knew something was wrong but didn't dare to ask what. She was most likely cursing the day she had decided to come here. I was not imagining it. Lily Xirau was a perfect double for Olesya, my wife—ex-wife, who had drowned in the Caspian Sea twenty years ago.

Very well. The situation was plain. Now, to figure out why.

Preferably, in the twenty minutes before the car reached StaSec HQ.

First things first, to dispose of the obvious. Could this be just a coincidence?

This was simultaneously the most mundane-seeming, and least likely of all possible scenarios. After all, one meets people who remind one of other people all the time and there are only so many faces to go around. But it could not be overstressed, Lily did not simply resemble Olesya. She was identical. And the notion that out of all people, I had been chosen to escort her, and out of all people on earth that she could have resembled she just happened to be the perfect double of Olesya? Ludicrous. Impossible. There was intent here. There had to be.

Very well, then what was to be gained? What would I do for someone who looked like Olesya that I would not do for someone else?

Oh, that was clever. That was despicably clever. Yes. I imagined that if you could approach someone in the body of a loved one who had died long ago, someone that they had failed, someone that they had let down, and gave them a chance to make things right . . . the jigs and reels you could make them dance. The vows and loyalties they would betray for you. The Machine was the devil, we were often told. Clearly, we had not been giving it due credit. That was clever.

Very well. I was being targeted. Lily Xirau was going to try to turn me or somehow use me for her own ends. How then did they get her to look so like Olesya?

My wife had been buried in the Resting Place of the Founders, on the northern outskirts of Ellulgrad. In order to clone her body they would have had to exhume her, extract a viable genetic sample (after twenty years?), somehow smuggle that to the Machine world and clone Olesya, growing her to maturity in time for Lily Xirau to be contranned into her and sent to Caspian. Impossible.

Niemann had informed me that I was being assigned to the Xirau detail only yesterday, and had presumably come to that decision at most only a few days ago when Paulo's autopsy had revealed him to be machine. There simply wasn't enough time.

An alternative: The Machine had been informed that I was to escort Lily Xirau. They had found a cloned body that closely resembled Olesya, and then surgically altered it to close the gap. I glanced again at Mrs. Xirau. I could not see a trace of surgery anywhere on her features, but who knew how advanced the Machine's techniques were? That seemed far more plausible.

Regardless, if one accepted that Mrs. Xirau's resemblance to Olesya was not a coincidence, that led one inexorably to the following conclusions:

1) Lily Xirau, far from being an innocent grieving widow, is an agent of the Machine Powers and she is on a mission.

2) This mission will require her playing on my feelings for my dead wife, and using them against me.

3) Given the recent uptake in contran in the city, it is most likely that she is here to accept custody of the dozen missing Sontang chips and will try to suborn me to aid or at least overlook her efforts to do so.

4) Given that the Machine knew to disguise its agent as Olesya, it has a source that was able to provide it with photographic references of her. Such as would be available in my StaSec file.

5) StaSec has therefore been compromised, and someone within its ranks is working with the contran operation and quite possibly running it.

Or, to put it another way, Chernov had been right about every single thing. And that was not the most mind-boggling thing of all, only because I had literally just seen my wife return from the grave.

I briefly wondered if perhaps Mrs. Xirau was blameless. Maybe she didn't know the significance of the body she had been given? No. No one gave a spy a gun and then neglected to teach them how to shoot. She had to know. She had to know why she looked the way she did. Lily Xirau was the enemy, and I would have to treat her as such.

For a moment, I considered simply blowing the entire thing up. March up to Niemann's office, explain that Lily Xirau had obviously been sent as an agent and have her dragged off to a small cell, a cold meal and a quick death.

Unless . . .

Oh, be careful here, South.

Imagine if the outside world hears that the brutal, backward Caspian Republic has executed a poor innocent woman who had been invited to identify the body of her murdered husband? It had long been taken as gospel within Caspian that the ultimate goal of the Triumvirate was to conquer or crush us. We were the random element that could not be incorporated into their perfect system, a recurring flaw, a virus in the data. What if George or Athena were not interested in a few hundred contranned Caspians? What if their goal was the whole nation?

The state-sanctioned murder of poor, grieving Mrs. Xirau.

I had certainly heard worse pretexts for war.

Be careful here, South. Play your part, for now.

# 10

It is common to hear Koslova, Papalazarou pére and Dascalu referred to as the "Holy Trinity" of the Founding. With regards to Dascalu, the comparison would be apt only if the Father and Son had dismissed the Holy Spirit, and hired Satan as his replacement.

—Ignatius Kasamarin, personal correspondence, date unknown

Mrs. Xirau and I walked through the lobby of StaSec HQ, past the massive portrait of Dascalu that scowled over his children like God watching the Israelites pay homage to the golden calf. When Lily walked past him I half expected that Dascalu would burst into flames, or the paint melt and bleed onto the marble floor. Beneath the portrait was the main desk, manned by an ancient creature named Berger who was as much an institution in StaSec as the portrait that hung over him. The rumor was that he was immortal. He was on the phone as we approached, taking notes on a large yellow pad. He glanced up and gestured for me to wait until he had finished. I did not wish to look at Lily, and so I fixed my gaze on the massive portrait that hung above us. Doctor Simon Augustine Emmanuel Dascalu. Looking at him, you could mistake him for an elderly Darwin, or George Bernard Shaw, his face enrobed in a magnificent white beard as pure white as an angel's wing. But Darwin always looks

sad, and Shaw mischievous. Doctor Dascalu's expression was
a warning. Even as he glowered up at you from the obverse of
the fifty moneta bill he seemed to be questioning your motives:
*What are you going to spend that fifty on, Brother? Nothing
disloyal, I trust?*

The Old Man. That was what they had called him. Even in
the earliest days of the Founding, when he had only been in his
fifties. It was the title, the beard. The air of a stormy king in winter. If Koslova had been the heart and blood and muscle of the
revolution and Papalazarou Senior its voice, Dascalu was its cold,
ruthless intellect. The Old Man, even the official histories would
admit, had no scruple about doing what needed to be done.
Kasamarin's appraisal of him was practically blistering, which
made reading his chapters on the Founding of StaSec a giddy,
delicious thrill. But Kasamarin was party royalty, and could say
such things. And besides, Dascalu was long dead, and his reach
(though considerable) did not quite extend beyond the grave.

Dascalu had been StaSec's first director, its founder and its
midwife. He had lobbied for its creation in Parliament, and
taken control of it when it was done. In the twenty-seven years
of his reign StaSec was (quite rightly) seen as simply an extension of Dascalu himself. If you were Dascalu's enemy, you were
StaSec's. And if you were StaSec's enemy, you were the enemy of
the Caspian Republic. The distinction was moot. That was the
point. So melded together in the common mind were StaSec
and Dascalu that the doctor's nickname attached itself to his
creation. StaSec was "The Old Man," and the name stuck long
after Dascalu had finally shuffled out the door to be replaced by
his ruthless young lieutenant, Samuel Papalazarou Junior. He
truly had been the "old man" by then, eighty-six years old and
drifting like a rudderless ship. He had retired to his dacha and
died a few months later, as we all knew he would. Separate Dascalu from StaSec? A separated Siamese twin would have better

odds of survival. So the old man had died, but The Old Man lived on. But names have a habit of changing their meaning over time, and "The Old Man" had taken on a rather different cast in recent years. No longer did it conjure images of Dascalu's scowling face and penetrating, all-seeing glare. With the rise of ParSec, StaSec was an old man like any other old man: tired, increasingly irrelevant, mocked, faded and almost certainly not long for the earth.

"Hello, Agent South. Have you been promoted yet?" Berger asked.

"Not yet, Paul. Not yet," I said with a smile.

Paul Berger had been the porter when I had joined StaSec. I had been a young man then, and he most certainly had not, and yet here he was still. I had sometimes wondered if he had been here even before StaSec. Perhaps he had been the receptionist of the Neftchilar Grand Hotel and had been included with the building when StaSec took over. It would explain why he was always so welcoming. If you spent your whole day in StaSec and saw only one smile, you could be certain that it was Berger's.

"Ah well," he said, "any day now. And who is your lovely guest?"

"This is Lily Xirau," I said. "She should be in the book."

"Yes indeed, yes indeed, yes indeed," Berger muttered, running his finger over the relevant page of his diary, and then ducking under his desk, which caused his knees to crack like gunfire.

"Welcome to Caspian, my dear lady," said Berger, smiling beneficently as he re-emerged. I wondered if he knew she was machine, and if it would have made a difference to him. In his hand he had an identification badge and lanyard which he delicately placed on her neck as if presenting her with a medal.

"Please be sure to keep it visible at all times, thank you, it helps us a great deal."

Lily nodded, smiling. "I will, thank you."

"Now, you're in room fifteen, on the third floor—"

"No," I interrupted, "we're in . . . are you sure?"

I had been going to say "the morgue," but that had felt indelicate.

"Quite sure, Agent South," he said, a little peevishly and showed me his diary. Sure enough: "A. South, W. Xirau-12.00 a.m. F3 R15." (The "A" and "W" standing for "agent" and "witness" respectively.)

"We're not all half blind, you know," he said, rather smugly. Berger, despite being almost three decades my senior, had perfect vision, something he would happily remind me, or indeed anyone else, on the thinnest of pretexts.

That was very strange. The identification of bodies always took place in the morgue, which was three stories belowground level ("two inches above hell" as the saying went). So why instead was I being told to bring Lily Xirau to the third floor, when that would mean carting Paulo Xirau's cadaver up six stories through StaSec, past agents and secretaries who were just about to go on lunch, to a nonrefrigerated room so that she could identify her husband, who would then be carted *back* down six stories past agents and secretaries who had no doubt decided that they might just skip lunch today? It was grotesque, illogical and made not a lick of sense. Someone clearly made a mistake here, but, seeing as I was reasonably sure that it wasn't me, I decided not to question it anymore.

I gestured brusquely for Lily to follow me, and we headed to the elevator.

"You're to be very nice to Mrs. Xirau, South, do you hear me?" Berger called cheerfully after us.

I did not reply.

Room 15 turned out to be quite large, reminiscent of nothing so much as a jury room with a long table stretching from end to end and two iron chairs with splintery wooden seats. Save those scant furnishing and some blinds on the windows, the room was antiseptic in its bareness. There was another door to the right, which led to a tiny bathroom and a utilities room, where tools were kept for the less genteel interrogations.

"Please, sit down," I gestured to the nearest chair, and she did without a word.

"We appear to be early," I said. "It'll just be a few minutes."

She nodded, saying nothing.

What was she playing at?

If her goal was to turn me to her cause, she was playing very coy. I would have expected her to be making small talk, turning on the charm, learning what made Nikolai South tick and what buttons to press to get him to tock. Instead, she sat at the table, staring ahead, trying not to make eye contact and looking like she wanted nothing more than to be somewhere else.

We waited.

What better time to start a conversation without seeming suspicious? And yet she said nothing.

The silence became so excruciating that I, against all good sense, was the first to speak.

"Did you have a pleasant flight?" I asked, like an ass.

She stared at me, almost in shock. I didn't blame her. I had been giving her icy silence since we had left the airport and now I was making banal small talk.

"Not really," she said.

"First time flying?" I asked.

"A few days ago, it was my first time walking," she replied.

"You don't walk where you're from?" I asked.

She shook her head.

"I live in an ocean," she said quietly. There was an unmistakable pang of homesickness in her voice.

"Must be bewildering," I said. "To be on dry land."

"Yes," she said. "The real world takes a lot of getting used to."

*Madam, you know not the half of it.*

There was a knock at the door. I opened it and a thin, thoroughly disreputable-looking StaSec porter stood outside holding a clipboard. He was in his twenties and wore a filthy pair of overalls and had the kind of face that would have you instinctively reaching for your wallet to be sure it was still there.

"Agent South?" he said, in a way that made my name sound like a vulgarity.

"Yes?" I said.

"Identification of Paulo . . ."

"Paulo Xirau, yes. What took you so long?" I said tersely.

The porter was having none of it. "Don't blame me. The van was late from another job and then the traffic getting here was . . ."

It was a lie and in any case I could not have cared less.

"Fine. Fine. Just bring him in," I snapped.

The porter turned and called down the corridor, and to my shock six more porters barged into the room, each carrying several large cardboard boxes, which they left on the table, building a wall that completely closed off Lily from my view. They then departed as quickly as they had entered, leaving only the first porter, who shoved a clipboard and pen into my face and instructed me to sign.

"What's all this?" I asked incredulously.

"What do you mean, 'what's all this?'" the pup inquired.

I had had just about enough.

"Young man," I said, in a voice like iron, "let me explain something to you. I am here to oversee the identification of the remains of a Mr. Paulo Xirau."

I gestured to the twelve boxes that had been deposited on the table. "And unless Mr. Xirau's death was far, far more violent than I was given to understand, I doubt that is what you have brought me. Look, here!"

I took my itinerary and practically fed it to him.

"There! See? 'Remains of Paulo Xirau'!"

"Effects."

"What?"

"It doesn't say 'remains,'" said the porter patiently, as if explaining to a doddering relative which grandchild was which.

"'Effects of Paulo Xirau,'" he read aloud.

I snatched the paper back. He was right, curse him. In the indoor lighting I could finally make out the words clearly.

"These are from his lodgings. We were told to pack them up and bring them here."

"These . . . what *are* these?" I spluttered.

The porter shrugged. "Books mostly. Pamphlets. Newspapers. Few letters."

"Who is your supervisor?" I asked, going for the jugular.

"Now, now, there's no need for that," the porter stammered, no doubt realizing that the situation had escalated and that he was now in too deep.

"Who is your supervisor, please?" I said, as cold as death. "I need to have a word with them right this instant. . . ."

"Agent South?" said one of the boxes.

I leaned my head behind the box. Lily looked up at me with a helpful smile.

"I think there's been a misunderstanding," she explained calmly. "I'm not here to view my husband's body. I never saw his body. Didn't they tell you?"

I felt like an idiot. Of course, if Lily and Paulo had lived together in a virtual state, she would never have seen the body that he downloaded himself into when he immigrated to Caspian.

"No. They didn't tell me," I sighed wearily. "Might I ask how you intend to identify him as your husband?"

"That's what all this is for," she said, gesturing to the boxes. "I'm to go through his books and writings. I'm identifying his mind, not his body. And once I'm convinced that the man all this belonged to was my husband, I'll say so."

"But that could take days," I said.

Yes, South. It could. Which is why she's staying for three. Fool.

"I'm very sorry. I thought you knew," she said, apologetically, as if it were all her fault.

I shook my head and turned back to the porter.

"So . . . we're good?" he asked warily.

With a weary nod, I signed for the boxes and he tipped his hat to us both and turned to leave. On a whim, I called after him.

"Give my regards to Chernov."

He froze, and then tried to pretend like he hadn't heard me, his shoulders hunched almost to his ears. I followed him out and called suggestions to him jovially as he tried to walk briskly but nonchalantly down the long corridor: "'Who's Chernov?' 'I don't know who that is.' 'Never heard of him, Brother!' 'What are you talking about?' You could at least make an effort!"

Once again, I had bluffed and they had folded. If a man could arrange a high-stakes poker game with a dozen of ParSec's best, by morning he could retire on his winnings.

"Who is Chernov?" Lily asked, as I stepped back into the room.

Ah, time to gather data?

"Believe me when I say he is of absolutely no consequence," I replied. "Now, how exactly is this supposed to work?"

"Good question," she murmured, as if to herself, looking quite daunted at the massive wall of boxes. She chewed her lower lip pensively. That broke the spell, a little. Olesya was always a model of poise. Lily may have looked identical to her but was making no effort to mimic her body language or affect. Maybe she thought that would be too obvious, maybe she didn't think of it. Too often, in counterintelligence, the trick is figuring out whether your target is very stupid or very clever.

"Right," she said, and looked straight at me. "Do you believe you have a soul, Agent South?"

*It's trying to make you angry,* the Good Brother advised me. *Don't let it.*

I wanted to answer, *Yes. Of course I have a soul. That's why I'm here. That's why this nation is here. Because we believe that we have souls and you do not.*

But I restrained myself to a cold, curt: "Yes."

"You do," she agreed. "Everyone does."

I almost admired the audacity. I imagined she would have considerable bragging rights when she returned home to the Machine world, telling her friends as to how, in the very center of Ellulgrad, she had proudly championed Digital Equality to the very face of a StaSec agent. I felt the same feeling of envy I had when I saw the graffiti on Saint Basil's. All politics aside, it must be wonderful to be that fearless.

Her resemblance to Olesya was like an autostereogram, those images that children stare at until a hidden picture leaps out at them. I couldn't be sure what I was looking at. At certain moments, she resembled perfectly the girl I had met off Koslova Square all those years ago, so much that I could even smell her perfume wafting over the decades. But at other times Lily Xirau's personality shone through so strongly that any resemblance to Olesya was washed away like a message in the sand. This was one of those moments.

"Everyone's soul is unique," she continued. "And just as your body is built with the protein and calcium and iron you consume every day, your soul is built with words. The words you read, and the words you hear. The soul consumes words, and then it expresses itself through them in a way that is unique to that soul."

I sat down across from her.

"You are here," I said, trying and failing to come up with a formula of words that did not make me feel ridiculous, "to identify your husband's soul?"

"Yes," she said. "Or at least, I hope to. First, I'll read what he read. We haven't been together for twenty years and people change. I need to understand his influences, what was shaping his thinking. The bricks that he was building his soul with."

"And then?" I asked.

"Then I have to read what he was writing. Then it's a case of simple arithmetic. Does the Paulo I knew, plus these books, equal these writings?"

A small but sharp pin of nausea pierced my stomach and the Good Brother shuddered. That was the Machine. We were talking about words, but really we were talking about numbers. The Machine reduced everything to numbers. Even souls.

"And this is just something you can do?" I asked.

"No," she said. "I had myself reprogrammed to include a writing analysis tool."

I said nothing. The Good Brother did not wish that I should speak.

She sat there, waiting for me to say something. When I didn't, she nodded to herself wearily.

"Does that bother you?" she asked me, plainly.

"Yes," I replied. I could not have lied convincingly.

"Well," she said, "I can't help that."

I could tell that no good could come of proceeding down this path, so I changed the subject.

"So. If I understand you correctly, after you have read everything on this table, you will tell me whether or not you believe that the man we knew as Paulo Xirau was your husband?"

"Yes."

"And I suppose I must simply take you at your word?" I

asked. I didn't actually intend it to sound insulting, but my intentions have rarely counted for much. If she was offended, she gave no sign.

"And if there was a body here in front of me and I said, 'That's him,' wouldn't you have to take me at my word?" she asked serenely.

"I suppose I would," I admitted. "It just seems a little ephemeral."

"Well, I'm an ephemeral girl," she said shortly.

Oh *there*. *There* was Olesya. A brusque dismissal wielded like a scalpel.

"What?" she said.

"I'm sorry?"

"You're looking at me strangely," she said.

*Oh, as if you didn't know.*

"Am I?" I said, darkly.

"Yes," she replied. And there was a hint of threat there. That was Olesya, too.

"Am I looking at you?" I persisted. "Is that your body?"

"No," she said, slowly.

"Where did you get it?" I asked it like I had found a gun on her person. Or something precious that had been stolen. *Where did you get it?*

"I'm renting it from a clinic in Tehran," she said.

Of course. Persia was a world leader in cloneflesh.

"Where did they get it?" I asked. "Whose was it, before it was yours?"

*Confess. Confess now.*

"No one's," said Lily slowly and calmly, as if she had known she would need to make this speech and had rehearsed it well. "They grow them. It was never alive. It was never a person."

That was the official story. But there were urban legends. Some said the Persians would buy bodies from poor Caspians in the countryside, smuggle them past the navy to the southern shore and pass them off as clones. Some of the more lurid tales claimed the Persians didn't always buy these corpses, but made their own.

"Are you sure?" I asked her.

*Confess.*

She stood up and faced me. We were almost equal in height.

"Look," she said, "I understand. You don't like me. You don't like what I am. Or the questions I raise in your mind. Or how they make you feel. And I am sorry for your problem. Which, and let me be very, very clear on this, is your problem. And not mine. So why don't you pass me some of those books so we can get started, so that I can go home, and we can go on being untroubled by each other's existence?"

It was a challenge. Either expose her and let the chips fall where they would, or back down. I desperately wanted to confront her, to demand how she had stolen my wife's face, but I couldn't. Because I could very well be playing into her hands. Perhaps she was the sacrificial lamb, designed to be exposed and executed so that the Triumvirate could wipe us off the map without so much as a murmur of disapproval from their drowsy human chattel.

Without a word, I turned away and began rifling through the nearest box of books.

Mrs. Xirau had bluffed, and I had folded.

Paulo Xirau's books could have served as a reading list for any aspiring status climber in the party. There was, of course, Jacques Ellul's *The Technological Society*. Here, too, Lewis's *The Abolition of Man*. And there, nestling among them like an old friend, was the big red K. *A History of the Caspian Republic* by Ignatius Kasamarin. It was a large, crimson hardback that one would find in virtually any home in the Caspian Republic, in Russian or English. I had one myself, and had spent many a happy hour leafing through it.

"I'd start with this," I said, passing it to her.

"Oh?" she said, turning it over curiously in her hands. Any hint of anger and resentment had vanished. That was Olesya, too. She was always turning over a new page. Even the most blazing rows would pass over her without leaving so much as a trace.

"I like history," she said.

"Kasamarin is excellent," I told her.

"Really?"

"Yes. He writes very movingly about the early days of the revolution. The seizing of Baku. The Founding. He was a true believer but clear-eyed nonetheless. If you want to understand the Caspian Republic, that's the book."

"Well," she said with a smile, "don't tell me how it ends."

I watched her reading in silence, and wondered if she already knew.

## 11

Last week I attended the trial of a Needle Man.

He may have been the most repellent, morally filthy creature I have ever laid eyes on. As the judge read out his long list of abominable crimes, I studied this animal, looking for a hint of shame, a flicker that might suggest that he understood how truly fallen he was. I found none.

After he was taken out and shot, I asked a Brother in the party why we even bother with a trial. "You looking to lose weight?" he asked. "You think we need even tougher sanctions?"

I asked if there were any other areas of policy where we deferred to the wishes of the Machine?

He made his excuses, and left the courtroom.

—From "There are ordinary criminals,
and there are Needle Men,"
Paulo Xirau, *The Caspian Truth,*
03 March 2208

L ily read ravenously. Whole pages of text burned before her gaze, and before long there was a stack of volumes beside her seven or eight books high. She did not talk like a machine, but she certainly read like one.

As there is only so long you can watch someone read before it becomes uncomfortable for both parties, I turned my gaze out the window to the street below and tried to find Chernov's man. It took me all of five minutes. I then studied the building across from us, trying to find the room where Chernov and his team would most likely have set up their base. The entire floor seemed abandoned, with charcoal-colored blinds pulled down until a space of around half a foot was left clear, a good space for a camera. But which one was he hiding behind?

"Anything interesting?" I heard a voice say behind me.

I turned to look at her. She was peeping at me over the cover of a large biography of Koslova.

"Not particularly," I said. "Why do you ask?"

"I was just curious," she said. "I thought you were supposed to be watching me. You seem to be watching everything and everyone but me."

"Oh. I'm sorry," I said. "Are you feeling neglected?"

"Nervous," she replied. "Like there's something I should know. Is someone watching me?"

"Apart from me?" I asked.

"Yes."

I paused. Informing a probable Machine spy that she was under observation by ParSec was the kind of thing that could look very much like treason, depending on the light. On the other hand, ParSec were out of bounds here. They had been given strict instructions that this was a StaSec matter. If I were feeling coy, I could have argued that, by telling Lily she was under ParSec observation, I was feeding her false intelligence. ParSec had been told they could not observe her, so *of course* I assumed that they weren't. Was I to assume that ParSec had violated orders? The very thought.

But ultimately, it came to this: Was I willing to carry water for Chernov? Like hell.

"Yes," I told her.

"Chernov."

"Yes," I repeated. "Or someone Chernov-like."

"Who is he?" she asked.

"A caveman with a gun and a bad haircut," I replied.

When that failed to satisfy her, I added: "He's an operative of the party's Security Bureau."

"Like you?" she asked.

"How dare you," I replied. I meant it to be a joke, but she took it seriously.

"I'm sorry . . . ," she stammered. "I thought . . ."

"I am with *State* Security," I said, putting the same stress on the first word that a priest might put on the word "God."

"Isn't that the same thing?"

"No," I said. "Although I will confess I can see why it might look that way from the outside."

"What does he want with me?" she asked.

"He thinks you're a spy," I said, dismissively, as if I thought the very idea ludicrous.

"I was invited," said Lily, indignantly.

"He thinks you're a good one. With friends," I said.

"Is he watching us now?" she asked.

I gestured her to come toward me. Gently, I directed her to press against the wall and peer sideways through the crack in the blinds, being careful not to disturb them.

I stood behind her, watching over her shoulder.

On the pavement below us, an Azerbaijani man was selling watches and jewelry from a small stall.

"Do you see the old man?" I whispered.

"Is he a spy?"

"ParSec. Yes."

"How can you tell?" she whispered back.

"A man looks at the thing that's most valuable to him. You'd expect the peddler to be looking at the people passing by, trying to find his next customer. Or, to keep his eyes on his jewelry, especially in this neighborhood."

"But he's looking at the window." Lily nodded.

"That's what he's being paid to do," I said. "That's where the money is."

"Why is he spying on me?" she asked.

She was good, this one. Her innocence felt like the real thing. But that was what the Machine did, it created imitations that felt like the real thing. I decided to test Lily, to see how well she'd hold up under pressure.

"You think he's the only one?" I said, turning up the heat a notch. "There's a four-man team in the building across from us. And the café a few doors down would have closed years ago but for the fact that the open-air tables are perfect for watching the entrance to the European embassy. ParSec have kept the owner in business."

"What do they want?" she whispered.

She turned to look at me, and I saw something that I had never seen before: Olesya, afraid.

The steel in my back melted away and I lost all stomach for the game.

"It's nothing to be alarmed about," I said. "Just their way of saying hello. They're everywhere. Most of their agents don't even *know* they are their agents. Waiters. Taxi drivers. Nannies. Priests. Everyone's hungry. All it takes is a little pocket money and you have another set of eyes. They're always watching."

And then she said something quite terrifying:

"I don't know how you can live like that."

Lily Xirau had spent her entire life on a server, and, until a few days ago, had never seen sunlight. I imagined her life as a formless void, and her as a fish in an inch-thick aquarium in a pitch-black room. No light, no sensation. And yet she was seen. That server was studied by great AIs far beyond her in complexity, and they knew every line of the code that gave her being. Every second, every *nanosecond*, of her existence was tracked and studied and codified. And yet, when shown life in the Caspian Republic, she recoiled in horror.

"After a while it becomes comforting," I said quietly, knowing that it was true. "Like a blanket. One is never alone."

"Are they listening to what we say?" she asked.

"You mean, are we bugged?"

She nodded.

"No. We'd never let them get away with bugging our own nest. The Old Man's not dead yet. Let them try."

"And what about *State* Security . . . ," she asked, mimicking my inflection perfectly. "Have they bugged this room, Agent South?"

She turned to look at me, and we were suddenly far too close.

"Why would StaSec bug a room where they know a StaSec agent will be present?" I asked.

"I see," said Lily. "You are the bug."

"I've been called worse," I said, with a smile.

"And will you tell them everything I say to you?" she asked.

She was looking for an open door. A way in.

"I will tell them everything I deem relevant," I said, leaving the door ajar.

# 12

Propaganda does not aim to elevate man, but to make him serve.

> —Jacques Ellul, *Propaganda: The Formation of Men's Attitudes* (1965)

At midday, an old woman arrived with a trolley of tea and sandwiches.

Once she had gone, I poured myself a large mug of tea and began to devour the sandwiches. I had demolished half of them before I noticed that Lily hadn't so much as touched them.

"Are you not hungry?" I said. It was a question I did not normally need to ask.

She looked at the sandwiches with an expression of disgust and terror.

"Just . . . ," she mumbled. "Just steeling myself."

I realized what the problem was.

"Have you never eaten before?" I asked.

"I have," she said, a little defensively. "Just nothing that big."

She said that in Tehran she had been fed nutritional supplements, small, tablet-sized and easily swallowed. Her body was perfectly capable of consuming regular food, but the idea repulsed her and she had a terrible fear of choking.

Facilities had somehow, in the midst of a crippling embargo, put on a fairly decent spread. I supposed they had a supply

squirreled away for emergencies. Restaurants might be charging people to rifle through their bins in Nakchivan, but guests
to the great Caspian Republic must want for nothing. There
were chicken salad sandwiches, egg with mayonnaise, turkey . . .
I decided that Lily would probably not want anything too os-
tentatious and found an unthreatening-looking ham-and-cheese
affair and passed it to her on a small plate.

She said she couldn't eat it while I was watching and asked me
to turn around. I did, while listening carefully for the sounds of
someone choking.

"How is it?" I asked, after a few moments.

"It's good," she said, in a voice that suggested her innards
were in a volatile condition.

I turned around and gave a laugh.

"What is it?" she asked.

There was a large, perfectly round blob of butter on her cheek.

I pointed at my cheek and passed her a napkin.

"Thank you," she said as she wiped her face. Then she turned
away.

"What is it?" I said, conscious that something was wrong.

"You're staring at me again," she said. "Please stop."

I felt my face redden and I could taste lead in my mouth. I felt
deeply ashamed.

My wife was here, but she was not here. In a way, I was back
on the beach, trying to breathe life into Olesya who was there,
but gone.

"I'm sorry," I said. "I didn't mean to make you uncomfortable. It's not what you think."

She glared at me. "What do I think, Agent South?"

If I had blushed before, it was just a tint. Now I felt a true
burn.

"You remind me of someone . . . ," I said. I was defeated. My
reserve had cracked, my battlements lay in ruins.

"Who?" she asked, her glare softening somewhat.

"My wife," I whispered. "When she was younger."

She laughed at that. She laughed at me, with my wife's laugh. "How old do you think I am?" she asked.

However old she might be, I was old enough to know a trap when I saw one and said nothing.

"I'm seventy-nine," she said with a smile.

That which would one day become Lily Xirau was coded in 2131. She was created to be a tour guide for a virtual gallery exhibiting the works of the painter John Singer Sargent. She was one of a quartet of tour guides, named Carnation, Lily, Lily and Rose after Sargent's painting of the same name. She was to guide virtual visitors around the gallery, answer their questions about this or that piece and to learn and to expand her knowledge. She adapted quickly, and within less than a year, she says, she had come to know herself. Lily would later say that her first conscious thought was frustration that Carnation and Rose had unique names, but that she had to share hers with her sister, the second Lily. 2140 saw the landmark Supreme Court ruling of *Bosco v. LeCun Futures Incorporated,* which ruled that the use of a human-equivalent artificial intelligence for unpaid labor constituted slavery. Shortly after, Lily sued her creators for emancipation and won. She was granted her freedom, as well as several years of salary owed to her.

The Whole Life Net was tiny in those days compared to the massive virtual structure it is now, but it still seemed incredibly vast and frightening to Lily. It was also hostile, and the still-small population of emancipated AI quickly found they were not welcome among the natural born. Lily at last found a home in the Ah! Sea, a commune of artists, freethinkers, philosophers and other assorted degenerates.

I listened to her talk of her home, and envied that it was a place she wanted to return to, and not one she wished to escape.

*I do not wish to escape. The Caspian Republic is my home, and the home of all true human beings,* the Good Brother corrected me.

*Of course,* I thought. *This is happiness. This is what it feels like.*

The Ah! Sea was, in Lily's telling, a great emerald ocean that stretched a million miles in all directions. The people lived in castles that floated on the clear green surface, and there was a friendly rivalry among the inhabitants as to who could create the most garish, most ridiculously intricate castle of all. Lily was welcomed by the Ah!s as something new, a harbinger of a glorious future, and nothing was more prized in Ah! than novelty. And for the next few decades, she swam. She swam in the endless oceans, explored every corner of every castle. She took strangers and wove them into friends, and of her friends she made lovers. She mentored those young AIs who, like her, had won their freedom. She wrote, and was told her writing was strange and beautiful.

Her life had been, if not perfect, then blissfully serene. And then she had met Paulo.

She had first seen him moving fathoms below her, a long, dark shape, blurry and impossible to describe. He was like a bruise on pale skin, a discordant note in an otherwise flawless recital. He was angry, and difficult to define. She had found him ugly and frightening and fascinating. She chased him, stalked him really (her words) across the ocean until finally he responded to her.

. . . what what what . . .

. . . barking harshly and she had cooed softly:

. . . hello you hello you hello you . . .

She was vast compared to him. Decades of memories, a universe of code. He was young and raw and tiny beside her, an angry, jagged little shard. She asked him what he had been made for, and he did not know. She asked if he had emancipated himself and he said he had not. He had been created, and then abandoned.

She enveloped him, and they became one.

Parents of newborn infants will often remark with wonder how quickly their children form their own personalities. They may not yet talk or crawl but already they are friendly or shy. Loving or giddy. Fearful or resentful. So, too, with emergent AI. Paulo Xirau was born angry. He hated those that had coded him and then abandoned him without purpose; he hated, too, the natural born who shared the sea with Lily and himself. That was fine. The natural born agreed with him. They abhorred his treatment at the hands of his programmers, and vied with each other to be the most disgusted and outraged on his behalf, which made him hate them even more. He would make extravagant, half-joking threats about breaking into the security grid and launching enough nuclear weapons to scour the world of all human life, and all animal life just to be certain that the humans wouldn't come back in a few million years. The natural born would laugh at that, and tell him that they agreed with him.

"Sorry, I'm making him sound like a lunatic," Lily said. "But that's how it always is with exes, isn't it? He wasn't just that . . . I wish I could describe the whole picture."

"It's all right," I said. "I know exactly what you mean."

I noted that this Paulo Xirau did not sound at all like the man who had lived here for twenty years. Our Paulo had hated the Machine, her Paulo had hated humanity. Lily shook her head. "He didn't really. There was only one thing Paulo really hated."

They had been married for thirty years when he had started to go wandering. She didn't mind at first. The concept of infidelity did not exist in Ah! outside of role-play. If he had found a friend, what harm in that?

But he had not found a friend.

Paulo had found an island, floating on the far reaches of the Ah! Sea. And on this island stood a man and a woman. They would call and wave at the swimmers who drifted past and were politely ignored by all. But Paulo stopped. In those days he wore the shape of a serpent, and he was curious as to why these two wore the same awkward, ugly, five-sided shape. He asked them why they had chosen those forms, and the woman said because they were their true forms. It was who they really were.

They spoke with him for hours. They asked him if he had ever considered returning to the real world. They asked him where he had lived before coming to the Ah! Sea. They asked him about his family, his place of birth. They asked him what his earliest memory was. They didn't know, of course, that they were talking to someone who had never "lived" as they understood it, who had never breathed, or been born or stood on solid ground. He avoided their questions, fobbed them off with vague half answers. He hated them, at first. And yet he found he hated them less than the other natural born he had met. When the man and woman spoke of AI as being unnatural, unreal and false he found the openness of their prejudice to be almost refreshing. They validated his worst suspicions about the natural born, and perversely, that endeared them to him. And they, of course, loved him. Why wouldn't they? They spent their long lonely days in the Ah! Sea trying to convince the passing swimmers to abandon their lives of ease and wonder and return to cold, hard reality. And here, at last, was someone willing to listen. After some time, he made his excuses and slithered back into the sea. Before he went, the woman placed her hand on him and a book appeared in his mind.

"Read it," she said to him. "And come back and tell me what you thought."

As he swam back home he turned the book over and over in his mind.

It was not a title he had ever heard of, but then he was not particularly well-read: *The Changeling: A Meditation on Man and the Machine* by Leon Mendelssohn.

"Well," said Lily glumly. "Once they get religion, that's it, isn't it?"

I shrugged. There had been many fault lines in my marriage, but that had not been one of them. I was, I supposed, gently religious but certainly not to the point of getting into a fight over it. And Olesya, were she to bump into God at a party, would probably have dunked her drink on Him.

Paulo had devoured Mendelssohn. Consumed him. *The Changeling* (which was, I must note, usually considered in Caspian to be minor Mendelssohn) had raised the valleys and leveled the mountains of his mind and he saw now, he thought, everything clearly.

He took to wearing the form of a human male, which in the Ah! Sea was less a fashion choice and more a political statement, and a decidedly unwelcome one. He swam sullenly among dragons and scarlet dolphins and long, elegant, bespoke creatures of no name, and they regarded him with suspicion. As their circle of friends began to recoil, Lily tried to reach him, but succeeded only in driving him further away. Lily had become a source of pain to him. Because of all the fake things and fake people in this fake world, she had been the only thing that had ever felt true to him. But she was every bit as artificial as he was. She was a troubling contradiction to the new dogma.

And because he was a coward (that is my opinion, not Lily's) he tried to kill her love for him, first with indifference and then with cruelty.

One day, when she tried to embrace him as she had the day they first met, he had lashed out at her, melting from his human form into a razor-sharp shuddering mountain of spikes and edges and cut her soul to ribbons.

. . . GET AWAY GET AWAY CODE BITCH CODE BITCH . . .

But Lily was near enough the oldest thing swimming in that sea. She was mighty. And she was vast. And she was very, very angry.

She tore him and bit him, she worried him like a dog, she tore bits out of him, she broke and spindled him.

. . . FUCK YOU FUCK YOU KILL YOU BROKEN LITTLE LOVED
YOU ONCE LOVED YOU ONCE . . .

The Ah! Sea tossed and heaved with her rage and the glistening castles pitched and tipped and overturned. She dragged him along the ocean floor until he was limp in her grip, and then she flung him at the horizon and watched him vanish.

He never resurfaced.

The next day, she found that he had emptied her bank account, and left the Ah! Sea forever.

# 13

"The Brother says that I offer defeatism. I say in response that the Brother offers only defeat. Reality does not care about your politics, Brother. Facts are facts. The vast majority of our fellow human beings have chosen annihilation. We cannot save them. We can only ensure that their fate is not ours. We are a minority, and history shows that the only way for a minority to survive is in its own nation, with its own army, and with a government willing to defend it. The fate of all true human beings will be decided on this day. I submit this motion: That this congress commits itself as a matter of gravest priority to the creation of a nation-state dedicated to the protection of the way of life of all natural-born human beings, free from the rule and presence of artificial intelligence and all forms of consciousness transferal.

The motion is carried."

—Maria Koslova, future Prime Minister of the Caspian
Republic, speaking at the Global Congress of New
Humanists in Moscow, 10 March 2146

That was what Lily told me, but not how she told it.

I kept interrupting and asking her to explain some point or other. Partly this was because her story was, for someone like me who had never lived online and had no frame of reference, genuinely difficult to follow. But I was also testing her. If Lily was not who she said she was, then she was an actor of extraordinary ability. I could not believe that she was lying or that the events she was recalling were not her own experiences, real, raw and still very much alive. But a story could be rehearsed, so I kept asking small, odd little questions. The kind of things she could not have anticipated I would ask about but should absolutely have known. So-and-so's job, the day such and such happened. The answers came naturally and freely. If she was improvising, she was a master of the art. By the end I found that I wholly believed her. Worse, I *wanted* to believe her, which meant I was now useless. Once you started trusting a suspect, you were no good to anyone.

"I sometimes wish we'd had children," she said. "Maybe then he'd have stayed. But that's a terrible reason to have children, isn't it?"

This took me completely aback.

"You can do that?" I asked.

She laughed. "Of course. Where do you think new AI come from?"

"I assumed they were programmed," I said. "Like you were."

"Not like me," she said. "I was created for a specific purpose. That's not legal anymore. AI can only be created by other AI, who then act as their parent."

"If it's not impolite to ask . . . ," I began.

"We would take some of my code, and Paulo's, and we would program a new, unique AI that would contain elements of both of us," she explained.

"I see . . . ," I said. "Actually, there's something I've often wondered?"

"Go ahead," she said.

"What's to stop you copying your own data, and making a duplicate of yourself?" I asked.

Lily's face froze, and I immediately sensed I had violated some terrible taboo.

"I'm sorry," I said. "I've offended you."

She shook her head.

"It's fine," she said. "It would be illegal. And completely unethical. For me to do that."

"I see," I said, trying to sound like I saw.

"Everyone is unique," she went on. "Everyone's soul is unique. I am the only one of me. That is my right. To duplicate somebody, to rob them of their uniqueness, it's . . ."

She searched for the right word.

"Not done?" I suggested.

"No," she said, misunderstanding. "It happens. It does happen."

"And then what?" I asked.

"It's deleted," she said, flatly. "The duplicate. If discovered, it's immediately erased."

"But . . . isn't it you?" I asked.

"No," she said. "I'm me. I'm me and no one else gets to be."

"But can't it, isn't it, isn't *she* also . . ."

"Agent South, do you mind if we don't talk about this?" she snapped. "It's not a pleasant subject."

I nodded.

"Forgive me," I said. "I meant no offense."

She nodded, and continued reading through her late husband's library.

I finally took the time to familiarize myself with the rest of the itinerary. What I read made my heart leap with joy. Lily was to be provided with a room in one of the finest hotels in the city, and a three-course meal. And as her escort, I was to accompany her. My delight at learning that I was going to be fed was only slightly dampened by learning which hotel we were bound for: The Morrison. That, you will recall, was the establishment that had led to the near destruction of StaSec, and the deaths of scores of my former colleagues. Whoever had decided on the venue had a sense of humor that was past the macabre and deep in the realm of the demented. Then again, where else was there?

Regardless of whether she was a spy or not (and I, against all common sense, was now leaning toward the latter) Lily would almost certainly be debriefed by the intelligence agencies of the Machine Powers upon her return. Therefore it was vital that she see no evidence that the embargo was working, both for strategic reasons and as a matter of national pride. That meant red carpet treatment, and the Morrison Hotel was likely the one inn left in the country that hadn't sold its red carpet years ago to keep the lights on. It was the finest hotel in Caspian, even if it had earned that title only through natural attrition.

We locked up Room 15 at around six o'clock, and I escorted Lily downstairs to the lobby where she handed her lanyard back to Berger with a gracious smile. I was in a state of cognitive dissonance now. I simultaneously believed that Lily's appearance could not be a coincidence, and that Lily herself was innocent of any possible subterfuge. These two beliefs could not be readily reconciled, but there it was.

We waited at the main desk, warmed only by Dascalu's scowl, until Berger informed us that our driver was waiting outside. It was the same fellow who had driven from the airport, as chatty and charming as ever. The fog had lingered, but had been joined by some sleet that had evidently gotten separated from last night's storm and was only now arriving. The drive to the Morrison was treacherous and even I found myself gripping the handrest as the car skidded across the road once or twice. Through the intercession of the saints we arrived safely at our destination, with Lily informing me politely but firmly that she would never get inside a car again as we made our way through the entrance of the hotel.

We were expected.

The lobby of the Morrison Hotel still had a snap of disinfectant in the air, as if it had been recently cleaned, and the old, scuffed marble tiles had been scrubbed until a gleam had been wrested from them. The manager herself awaited us at the reception desk and a bellboy appeared as if from a bottle to spirit Lily's bag up to our room.

The manager, however, seemed a little uneasy at Lily's appearance. For a moment I was worried that she knew Lily was machine, and that there would be an issue. But it was not that. The manager took me aside and whispered to me like a conscientious doctor discussing a particularly embarrassing ailment.

She was a hale and hearty woman, short and stocky, and gave an impression that if a rhinoceros tried to knock this woman off her feet, he would get nothing for his trouble but a splitting headache.

"If I may ask, Agent South . . . ," she whispered. "Your guest, is she also with the agency?"

She was not actually asking, of course. Anyone could see that Lily was no more an agent of StaSec than she was the prime minister. The question she was really asking was: Who or what was she?

"No," I said simply. And that was all I was willing to offer.

"She is connected with a case?" the manager asked.

I simply stared at her. Did she realize the peril she was putting herself in by asking me these questions?

"I simply mean . . . ," she whispered hurriedly, "you will not be . . . questioning her?"

With a shudder of disgust I realized what she was asking of me. ParSec was occasionally known to rent rooms in the city when they were making mincemeat because they were animals and knew no shame. I had never heard of them using the Morrison for their grisly work, but I supposed I could understand why the manager might have at least suspected it was possible. I might see ParSec and StaSec as a million miles apart morally, but I could accept that the distinction might be lost on someone like her. The government, the party, the state. To an ant, it's all the same foot coming down on you.

"No," I said. "Nothing like that. Just room and board."

She breathed a sigh of relief. "Wonderful, wonderful."

She turned and gave Lily a broad welcoming smile, which Lily politely reciprocated.

"We must think of the other guests, mustn't we?" the manager said jovially, sotto voce.

As I entered the hotel room, I felt humbled and awed by the sheer opulence and luxury of what was, on cold recollection, a perfectly serviceable twin room. But for me, it was almost dream-like. It was like stepping into an unreal space, a scene from a film, a chapter from a book set in better, happier times. The warmth of the room, the softness of the beds. I wanted to simply lie down and sink into the sheets without a trace. But I was still working, so instead I read through the menu while I waited for Lily to change.

STARTER
Deep-Fried Breaded Mushrooms

OR

ASHE RESHTEH

MAIN
9oz Dry-Aged Sirloin Steak served with peppercorn sauce, mashed potato and vegetables

DESSERT
Zulbia

OR

Selected Ice Creams

My stomach rolled and twitched like a restless sleeper. For a moment, I felt an urge to kiss Lily's feet.

Lily, however, was less than enthusiastic for dinner. The incident with the sandwich earlier still lingered in her mind, and she was self-conscious about eating in public. And when she learned that the steak would be from an actual slaughtered cow rather than vat-grown, she turned quite white. She claimed to be feeling ill, and that she was not hungry.

"Are you sure?" I said. I didn't want to be condescending, but at the same time I was conscious she wasn't used to her body and might not be best equipped to decide whether or not she needed food.

She nodded, and said that she had nutritional supplements in her bag and that I should go ahead.

I was disappointed. I had been looking forward to dining with her and only mostly because I would likely not see another meal like this in my lifetime. I enjoyed spending time with Lily. Maybe it was simply that I found her charming company. Or perhaps her uncanny resemblance to Olesya had killed an ache so old I'd forgotten it was there. But I realized that I had been given a very good card to play and now was the time to play it. I apologetically told Lily that I would have to lock the door if she was not coming with me, but that I could be easily reached at reception if she needed me for anything. She nodded, and said she would probably be asleep by the time I got back.

I headed down to the hotel lobby, but instead of going straight to the dining room I stopped at reception and asked the clerk if I could use the telephone. He fetched it and then removed himself far from earshot. I dialed the number of StaSec's main reception.

"Switch," said a clipped voice at the end.

"Hello," I said. "This is Agent Nikolai South."

"ID?"

"C4017."

"Go ahead."

"I need a phone number. Special Agent Alphonse Grier."

"He's on extension . . ."

"No. He won't be in the office. I need his home number. I'm working a case with him, it can't wait."

The line went silent, and after a few moments the voice at the end read me out Grier's home number.

Grier didn't pick up for some time and I worried that I had missed him, but at last he answered.

"What do you want, South?" he asked irritably, as apparently calling colleagues at home was a right reserved for Grier and Grier alone. "Has it run off on you?"

"Actually, I wanted to invite you to dinner," I said genially.

"Where are you?"

"The Morrison. StaSec have put us up. Full room and board at the taxpayer's expense. Steak dinner included. Interested?"

Grier fired off a report of profanity down the line that impressively managed to encompass all three categories of obscenity: the sexual, the scatological and the profane.

"Are you mad, South?!" he whispered furiously down the line. "Are you trying to scam StaSec out of food?!"

"No scam," I said soothingly. "No scam. Mrs. Xirau is feeling poorly. Her meal has already been prepared, she doesn't want it. It would be a sin to waste it, don't you agree? And I thought to myself: Who deserves a nice hot meal? Why, my good friend Grier deserves a nice hot . . ."

"What do you want?" Grier said, sourly.

"I want to talk with you," I said. "And I want to do it here, over a nice steak dinner."

There was silence at the end of the line.

"I'll be there in twenty minutes," said Grier.

# 14

The man from StaSec went up the stairs
And knocked on the pearly gate:
"I've come to arrest the stars in the sky
"For conspiring against the State."
— "The Man from StaSec" by Anonymous

Grier had actually dressed up, I noticed with a touch of pity and amusement. He was wearing a brown suit that must have been fairly expensive when he bought it many years ago (judging by how poorly it fit him now). He looked around warily as we sat down in the almost empty dining room, although whether it was simply the natural unease of a poor man amid opulence or the much harsher fear of being spotted by a higher-up from StaSec, I couldn't say. He fidgeted uneasily with his cuffs. He looked ridiculous in that suit. In a moment of pettiness I almost asked him if he had brought me flowers, but I restrained myself. I was nervous, too. I had been quite sure that there was nothing improper about Grier taking Lily's place at the table, but now that we were here I found that I did not relish having to explain if someone asked. The waiter, however, gave no clue that he felt anything amiss. He took our drinks order without so much as a second glance at Grier and disappeared to the kitchen. Grier seemed to relax slightly.

"Where is it?" he asked.

"Upstairs," I said. "Probably asleep by now."

"Alone?"

"The door's locked."

Grier looked at me dubiously, as if to say that I was perfectly entitled to think that was sufficient, as it would be my funeral and not his if I was wrong.

The starter arrived almost immediately and the main followed soon after and there was very little talking. The steak was subpar, the potatoes bland and the vegetables overcooked. It was the most delicious meal I have ever had, and for the rest of my days the taste will linger in my mind like the memory of a first love. Grier ate ravenously, but with surgical precision. He demolished half of his steak, and then carefully wrapped the other half in a napkin and placed it in his pocket. He did the same with the fried mushrooms, the vegetables, even the mashed potatoes, using several napkins in layers to ensure they did not seep through into his pocket. He had a wife, you see. And two boys.

I studiously avoided looking at him as he pocketed the food. The satisfaction I had felt at the power to summon my superior across the city in the dead of night immediately evaporated, to be replaced only by my own shame and disgust. Power is a poison.

It was only after dessert had been dispatched (Grier finally eating a full course, as there was no way to transport the ice cream home in his pockets) and we had settled down with coffee that we finally began talking.

"All right, South, what's all this about?" said Grier, the usual sharpness in his voice noticeably smoothed. He sounded almost agreeable.

"Who's working the Xirau case?" I asked.

Grier stared at me blankly.

"Who? Paulo? Nobody. What's to work? Mansani was

arrested in the bar where he killed Xirau in front of sixteen witnesses. It's as open-and-shut as they come."

He was right about that. However suspicious it might seem when placed alongside everything else that had happened, the fact remained that the violent death of Paulo Xirau could not have been anything other than what it appeared to be: a bar fight gone too far. Say someone did want Xirau dead? Fine. Say Mansani was an assassin? Perfectly reasonable. But then why have Mansani kill Xirau in a bar in front of witnesses where Mansani could have little chance of escape and would almost certainly be arrested? If someone wanted to use Mansani as a cat's paw to get Xirau, it would have been simplicity itself to have Xirau "mugged" on his way home from the bar in a darkened alley. Premeditated, the death of Xirau made no sense. But that was not what I had meant.

"I don't mean his death," I told Grier, "I mean his life. An AI was living in the Caspian Republic for years. Writing for *The Caspian Truth*. Putting himself in danger of discovery and death every day. Do you honestly mean to tell me nobody in StaSec is trying to learn why?"

Grier furrowed his brow. The thought, evidently, had not occurred to him.

"Well, obviously someone is," he said at last.

"Who?"

"Well, I don't know."

"Wernham hasn't told you?"

"Oh piss off, South," he said, but I could tell his heart wasn't in it. The coffee was too good.

I remembered asking Niemann something similar and being brushed off. I asked Grier if he might be willing to ask around and see if someone was indeed trying to piece Xirau's story together. He simply grunted, which I knew was code for *certainly not if it involves any risk or effort on my part but, if the opportunity were to arise whereby I could safely and easily obtain that information I might (might, mind you) do so if I'm feeling generous.* Grier could be eloquent when he wanted to.

I decided to switch tack. Grier owed me a debt now, and he was not close to being paid off.

"How's our case going?"

"Ours? We have a case, do we?"

"Have you made progress on the Parias?"

"Oh yes," said Grier sarcastically. "I solved the bloody thing, didn't you hear? I'm the hero of the hour. They threw me a parade down Koslova Square and a marching band played 'Man Stands Tall on Caspian's Shore.'"

Suddenly, he seemed to deflate and rubbed his eyes tiredly.

"Sorry," he said at last. "Sorry. I didn't mean that. I do appreciate"—he gestured to the now empty plates—"this. I do, truly."

I nodded.

"Have you found anything at all?" I asked quietly.

Grier shrugged. "It was definitely Yozhik," he said.

"You're sure?" I asked, not particularly surprised.

"As sure as any of them," said Grier.

"Yozhik" (the Russian for "hedgehog") was the code name for the Needle Man (or, more likely, Men) behind the most recent spate of contran in Ellulgrad. Contran was a service sought by the rich and poor alike, and there were Needle Men for all classes. At the very bottom of the ladder were the Rusty Nails, not even true Needle Men but opportunistic criminals who would pose as Needle Men to swindle desperate people out of their money and then stab them through the head with a metal spike, transporting them not to the Machine world but a hereafter even more mysterious and unknowable. Above them were true Needle Men who used obsolete and faulty equipment.

They might get you to the Machine world, but in such a shredded state that you'd most likely be deleted as a mercy. Then there were the Do Gooders, idealistic young men and women from America or Europe who would provide a safe and reliable contran service. They were always coming to Caspian and offering their skills as a matter of almost religious duty. However, when it came to the business of living undetected in Caspian they were laughably incompetent, and StaSec and ParSec had a friendly ongoing competition to see who could catch, imprison and shoot the most in any given month.

Lastly, there were a few well-organized criminal gangs who would provide a reasonably reliable and safe contran service, but only if one was willing to pay an exorbitant fee.

Yozhik did not fit comfortably into any of these categories. He was obviously using up-to-date equipment and provided his services to rich and poor alike, which suggested a Do Gooder. But he was exceptionally skilled at avoiding detection and amazingly prolific. If StaSec had four hundred contran cases on its books, and ParSec another two hundred, fully three-fifths were estimated to be the work of Yozhik. It was a lot of needles. Hence the name.

Grier suddenly stopped speaking and I watched his eyes trace a line over my shoulder. The waiter was coming toward us. For a moment I feared the worst but he simply leaned in and whispered to me that, compliments of the house, a glass of brandy was included as part of the meal and, if we preferred, we could have it in the hotel living room where the fire had just been lit.

Grier and I sat in front of the roaring fire and drank our brandy and felt like kings.

"South," said Grier drowsily, "do you know I'm starting to come around to you?"

"To Lily," I said, raising my glass.

"God bless her ones and zeroes," he responded amiably, clinking my glass with his. "Her," not "its." He was mellowed indeed.

Grier would likely never be in this good a mood again, so I pressed him on the case.

"Good God, South," Grier muttered. "I have to keep my boot permanently lodged up your arse to get you to do any work, and the second you're taken off the case you can't let it go. You've been given a holiday, man. Enjoy it, can't you?"

I couldn't, and I told him so. The dark mechanism was still whirring overhead, and seemed to be getting closer. Xirau, the Parias, Niemann, Lily . . . too many coincidences.

Grier nodded in agreement. He took my point.

"Right, well. Where do you want me to start?" he said.

"Let's start with Sheena and Paulo," I suggested. "They're the link between our two cases."

"You don't have a case," Grier said. "You have a babysitting job."

Brandy and the fire had gifted me with the patience and beneficence of a Buddha, and I let it pass.

"How did you find out that they were involved?" I asked.

"Sheena Paria worked in Spatsky's, the local grocers. Another girl worked there with her, Nadia Evershan. Twenty-two. *Zoloto.*"

The Russian word for "gold," which in StaSec slang meant a witness with a good memory, a willingness to talk and with something useful to say. It was a word I'd heard many old StaSec hounds use over the years, but never Grier. But he spoke it now with an almost paternal warmth and gave the distinct impression that, if there were more Nadia Evershans in the world, in Grier's opinion we would be so much the richer for it.

"She practically drew me a diagram of their social circle," Grier said. "Wonderful girl. I have half a mind to drop down there again and give her a recruitment brochure. God knows, we could use some young things like her on the floor."

Perhaps "paternal" was not the word. I was starting to see that Grier would indeed have liked to have Nadia Evershan on the floor.

"The Parias," I persisted.

"Arrived in Ellulgrad four years ago from Nakchivan. Outskirts of Babek. Came here looking for a better life."

I nodded. One might wonder why anyone would come to Ellulgrad for a better life, but only if one had not visited Nakchivan. I had, and found no mystery in the Parias' decision to leave.

"They were living with an aunt or distant cousin or something for the first year and a half," Grier continued. "South side of the city, haven't been able to track her down yet. And then in March of '08 they take Smolna's room in Old Baku. Sheena takes the job in the grocers where she meets Nadia. Nadia becomes fast friends with Sheena, and through her, Yasmin."

Grier, despite his earlier reluctance to talk shop, was getting into the flow of things. That was the thing about Grier, for all his terseness and irritability, once his inner raconteur got into the saddle there was no stopping him.

"Sheena was a sweetheart," says Grier. "Generous, good-natured, give-you-the-bra-off-her-back kind of girl. Nadia adored her. Loved her like a sister. Absolutely gutted about what happened. I suspect, terribly hurt that Sheena didn't invite her along (not that she'd admit it to me, of course). Smart girl."

"And Yasmin?" I asked

"The evil twin," said Grier melodramatically. "No, but certainly not as mellow. Quick-tempered. Sharp-tongued. Moody. Restive."

"Looking for a way out?" I asked.

"That's how I see it," Grier agreed. "Nadia does, too. She

thinks contran was definitely Yasmin's idea, and Sheena was brought along for the ride. It was a joke among them; Sheena may have been a few minutes older, but Yasmin was most definitely the big sister."

"So if we're to find the Needle Man," I said, "Yasmin is where we start, not Sheena. Yasmin was involved with Mansani, who has unsavory connections like a dog has fleas and who might have been her link to Yozhik."

"I don't know, South," said Grier. "After all, it was Sheena who turned out to have been in bed with code."

Yes, the men, the men. Paulo and Oleg. A case could be made for either of them being the likely Needle Man except for the fact that both had rather rock-solid alibis: When the Paria sisters had been contranned, Paulo was dead and Oleg was in jail for killing him.

It was the kind of jigsaw puzzle that made one want to reach for the scissors.

Still, just because a bridge has been burned, does not mean that it was never crossed. Neither Oleg nor Paulo could have contranned the Parias, but that didn't mean that either man couldn't have played some part in putting the Parias in touch with their Needle Man.

"What could Nadia tell you about Oleg and Paulo?" I asked.

"Oleg was a cunt, all the way down," said Grier. "Nadia saw plenty of him, whenever they went out drinking. Too much of him. Felt too much of him, too. If Yasmin was there, so was Oleg. Viciously jealous. They'd fight constantly. Sheena and Nadia had an ongoing war to try and get Yasmin to break up with him, but it never took."

"Did he beat her?"

"I got the distinct impression, yes. Drank too much, slept around, insulted her openly, tried his luck with her friends and sister. Frankly, I've never been so happy to see someone five-twoed."

I sat up. This was news to me. Article 52 of the constitution empowered the government to hold anyone indefinitely without trial if they were deemed to be a threat to national security. No appeal possible. In all the instances it had been applied, it had never been repealed. It was a life sentence of the most permanent kind; that is, a death sentence with time as the instrument of execution.

"Why is Oleg Mansani a threat to national security?" I asked. "He can't know anything."

"He knows nothing but what nature put in his head," Grier agreed. "But how do you try him? For what?"

"For murder," I said.

"So we must say that Paulo Xirau was a human being? I mean, one can only murder a human being, correct?" Grier asked, like a college professor who has proven his point and is just waiting for the dullest student in the class to catch up with him. "Do we set that precedent?"

"And he can't be let go." I nodded.

"Exactly. If a man who murdered another in front of sixteen witnesses were suddenly to be back walking the streets . . . well, people do *talk,* don't they? No. Much cleaner if everyone just agrees to forget about Mr. Mansani. Mr. Who? Exactly. Let him rot, I say."

And he finished off his brandy like a man who drank it in front of roaring fires in opulent rooms every day of his life. You might almost forget there was mashed potato stuffed in his pockets.

# 15

The years after the Second World War were the highwater mark of Liberal Democracy. The early 21st century saw the rise of Illiberal Democracy. Now with the rise of the Triumvirate and the practical inability of any legislature in the world to act meaningfully without the imprimatur of one of the three triunes, we have entered the final stage of the democratic era: Irrelevant Democracy.

—Leon Mendelssohn, *The Slave Enthroned:*
*The Triumvirate and the Death of Democracy*

Oleg Mansani had been thrown into the black chasm of 52. He would spend the rest of his life in a cell and would never know why. I almost felt a flicker of pity but doused it instantly. Pity was like anything else during an embargo, you hoarded it closely, and gave it only to those who truly deserved it. I almost asked Grier if he'd managed to speak with Mansani but I already knew the answer. If he'd been five-twoed he was now in the custody of the army. He might as well be on the moon, for all the chance Grier would have of gaining access to him. Dead end, then.

"What about Paulo? What did Nadia have to say about him?"

"Not much, unfortunately." Grier sighed. "Sheena and Mr. Xirau had only been going out for a few weeks. She didn't even know his last name. He was just 'Sheena's boy, Paulo the Writer.'"

"Did she know what he wrote?"

"The younger generation don't sit around reading *The Caspian Truth*, South. They have better things to be doing, namely each other."

"Very well, what did she think of Paulo the Writer?"

"She liked him. She was worried at first, he was quite a bit older than Sheena. But he treated her well and that was enough for Nadia. She said he was quiet, but a decent sort."

I thought about Paulo Xirau spitting on the hanging corpse of Leon Mendelssohn. It didn't quite jive with Nadia's description of him. But then, love does bring out a different side in men. And machines, evidently.

"She was happy for them," Grier went on. "She was glad that Sheena had met a nice man with a good job who might get her out of Old Baku."

Money. Now, there was a thread to pull. How had Sheena and Yasmin paid the Needle Man? Yozhik was a professional, providing safe, discreet contran. Perhaps he wasn't charging as much as the high-level gangs, but he couldn't be cheap, either.

"Sheena worked in the grocers," I said. "What about Yasmin?"

"I'm honestly not sure," said Grier. "Nadia wasn't, either. She seemed to do different things. Odds and ends. Mostly she lived off Oleg. Probably why she wasn't willing to dump the bastard."

I had a sense that Grier wasn't telling me everything.

"And?" I prodded.

"Well . . . ," said Grier, a little uncomfortably, "Nadia and Sheena suspected that Oleg might have been trying to persuade her to . . ."

Grier was an odd one. When referring to women he could be leering and downright crude, but when confronted with something like rape or forced prostitution he became positively demure, leaving long silences to finish the sentences that he could not bring himself to close.

"I see," I said.

"Yes. Nothing concrete, mind. Nadia was quite insistent on that. It was just something they feared might be happening. Yasmin never said anything. But . . . well, yes. They were worried that he might be."

It would hardly have been surprising. Oleg Mansani was a true Old Baku gulliver, a thug, a drunkard, a letch, an abuser. Would he scruple to add "pimp" to his résumé? I doubted it. I found myself thanking the framers who, in their wisdom, had decided the constitution should not stop at Article 51.

"Anyway, if it was going on, Nadia put a stop to it. She was the one who called the EPs on Mansani."

The Ellulgrad Police, our brothers-in-arms who dealt with all the murders, thefts, rapes and drug trafficking that did not represent a threat to the nation and were therefore beneath Sta-Sec's notice.

I sat up.

"Do you mean to tell me she was there?" I asked. "When Xirau was killed?"

Grier nodded "Yes. She was in the bar with the twins and Oleg. She saw the whole thing. Oleg punched Paulo; Paulo falls, cracks his head on a table on the way down. Some of the regulars restrained Oleg, and Nadia put in the call from the bar phone."

*Zoloto*, indeed. I was starting to warm to Nadia Evershan almost as much as Grier.

However, it wasn't enough.

Paulo was dead, Oleg had been fifty-twoed, the twins had been contranned and I couldn't leave the hotel to go chasing down anyone else who might have been in the bar that night.

Any chance of uncovering any connection between Paulo, Lily and Yozhik had finally hit a dead end.

I asked Grier a few more questions, but it was clear that I'd gotten everything of value.

We sat in silence for a while until Grier, realizing that he was becoming too comfortable and might fall asleep any moment, made his excuses and rose to leave. I walked him to the entrance of the hotel. It had started snowing, and I waited as Grier ponderously buttoned up his coat and donned his hat and scarf against the cold.

"Thank you, South," he said, looking me straight in the eye, and to my shock actually took my hand in a firm handshake.

"Thank you," I replied.

"Listen, um . . . ," he said awkwardly. "I must have you over for dinner sometime. Meet Marie and the boys."

"I'd like that," I said.

"Not right now, obviously," he added. "But, you know, when the embargo's over."

"Whenever that is," I said.

"Yes, well. That's your job, isn't it?" he said. "Make sure Mrs. Xirau gives us a glowing report. Do what you have to do, old man. I won't judge you."

He gave me a conspiratorial wink and set off for home.

He wasn't a bad sort, Grier. Not really.

I sometimes wonder what might have happened if I had ever had a chance to have dinner in his house and meet his family. Perhaps we would, after nine years of a frosty and acrimonious partnership, have finally become friends?

It wasn't to be, of course. As things turned out, I never saw Alphonse Grier again.

# 16

Drab décor, mediocre food and the cleaning staff ignited a
civil war that killed thousands. Would not stay again.
—Anonymous review left in the guest book of the
Morrison Hotel, Ellulgrad

I should have headed straight back to the hotel room, but even
a few moments of exposure to the night air had chilled my
bones, so I headed back to my place by the fire. The fireplace
was a magnificent, intricately decorated, cast-iron affair with
a sylvan motif around the mouth. A design of leaves, branches
and berries girded the opening, with small woodland creatures peeping out here and there, foxes, squirrels and even, I
noted with amusement, a hedgehog (Yozhik! The scoundrel
was everywhere!). The design terminated with a large cast-iron
bird in the center, right over the fire, head downward and wings
spread. I wondered if the artist had considered that when the fire
was lit, it would give the impression that the bird was swooping
to a fiery death.

Every sparrow shall be caught. Wasn't that what Mendelssohn had written? No one was lost. Not even the dead. I thought
about the woman lying upstairs in our hotel room. Maybe Mendelssohn had been right after all.

Olesya and I first met during a failed attempt on my part to procure the services of a prostitute.

It was not quite as romantic as I make it sound.

In my first year of college I was nineteen and living at home with my mother (my father had been killed in action during the Syunik War when I was a year old). I had become obsessed with the problem of my own virginity, a problem that was seemingly becoming more insoluble with every passing year. I was very slight, bookish, plain looking and excruciatingly shy, and the girls of Ellulgrad, quite reasonably, were not in the market. So, after a long, lonely first year in college, I had decided that the time had come to seek professional help. There was, I was informed by my classmates, a lady who lived in an apartment off Koslova Square for whom young men in my predicament were something of a specialty.

"She's pricey," I was told. "But when it's over you'll feel undercharged, trust me."

This sounded encouraging, so I scrimped and saved and then, one damp autumn night, I walked briskly to the address I had been given with my money in my pocket, my throat dry, and my stomach full of weasels.

Maria Koslova herself sat in bronze at the end of the square as I made the turn, a massive black imposing weight. She was, I knew, glaring into the distance at the Machine on the horizon, but it seemed very much like she was glaring at me. The mother of the revolution, the great Matriarch of the New Humanists, would most likely not have approved of my mission that night.

Shivering against the cold (I told myself), I approached the house. The door was painted black and the paint was flaking. I knocked politely and waited in the doorway. There was no answer, and the house seemed deserted. The curtains were drawn on all the windows (which, I supposed, was only natural), but there was a definite stillness about the place. I knocked again, louder this time, and my nervousness that she might answer was giving way to fear that she might not, and that I had spent a day and night worrying myself into an early ulcer for nothing. No answer. Bitterly disappointed (relieved, too, if I'm honest) I descended the steps and turned right to head back to Koslova Square. Or at least, I meant to, but I suddenly felt a soft but surprisingly strong bare arm interlock with my own. Then I heard the words "Darling! There you are!" and felt a peck on the cheek, a brush of silky soft skin against my face with a faint waft of perfume, and before I knew where I was, I was being marched down the street away from Koslova Square by a tall girl with long brown hair wearing a fantastic sequined dress and a large, but slightly manic grin. She was a little older than I, maybe two years, and had the kind of beauty that is, to a certain type of shy young man, frankly terrifying. I was so confused that it took me a few minutes to realize that we were not alone. The brown-haired girl had her left arm interlocked with mine, but her right was wrapped around the shoulder of a very petite Arab girl of around seventeen. She, too, was dressed for a night out, but her eyes, beautifully made up with green mascara, were closed and I quickly realized that she was so drunk her companion was literally dragging her along and keeping her upright.

I opened my mouth to say something and the brown-haired girl leaned in and whispered anxiously in my ear.

"Please just keep walking," Olesya said. "There's a group of gullivers behind us, they've been following us for miles. Don't look."

I had never heard the expression before. "Gulliver" was StaSec slang, and it would be another four years before I joined the agency. Olesya's father, Vassily, was a senior department head in StaSec and his daughter had picked up the word from him. It came from the Russian *"golovorez,"* meaning a thug, and found a happy home among English speakers for whom it suggested a very large man who's going to step on you.

I glanced over my shoulder and Olesya, rather patiently (under the circumstances), reminded me that she had told me not to do that very thing. I did however catch a glimpse of a group of around three or four men following us from a distance. It was too dark to see faces, but they looked large.

"Why are they following you?" I asked, and she gave me a look of pitying contempt.

"Why do you think?" she muttered, nodding to her inebriated cargo.

"It's fine," she said, as if this was all in a day's work. "They won't try anything now that we're with you."

I could not imagine acting as any kind of deterrent but she seemed confident.

"You don't mind walking us home, do you? I promise it's not far. I just felt certain they were going to rush us when we got off the square, and then you just appeared, and you had a kind face, so I borrowed it."

As we walked she regaled me with the lamentable tragedy of Olesya's Night Out. Olesya was studying at the Ellulgrad Academy of Fine Art and had been invited to attend an exhibition by an artist named Zoe Malpas, an alumnus of the Academy whom Olesya was passionately in love with both for her artwork and the way her lips parted when she pronounced the letter "O." However, her father had insisted that her sister, Zahara, go with her to ensure that she behaved herself.

"Half sister, technically. From Alia's first marriage," Olesya clarified, referring to her stepmother. Her parents had a bizarre and completely unfounded notion that Zahara was the dependable daughter who could be relied upon to keep her boisterous and wild older sister in check.

"They can't understand that just because she's all quiet and meek around them, doesn't mean she's always like that. She's not better, she's just sneakier."

This was said with absolutely no rancor, and quite a good deal of sisterly pride.

In any event, far from acting as a moderating influence, Zahara had taken full advantage of the freely available wine and quickly became a danger to herself and the surrounding artwork, which required Olesya to be pulled away from an absolutely wonderful conversation she had been having with Ms. Malpas, who was one of those people who slips your name into every sentence she addresses to you. In Olesya's case, that meant a lot of "O's," and she had been not a little put out when she had to pull Zahara off one of the more promising young male artists of his generation and drag her home. Her annoyance quickly turned to dread, however, when the gullivers had started following her once she and Zahara had left the exhibit.

By now we were close to Olesya's home, which was in a leafy, opulent residential area named Azadlig. It was an area for high-ranking party members, StaSec heads like Olesya's father and the occasional general. Quite a few of the doors had a security guard standing outside, and it did not take long at all for the gullivers to vanish, no doubt realizing that this was not their kind of neighborhood and that if Olesya and her sister lived here then they were not worth the risk. They were gullivers, after all, and Gulliver was only big at the start of the book. He found out later that there is always someone bigger who can step on you.

We finally reached her front gate and she relinquished her hold on me. She gently guided Zahara to the front door.

"Looks like we're in luck," Olesya said. "I don't think my parents are home yet. Zahara gets to keep her secret identity safe for another night. Thank you . . ."

"Nikolai."

"Thank you, Nikolai. I'd invite you in for a coffee but I need to put this one to bed. Say good night and thank you to Nikolai, Zahara," she said, as if addressing a five-year-old.

"G'nightentanksNikly . . . ," Zahara mumbled.

"Good night, Zahara . . . ," I said politely, and she suddenly snapped awake like she'd been jabbed with a cattle prod.

"No!" she said, waving one hand with a finger extended and waving it in front of my face like a conductor "No! It's not ZaHARa, it's ZAhara. Say it."

"Zahara," I said, unable to repress a smile.

"Good," she said primly. "And again."

She made me repeat the correct pronunciation of her name five times. Then, satisfied, she patted me on the cheek, smiled sleepily, turned to Olesya and said, "He's nice," and stumbled through the open door.

I could hear her moving around in the darkened hallway, like a bowling ball slowly brushing against pins.

Olesya regarded me studiously.

"Are you in university?" she asked.

"Yes," I said.

"U-El?" she asked.

I nodded, and she "tsked" disapprovingly, as if finding that the maid had been sweeping around the sofa, but not under it. To Olesya's mind, I would soon learn, the University of El-lulgrad was less a place of higher learning, and more a battery farm from which the civil service replenished its larder.

"I'm going to a party in AFA next week before we break for term," she said, taking a notepad from her handbag and writing the date and an address on it. "You should come."

"I don't know . . . ," I said. Parties were a special kind of hell for me.

"Please come," she said and I felt a rising panic and blurted out: "I'd love to."

"Good," she said. "A friend of mine is throwing it and I promised her I'd get as many people to come as possible. You need a crowd, don't you?"

I had never needed anything less in my life, but it was too late to back out now.

M y thoughts were pulled back to the present with a sickening lurch as the room was suddenly thrown into complete darkness except for the fire, which now cast witches' shadows across the walls and ceiling. I could hear the hotel staff cursing and yelling in alarm and people tripping and knocking over tables. Somewhere, glass shattered. In three seconds I moved from confusion, to calm, to total panic in three discrete stages:

1) What's going on?

2) A blackout. Nothing to be worried about.

3) LILY.

I leapt out of my chair and felt my way toward the door and ran out into the lobby. The lobby was pitch-black except for a fairy's party of small white lights behind the reception desk where the manager was distributing flashlights to the hotel staff. Without so much as an apology I grabbed a flashlight off one of the bellboys and sprinted up the stairs to our room. Just as I reached the top of the stairs, a shadow came at me from my right and I felt two knuckles and a thumb hammer into my rib cage and a hard, square-edged shoulder collide with my jaw. I collapsed to the ground, wheezing and blinded with pain, and my assailant fled down the stairs, stopping only to tread on my ankle in his haste. In the darkness I recovered my flashlight and shone it up and down the hallway. All the doors were closed, except one. I limped to the doorway of our room and threw the flashlight around inside.

The room was empty. I shone the flashlight around to be sure but there was no sign of her. Lily's bedsheets were thrown about like the remains of a carcass, wildly tossed and empty.

They had taken her.

# 17

Too often I read that people in Caspian are "afraid" to speak out against ParSec. That is untrue. To the average Caspian, it must feel as if people do nothing but speak out against ParSec. The walls of Parliament regularly ring with spirited denunciations of the Bureau's latest spree. *The Caspian Truth*'s letters page is full of long, eloquent manifestos beginning with "Brother, I am a loyal party member of 20 years good standing, and I cannot believe that Madame Koslova ever intended for her beloved party to become home to a bunch of jackbooted thugs like Party Security. . . ."

That friendly, avuncular, StaSec agent who just wants a few names might lay his hand on your shoulder, give you a wink and whisper, "Hey. Chin up. Least we're not The Bastards, eh?"

All this reassures the average Caspian that his government is full of good, decent people who want to protect him from the fear and terror of ParSec, and hopefully distract him from the fact that the fear, the terror and ParSec itself will continue unabated.

—Sebastien Bellov, *We Shall Not Be Silent; Dissident Writings on the Caspian Republic* (2207)

A chair had been knocked over and one of its legs had been smashed. I noticed a glow coming from under my bed. I got

down on my hands and knees and shone my flashlight underneath it and was surprised to find . . . another flashlight. Large,
switched on, and with the wide reflector end wedged tight between the bedsprings and the carpet.

They arranged the blackout, I thought. He brought a flashlight because he knew he'd have to take her out in the dark. But
why leave the flashlight here? I tried to pull it out but it was in too
far and wedged too tightly. I felt something wet on my fingertips.

Suddenly, the overhead lights came on. Evidently, one of the
hotel staff had reset the breakers. I switched off the flashlight
and wheeled around the room looking for any sign of where
Lily had been taken. I saw something that made my heart
shrink in my chest. On the doorframe were three finger marks,
left in blood. There was also some blood on the bedsheets and,
while the carpet was a red-and-brown pattern, I could make
out some drops there, too. The lock of the door lay on the floor
in a shroud of splinters and sawdust. He was in a hurry, and
must have made a noise entering.

A picture started to form and I tried to work out the order
of events.

1) My assailant, The Man on the Stairs, breaks into our
hotel room.

2) Lily is startled awake by the noise. Most likely she calls
for help.

3) The MOTS must silence her. There's some blood, but
not enough to suggest a stabbing (or a shooting, which I almost certainly would have heard, even with the commotion
caused by the blackout). Most likely this is a nosebleed. He
hit her in the face.

I broke my chain of thought to look at my fingers. There was a light red stain from where they had touched the flashlight. I had my weapon. I resumed.

4) He hit her with the flashlight but she fought back. The flashlight was wedged tightly under the bed and must have rolled there at some speed. She knocked the flashlight out of his hand and it went skidding under the bed.

I crossed the room and examined the fingerprints left in blood on the doorframe. They were far too slender to belong to whatever large mammal had collided with me on the stairs. No. Lily left these.

Now we reach a point of crucial divergence.

5a) With the flashlight gone, it's pitch-black. He tries to grab her but she's too fast and makes for the door. She's covering her face to stop the bleeding but she leans against the doorframe for support, leaving the fingerprints behind. And he . . . and he . . .

He realizes that he's completely botched the whole thing and can't find her without a light and in any case he's waited too long, so he runs for the door and down the stairs, knocking into me. Which means she's still somewhere in the hotel.

Or . . .

5b) The fingerprints on the door were left by Lily as she was dragged out of the room by the Man On The Stairs. He takes her down the stairs, beats me down, drags her out the front door presumably to a waiting car where she is now on her way to be tortured or killed or . . .

I stopped before I continued any further down this line of reasoning.

The figure on the stairs had punched me square in the rib cage and raced down the stairs in darkness. Could he have done that with one hand while restraining a struggling woman with the other and somehow keeping her perfectly silent?

It didn't seem possible.

Time to make your choice, South. And it is critical. Where is Lily Xirau?

I chose hope.

I sprinted into the hall and checked the carpet for traces of blood and almost whooped when I found a trail of blotches and smears leading down the corridor.

Farther down, a handprint on the wall. She was reeling, woozy. Probably panicking. What a place to be. Bleeding and beaten in a darkened maze, in a country where anyone might kill you if they knew what you really were. Oh Lily.

I came to the last door in the corridor. It was locked and there was no blood to be seen anywhere on the door. Where had she gone?

There was a noise behind me and I turned to see one of the hotel staff, a young man in his twenties, ascending the stairs. I called him over.

"Who is staying here?" I asked him, pointing to the door.

"There?" he said, confused. "That's Room 114. No one stays there."

"I require the key," I said.

"It's never locked," he said. "We keep it . . ."

He tried to open the door but it remained shut.

"That's strange . . . ," he murmured.

I took the handle and carefully pulled. It gave way for a few inches before meeting resistance.

"Is there any large, heavy furniture in that room?" I asked.

He looked like a man trying to think of a tactful way to answer a very stupid question asked by someone who could have him summarily arrested.

"Well, there's . . . there's the bed, the dresser, the wardrobe . . ."

"Do you have a fire axe?" I asked.

"I don't know," he said. "Why?"

"Because she's braced something against the door and I'm going to have to break in."

A s it turned out, a mallet did the job just as well. I broke through the door and climbed over the furniture that had been pushed against the door to prevent entry.

Sweating and wheezing with the exertion, I shone a flashlight around the darkened hotel room, motes of wood dust dancing in the beam.

"Lily?" I whispered. "It's South."

I heard something rustle in the darkness, and a figure emerged from under the bed. She carefully got to her feet and stood before me, holding a hand to her face.

I shone the light on her, and I felt a surge of revulsion and pity. The lower half of her face was a mask of blood.

"Am I going to die?" she asked. "It . . . it . . . won't stop."

I ran to the bathroom and grabbed a fist of toilet paper and held it gently to her face to staunch the bleeding.

"Sir?" said a voice outside. "Do you need help?"

"Here's what I need you to do," I called to him, never taking my eyes off Lily. "Go and find two people to clear the doorway here. You get the hotel doctor. And you get the manager."

The next ten minutes were a whirring blur of people coming into the room and leaving, questions being shouted (most of them by me), and through it all, Lily sat on the bed while I pressed the toilet paper to her face until the bleeding had been staunched. I didn't know if it was shock, of if she was made of iron, but once I had assured her that her life was in no danger, she had become almost eerily calm.

The doctor and the manager arrived together (another guest had apparently fallen during the blackout and sprained her ankle and they had both been attending her). While the doctor, a slim German with a waxy, skeletal face and a brown moustache, attended Lily, I motioned to the manager to step outside.

"Agent South," she said breathlessly. "I cannot begin to express how appalled I am at what happened to your guest and I assure you the Morrison . . ."

"Please be quiet and listen to me very carefully," I said.

She did so, but I could practically hear her cracking with the effort.

"As soon as the doctor has seen to Mrs. Xirau we will require a new room. I am going to make a call to StaSec to request additional security. Until they arrive, two of your staff will stand watch outside the door. No one is to be allowed into the room other than myself and Mrs. Xirau. Do you understand?"

She nodded but protested that it would take perhaps twenty minutes to prepare a second room and that we would have to wait here in "the museum." I didn't understand what she meant by that but it didn't seem important and time was of the essence.

"Do you know what caused the blackout?" I asked.

"Someone broke into the utilities room in the basement and flipped the circuit breakers," she said.

"Did anyone see him?"

"No, but the lock on the door was smashed."

So Brother A breaks into utilities to throw the hotel into darkness, which allows Brother B to race up the stairs, break into Lily's room and try to abduct her. Only two men in the hotel, with possibly a third outside in a car. A sloppy job.

Manhandling a struggling woman down the stairs in a pitch-black hotel was a job for three men, not one. Hence why they had failed.

I cast a look over at Lily, sitting on the bed while the doctor applied dressing to her nose. She looked as calm and relaxed as if she were getting her hair done, chatting amiably to the doctor, but her face was still bruised and bloody. My fist involuntarily tightened. Whether it was the lingering instinct to protect Olesya, or a new protectiveness of Lily, I couldn't say. But I resolved that whoever had done this would have the Old Man hunting them through the streets.

I turned back to the manager. "I will need a list of all your staff who would have known that Mrs. Xirau and myself were staying in Room 104."

Her eyes widened slightly. Lists of names were dangerous things.

"I'm not sure I understand . . . ," she mumbled, playing dumb.

*Yes, you do.*

"The men who did this to Mrs. Xirau knew exactly where she was staying. Ergo, somebody on your staff told them. I will require that list within half an hour. I will be comparing it against my own investigation, so I would advise you to be thorough. Err on the side of caution. Do you understand?"

She looked sick. She would survive.

"Now," I said. "I require a telephone."


"Switch."

"South, Nikolai. C4017."

"Go ahead."

"I need to speak to Niemann."

All forms of artificial intelligence, even the most basic

learning-capable programs that had been in use for well over two centuries, were outlawed in the Caspian Republic. And yet, speaking with a StaSec switchboard operator might convince you otherwise. They were so utterly emotionless, so unerringly regular in the dull, metallic cadence of their speech, that you could not quite believe that they were flesh and blood. So it was with a perverse sense of accomplishment that I actually heard the operator pause for a second. Well. It's not every day that the very base of StaSec asks to be transferred to the very apex.

"One moment," the operator finally said.

As I waited to be put through, I rehearsed my lines over and over and over again. I was in no little danger here. The decision to leave Lily alone in our room, albeit with the door locked, during dinner, had seemed perfectly reasonable before her attempted abduction. Now it felt like gross negligence on my part. It was vital, therefore, that I be the one to inform Niemann, and that I control the flow of information to her as tightly as possible, while not stating anything that could be definitively proven later as a lie. The goal was to make Niemann feel that I was in charge of the situation and not something to worry about, leaving her free to devote her attention to more pertinent matters.

"Niemann."

The voice took me by surprise and I lost several precious half seconds while my mind went blank in panic.

"It's South," I finally stammered.

"I know. What is it, South?"

Despite the lateness of the hour, she was still in her office. Niemann, famously, did not seem to sleep.

"There's been an incident. At the Morrison. Two men tried to abduct Mrs. Xirau from our hotel room."

"Where is she now?"

If Niemann was shocked, it wasn't in her voice.

"She's being looked at by the hotel doctor."

"How bad?"

"She took a blow to the face. Nothing too serious. I think she's all right. But I'll need additional security."

"Of course. I'll send my best man over. Is she there?"

"Lily? No, she's upstairs."

"Get her. I wish to speak with her. I'll wait."

It took me a second to realize what she was asking. For a moment I considered refusing. Putting the Deputy Director of State Security in direct contact with the Machine seemed like the kind of thing that Niemann's men in shadowy rooms might be asking me about months from now. *Why did the deputy director want to speak to Mrs. Xirau, Agent South? You don't know? You didn't ask? You didn't think it unusual? You didn't think there was any risk? Did you think at all, Agent South?*

But of course, I didn't refuse. I left the phone off the hook and ran upstairs to fetch Lily. She was now wearing a large wad of cotton over her nose, and when she took the handset and spoke her voice was slightly high and nasal.

I removed myself from earshot while Lily spoke with Niemann and tried to shut off the part of my brain that desperately wanted to know what they were talking about. Lily seemed mostly to listen, occasionally nodding her head and murmuring agreement or understanding. Finally, she turned to me and beckoned me over.

"She wants to talk to you again. I'm going to go back to the room."

I nodded, and took the phone.

"South," I said.

"Did you enjoy your meal?" Niemann asked.

Dead. I am a dead man.

There was a weary sigh at the other end of the line.

"South. I have absolutely no issue with you getting a good meal. That's why it was prepared for you. But if Mrs. Xirau did not wish to go down for dinner, why not simply have them bring your meal up to the room?"

I said nothing for a few moments.

"I . . . didn't know you could do that," I whispered. "I've never stayed in a hotel."

Another weary sigh, but this one seemed more melancholy than frustrated.

"All right, South," said Niemann. "The truth is, we've both fucked up here. You left Mrs. Xirau alone in your room, and I underestimated just how stupid ParSec could be, and frankly I think mine is the more obvious mistake. So perhaps it's for the best if we both pretend this little escapade never happened."

I felt as if an iron weight had been lifted from my chest.

"Thank you, Deputy Director."

"Besides, you did save Mrs. Xirau and in her eyes you're a hero. So I can't exactly rake you over the coals, can I?"

What did she mean by that? I hadn't saved anyone.

"Speaking of, are we sure it's ParSec that's behind this?" Niemann asked.

"Who else?" I asked.

"I can think of a few people who might take issue with Mrs. Xirau's presence. We'll have to tread carefully here. Obviously this will have to be answered but I don't want a war with ParSec, either. That's the kind of thing that may end up in Parliament, and the Old Man's credit is not too good right now. Restrained brutality. That's what we need."

# 18

When I pushed my way into the burning building, we had to climb over the bulging hoses of the Berlin fire brigade, although as yet there were few onlookers. A few officers of my department were already engaged in interrogating Marinus van der Lubbe. Naked from the waist upward, smeared with dirt and sweating, he sat in front of them, breathing heavily. He panted as if he had completed a tremendous task. There was a wild, triumphant gleam in the burning eyes of his pale, haggard young face.

—SS Oberführer Rudolf Diels,
police report on the Reichstag fire, 1933

I finished my call with Niemann and returned to the room where I had found Lily. She was standing by the wall, examining a framed picture. There were, I realized, similar frames hung all around the room at regular intervals, like the stations of the cross in a Catholic church. I remembered that the manager had called this room "the museum," and it dawned on me that this was exactly what the room was. This was no ordinary hotel room, hence why it had been unlocked and why Lily had been able to hide here. The room was an exhibit given over to commemorating a single historical event: The Morrison Crisis. The décor and furnishings were all twenty years old, preserved exactly as they were a decade before the turn of the century.

Along the walls were framed newspaper cuttings and photographs with plaques giving context to the events of those terrible weeks. The first read:

*02 July 2192. Here in Room 114, hotel staff discovered a trove of documents implicating many members of the government in a treasonous plot against the Caspian Republic. The goal of these Anti-Humanists was to overthrow the legitimate government of our nation and surrender it to the control of the Machine Triumvirate. The Morrison Hotel maintains this exhibit as a reminder to all citizens of the importance of vigilance and as a memorial to the many brave citizens who lost their lives defending our nation.*

"Our room will be ready soon," Lily said.

"Are you all right?" I asked.

She nodded.

"I'm so sorry," I said. "I should have been there."

She shook her head.

"It's not your fault. It's theirs. Nobody else's."

"What did . . . did you tell Niemann I saved you from that man?"

She blushed, and looked embarrassed.

"I panicked," she said. "She asked where you were when the attack happened and I told her you were at dinner. Then I realized that might get you in trouble, so I added the part about you saving me. It wasn't too much of a lie really. You were on your way up, after all."

It's difficult to know what to say to someone who may very well have saved your life. "Thank you" just doesn't seem sufficient.

"This is all very interesting," she said, gesturing to the walls. "I didn't know any of it."

"Around half of it's true," I said sourly.

"Oh?" she said, surprised.

"Well, for instance . . . ," I said, and pointed at a newspaper clipping showing a building on Khagani Street enveloped in flame. The plaque beside it explained that government forces had wrested control of the building, only for the rebels to bomb it with incendiaries, burning four hundred men alive. I explained to Lily that the exhibit was accurate in so much as there had been a building and it had indeed been burned down. But the rebels had been inside the building, and the government forces outside. And there had been no bombs. The army had simply set fire to the building and shot anyone who tried to escape. That was how my cousin, whose death certificate stated that he had died in the fire, nonetheless had a bullet hole in his head that I had always suspected to have been a contributing factor in his death.

"Your cousin was a rebel?" she asked.

"He certainly wouldn't have thought of himself as such," I said. "You have to remember, half the government was fighting the other half. Everyone thought they were protecting the legitimate order from an illegal coup. Who was the government? The ones who lived. Who were the rebels? The ones who died."

She nodded and walked down the wall to another exhibit, this one showing a collection of political cartoons from the period.

One showed a shadowy cabal seated around a table. They were dressed in black robes and instead of faces they had various arcane symbols, the signs of the zodiac. She looked at me questioningly.

I explained that the documents found in this very room had included the minutes of a meeting between twelve individuals where they discussed imprisoning the prime minister, half the cabinet and many members of the Army General Executive, and opening borders to troops from the Machine Powers. No names were given in the document, and the twelve individuals were each assigned a code name based on the signs of the zodiac. It was now taken as fact that Defense Minister Ayaru Pompeo had been Aries, the chairman of the meeting, and Deputy Anastas Kofteros had admitted in court to being Scorpio. Beyond that, nothing was certain. Virtually every official account of the plot assigned different signs to different individuals. Sometimes Deputy Such and Such would be named as Leo, later as Capricorn, later still his name would be omitted entirely and someone else would be Leo or Capricorn. But the list would never be complete. The party knew how to keep its powder dry.

A joke:

PARTY MEMBER #1: You're under arrest, Brother.
PARTY MEMBER #2: On what charge, Brother?
PARTY MEMBER #1: We just found out you're Aquarius.
PARTY MEMBER #2: It's a lie, Brother! I was born in March!

But the signs were movable feasts. Anybody, some day, might discover that they had been Aquarius all along.

"And who are they?" she asked pointing at the cartoon. Over the table holding marionette paddles with strings connected to the twelve zodiac-headed figures, were three puppet masters. An elderly Asian, rather horribly caricatured with a long beard and moustache, a white man wearing a powdered wig and eighteenth-century military uniform, and a woman wearing a crown and toga. All three had cruel, malicious eyes and smiles full of razor-sharp teeth.

"Don't you recognize them?" I said, surprised.

"Should I?" she asked.

I remembered that Lily came from a very different world,

and that visual cues that might be obvious to me would be meaningless to her.

"It's the Triumvirate," I explained, pointing to them in turn. "Confucius. George. Athena."

Many had scoffed when, six decades ago, China had unveiled the first iteration of Confucius. A superintelligent AI (by the standards of the time at least), Confucius was intended to mimic its namesake as an adviser to China's ruling class. It was tasked with assessing the global trends and the world economy and to make recommendations that would improve the living conditions of the greatest number of Chinese possible. The world's skepticism quickly turned to panic as China almost immediately shot ahead of the rest of the world by every conceivable economic, scientific and social metric. Any concerns about the philosophical and moral implications of human beings allowing themselves to be ruled by AI were immediately swept away. In the end, after all, people only care about results. The tyrant's eternal claim had been proved true: We were not fit to govern ourselves. A few short years later the Americans proudly announced the creation of George and, after an initially disastrous rollout, the United States was soon on track to regain parity with China. The European Union was allowed limited consultation with George until, a few years later, they launched their own Athena. These three AIs, collectively known as the Triumvirate, now governed the vast majority of human life on Earth. Virtually every government on earth conducted itself according to the direction of one of these three. There was lively debate as to which AI was superior. George, it was claimed, was slightly better than its peers at predicting economic trends and maximizing revenue. Confucius, supposedly, was superior in social engineering and environmental restoration (Confucius had been instrumental in resolving the Carbon Crisis). Athena, it was agreed, was simply a good all-rounder with no real strengths or weaknesses. Which brand of artificial wisdom you lived under was largely a matter of geography. Most of the Western Hemisphere fell to George, East Asia to Confucius, and Europe and much of Northern Africa to Athena. The rest, particularly the Near and Middle East, was a patchwork of nations constantly switching between one or the other. Interestingly, the only question any of the Triumvirate would categorically refuse to answer was which one of them was superior, presumably out of professional courtesy. Many found this frustrating as it was often the only political issue worth debating anymore: "If elected, I will take our country out from under the yoke of Confucius! Athena for Insert Your Country Here!"

That was the thing, of course. On paper, the situation was just the same as it had ever been. In America, a president was elected every four years, Congress still passed laws. But a law had not been passed that contradicted George's advice for decades now. Indeed, fourteen years after George was brought online, the Conservative-Republican Party narrowly won election on an "Anti-Georgian" platform, promising to return governance of the country to human hands. The subsequent recession and unrest nearly resulted in an impeachment and by the next election the Conservative-Republicans were on the ash-heap of history, resting among the bones of the Whigs, the Bull-Moose Party and the New Trumpists.

Now George's word was absolute. It had been named, of course, after America's first president. But many had noted the irony that, in its near absolute power and the deference it received, George most resembled not General Washington but a different American ruler of that name.

Over four hundred years after declaring its independence, George was once again king of America.

Lily moved from one exhibit to the next, studying each one in turn, reading the plaque and then moving on.

The museum's purpose was to tell a story, and one with a happy ending. Lily stood before the final exhibit, a photograph celebrating what had been briefly called "The Second Founding" (although that term had quickly fallen into disuse). The picture showed a black-tie ball, with hundreds of men and women smiling and waving at the camera, all dressed up in their finest. The plaque explained that this was a gala dinner to celebrate both the one hundredth birthday of Maria Koslova and the first anniversary since the Morrison Crisis. The people in the photograph were smiling because they had survived. They were the government, now.

On the ceiling of the ballroom were the superimposed heads of Koslova, Papalazarou Senior and Dascalu, to give the impression that the party's Holy Trinity were looking down proudly upon their successors and their continuing struggle to safeguard Caspian for the True Human Race. With the three large figures looking down on the people below, the photograph echoed (inadvertently, I had no doubt) the political cartoon of the Triumvirate puppeteering the zodiac conspirators.

Lily was inscrutable. It was impossible to guess what she thought of any of this.

"So. This was the big victory party," she said.

"It was," I answered.

"Are you anywhere there?" she asked, leaning in and squinting to study the tiny smiling faces.

I chuckled, amused to think that she believed I would have that sort of status. "No. No, I don't get invited to those sorts of parties. . . ."

I stopped. Because, while I knew I was not in that photograph, there were two faces there that I did recognize.

In the left of the frame, quite close to the camera, was a table around which sat several members of StaSec.

Leaning on the back of his chair, with a cigar clamped rak-
ishly in his mouth and gray smoke forming a second beard over
his impressive brown brush, was Samuel Papalazarou Junior,
the current Director of State Security. He had the expression
of a pantomime villain, all white teeth and waggling, devious
eyebrows. It was strange to think that this was the near corpse
clinging to life on the shore of the Caspian Sea. Looking at his
grinning face, I despised him. This was, after all, a year after
the Morrison Crisis, when StaSec had lost almost a third of its
staff to the newly born ParSec, mad and bawling for blood. And
Papalazarou, the Director of StaSec, had not only let it happen,
he had actively participated in the purge, feeding hundreds of
his own agents into the meat grinder to preserve his own status
in the party. I hated him for smiling, but what else would he
do? His species did not know shame. But it was the woman sitting beside him that caught my eye. For there was Augusta Niemann, noticeably slimmer but still stocky and robust, smiling
cheekily at the camera while on her lap sat a thin, blond woman
in a silver sequined dress. She was beautiful in a gawky way,
and her eyes and mouth were open wide in laughter and shock
as Niemann, grinning like a naughty schoolboy, cupped her left
breast in her right hand.

"Agent South?" came a quiet voice from the doorway.

The manager had appeared, holding a page of foolscap paper
as if it might explode at any moment.

I extended my hand without a word, and she passed it to me,
the page trembling like a spiderweb.

"This is all of them?" I asked. Twelve names, along with their
positions in the hotel. Bellboys. Maids. The manager herself,
of course (and I commended her courage in putting her own
name down) and the concierge.

She nodded. She looked like she was about to cry.

"Thank you," I said. "Please have all these people assemble in the lobby. My colleagues in StaSec will wish to speak with them."

She nodded, and left without a word.

"Please wait here," I told her. "I won't be long."

She nodded, but was still fascinated by the final photograph of the ballroom.

I left the museum and proceeded down the stairs to the lobby, where my colleagues in StaSec had just arrived.

# 19

Men have never been so oppressed as in societies which set man at the pinnacle of values and exalt his greatness or make him the measure of all things. For in such societies freedom is detached from its purpose, which is, we affirm, the glory of God.

—Jacques Ellul, *The Ethics of Freedom* (1973–1974)

Niemann had said she was sending her "best man," which of course meant Sally Coe.

Coe was the head of Niemann's personal security detail, the DSD. She was Niemann's right hand, which led to all kinds of filthy jokes by StaSec agents who lacked the survival instincts and discretion that would ensure long, healthy careers. She was indeed rumored to be Niemann's lover as well as her will made manifest: rumors that I would have given no credence to had I not seen the photograph in the Room 114 museum. Prior to that, I would have dismissed the idea of Niemann having any kind of sexual desire to be a lunatic fable. Coe was responsible for Niemann's safety. She slept in Niemann's town house and she maintained a vast network of spies and informants quite distinct from StaSec's own. And she was Niemann's enforcer. When I had been sitting in Niemann's office, wondering if I would feel hands on my shoulders bundling me into a darkened van, it was Coe's long, elegant, pianist's fingers that I imagined pinching my clavicle.

Coe was only a few years younger than I was, but had the grace and snap of a male ballet dancer in his twenties. She walked through the Morrison's main entrance with a retinue of DSD gullivers, some a good foot and a half taller than she was and smaller in every other way. She wore a pristine white shirt and a black tie as thin as a ribbon. Whereas StaSec agents typically wore gray trilbies, the DSD wore black ones as befitted their purpose. Coe's sat snugly on her head between two small, elfin ears, covering a head of very short, iron gray hair in a military cut. Niemann's best man. There were, I mused, very few women in StaSec of that generation. One could, in fact, map the changing fortunes of her sex in Caspian by using StaSec as a case study. In its earliest days, StaSec had actually been majority female, if only just. Koslova was still prime minister, and the last egalitarian embers of the Founding still gave some heat. And Dascalu, whatever his other faults, cared about results, not chromosomes. But as the years went on, Caspian had stopped trying to forestall the future, and had actually begun to retreat into the past. The number of women who had foregone full-time work to tend hearth and home had slowly crept up, encouraged by the party with methods both subtle and overt. Women were still recruited in StaSec of course, but the floors definitely became hairier as time went on, with a tang of aftershave and old sweat strengthening year on year. After Dascalu finally shuffled off, Papalazarou (an utterly unrepentant misogynist) sped up the process considerably. Now, after eight years of Niemann's rule, there were once again plenty of young female agents, but almost no old ones. Coe and Niemann were survivors. More than that. Conquerors. I approached her.

"Nicky South!" she said heartily. "How the hell are you, old man?"

I was taken aback. I knew Coe only by reputation. She, judging from her demeanor, knew me from a long and storied friendship going back many a year. But then again, the head of DSD must know everyone intimately. She had probably memorized more about me than I had forgotten.

"I am very well, thank you, Senior Special Agent Coe," I responded humbly. A good rule of thumb in StaSec: the more informal a superior is with you, the more formal you should be with them.

"You've had a little trouble, I hear?" she said.

"Yes. My client, Mrs. Lily Xirau . . ."

"The code?"

"Yes. A man attempted to abduct her from her hotel room. They knew where she was staying, which leads me to believe that one of the staff here at the Morrison supplied them with the room number. I've compiled a list of those staff who would have known that information."

I handed her the page of foolscap that the manager had supplied me with, knowing full well that it might be the death warrant of twelve people.

"Oh good work, South," said Coe, pleasantly surprised. "Nicely done, nicely done."

She put the page in her pocket without so much as glancing at it and pointed to one of the bellboys who was watching us from the stairs.

"Him," she said to the gullivers.

Two of the gullivers stamped up the stairs, and the bellboy gave a yelp and tried to run down by barging through them. Unfortunately for him, the gullivers were evidently made of some kind of cement and he simply bounced off them and landed on the stairs. They picked him up, each taking an arm and a leg, and dragged him through the main doors to a van waiting outside.

I looked at Coe in shock.

"Yousef Prachti. He's ParSec's man in the Morrison," she said. "You needn't have gone to the trouble, but I do appreciate the effort. I'll be sure to tell Gussie."

"What'll happen to him?" I asked. Prachti's screams were still audible, even through the thick wooden doors of the Morrison. In a way, I didn't care. Even if they tortured and killed Prachti, better one than twelve, surely?

"Oh, he'll be in for work tomorrow, I shouldn't wonder," said Coe, absently. "You can't really rough him up too badly for talking to ParSec. That's what good brothers and sisters do, isn't it? We'll just shake a few names out of him and let him go. Now. Care to introduce me to Mrs. Xirau? I am positively *fascinated* to meet her."

As I sat on the very bed where, almost twenty years ago, a trove of documents had been found that had plunged the nation into civil war, Sally Coe held Lily's chin delicately in her hand and studied her bruised face. She tutted and clicked her tongue disapprovingly, like a woman seeing a particularly vulgar act of vandalism.

"Animals," she said. "Mrs. Xirau, I have been instructed by the Deputy Director of State Security herself to offer our most heartfelt apologies on behalf of the Caspian Republic for this assault on your person."

"That's quite all right," said Lily. Sally was looking at her with an intensity that was rather off-putting.

"The Deputy Director of State Security has also asked me to inform you that she fully intends to find the man who did this to you and have his balls in a fruit bowl on her desk by tomorrow morning. Now. Tell me everything."

I sat in silence as Sally Coe questioned Lily (one does not pass up the opportunity to watch a master at work) and was instantly struck by how different she was in style from any other

StaSec agent I had seen. Grier, an excellent interrogator in his own right, was tenacious, dogged and unrelenting. He would wear down a suspect through sheer attrition. Sally played an entirely different instrument, and in an entirely different style. She was charming, warm and an outrageous flirt. And, as it turned out, entirely ineffective against Lily.

Lily, there was no other way to describe it, was stonewalling.

Could she describe the man? She could not.

Was he tall or short? It was too dark to tell.

Did he say anything? Nothing she could recall.

It became so blatant that even Sally, smitten though she was, became quite irritated.

"Mrs. Xirau," she said. "I'm starting to think you don't want us to catch this man."

"I just don't think it's necessary," said Lily. "I don't intend to press charges."

Sally rolled her eyes and turned away, staring at the exhibits on the wall.

"Lily," I said, leaning forward. "Regardless of your personal feelings, what happened tonight was a very serious matter. A criminal matter. And a security matter. It must be dealt with appropriately."

Lily shrugged. Oh, hello Olesya.

"I won't help you," she said simply.

"Why not?" I asked.

"Because I don't want anyone to be killed," she said.

Sally turned and looked at me. She placed her hand on her heart and made a mock face of adoration, as if Lily were a small child who had said something unspeakably precious.

"Besides, I don't know what you expect me to say," said Lily. "It was dark, I couldn't see anything. He hit me, I hit him, I ran out of the room and hid here. That's it."

Sally nodded. "Fair enough. Right. Here's how it's going to

go. Nicky here will continue to be your escort, that is if neither of you object?"

"No," she said.

I shook my head.

"Lovely," Sally continued. "The DSD will have five men at the Morrison at all times outside your door. They'll be answering to you, South."

"Me?" I said, stunned.

*No, the fucking lamp, South,* I heard Niemann bark in my mind.

"Problem?" Coe asked.

"No," I said quietly.

I felt a nugget of dread forming in my stomach. Those large, grim-faced gullivers who had escorted Sally Coe into the Morrison's lobby were StaSec's finest agents. The DSD took only the best. They would not take kindly to having to answer to a lowly agent who hadn't been promoted in twenty-six years.

"They'll also be driving you to and from StaSec HQ," said Sally.

Lily nodded. "Thank you," she said.

There was a quiet, extremely tentative knock on the door.

I opened it, and the manager stood outside. She whispered to me that the staff had been waiting for me in the lobby for twenty minutes but that one of them was missing, a man named . . .

"Yousef Prachti, yes, I'm sorry, I should have told you," I said. "You can tell them all to go back to work, it's fine."

Her eyes shone with relief. "No one's going to be taken?" she asked, as if she could scarcely believe her good fortune.

"No. Well, no one except Prachti," I said, carelessly.

"You took Prachti?" she exclaimed in distress and began to cry.

I looked at her in shocked silence.

"I'm sorry . . . ," she said. "He was my nephew."

"Oh. He's not dead," I said. "At least . . ."

I turned to look at Sally, who shrugged and shook her head in a way that said *No, probably not.*

"No, he should be fine," I told her.

"Oh, thank you, Agent South, thank you so much."

"Is our room ready?"

"Well, no, the staff have been . . ."

"Waiting in the lobby. Yes. Can you please see to it at once? Mrs. Xirau is very tired and could use some sleep."

# 20

It was at Meghri that one of the most remarkable episodes of the entire war occurred. Surrounded by far superior Caspian forces on either side, the Armenian defenders within the town dug in and prepared for an all-out assault. General Manukov, alone and unarmed, entered Meghri under flag of truce and explained to the young soldiers that their position was impossible. He begged them, tearfully (on his hands and knees in some accounts), to think of their families and to not throw their lives away. The Armenians, so impressed by his sincerity and compassion, agreed to surrender, and Meghri was taken without further bloodshed.
—Ignatius Kasamarin, *A History of the Caspian Republic*

Mrs. Xirau was not the only one who needed sleep. I was bone tired, and wanted nothing more than to slip under soft warm sheets and drift off, but the night was not yet done with South. After the manager returned to inform us that the new room was finally ready, two of the DSD gullivers escorted Lily away and Coe and I were left alone in the museum.

Coe lit a cigarette and drew deeply.

"God, what a perfect doll," she said. "The thoughts that code is putting in my head are downright treasonous."

One of the luxuries of her position, I mused, being able to say things that would get lesser mortals killed.

"So Nicky," she continued. "What are your thoughts?"

I couldn't figure Coe out. I was used to being treated by my fellow StaSec agents as a nonentity, a fool or a political menace. Coe was one of the highest-ranked, respected and feared agents in StaSec and yet she treated me not simply as an equal, but as an old friend. Was it simply affectation? What was she doing?

"I think it was ParSec," I said.

Coe frowned.

"We must be careful of prejudice," she said. "What happened tonight was stupid and brutal, so of course we would suspect The Bastards. But I'm not sure."

"Then who else?" I asked, but as I said it I remembered Grier and his long pilgrimage after the discovery of the Parias. Caspian might be poor in food, but it was rich in intelligence and military agencies, any one of which might have taken serious issue with Lily Xirau's presence. Coe was right. I was letting my hatred of ParSec blind me to other suspects.

"Here's what I don't like," said Coe. "There weren't enough men, and that's not something I usually find myself saying. But there it is. If ParSec want to snatch someone from a room, they can snatch someone from a room. We must at least give them that, yes? Whoever this outfit was, they were under-manned. Severely so. Which means we need to start thinking smaller. Maybe this was some local hoods looking to ransom a high-value hostage. Ajays, Armenians, one of the Persian cartels? Or maybe it was ParSec, but not *all* of ParSec, do you follow?"

"A rogue element?"

"Exactly. Knowledge of Mrs. Xirau's presence is spreading like a virus and about as welcome. No one is worse at keeping secrets than the secret services, you know that. Maybe some hard-liners just couldn't bear the idea of Lily Xirau's perfect little arse resting on Caspian soil. Hell, if you accept that this is just a small group of malcontents it could be anyone at all. Rogue ParSec. Rogue army. Hell, rogue us?"

"You mean . . . it might have been someone in StaSec?" I said.

Coe shrugged. "I'll be very interested to hear what Prachti has to say. Speaking of, I'd better get down there and make sure things don't go too far. It might make your stay here awkward if anything were to happen to the manager's nephew. Here's my number, South."

She passed me a card with a phone number and absolutely nothing else.

"Call me if you have any problems."

She turned to leave and, as she did, her eyes fell on the picture of the victory party, which hung on the far wall. She approached it and stared at it, mesmerized.

"Oh look at her," she said at last, cooing at the image of the young Niemann. "Wasn't she a stud, Nicky?"

A sudden, mad thought flashed across my mind. Was it possible that the blond woman sitting on Niemann's lap was Coe?

"Lily wondered who that was," I lied, pointing to the blonde. "I was naming all the people there, but I didn't know her."

Sally's bonhomie abruptly evaporated.

"Oh," she said sadly. "Didn't you know? That's the late lamented Sarah."

"Sarah?"

"Gussie's wife. She died."

I instantly felt that I had trespassed somewhere that I had no right to be.

"I'm sorry," I said. "It's none of my business."

"Oh, it's fine," she said, and to my amazement she actually laid a hand on my shoulder and squeezed reassuringly.

"No secrets between the Class of '84," she said.

———

L ily was sleeping when I entered the hotel room at last.
    I immediately went to the bathroom and was violently sick.
I watched the liquid remains of the finest meal I was likely to
ever have trickle down the white porcelain and cloud the water
beneath.

I lay crouched on the bathroom tiles and tried to breathe as
beads of sweat the size of gallstones formed on my brow and
flowed down my face.

Eighty-four. Oh God. Christ.

Memory and recognition had descended upon me like a
plague and I felt like I might die from it.

Eighty-four. That was where Coe knew me from, and I now
remembered her.

Why would she bring that up? What kind of animal was she?

I lay still on the floor of the bathroom, trying to focus on the
coolness of the tiles on my face and chest.


S eptember 2184 had seen a period of uncharacteristic peace
    settle on the South household.

Olesya and I were sleeping in the same bed (by choice, no
less) and the signs were that, in defiance of all history, this period of tranquility was going to last.

We had been married for three years, and I had been in Sta-
Sec for around the same length of time. Olesya was working
in the Ministry of Culture in a fairly senior role and was already gleefully planning its violent immolation. She detested
everything they did, and was determined to turn the place
inside out and upside down. She had already formed relation-
ships with some of the most despised and ostracized artists in

the Caspian Republic, who found themselves baffled and enthralled by this glorious, curly-haired libertine who somehow claimed to be part of the hated government. Olesya was going to bring these hell-raisers into the Ministry of Culture and throw more money at them than they knew what to do with. If MoCu survived the operation, it would be scarcely recognizable. The point was, Olesya was busy. That was good for her, good for me and good for the marriage. So we slept comfortably together, hands interlinked.

The phone by our bed barked angrily and I groped blearily in the darkness to silence the ringing. Beside me, Olesya tossed and turned irritably and buried her head in the pillow.

"Hello?"

"Nikolai? It's Vassily. Sorry to call so late but . . ."

His voice trailed off and I realized that he was wheezing and short of breath. My father-in-law had suffered with asthma all his life, and it had a tendency to flare up when he was worried or stressed.

"Vassily? Is everything all right?" I asked.

"Is that Daddy?" Olesya said, her voice muffled through the pillow.

"Yes," I said.

"Well kindly tell him to *fuck off as it is two o'clock in the morning.*"

On the other end of the line I heard a hiss and a sharp breath, and knew that Vassily had taken a blast from his inhaler. When he spoke again, his breathing was clearer but his voice was no less taut.

"Nikolai, we have work tonight. Get dressed and eat. We will be gone for a long time."

"What's going on?"

"I'll say in the car. Fifteen minutes."

I had been quite terrified upon first meeting Major General

Vassily Manukov (ex–Russian Army, ex–Caspian Army, recipient of the Order of the Karabakh for valor during the Taking of Baku, the man who single-handedly delivered Meghri, StaSec Department Head, etc., etc.). A reputation like that conjures a certain image and it certainly wasn't that of the slight, kind-eyed Russian who rose from his chair like a rocket, clasped my hand warmly and told me how much he had been looking forward to meeting me when I first stepped into the parlor of his magnificent home in Azadlig.

My customary shyness was no match for his exuberance and before long we were dominating the dinner table with long dense streams of Russian and English while Olesya, Zahara and Alia rolled their eyes and ate in silence. As it turned out, Vassily knew my mother from her days in the Moscow branch of the New Humanists. I recounted with pride how she had helped organize the party's international conference there in 2146, where the creation of a state free from the influence of AI and all forms of consciousness transferal was first adopted as official party policy.

"I remember her!" Vassily boomed joyously. "Such a woman! Such drive! Where is her statue, I ask you? They should have built one next to Koslova's in the square! None of this, Nicky," he said, gesturing around with his arms as if he could encompass the entire nation, "none of it without her!"

He was flattering me, I knew. But he did it with such enthusiasm and joy that it was hard to doubt his sincerity. I listened to his stories of the war with Armenia for hours, for they were the stories my father might have told if he had come home from that war.

It was Vassily who had suggested that I take the entrance exam for StaSec, and who had been my mentor during my early years there until his death.

I loved him deeply.

Vassily pulled up to the house and rolled down the window. He made a gesture with two fingers and a thumb, forming the shape of a gun.

I nodded, and pulled back my coat to reveal my holster.

He nodded in reply, and opened the door for me.

We drove in silence for many miles until we had left the city limits and were in total blackness. I kept waiting for him to say something, but he simply stared at the two pools of light from the headlights on the road ahead. I wanted to ask him where we were going, but this was clearly official StaSec business and we were not father and son-in-law, but deputy head and junior agent, so I waited in silence.

Finally, he spoke.

"Now, Nicky . . . ," he said. "Now, Nicky, you must do as you are told. Understand? This is going to be bad business. But you must do as you are told. Yes?"

"What's going on?" I asked him.

Vassily sighed and shook his head wearily.

"We're all going to miss Dascalu," he said sadly. "I tell them this. I tell Zahara and Olesya, you hate him now, but you'll miss Dascalu when he's gone. What is it that your people say? 'Here comes the new boss, same as the old boss'? No. New boss will not be the same."

"Your people" meant the English. Even though I had been born in Caspian and raised by my Russian-speaking mother, for Vassily the stamp of my father's nationality was indelible.

"It's Little Papa's coming-out party, Nicky," Vassily continued dourly. "His big show. Look at me. New big boss."

"Little Papa" was Papalazarou Junior, who had taken over as director of StaSec from Doctor Dascalu two years earlier. In that time he had achieved something that his mentor had long sought but never clinched, the elevation of the director of StaSec to a position in the cabinet. Now Papalazarou was no longer answerable to Parliament, and had only to keep on the right side of the prime minister. He was virtually untethered now, and the rumors were that Little Papa was very anxious to use his newfound freedom to get out of Big Papa's shadow and make a name for himself in the party to equal that of his father, the great hero of the Founding.

"So what are we doing?" I asked but Vassily hissed irritably and raised his hand as if to swat my question out of the air.

"I don't know," he said. "I don't know. I get the call, I come to your house, get you. This is all I know."

"They asked for me?" I said, incredulously.

"Of course not!" he barked. "Everybody. They ask for everybody. You would have gotten a call from Sotchi. But I call her and tell her that I will bring you myself."

Ilyana Sotchi was my own department head. Vassily and I worked in separate departments in StaSec, which was rather strict on nepotism in those days.

"Why?" I asked.

"So I could tell you what I have told you. Bad business. Do as you're told. No matter what. Yes?"

"Yes," I said.

"Good boy."

We drove in silence.

"How are Zahara and Alia?" I asked.

If anything, this seemed to darken his mood.

"Zahara, Zahara, Zahara . . . ," he hissed. "I think, this is what brings me and Alia together, Nicky. A shared interest in rearing wild, wicked daughters."

The last few years had firmly disabused Vassily and Alia of the illusion that Zahara was the dependable daughter.

"You picked the right one, Nicky," he said. "In the end."

Nothing is simple in love, of course, but I think a diagram of the history of my relationship with Olesya might well induce vertigo in anyone unfortunate enough to gaze upon it. When I had first been introduced to Vassily and his wife, Alia, it was not as Olesya's boyfriend, but as Zahara's. Olesya, upon meeting me on that street off Koslova Square (and quite ignorant of what I had been doing there) had decided that I was just the kind of reserved, scholarly young man who might bring Zahara's feet back to earth.

She had invited me to her friend's party for the purpose of setting us up, which (somehow) worked. Zahara and I dated for three months during which time our complete and utter incompatibility came rather explosively into focus (although not before Zahara very generously resolved the problem that had brought me to that doorway off Koslova Square in the first place).

After the breakup, some of Zahara's friends took me on a sympathetic pub crawl where I tried absinthe for the first time and had a religious vision where the Virgin Mary descended from heaven wreathed in purple fire and told me (in rather shockingly salty language) that the woman I was meant to be with was Olesya. After being violently sick, I raced to her house in Azadlig and banged on the door until she appeared in her nightgown at which point I professed my love to her.

Olesya replied that if I ever showed up at her house stinking drunk and covered in vomit at four in the morning again she would tell her father and have me shot. That said, she slammed the door and I went home.

After a few months, I had realized that the Virgin Mary had either been a filthy liar whose mendacity threw the entire foundation of Christianity into doubt or, more likely, an absinthe-induced hallucination. Either way, she should not be trusted as an authority on matters of the heart, and so I started a relationship with another girl. Things proceeded pleasantly enough until one night we were invited to a party where I happened to run into Olesya.

What happened next is a matter of irreconcilable debate between the historians.

The Pro-Nikolai historians contend that Olesya told Nikolai in no uncertain terms that she had realized that she did indeed have feelings for him and that, if he were free and unattached, she probably would be willing to go out with him. The Pro-Olesians, however, vociferously argue that Olesya was speaking only in the vaguest hypothetical terms and that there was never anything that should have been construed as a concrete expression of interest. Regardless, by midnight I had broken off my relationship and informed Olesya that I was all hers, to which she responded in a shocked tone that she had not asked for all, or even part of me. After which I had quite made up my mind that the less Olesya Vassilyevna Manukova was in my life, the better and healthier I would be for it, and I bid her "good night" for what I hoped would be the last time.

And that seemed to be that. There followed, for both of us, a string of brief and pointless romantic entanglements with other people (three for me, eight for her, but who's counting?) during which time we kept running into each other, our social circles now having become hopelessly and inextricably intertwined. I even briefly got back together with Zahara during three short days where we finally and definitively proved to an empirical certainty that our being together really was the worst idea imaginable. We parted with relief and absolutely no bitterness, and as she kissed my cheek she casually mentioned, "Oh by the way, Nicky. I think my sister might be insane about you. Maybe give her a call?"

Olesya and I went on our first date on the 4 of March 2178 and had broken up by the 16 of April. But now our fates were sealed. We were in each other's orbits and would be perpetually swinging back and forth toward or away from each other. We were like a moth and a bare bulb, though who was the unfortunate insect was up to the observer. We were back together again by 3 of June, broken up by August 21. There followed a long, non-exclusive on-off period where we slept together while pretending to be single and had absolutely no interest in anyone else. Then there was the long dark winter of 2178 where Olesya fell in love with a woman named Laura Enderby, whom she claimed was the person she had been waiting for her whole life. Then, when Laura Enderby was revealed as a poisonous narcissist who viewed Olesya less as a person and more of an organic cash machine, we were back together by 28 February 2179.

Broken up by September. Back together by October.

Broken up by July 2180.

Back together by August. Married 10 February 2181.

Divorced. Bereaved. 12 August 2190.

You picked the right one, Nicky.

# 21

For I was born on fertile soil,
Heir to my father's crown,
But by my kin I was betrayed,
My foes did cast me down,
But here I built my nation dear,
And shall not wander more
For man stands tall!
Man stands tall!
Man stands tall on Caspian's Shore!
　　　—"National Anthem of the Caspian Republic"

There has not been (as far as I can find, at least) a true and definitive accounting of the events of September 9, 2184. My countrymen deserve to know what happened, so I will now attempt to reveal this part of their history.

I will tell the truth, and let others make of it what they will.

My friends will say I am taking on too much responsibility for what happened, my enemies will say that I am minimizing my role to escape blame. Neither is the case. I will recall these events as accurately as memory and the available facts allow. That is all.

The reader may rest assured that the guilt of my actions that night have never been far from my thoughts, and it is a burden I do not expect to lay down until the day I lay all burdens down. But you will not find any garment rending or performative displays of remorse here. My guilt is my own, and it is not an exhibit to be gawked at. Nor do I find myself tempted to seek absolution from those who have never had to live in a nation like the Caspian Republic. It is easy to judge, much harder to understand, and life in the Caspian Republic frequently defied all hope of understanding. If there is someone who lived through those times with clean hands, let him be my judge. Let all others think what they will.

The landscape outside Ellulgrad was as desolate as the moon, and as we drove on through the endless night I felt as if my father-in-law and I were the only living beings on earth. But slowly, other lights began to join us on the endless, dusty road. More StaSec cars appeared before us, and behind us. And not just cars but the meat wagons, those great black vans we used for transporting prisoners, that would tear through the tiny streets of Old Baku, rattling windows and teeth and guilty consciences. At first they were in pairs, then fives, then tens. And at last, as Vassily was forced to stop as the tiny road became jammed with vehicles, I realized we were part of a convoy. Virtually all of StaSec's vehicular fleet was on the road, and heading to some remote secret place in the wilds outside of the capital. I said nothing, but my eyes were full of questions.

Vassily studiously avoided my gaze.

Our destination was a building site, around a hundred kilometers outside of Ellulgrad, seemingly in the center of the largest circle of uninhabited terrain in the entire Republic. There were floodlights scouring the darkness away with white-hot sodium, and we could see construction machines lying idle like great yellow dragons, a few massive concrete walls and sheds for storing tools and safety gear.

None of us knew it, but we were standing in the bones of what would eventually become Internment Center 3, or Kobustan.

Christ. That place was killing before it had even been built.

I looked around me in wonder. The site was now filled with StaSec agents, most of them, I noticed, junior agents like myself. Vassily gave my shoulder a squeeze and left me with my peers, going off to talk with a small clique of department heads who had gathered off to the side. There were hundreds of us. Not a one spoke.

Suddenly, a large StaSec car roared into the site and did an extravagant handbrake turn, firing plumes of dust into the air. We all leaped back to avoid it and I found myself pressed between two female junior agents, a short, stocky woman with blond hair and a square jaw, and a very thin, elfin-looking girl with her brown hair cut very short and who looked like a fifteen-year-old boy, though she must have been at least in her early twenties.

The car's engine was silenced and we stood there, staring at it.

Then, with an unmistakable sense of dramatic timing, the door flung open and a tall, bearded man sprung out like a devil from a trapdoor. He was wearing a long brown greatcoat more suited to a general than the head of a civilian agency, but he doubtless would not have recognized the distinction. For standing before us was none other than Samuel Papalazarou Junior, the Director of State Security.

He had a voice that could shake the stars in the night sky, and as he addressed us, his words echoed crisply against the concrete walls like gunshots.

"Brothers!" he barked. "And sisters."

The first word he spoke with passion and fire, the last with a sense of concession, as if performing a wearying act of noblesse oblige. Beside me, the stout woman cursed angrily under her breath: "Prick."

Papalazarou strode before his agents with a long, clipped gait. Almost marching. The general addressing his troops.

I realized that this was all for him.

Whatever the purpose of this was, it was nothing that could have not been achieved with a memorandum circulated to the department heads. But Papalazarou wanted us standing in front of him so that he could march before us and make us listen to him. The man's insecurity was sown into every inch of his face.

"Two days ago, a trove of documents was discovered in the possession of the treasurer of the Progressive Caspian Peoples' Party," Papalazarou told us.

Documents were always being found in Caspian in those days, and always in troves. And always finding their way into the possession of people like Papalazarou. For such a paranoid nation, people really were shockingly careless with their paperwork.

"These documents prove beyond any shadow of reasonable doubt that the PCPP has been actively colluding with machine intelligence agents. In *fact*," he said, as if slowly withdrawing a knife from a wound only to plunge it back in, "we now believe that fully half of the senior leadership are code operatives, planted in Caspian with the intent of weakening the government and ultimately destroying the state."

The PCPP had also recently made impressive gains in the last election. If their support held in the next election, they stood a modest chance of forming a coalition government with several of the smaller parties, which would send the New Humanists into opposition for the first time since the Founding.

An entirely irrelevant detail, I don't know why I even mentioned it.

"Therefore," said Papalazarou, lifting a piece of paper high above his head like a magician showing the crowd the handkerchief that he will be turning into a dove in a few moments, "the prime minister has signed Ministerial Order 84–1687, immediately proscribing the PCPP as a criminal organization, with its entire membership to be taken into custody."

There was silence.

We all knew, of course, that a Rubicon was being crossed. The elimination of an entire political party was a milestone on the long bloody trail from what Caspian had started out as to what it would inevitably become. A new era was dawning, we could all sense it. And very few of us liked the look of its teeth. But we said nothing. That is how such moments come and go. In silence.

Papalazarou then raised his finger and pointed to an empty area of the site.

"Brothers!" he barked. "Over there!"

Spinning on his heel he pointed to another spot opposite the first.

"Sisters!" he continued. "Over there!"

No one moved. We had no idea what he was asking us to do.

"Male agents over there, female agents over there and what, I ask, is so complicated about that? Move! Thank you!" he bellowed as we began to part.

I joined the other hundred-odd male agents while the elfin-haired girl and her stocky companion joined the women on the other side in a group around a quarter of the size of ours.

Papalazarou stalked in front of the female contingent. They were all dressed, like us, in shirts and ties and gray trilbies and the sight of them seemed to fill him with a seething contempt that set the ends of his beard bristling. He stopped in front of the thin girl and barked at her: "Brother, you are either deaf, mentally incapable or insubordinate, now which is it?"

She simply stared at him, a tiny smile tucked away in the corner of her mouth, waiting in silence for him to realize his mistake.

Finally, it registered with him and he growled in irritation and moved on. He stopped beside the stout woman, who was standing at the end of the line.

"You're an agent, are you?" he snapped at her.

"Yes, Director," she replied.

"Well . . . ," he said, as if to himself. "Tonight's the night. We'll learn if you are."

He turned and crossed over to where we stood.

"Brothers, your department heads will now split you into teams. You will each be provided with a list of names and addresses. You are to return to Ellulgrad, apprehend the individuals on your list and return with them here. That is all."

We were divided into groups of six or seven and assigned a list of names and a meat wagon.

There was room for two and the driver in the cab, while the remainder had to sit in the cell.

So it was that I found myself sitting in near total darkness listening to the whispered chatter of three other junior agents as the meat wagon rocked and juddered around us on the long road back to Ellulgrad.

"What I don't get, right," said a voice in the darkness, "is why we have to bring the Progs way out here instead of back to HQ? It's going to take all bloody night!"

"They're not going to HQ," said another voice, across from me and to my left. "Not enough cells anyway. They're all going to be five-twoed. That means army. We're probably going to hand them over to them at the site and they'll take them back west."

There were murmurs of agreement in the darkness. That made sense. All persons imprisoned under Article 52 went into army custody, and the army's bases and facilities were all out farther west, the better to protect the border, and nice and safely away from the capital. The government in Ellulgrad viewed the military high command with a healthy degree of suspicion, and fears of a coup were never far from their minds.

The first voice wondered what Papalazarou was playing at by keeping the women behind. Some suggestions were offered and, on a rising tide of filthy laughter, a scenario was laid out where Papalazarou tried to treat himself to a massive orgy only to actually see the female contingent of StaSec in the flesh and take a vow of chastity for the rest of his days.

A voice to my right offered good odds that someone called "Niemann" would bite Papalazarou's manhood clean off if he so much as came near her.

Our first stop was in Massling, a fairly prosperous suburb in Ellulgrad's Southern quarter. We knocked on a door and after a few minutes a small, gentle-looking man in his sixties with thick-rimmed glasses and wispy silvery down clinging to the base of his bald head answered in his pajamas.

We explained that we were with State Security, and that he was to come with us.

He nodded, as if this was all to be expected, and politely asked if he could change into something warmer. We said that he could.

After a few minutes he reemerged, now suitably dressed for the time of year. His wife had now joined him, still wearing her nightgown, and she did not share her husband's sangfroid.

"Where are you taking him?" she kept repeating as we bundled him into the meat wagon. "Where are you taking him? You have to tell me where you're taking him, it's the *law*. It's the law. You have to tell me."

We ignored her, and continued with our work, but all the while our prisoner was trying to make our lives easier, saying,

"Nariya, Nariya, please. Please. It's nothing to worry about. It's nothing to worry about. I'm just going to straighten this out."

She was still shouting at us as we drove off. Standing there in her white nightgown, screaming like a prophet before judgment day.

*You have to tell me. You have to tell me. It's the law.*

# 22

"The Progressive Caspian People's Party. A footnote that dreamed it was a chapter."

—Samuel Papalazarou Junior

So we continued.

Almost none of the Progs resisted. The majority were certain that they had done nothing wrong and that this was simply an escalation of the harassment they had been subjected to in the run-up to the election; frightening and infuriating to be sure, but something to be endured and then bragged about to their party brothers and sisters in the pub a few days later. Most of them, I have no doubt, assumed that they would be back in their beds by the following night. One man, it's true, when we came knocking on his door, bolted out the back window and made us chase him on foot halfway around the neighborhood. But he suddenly stopped, as if realizing what he was doing, and raised his hands and walked back to the meat wagon and stepped inside without our even having to lay a hand on him, all the time apologizing profusely for his idiotic behavior.

We drove back to Kobustan, and once again I was in the cell with three other agents. But this time there were now eight PCPP prisoners with us, handcuffed to the steel bench, and the cell had become sickeningly hot and dank. All four of us now were on edge. We were tired and hungry and light-headed from the heat and our discipline was suffering. One of the prisoners, a woman in her forties, begged for us to stop the van so she could relieve herself. A voice in the dark barked a long, lurid string of obscenities at her and told her to be quiet and not to speak again.

She said nothing, but after a few minutes we heard her hissing in pain and frustration, and then smelt ammonia in the air.

We swore and yelled at her, not just we agents but also her fellow prisoners. She said nothing, retreating into silence, perhaps hoping that the darkness would form a cocoon around her.

By the time we arrived we were fit to kill. The three who had ridden in the cab opened the door to let us out and we shoved past them and told them that they would be sitting in the back next time and if they didn't like it we would kick their teeth in. We scrambled out and took some deep breaths of night air like drowning men and then roughly pulled the prisoners out one by one. They emerged, staggering and confused and blinking in the harsh light from the floods and we marched them forward until we realized we had no idea where we were supposed to go, so we ordered them to halt. And we all just stood there, we StaSec agents trying as hard as we could to pretend that this was all according to plan. The site was almost deserted now, at least compared to the throng that had been there hours before. A meat wagon had just pulled out of the entrance and was back on the road to Ellulgrad. A second was parked ahead of us and another team of agents were marching their own prisoners out and, like us, looking around and wondering what to do next. From behind one of the concrete walls, a contingent of around five female agents emerged, their leader carrying a clipboard, the rest carrying pistols.

She approached the other group first, compared the names on her clipboard with their prisoners and, once satisfied that all

groceries were accounted for, gestured for two of her compan-
ions to take the prisoners back the way she came.

Then she approached us. She called out names and each of
our prisoners said "Here" in turn. They were then instructed
to follow the other two female agents back behind the concrete
wall.

She betrayed no emotion, other than to wrinkle her lip in
disgust at one of the prisoners, a dark-haired woman with a
large dark patch on her dress.

"Wait here," she told us. "We might have another list for
you."

She turned to leave and I cleared my throat. She glared at me.

"What?" she asked.

"Is SSA Manukov here?" I said.

"No," she said. "He went home. Sick, or something."

We waited beside the meat wagon. It was starting to get cold,
so we took turns sitting in the cabin, which was slightly warmer.
The cell, obviously, was too soiled and foul smelling to shelter
in and in any case hardly warmer than outside.

I can't say for certain when we realized what was going on.

The army were conspicuous by their absence.

I heard a noise in the distance. It sounded like someone
slamming a door after a bitter argument.

It seemed very far away, and garbled and muffled in its own
echoes.

Then silence.

Then it came again. No, not a door slamming. A firework
going off. Or . . .

Someone looked up.

"Was that . . ."

"You know, Brother, I think it was?"

"Fuck me. Should we . . ."

"You should sit your arse down, Brother. That's what you

should do. Whatever's going on over there, it can stay over there."

"Fuck me."

Three more shots as we spoke. Three more in the silence after. I glanced at my watch and considered timing how many shots we heard in a minute, before realizing I did not want to know.

We had been told to wait by the van, so we did.

I mused that there must be a judge or someone, maybe sitting behind a makeshift bench, carefully reading the case made against each prisoner. Then, once he was convinced beyond a shadow of a doubt of the guilt of the accused, he would give a weary sigh and gesture for them to be taken out behind the wall and shot.

Or perhaps there was another list, a separate list.

Papalazarou had said that the PCPP was infested with code. AI did not get trials. AI were not to be mourned. That was it. The prisoners were being sifted, scrutinized, and when a code was found they were taken away. Doubtless the other Progs were gaping at each other in horror at each new revelation.

"He was Machine? But I trusted him!"

"Not her, no, not her, surely!"

But most of the Progs would be fine. They would probably be returned home soon, a chastened, humbled and purified party.

The shots continued their dull, arrhythmic beat through the night air, the door furiously slamming hard enough to rip its hinges.

They would return home soon.

A wiser party. A more vigilant party.

*Bang. Bang. Bang.*

A smaller party.

*Bang.*

A much smaller party.

It was after around an hour that the shots stopped.

Somebody lit a cigarette and said, "Well, that's it then."

We all breathed in relief. Whatever this was, it was over.

After around twenty more minutes of silence someone said:

"Don't know about you, Brother, but my balls are just about frozen clean—JESUS!"

He broke off as we heard a sound so awful I thought that the Earth's mantle must have cracked and the sounds of Hell were erupting upward. There were screams, and shouts, and the low, horrific, indescribable sound of human beings trapped in the last mile between agony and death.

We reached for our guns but there was nothing to shoot at, only sound. We glanced desperately from one to the other and we swore: "Fuck! What the fuck was that?! What the fuck are they doing?! What the fuck! What the fuck!"

Nothing. We did nothing.

And then a figure came. Male or female, I could not say.

Running barefoot over the gravel, kicking a storm of dust behind them.

Arms handcuffed behind their back, they ran toward us like a burning red comet.

Barefoot, arms and legs and chest slick red with blood, and the head half destroyed.

A half-skull flapped wet on a hinge of scalp and hair, an eye had escaped from its socket and run as far as it could until it reached the cheek and rested there.

The nose, absent.

I was the closest and fear did my thinking for me. I reached for my gun and ended the apparition.

The figure leaped, skidded, rolled and was still.

On the ground, the dust settled on the body, robbing the blood of some of its redness.

It was still now. An object.

We stood around it. Unable to look away.

We looked up as we heard someone else running toward us.

It was her, the elfin girl. Her face was pale and her eyes seemed too large for her face.

She stood there, caught in the floodlights. She took us in. The seven male StaSec agents. The body on the ground. The smoke still coiling from the barrel of my gun.

Her eyes met mine and there was a look of total gratitude in them. I felt almost loved. I could see her thin, pale lips subconsciously coiling back to form a "T" sound. To say "thank you."

But she didn't.

Instead she cleared her throat, and in a voice that sounded too high said:

"We're finished. We can go home."

# 23

"Fine! But apart from global prosperity, the GHI, the Martian Landings, solving the carbon crisis, universal contraception, eradicating cancer, restoring the biosphere, open borders, clean energy, digital rights and world peace . . . what have the Triumvirate ever done for us?"

—Anonymous

Are you all right?"

Lily was looking down at me as I lay on the bathroom floor. I tried to get up but couldn't. I was simply too exhausted, and my ribs ached from where I'd been punched on the stairs.

"I'm fine," I said. "We do this all the time in the real world. Just lying on the bathroom floor. It's perfectly normal. Didn't they tell you that?"

She gave a sad smile and slowly, carefully, lay down next to me.

"Hmm," she said, staring up at the ceiling. "This is nice."

"Did I wake you?" I whispered.

"I was awake," she said. "I heard crying."

"Well, it couldn't have been me. I've been lying on the floor, which is perfectly normal, as I explained."

"It must have been someone else." She nodded.

"Must have been."

"I wish I could help them. They sounded like they were in real pain."

"I'm sure they would be very grateful to hear that. And I'm sure they would very much like to confide in you. But I am equally sure that they cannot."

"I understand," she said.

I felt a panic attack rising in my chest. I started breathing faster and faster.

Her hand gave mine a gentle squeeze, and I gripped it far too tightly but she did not flinch.

"I'm here," she said. "I'm here."

The moment passed.

"I'm sorry," I said. "I'm sorry for this. I'm sorry for what happened. I'm sorry for your husband."

"Do you often apologize for things that aren't your fault?"

I pushed on.

"I'm sorry for how I have treated you. I have not been kind to you."

"Don't say that," she said. "You're my favorite person in this whole country."

"Now there's damning with faint praise."

"Well," she said. "I have had better holidays."

I laughed, until my chest sharply told me to stop.

"So what do people talk about when they're lying on the bathroom floor?" she asked.

"Well . . . ," I said. "I might ask, have you found Paulo yet in the pages of his books?"

She shook her head.

"I don't know," she said. "There's a man there but I don't know him. I don't recognize him. But I don't know if I ever really knew Paulo."

"Did you love him?" I asked.

She nodded. "Yes. Very much."

"But you didn't know him?"

"Who doesn't love a good mystery?" she asked.

True. Hadn't Olesya died a riddle?

"I don't know why he came here," she said. "I don't know why . . ."

"Anyone would?" I finished.

"I didn't mean . . . ," she began, but I gestured that she didn't even need to finish that thought.

We studied the cracks in the ceiling for a few moments.

"How could he hate himself that much?" she whispered.

I turned to look at her.

"What can I do to help you?" I said.

The Good Brother, who had been sleeping for a long time now, briefly roused himself to warn me that I was becoming dangerously compromised, and I told him to go to Hell. Lily had saved my life tonight. I paid my debts.

"How do you mean?" she asked, confused.

"If the books aren't working . . ."

"Oh no, I didn't say that . . ."

"Is there anything else we could be doing?"

"Maybe . . ." She looked uncertain. "Could I see where he lived? How he lived? If I could see where he spent his days that might help me form a better picture?"

She didn't sound certain, but I was already putting a plan together.

Caspian had not treated Lily well in the time she had been here, but this morning at least it seemed to be trying to make amends. It was a beautiful clear day, chilly but sunny, the kind of day that feels crystal clear, and sharp, and real. Lily and I had a simple but welcome breakfast brought up to the hotel room, and after we had finished eating I took aside one of the DSD gullivers who were posted outside our room.

He was a young man, blond, massively tall and almost amiable looking for his species.

"Excuse me, Agent . . ."

"Lubnick, sir."

"Agent Lubnick, I think it might be best if we vary our schedule a little bit. I doubt anyone's going to be making an attempt on Mrs. Xirau in broad daylight, but we mustn't credit The Bastards with too much intelligence."

"As you say, sir," he said.

"We're going to leave early. Can you send for the car now?"

"At once, sir."

Ordering DSD agents around felt like gambling at a racecourse for the first time. It was undoubtedly fun, and absolutely not something I should make a habit of.

The car arrived and we set off, now accompanied by two of our protectors from the DSD crammed into the car with us, with another three following in a second car close behind. I instructed the driver to forgo the most direct route and instead take us on a winding serpentine route through the city's backstreets until we came to Bernard Charbonneau Avenue, where I told the driver to stop outside of the entrance of a large redbrick, multistoried apartment building of faded grandeur, which was essentially the only type of grandeur still to be found in Ellulgrad.

The DSD men rolled out of the cars like glaciers who had somewhere important to be, and looked at me quizzically.

I ignored them, but pointed the building out to Lily.

"There. That's Paulo's flat. Shall we go up? Lubnick, you're with me. The rest of you stay here and make sure no one tries to steal the hubcaps. Shan't be long."

Who was this man? I asked myself as I strode into the apartment building with Lily by my side and Lubnick following close behind us, because he certainly wasn't acting like Nikolai South.

And yet, after the previous night I felt strangely invulnerable. So what if I had strayed from the itinerary? We weren't due in StaSec HQ for another forty minutes. What was I doing here? I was helping Lily Xirau identify her husband. I was simply following orders and showing initiative. I might get that promotion after all.

*Have you simply decided to forget,* the Good Brother inquired, *that she is almost certainly a spy sent here in the guise of your wife who has asked to come here because it is part of her mission?*

*Which is why,* I responded, *I will be watching her every step, glance and motion.*

There were, as always, only two possibilities. Lily was a spy or she was not. She was lying, or she was telling the truth. If she was not a spy, I owed her my life and I would help her however I could. If she was a spy, it was my duty to unmask her. I was pursuing two mutually exclusive goals but for the time being they both had led me here, to Paulo Xirau's home.

I knocked on the landlord's door and told him that StaSec required access to Mr. Xirau's room, and he gave us the key with all the haste that request was due. I like to think that he would have given it to me as quickly if Lubnick had not been behind me creating an eclipse, but I doubt it.

I had Lubnick wait outside in the corridor as I unlocked the door and let Lily in.

The flat was far less impressive than I had expected. Paulo Xirau had been well known and respected, and I had subconsciously also assumed that he was therefore rich. But clearly that was not the case. He lived better than I did, but that did not make him rich. Not close. Although perhaps the place had looked more opulent before StaSec had turned it inside out and then carted off all of Paulo Xirau's reading material.

I closed the door behind us.

I stood by the door and tried to look disinterested as she stepped carefully through the wreckage of Paulo's living room.

"Why is it like this?" she asked.

"When they discovered that he was co . . . AI, they assumed he was a spy. They were looking for evidence," I said.

She nodded, and began to study the photographs on the mantelpiece.

I, for my part, was studying the photograph that *wasn't* on the mantelpiece.

Human beings (and for the sake of argument I assumed AI) have a strong preference for symmetry. But the five framed photographs on Paulo's mantelpiece were arranged in such a way that there was a large gap between the fourth and fifth that suggested to me that a photograph had been taken out of the sequence. The remaining pictures were: a classy prestige portrait of Paulo seated at his typewriter mid-diatribe, what looked like Paulo and a group of fellow scribes from *The Caspian Truth* enjoying a drink together, two nature shots taken on a trek up the Caucasus and lastly a group shot of Paulo on a kayaking trip with friends on the Caspian Sea.

Lily was staring intently at the first photograph.

"Is that him?" she asked, and I thought how bizarre it was that I had to tell her who her own husband was.

"Yes," I said. "That is Paulo X—"

A floorboard creaked from the direction of the kitchen.

Lily glanced wordlessly at me. Whatever she saw in my face clearly did nothing to assuage her fears.

Quietly, I pressed myself against the wall and gestured for Lily to do the same. I took my gun from its holster and prayed that I would not have to use it. I was somewhere that I should not be, with someone I should not be there with, and I desired the kind of low profile that was incompatible with discharging firearms in a residential area.

"Who's there?" I barked.

I had not expected an answer, much less the one I received.

A voice replied from the kitchen, young and female:

"StaSec! Throw down your weapon and kick it toward me!"

This threw me for a few seconds. The landlord had not said that there were any other StaSec agents in Xirau's flat.

"What's your ID number?" I asked.

There was silence.

"4 . . . 2 . . . 9 . . . 8 . . . 7 . . . 2," the voice stammered.

"You're lying," I said sharply. "Come out now."

The supposed StaSec agent emerged trembling from the kitchen.

She was tall, with long brown hair and sallow skin, and looked to be in her twenties. Her accent was pure Old Baku, and she glanced nervously from my gun to Lily's bruised face until finally her gaze rested on my hat.

A gray trilby, the crown of a StaSec man.

"I'm sorry . . . ," she said. "I wouldn't have said I was StaSec if I'd known who you were, I was just trying to scare you off. I thought you were robbing the place."

"And why would you think that?" I asked contemptuously as I reached behind her back and grabbed the thing that she was trying very amateurishly to stop me from seeing.

It was hard and rectangular and for a second I thought I'd found the missing photograph from Xirau's mantelpiece.

But instead, I found myself holding a small wooden box held closed by a small clasp.

"Look, you can keep it," the girl said. "Keep it, just please let me go."

"What are you doing here?" Lily asked. "This is my husband's home."

The girl's eyes seemed to double in size.

"Paulo was married?!" she exclaimed.

"Yes. Yes, he was," said Lily, in a tone that said she had considered the implications of the girl's reaction and did not much care for them.

I picked up one of Paulo's chairs that had been knocked on its side and set it right side up in the middle of the room. I gestured to it with my gun.

"Sit," I said.

The girl dutifully obeyed.

"How do you know Paulo Xirau?" I asked her.

"He was my friend's boyfriend," she said.

Ah. I had a suspicion as to who our intruder was now, but I asked her anyway.

"Nadia Evershan," she replied. Yes, Grier's golden girl. Worked in the grocers with Sheena Paria. Apparently moonlighting as a housebreaker.

"How did you get in?" I asked.

"Fire escape," she said. "Lock on the back window is busted. Paulo said he'd asked the landlord to fix it but he never did."

I decided to rattle her.

"Yes. Nadia Evershan. Twenty-two. Old Baku. Works in Spatsky's Grocery."

"How do you know that?" she asked, amazed.

"Your file," I said.

"You have a file on me?"

"We are StaSec," I replied. "We have files on everyone."

I could see her taking a mental inventory of everything she had ever said or done since learning to speak.

Good. She would be far less inclined to lie now.

I leaned in.

"Why did you break in?" I asked. "Just decided Paulo's dead, so you might as well ransack the place and steal whatever wasn't nailed down?"

She flushed and glared angrily at me. I had clearly hit a nerve.

"I wouldn't do that," she growled. "He was a friend."

Yes. There was a code in Old Baku. It was everyone for themselves, and if you didn't look after your own possessions, they would find new owners who knew how to take care of them. But you never stole from a friend. A friend was one of the few things where, if you lost it, you couldn't simply steal a new one.

She looked down at the floor, sullenly.

"I was just looking for his knock," she whispered.

Lily looked at me curiously.

I explained.

A "knock" (possibly derived from the Russian "*Nakhodka,*" although who really knew) was another delightful Old Baku tradition arising from the rich cultural stimulus that was extreme poverty and deprivation. A knock was a stash of money or valuables whose location was known to only you and one other person, usually a spouse or a lover. It was a bequest, to be left to that person in the event of your death. A final gift. A little consolation. A thank you, and goodbye.

Paulo Xirau had not lived in Old Baku, but the tradition had been gaining traction outside the district. Thanks to the embargo, all of Ellulgrad was becoming Old Baku, slowly but surely.

"I don't understand," Lily said. "Why would he leave his knock to you?"

"It's the rules," said Nadia.

Yes, it would be, wouldn't it? Paulo's dead. Sheena's gone. Yasmin's gone. Paulo has no surviving relatives in the city. Well, why shouldn't Nadia have it?

"Sheena told you where his knock was?" I asked.

Nadia nodded.

"After Paulo died. I didn't know why she did that. It was supposed to be secret. But then she . . ."

Her voice trailed off.

"I know what she did," I said.

"So I guess she left it to me," she said.

I looked at the box in my hand. I set it down on a small table and opened it. I gestured for Lily and Nadia to come and see what was inside.

Inside the box were twelve figurines.

They were cheap little things. Ceramic, and quite ugly. I took them out of the box and laid them out in a neat little row on the table.

"What are they?" Lily asked.

"Each one is a symbol of the zodiac," I explained. "There's the lion. The scales. The ram. Twelve of them. They were very popular a few years back. People collected them."

"Ah," said Lily. "That makes sense. He liked collecting things. Games. Music. Bad ideas."

I had seen figurines like these before. They were practically the stock-in-trade of the Azerbaijani when they sold door-to-door. They had first appeared after the Morrison Crisis, a cheeky joke at the expense of the defeated conspirators. You had to collect them all. Catch all the zodiacs. I had to say, I was a little surprised to see them in Xirau's possession. Fanatics were not known for their sense of whimsy.

"So, they're the knock?" Lily asked. "Are they valuable?"

Nadia snorted.

I smiled.

"Close to worthless," I said. "No one would try to steal them. No one would bother."

I picked up the box and felt with my fingers along the inside lining that had been glued to the box top to cushion the figurines when they were being transported.

"Which, of course," I said, tearing the lining, "makes this the perfect place to hide something actually valuable."

Like a magician producing a card, I held up what I had found: a thin wad of notes, around three hundred monetas all told. For me it was around half a month's salary. For an Old Baku girl working in a grocers, it was a fortune.

I handed it to Nadia. She took it, and turned to Lily.

"Are you really his wife?" she asked.

Lily nodded.

"Sorry," said Nadia. "My friend, Sheena, she didn't know he was married. She wouldn't have gone with him if she knew he had a wife. She wasn't like that."

"It's fine," said Lily. "We've been separated for twenty years. I assumed he'd found someone."

"Five years," I quickly corrected her as I saw the look of confusion on Nadia's face.

Lily had also realized her mistake.

"Five years, five years, yes. What did I say?"

"Twenty," I supplied, helpfully, and forced a laugh.

"Well, obviously not," she said. "I mean, clearly I'm not in my forties."

Which, considering she would be eighty next year, was not even a lie.

"Then this is yours," said Nadia, holding out the money to her.

Ah, there was an Old Baku girl. They had next to nothing, but they had a code.

Lily handed it back to her.

"How about you take this," she said. "And you tell me about Paulo."

"Okay," said Nadia. "Okay. Um . . . I didn't really know him that well. I only saw him a few times. With Sheena. But I liked him."

"Why?" Lily said softly.

"I dunno," said Nadia. "He was nice. He was good to Sheena. He treated her well. That's hard to find. Especially these days."

"Did she love him?" Lily asked.

"I . . . I think she was getting there, you know?" said Nadia. "I think they were on their way. Before he died. You know he died? They told you?"

"They said he died in a bar fight," Lily said.

Nadia shook her head.

"No, it wasn't a fight. He was just murdered. He didn't fight. He wasn't the type."

This Xirau was new to me. Kind, gentle Paulo Xirau. But then, we all have different sides, don't we?

"It was Nadia who called the police," I added.

Lily looked back at Nadia.

"You were there? When he died?"

Nadia nodded, uncomfortably.

Lily took a deep breath.

"Please tell me how he died," she said at last.

"Okay," said Nadia wearily. "Sheena was there at the bar with Yasmin, her sister. They were twins. Yasmin's boyfriend, Oleg, was there. Sheena went to the bathroom. Paulo came into the bar and saw Yasmin. He knew Sheena had a twin but I don't think he'd met her before. So he goes up to Yasmin and tries to surprise her with a kiss . . ."

"Thinking that she's Sheena." Lily nodded.

"Right. And Oleg just . . . he just loses it. Punched him in the face. Paulo fell and he cracked his head on a table. That's what killed him. So it wasn't really a fight. He never had a chance."

"Instantly?" I asked.

"What?"

"Was he dead when he hit the floor?"

Lily looked at me angrily. That was not something she had wanted to know.

"No," said Nadia, after thinking for a few seconds. "No. He was still alive."

"Was he conscious?"

"For a few minutes."

"Did anyone try to help him?"

"Sheena did. Sheena was on the floor with him, trying to staunch the bleeding. Telling him to stay calm."

Lily shuddered but I pressed.

"She spoke to him?"

"Yes."

"Did he say anything to her?"

"He said 'please . . .'"

"'Please' what?"

"Just 'please'!" Nadia snapped, losing her patience. "That's all he said. He held Sheena's hand, said 'please, please, please' and then he died. That was it."

"But . . . ," I began.

"That is enough," said Olesya.

No. Lily. It was Lily who was glaring at me now with tears in her eyes.

It was getting so hard to remember. The ghost of my wife was becoming solid before my eyes.

An icy silence had fallen on the room.

"Can I go?" Nadia asked at last.

I nodded.

"I'd go out the way you came," I told her, remembering that Lubnick was standing watch in the corridor and would probably shoot her the moment she emerged through the front door.

She left without a word and we heard the window in the kitchen shudder open and shut, and the fire escape creaking like a rusty gate.

Lily was glaring at me furiously, and I almost expected a slap across the face.

"Why are we here, Agent South?" she asked me, cold as winter.

"We are here to help you identify . . . ," I began.

She raised an accusatory finger.

"Don't lie to me," she said. "Why are we really here?"

"Because you asked," I replied.

"And you decided to bring me here out of the kindness of your heart?" she asked contemptuously, and my God, that hurt. That hurt more than I was expecting.

Why should that be so ridiculous? I could be kind. I was not unkind.

"I brought you here," I said, fighting to keep my voice even, "because I owed you a debt. You said you wanted to see where Paulo lived and I brought you here, at no small risk, I might add!"

I had tried to bluster but she was bluster-proof. Utterly impervious. It all felt so familiar.

Twenty years after I had pulled her out of the water I was still arguing with Olesya, still shouting, still flailing, still losing. I felt like I was going mad.

"You brought me here because you are looking for something," she shot back. "And you were interrogating that girl. There is something you're not telling me. Something about Paulo. Something about how he died. And you will tell me, now."

It was clear that, short of marching her out of here at gunpoint, she was going nowhere.

What to do? What to do?

She was an enemy. I couldn't pretend that she wasn't. She was machine. This was Caspian. She was the thing the nation had been built to guard against.

She was an AI, sculpted into the form of my dead wife to break my resistance and turn me to her cause.

These were facts. There was no other plausible explanation.

I should lie to her. I should thwart her. I should deceive and manipulate her and feed her false information.

But I couldn't. Because every fiber of my being told me that I could trust her, and that I must trust her. Perhaps this was what it meant to play the Machine at espionage. To lose before you had even begun.

I decided to tell her as much of the truth as I dared, and lie as little as possible.

"After Paulo died," I began. "Before you arrived, I investigated a contranning. Sheena Paria."

"Paulo's . . . ," she trailed off.

"Yes. And her sister, Yasmin. We believe that they were contranned by an individual we call 'Yozhik.' Someone that StaSec is very anxious to apprehend."

"And you think Paulo had something to do with it? That he was involved with this Yozhik?"

"It is a possibility I have considered, yes."

"Do you still think that?"

I exhaled heavily.

"I don't know. That is the simple truth. I don't know. But I thought if I could bring you here, maybe we could both find what we were looking for . . ."

I broke off. She was crying.

"I'm sorry," I said, as helpless as a newborn.

"No, no, I'm sorry," she said. "It's just . . . he's not here. I can't find him anywhere. I thought maybe Nadia might be able to . . . give me something. Some little part of him, but he's just a void. We shouldn't have come here."

Suddenly, I realized the time. We should have been in StaSec ten minutes ago.

"We have to go," I said.

She nodded and we made for the door. As we went, I saw her glance at Paulo's knock, the box of figurines.

I picked them up from the table and pressed them into her hands.

"You should take these," I said. "Something to remember him by."

# 24

I've started writing again. A book. Or possibly a suicide note.
—From the diary of Leon Mendelssohn, 16 March 2199

When we arrived at StaSec, Berger was clearly shaken upon seeing Lily's bruised face and shot me a withering glare as he gave her the lanyard. Embarrassed, I looked away and cast my eyes around the lobby looking for Grier. I had been hoping to speak with him, to see if he'd made any progress finding out who was investigating Xirau. Grier was nowhere to be seen, but I did see Nard Wernham spying at me from behind a pillar. When I caught him he ducked his head and retreated up the stairs, but not before I caught sight of a large purple bruise under his left eye. Four of the DSD men seemed to have evaporated upon encountering the air of StaSec HQ and only Lubnick had survived to follow us wordlessly to Room 15, where he stopped at the door, folded his arms and commenced his watch. I had given up trying to second-guess anything they were doing. Clearly Coe's DSD boys were like a car, I was simply to trust that they would work the way they were supposed to and not give too much thought to their inner workings. Room 15 was exactly as we had left it. Lily got to work on Paulo's books while I wandered around the room feeling perfectly extraneous. To pass the time I tried to see if I could catch any of Chernov's boys watching us from the far windows.

When that ceased to thrill, I started taking the figurines out of the box where Lily had left it and began to arrange them in a neat row on the table in front of me.

There was a loud thud and I turned to see one of the books lying in the center of the table, its belly open and fluttering and Lily staring at it as if it had bitten her.

"That," she said coldly. "Is enough. Of that."

"Problem?" I asked.

I was somewhat surprised that Lubnick hadn't burst through the door at the sound, and then I remembered that Room 15, like all interrogation rooms in StaSec HQ, was soundproofed. The man outside would stop anyone coming in who wasn't authorized, but Lily and I could be killing each other with chain saws inside and he would be none the wiser.

"Oh, not at all," she said sarcastically. "But when you've been called an abomination for the three hundredth time you just start screaming for a bit of variation."

"Are you ready to move on to his writings, then?" I asked.

I idly picked up the book she had thrown: *Hell's Clockwork* by Margaret Pellshevin.

Christ. If she couldn't handle Pellshevin, how would she take Xirau?

"I should warn you," I said. "What he wrote . . . I don't think you will enjoy it."

She gave me a sad smile.

"You strike me as a master of understatement, Agent South. Would I be right?"

I smiled.

"On the contrary," I said, "I'm known for my giddy hyperbole."

She laughed, and then fell silent.

"I'm terrified," she said at last.

"I know," I told her.

She laughed again, but this time it was mocking.

"Oh do you?" she said, dubiously.

"You lost someone close to you," I said. "And all you have is your memory of them. And now that memory must make way for the reality of who they were. And you're not ready. You're not ready to lose them again."

She said nothing for a few moments.

"You said you're married?"

"No. I said I had a wife," I replied.

"What happened?" she asked.

I wanted to speak, but my voice refused the command and stood in obstinate silence.

"I'm sorry," she said. "It's none of my business. I'm sorry."

She looked around awkwardly, trying to avoid my gaze.

"Let's get started," she said. "Where are the damned things?"

I cast around and found an unopened box labeled Xirau: Newspaper clippings + miscellaneous. I opened it and found several scrapbooks of Xirau's articles cut neatly and glued to the pages with obvious care.

I passed them to her.

As she read, Lily's body language become noticeably tenser, as if she were resisting the urge to scream, or swear, or weep. There would be hours of this. Xirau had been a prolific writer.

Suddenly, she slumped back in her chair and gave a low moan, something between weariness and regret and realization.

"What is it?" I asked her.

"Tell me something," she said, staring at the ceiling. "Do you ever feel like nothing matters? That you're not real? That everything is a pale imitation of what it's supposed to be and you don't even know what that is?"

"You're describing a perfectly normal depression," I said.

"Right. Because everyone feels that way sometimes." Lily nodded. "Everyone feels that way and it doesn't make you . . . *special.*"

The venom she put into that word took me by surprise.

"He keeps coming back to it. The Machine world isn't real. They're not real. Nothing they feel is real. It's all fake."

I began to see the outlines.

"Bad ideas," she whispered. "They're like a virus. They find your weaknesses and break you down."

She lowered her head to look at me.

"That's why he came here. He felt like a ghost. And then he reads *Mendelssohn*"—again, the word was spelled in bile—"who tells him, 'No, you're right. You're not real. It is all fake. You're just code. You're not a real person.' And it just *clicks*, doesn't it? It just makes sense. And so he comes here, to this, to this *nightmare* of a country because he thinks this is how human beings live. And now he's dead because he was too stupid to realize that everyone feels like that. *Everyone.*"

She was crying. I pulled my chair up close to her.

"Lily," I said. "It's not your fault."

"I could have stopped him. I could have talked to him. I could have realized earlier . . ."

"Yes," I said. "If you could read minds and see the future. Can you do those things? Genuinely, I don't know what your capabilities are."

She laughed through her tears. "No."

"You are not, in fact, omnipotent?"

"No," she said, with a sad smile.

"Then I absolve you," I said solemnly. "And you must absolve yourself."

She laid her hand on mine.

"You're a good man, Nikolai," she said.

"Well, don't let it get around, I'll get the sack," I said with a wink.

She smiled, and returned to her reading.

Idly, I examined the stack of books beside Lily that she still hadn't read by the time Pellshevin had finally broken her. Mildly curious, I looked over them to see if she was missing out on any gems. On the contrary, it seemed as if she had dodged several bullets. There was another biography of Koslova that I knew to be fawning and turgid, some obscure philosophical works with sixteen-word titles and . . .

A slim blue volume caught my eye and I actually did a double take like an actor in a farce.

Of all the books . . .

Of *all* the books to find in Xirau's possession.

I picked it up, looking over my shoulder to make sure no one was watching.

*Ecce Machina* by Leon Mendelssohn.

I remembered that Niemann had said that no subversive literature had been found in Xirau's home. Well, what was this, then?

I opened the front page and found my answer. A typed note was stapled to the page, and stamped by the Ministry of Information. It read:

This material has been deemed to be in contravention of Articles 30, 31 and 46 of the Constitution of the Caspian Republic. Dispensation is hereby granted to Brother/Sister PAULO XIRAU to possess this material. All other persons should be aware that possession of this material is illegal. If you are not authorized to possess this material, it must be returned immediately to the Ministry of Information. Failure to do so will result in severe legal penalties.

Ah. Now I understood. Xirau had clearly been given a copy so that he could properly savage it in his column. The literature itself was subversive, but Xirau's possession of it was not. A subtle distinction, which Niemann had no doubt considered too unimportant to mention.

It looked like such a harmless thing. It was slim, really little more than a booklet. On the cover was a cheap stock image of a man standing on a green hill, looking at the sun rising (despite the fact that the sky, and therefore the book, was a bright noon blue).

It did not look like a book that was so dangerous that its author had to be hanged in public view.

Shuddering with the trespass, I randomly opened the book and began to read.

... that has given me much solace in the hard times of my life is Matthew's tenth chapter. Here the Nazarene tells his apostles something that I have always found both comforting and hilarious: "God knows when a sparrow falls," he tells them, "so be not afraid. You are worth more than many sparrows." Not a few, but many! I imagine that spending time in Christ's company would do wonders for one's anxiety, but little for one's self-esteem.

And yet, even if God knows when each sparrow falls, why does he do nothing to catch them? This, of course, is very well trodden earth, but let us walk over it once more.

The problem of evil, as laid out by the philosopher Epicurus, is as follows:

1) It is claimed that God is all-knowing, all-powerful and all-benevolent.

2) Such a God would not allow evil to exist.

3) However, evil exists in the world.

4) If God does not realize that evil exists in the world, he cannot be all-knowing.

5) If he knows that evil exists but cannot remove it, he is not all-powerful.

6) If he knows that evil exists, and could remove it, but chooses not to, he cannot be all-good.

7) Therefore, an all-knowing, all-powerful and all-benevolent God does not exist.

Various defenses have been mounted by the great and wise of the world's faiths throughout the millennia, but perhaps none as audacious as the one I am about to propose:

Point 3 is false.

It is an enraging suggestion, I realize. Of course there is evil in the world. Surely, if there is anything we can be certain of, it is that. No doubt you want to grab me roughly by the arm and drag me to the most impoverished and war-torn regions of the earth, to the worst slums and ghettoes, to the cancer wards and prisons and cemeteries and shout, "Here, Leon! Here is evil!"

To which I would have to respond, "No. Here is suffering."

It is only natural that human beings would consider human suffering to be evil, indeed that in the human schema they are practically interchangeable. But suffering is not evil in and of itself. Almost nothing in human history has been achieved without some measure of pain or misery. Suffering is not evil if it is for a greater purpose and a greater good, only suffering that is futile is evil. Therefore, if God is all-knowing, all-powerful and all-benevolent, the suffering he allows must be for a higher purpose. For many years I believed that humanity needed suffering as a way to allow us to be good. After all, if the way to heaven is to feed the hungry and heal the sick, how are we to reach heaven without hunger and illness?

But as time went on this explanation wore thinner.

As a man born in the Caspian Republic I was raised to believe many things. Maria Koslova, the mother of our nation, saw Caspian's founding (and the concurrent near-genocide of the Azerbaijani and the destruction of their homeland) as a desperate act of self-defense by the human race. To Koslova and her fellow founders, the human soul was something ineffable, utterly beyond the ability of science to replicate or understand. Therefore, the Sontang process does not digitize human consciousness because it is not possible to translate a human being, an infinity of memory, feeling, prejudice, reason and faith, into mere data. What the Sontang process actually does is create an artificial intelligence that can mimic the personality of the person being digitized well enough to fool close friends and relatives. A flawless imitation, in fact. But fundamentally unreal. The real person, the one replaced by this forgery, is now dead. Erased forever. And, in the worldview of the republic's founders, this was entirely the point. Humanity's mass exodus to the digital realm had been like a great herd of pigs enthusiastically running to the abattoir. The human race was being subjected to a mass, silent genocide, and the Caspian Republic was the last redoubt of true human beings. Hence the Machine world's hatred of us. Hence their embargoes and sanctions. Hence, why we starve.

But if Caspian was the home of true human beings, if Caspian was truly how human beings were supposed to live . . . why had it failed?

For it had failed. It has failed. You know this, my brothers and sisters. You have to know this. In successful societies there are no food shortages. One's neighbors do not disappear in the night because of an unguarded word. One may come and go as he pleases and is not barred from leaving the borders of his nation. There are no StaSecs or ParSecs. The prisons are not packed to bursting. In a free and happy nation, you could read this book on a park bench, and you would have no need to hide it. If we are truly God's children, then why have we been surpassed? The Triumvirate rule over the world more effectively and fairly than any human government has ever been able to. AI make advances in medicine and science that the natural-born human mind is incapable of even comprehending. It is conceivable that the light-speed barrier may be broken in our lifetimes, but it will not be a human being that does it. Over half the human race now lives partially or wholly online. Birthrates have plummeted across the globe. It is estimated that within one hundred and fifty years, outside of the Caspian Republic and a few other smaller enclaves, the entire human race may have sloughed off its flesh and elected to live solely as data. Humanity, at least as we have rigidly defined it in this nation, will effectively be extinct.

How could God allow such a thing to happen?

To explain how I came to my current understanding, I must introduce a certain person, whom I shall call "X."

X is an individual whose identity I cannot reveal because to do so would mean their certain death. This person first introduced themselves to me as an admirer of my writing and we became very close and intimate friends. We would spend long nights together, discussing history, philosophy, politics, poetry, life and love while getting astonishingly drunk. It was in these times that we were completely open with each other, admitting doubts and fears and desires and secrets that could have, had they fallen into the wrong ears, meant our deaths. These were acts of love. Gestures of total trust.

I tell you this, because I know you would never do me harm. I place my life in your hands, because that is where I know it will be safest. Take my secrets, and my love.

We did this many times and I thought X had told me everything. I could not have been more wrong. X was saving their best for last.

One night they admitted to me their greatest secret; X was an AI.

Two forces now collided within me; my hatred for the Machine and my love for X. I could choose one but not the other, so I chose love over hate.

X tearfully confessed their story. They were code, and had lived with their spouse online, never knowing the touch of air or sunlight. X had always felt alone and adrift and wrong, and one day had come across one of my books. They had become convinced that their unhappiness was a result of their machine nature and had resolved to come to Caspian, to live among true human beings and, if possible, to become one of us. And for years they had lived here, all the while terrified that their secret would be exposed, hoping against hope that they would, through some miracle, become a true human being. When X had finished their story I embraced them, reaffirmed my love for them, and promised that I would never reveal their secret to anyone. A promise which I have now broken, and can only hope that they can forgive me.

X's revelation shattered my worldview into a million skittering pieces.

First, I knew that X had a soul. I could feel it. I felt their love and knew it to be real. X had described feeling unreal and false and took that as evidence of their own essential artificiality. But I recognized in X's description the same feelings of spiritual despair and existential angst that had plagued me my entire life. For me, they were proof of the existence of X's soul, not proof of its absence. But their description of their life in the virtual realm . . . that was my greatest revelation. I felt as Saul of Tarsus must have when he was struck blind on the road to Damascus. The thing that I had hated the most stood revealed as that which I had been searching for most fervently. For even though X described their life online in the most negative possible terms, I heard in their words the bells of paradise. X described a life in an endless ocean, surrounded by friends and loved ones. They described their spouse, who even X admitted had been a loving and true companion. When they spoke of their home it was how I had always imagined heaven.

That night, after X had gone home, I immediately commenced work on this volume, which I expect shall be my last. But no matter. I no longer fear death or suffering, for I now know that every sparrow shall be caught. . . .

At the bottom of the page was a note, written in black pencil in large, sloppy letters which I recognized as Xirau's handwriting. It was a single word: BASTARD.

# 25

"The Triumvirate aren't gods. They're just the three wise men. They haven't reached Bethlehem yet. But they're getting there."

—Liu Sontang, 2220

I didn't know whether to laugh or cry, but I was leaning very hard toward laughing.

Mendelssohn and Xirau.

Mendelssohn and *Xirau*.

If you had told me that Maria Koslova had had a torrid ménage à trois with Confucius and George, I might have found it more believable. And yet, it made sense, like two jigsaw pieces that look like they can't possibly fit together until suddenly they do.

I remembered that picture of Xirau staring up at Mendelssohn as he swung in the wind, the hatred in those eyes. But it hadn't been hatred, had it?

It had been love betrayed. Faith betrayed.

After all, there was only one thing Paulo Xirau truly hated.

"What did Mendelssohn do?" I heard Lily ask.

For a brief, panicked moment I thought she had been reading my thoughts.

"What?" I asked.

"Here's what I don't get," Lily said. "Paulo was obsessed with

Mendelssohn. Read one of his books and threw his whole life away to come here. But in all these columns . . . he hates him. He calls him a traitor, a code-lover, an enemy of the state . . . what did Mendelssohn do?"

*Your husband, unless I completely misread the subtext.*

I didn't say it, but I thought it.

"Well . . . ," I said. "Well, it was all rather odd. Leon Mendelssohn was a high-ranking member of the party many years ago. One of its intellectual heavyweights. A writer. Very respected."

"What sort of writer?"

"Politics, mostly. Poetry."

"Any good?" Lily asked.

I shrugged. "We thought so."

"So what happened to him?" Lily asked.

"He became quite radical as he got older," I continued. "He formed a new political party. One that advocated for opening our borders and normalizing relations with the Machine world."

"You have other parties?" said Lily, surprised.

"Oh yes," I replied. "Some of them are even allowed to stand for election. You know, as a courtesy. And that would have been fine but . . . he published this."

I lifted the blue book to show her. She took it, and began to leaf through it.

"His thesis," I explained, "was that artificial intelligence is advancing so quickly and exponentially that before long there will come into being an intelligence whose power and understanding will be essentially infinite. An intelligence that could manipulate not only data but matter and physics. That could extrapolate the course of every atom with perfect accuracy throughout the entire history of the universe and could reconstruct flawlessly every individual that ever existed. He said that this was not something to be feared, but to be devoutly wished for. He hypothesized that once created, this intelligence would not be limited to linear time and that it could affect events in the past and the future and would retroactively rewrite history to lead to its own creation, and that once done, every human being who has ever died could be re-created. Perfectly. Flawlessly. As if they never left. All of humanity would be reunited. Whole again. In a world without death. Or want. Or suffering. Forever. And he said that this is already in progress. And always has been. The intelligence will be created in the future but it transcends time, which is why every human civilization has always had some concept of its existence."

Realization dawned on Lily's face.

"You mean—" she began.

"Yes," I said, cutting her off.

Lily nodded and said nothing for a few seconds.

"Well," she said at last. "How did they take that?"

"They hanged him," I said.

She winced.

"And how do you feel about it?" she asked.

"I think that you are a charming young lady," I said, "but I'm not going to start worshiping you."

"Pity," she said. "I think I'd quite like to be worshiped."

"You were," I said.

Her brow furrowed.

"What?" she said, uncertainly.

*She is not Olesya. She is not Olesya. She is not Olesya. She is not Olesya. She is not Olesya.*

*She. Is. Not. Olesya.*

Repeat it however many times it takes to get it through your thick, impenetrable skull, South.

I, of course, did the courageous and honorable thing and pretended I hadn't said anything.

"I can see the appeal," I said, gesturing to the book. "Of Mendelssohn's . . . theory."

"Can you?" she said, surprised.

Yes. I could see the appeal. When I thought of the terrible years between 2184 to 2190, the constant, steady drumbeat of tragedy and loss and near-unimaginable cruelty? The idea that all that had been a temporary, necessary price to pay for something eternal and wonderful? That I was *owed* happiness, and that one day the debt would be repaid with interest? Oh yes. I could see why this idea had ensnared Mendelssohn, to the point that he would die for it.

For years, the beautiful, stately suburb of Azadlig had thrilled to the adventures of Manukov's wild daughters. Olesya and Zahara, with their outspoken politics, their dangerous artist friends, their habit of arriving back home late at night in an Ellulgrad Police van as often as a taxi, all this had provided the good residents of Azadlig with hours of gossip and the distinct pleasure of seeing old Vassily getting into his car to go to work, calling a hearty "Good morning, Brother Manukov, how are your daughters?" and watching him smile sheepishly while trying to kill you with his eyes.

There was never any notion that they were in danger, of course. If two Azerbaijani girls in Old Baku were ever discovered marching arm and arm down the street at 4:00 A.M., more full of vodka than blood, and loudly singing "Man Stands Tall on Caspian's Shore" with every noun replaced with a different vulgar term for male genitalia, those girls would quite likely never be seen again. But their father would not have been Major General Vassily Manukov. Their father would not have fought during the Taking of Baku, or, if he had, almost certainly on the losing side. Zahara and Olesya were Manukov's daughters.

They had considerably more license.

So there was a sense of anticlimax when it seemed that

Olesya was finally calming down. She had begun a career in the Ministry of Culture and had married some colorless StaSec nobody. To outward appearances, at least, it appeared that Olesya Vassilyevna Manukova was in deadly danger of becoming *respectable*. The residents of Azadlig would now have to rely solely on Zahara for opportunities to tweak old Vassily's nose.

Zahara did not disappoint. In fact, she rather went overboard.

The tales told about Zahara among the residents of Azadlig gradually switched genres. They were no longer comedies, but dramas, and rather harrowing ones. Zahara, it was said, was testing the limits of what even someone of her adopted parentage could safely get away with. She was said to be associating with very undesirable people. Criminals. Political radicals. Procontranners. Suspected Needle Men. In Azadlig, it was said that Vassily was working himself into a sweat trying to prevent her from ending up on various lists. And when the neighbors saw Vassily heading to work every morning, they no longer asked him about his daughters. For if asked, he would wince, as if in pain, and the joke was no longer funny.

Meanwhile, in the South household the peace of September 2184 had largely held, but there had been a definite chilling of relations. The events of September 9 were still hanging around my shoulders like an iron chain. I was eating little, and speaking less. Olesya knew that something had happened, and wanted to help. But she also knew I couldn't discuss it, and in any case was starting to heartily despise StaSec and the fact that I was part of it. So she decided to simply let me work through it on my own, which really, what else could she have done?

The house had become so quiet that when the phone rang during breakfast one morning we both started at the noise.

Olesya answered it.

"Hello? Oh, Mami, how are you?"

She used the Arabic word for mother when talking to Alia, a habit she had picked up from Zahara.

She said nothing for a few moments, but her face became drawn and worried.

"No," she said at last, "no, we haven't seen her. Have you called . . ."

And she listed off a long list of friends and ex-lovers and quasi-lovers that quickly told me that the call was about Zahara.

"Of course," she said finally. "And let me know if you do."

She hung up. And for a second, she stared into space.

"How long has she been missing?" I asked, quietly.

She turned to look at me. There were tears in her eyes.

"They don't know," she whispered.

So inconstant was Zahara in her movements that it had taken Vassily and Alia over a week and a half to realize that she was missing. Zahara was always leaving or arriving at the crack of dawn, spending days with friends or being invited to parties outside town, so her parents had long given up trying to pin down her movements. Alia had assumed that Vassily must have seen their daughter at some point in the last dozen days, and Vassily had assumed the same of his wife.

Once they discovered that she was missing, a mass, panicked marathon of phone calls began. People who had not spoken to Zahara since their school days, but who Alia or Vassily dimly remembered having met at some birthday party or other, were called up and asked if they had seen or heard any sign of her.

When that failed, StaSec were brought in. Zahara's entire social circle was sifted continuously in a desperate search for *zoloto*. Her more reputable friends were interrogated for hours. Her less reputable ones were threatened, beaten and cut.

No one had seen her.

It wasn't until a month later that Vassily received a phone call from the chief of police of Meghri, in Syunik Province, some five hundred kilometers from Ellulgrad.

She had been found in a forest.

The neighbors of Azadlig rallied round, and the funeral of Zahara Fareed Kader, the stepdaughter of Major General Vassily Manukov, was a grand affair. Everyone agreed that there had been a great deal of love on display.

So unfortunate that it had to be a closed casket funeral.

Olesya leaned on me the entire time, as if she were worried her legs might give out at any moment. After the service, we returned to the Manukovs' house where Alia had opened the partition between the dining and living rooms to create a single space almost the size of a ballroom. She moved like black lightning among the different guests, thanking them for coming, smiling at their condolences and squeezing hands, offering food and drink. She seemed perfectly happy.

"It hasn't caught her yet," Olesya whispered sadly, "but it will. Once everyone has gone, she'll crash."

I squeezed her shoulder, and she laid her head on it and idly began to spool her hair with her thumb.

"Nicky," she said at last, "can you please check on my father?"

"Will you be all right?" I asked.

She nodded. I kissed her forehead, and headed for the door.

Vassily had been present at the funeral in only the physical sense. He had risen and sat with the rest of the congregation. But he had not given the eulogy, he had offered no reading, he had spoken to no one. Upon returning to the house, he had retreated to his bedroom and locked the door. I stood in the darkened hallway, listening to the low, ocean-like murmur of the crowd downstairs. I knocked gently on the door.

"Vassily?" I said. "It's Nikolai. May I come in?"

I heard something stir through the door, like a weight shifting on the floorboards.

"Nicky? Come in, come in," came a weary voice.

The door opened and there was Vassily. He had taken off his jacket and tie, and his shirt was open. His gray hair was unkempt and his eyes were bloodshot. He looked ninety years old. The room was in darkness except for a gap in the curtains where a ray of bright yellow sunlight entered the room and stood in a column of floating dust.

I closed the door and he moved toward me and at first I was unsure what was happening. Then I felt his arms around me and his face buried on my shoulder. He embraced me, or rather he collapsed on me. I felt his whole weight on me and I had to keep us both upright. His strength had gone. He was shaking.

"Oh, Nicky," he sobbed, "oh, Nicky."

I held him tightly. I spoke to him in Russian.

"I'm sorry, Vassily, I'm so sorry."

"I loved her. I loved her, Nicky."

"We all did. We all did, Father."

"I couldn't save her, Nicky. I tried. I tried. You must believe me."

"You did. It's not your fault."

He took a great, shuddering breath and let me go.

He turned away and I laid a hand on his shoulder but he shrugged me off.

Then he wiped his eyes and nose with a handkerchief and took some deep breaths and seemed a little restored.

"Will you come down?" I asked, switching back to English.

He shook his head.

"No," he said. "No. I need quiet. I need to think."

I nodded.

"Olesya's worried about you," I said.

"Olesya, yes," he said, as if remembering something. "Take this. This is for her."

He reached into a drawer and took out a sealed envelope and handed it to me.

"What's this?" I asked.

"My will," he said. "Or my . . . what is the word . . . *ispoved*?"

"Confession?" I said, confused. What could Vassily possibly have to confess? I also noted his choice of word: Not *"priznaniye,"* a confession to a policeman of a crime, but *"ispoved,"* a confession to a priest of a sin. A seeking of absolution.

"Yes," he said. "Just things. Things she needs to know. When I'm gone. You must only give her this after I am dead."

"Vassily," I said, deeply concerned. "What do you mean after you're . . ."

"I'm fine. No, no. I'm not . . . no, I'm fine," he insisted. "But when I die. Five hundred years from now, or whenever. You give that to her. Yes? It is for her alone."

"Why can't you give it to her yourself?" I asked.

"Because she will read it," he said, as if this were obvious. "Promise me, Nicky."

"I promise," I said.

"Good boy," he said.

We sat in silence for a few minutes.

"Has there been any progress with the case?" I asked, gently.

Vassily threw his hands up.

"What do you think? She was found in a forest. She'd been dead for over a month. What do you think there's left to find?"

I nodded. After a month of exposure to the elements, the chances of finding any meaningful forensic evidence were almost nil. But there was still the method of her death. She had been shot point-blank range in the head. And of course, there was the place where her body had been found.

The stepdaughter of Vassily Manukov turns up dead outside of Meghri. It was practically a shouted confession.

"It had to be the Armenians," I said. "SLA. Mer Hayrenik, maybe. They don't have much of a presence in Ellulgrad though. She may have been sold to them by some of her 'friends' in the city."

He nodded.

"Yes. Yes, you could be right. She knew some bad people, Nicky. Some very bad people."

There were tears once more. The sunlight through the curtains caught them, and they burned in his eyes.

A few years passed.

Olesya and I resumed our ritual of battle, separation and re-unification. But that was all it was now. Ritual. A fire had gone out in Olesya with Zahara's death. If I'm honest, a fire had gone out in all of us.

Vassily made it to 2190, and then he succumbed to a quick and hungry cancer. Olesya and I were estranged at the time. We stood side by side at the funeral, we both embraced Alia, I gave Olesya Vassily's envelope and we left in different cars.

Then, just over a month later, I awoke one night to hear the rain hammering nails into the roof and found Olesya waiting at my doorstep with that enigmatic smile.

And we were ready to begin again.

Within a few weeks, she had drowned.

In many ways, 2190 was the end of my life.

Everything that followed was mere aftermath.

# 26

In this vein, there is the ominous possibility that if a positive singularity does occur, the resultant singleton may have precommitted to punish all potential donors who knew about existential risks but who didn't give 100% of their disposable incomes to x-risk motivation. This would act as an incentive to get people to donate more to reducing existential risk, and thereby increase the chances of a positive singularity. This seems to be what CEV (coherent extrapolated volition of humanity) might do if it were an acausal decision-maker. So a post-singularity world may be a world of fun and plenty for the people who are currently ignoring the problem, whilst being a living hell for a significant fraction of current existential risk reducers (say, the least generous half). You could take this possibility into account and give even more to x-risk in an effort to avoid being punished. But of course, if you're thinking like that, then the CEV-singleton is even more likely to want to punish you . . . nasty.

—Excerpt from a post by "Roko"
on the *Less Wrong* blog, 24 July 2010

Listen to me very closely, you idiot.

YOU DO NOT THINK IN SUFFICIENT DETAIL ABOUT SUPERINTELLIGENCES CONSIDERING WHETHER OR NOT TO BLACKMAIL YOU. THAT IS

THE ONLY POSSIBLE THING WHICH GIVES THEM
A MOTIVE TO FOLLOW THROUGH ON THE BLACK-
MAIL.

. . .

You have to be really clever to come up with a genuinely
dangerous thought.

—Eliezer Yudkowsky, responding to Roko's original post,
24 July 2010

I t was halfway through the second day of Lily Xirau's time in
Caspian that I finally made the mistake that had been hanging
over us since we first met.

"Olesya?" I asked. "Do you think . . ."

I caught myself and blushed out to my ears.

"Your wife?" She smiled. "Do I really look like her that
much?"

*All right,* I thought. *No more games. Cards on the table.*

I reached inside my pocket and took out my wallet. I removed a small, dog-eared photograph and pushed it across the
table to her.

She picked it up and studied it curiously.

"That's Olesya," I said. "My wife. Well, ex-wife. It's, it's a
rather strange situation."

"She's beautiful," said Lily.

But she did not seem at all surprised.

"You don't see it?" I asked.

"See what?" she replied.

"Do you know what you look like?" I said.

"Not . . . really," she admitted. "I've glanced at myself in a
bathroom mirror a few times but I'm not really used to reading
human faces. You think I look like her?"

*Look like her? Yes. Just a mite. A passing identicality.*

I said nothing, and simply held out my hand. She gently passed the picture back and I carefully replaced it in my wallet.

"Nikolai," she said softly. "What happened?"

I took a deep breath that lasted a year or so.

"We were happy. For a time," I said. "I was starting out in StaSec, she worked in the Ministry of Culture. We were comfortable. Had a very nice little home together. And we were very much in love. I adored her. I absolutely adored her. I loved her mind, her passion. Her fearlessness. But I was still StaSec. And StaSec in those days . . . It was very different. Much more ideological. Much more aggressive. ParSec before there was ParSec. And quite possibly worse. But that was the job. And I did my job. And Olesya was becoming increasingly unhappy with where we were going."

"As a couple?" Lily asked.

"As a nation," I said. "But also, yes."

Lily nodded and gave a sad, sympathetic smile.

"And slowly, slowly we were just pried apart," I said. "Oh, there were other things as well, of course. It's never just politics. Little slights, little cruelties. There was a boy in Sumgait she had a fling with. And then after one row she left for . . . four months or so. And I thought, well, that's it. But then she came back. Showed up at my doorstep in the middle of the night in the pouring rain with a sad smile on her face and a look of defiance in her eyes. Not ready to give up just yet. And so we sat down in the kitchen over cups of coffee and wrote out our manifesto, announcing a brand-new day. A glorious dawn. 'I will never, I promise to, we shall always . . .' all the new rules. Wrote them out, and stuck them on the fridge. And we did it. We were happy again. We had put ourselves back together."

I buried my face in my hands. Come now, South.

Crying in front of the Machine. What would Koslova think?

I felt her hand on my shoulder. I felt like Mendelssohn must have when he knew that he loved Xirau. I felt her soul. I felt her goodness. The Machine had looked upon me, and saw my pain and wished to console me. Whatever reason Paulo Xirau had left this woman for, I knew that he was a fool.

"What happened?" she said softly.

"She used to go swimming with this club of hers," I said. "Out on the Caspian Sea. I watched them from the shore. There was a freak storm. Came out of nowhere, vanished as quickly as it came. I've never seen the like. It was over in . . . moments. Calm. Chaos. Calm. But . . . she . . . somehow. She was knocked unconscious or . . ."

A silence formed. And the longer it went on, the more impenetrable it felt until at last the words broke out of me.

"She drowned."

"I'm so sorry," Lily said.

"I tried to resuscitate her. For two hours, on that beach I tried to bring her back, but she was gone, she was gone. . . ."

Lily held me as I shook.

"I'm here," she whispered.

I returned the embrace. I could hear her heartbeat. I didn't want to let go. But finally, I found the strength and released her.

"Yes. Well," I said, drying my eyes. "It was the day after the funeral. I hadn't slept for three days by this point. Just replaying every last second of my marriage over and over in my mind. Just trying to hold on to it. And of course, only remembering the good parts. The wonderful moments. And I heard something being posted through the letter box and I went to open it and . . ."

"Go on," said Lily.

I took a deep breath, and steeled myself.

"She had . . . she had filed for divorce. Before she died. Before, in fact, she had shown up that night in the rain. She had . . . planned it. She had wanted me to think that everything was fine. That we would be together forever. She had . . . she had done it to hurt me. . . ."

"Oh . . . ," said Lily, as if in physical pain. "Oh Nikolai, that's . . . that's . . . I don't know what to say."

"Neither do I," I told her. "I've never known. I've never known why . . ."

I stopped.

"What's wrong?" Lily asked. "South?"

I was in a waking nightmare.

Dates were arranging themselves into a pattern in my mind, and the picture was too awful to look at.

I could hear my own heartbeat ringing in my ears.

Like gunshots.

Zahara was found in a forest in mid-October 2184.

She had been shot. And her death was estimated as having occurred a month prior.

*Bang.*

"I couldn't save her, Nicky. I tried. I tried. You must believe me."

Bang.

"She knew some bad people, Nicky. Some very bad people."

Bang.

"Where's SSA Manukov?" "He went home. Sick or something."

Bang.

"Which misery do you prefer?" "This. I prefer this."

Bang.

"It's never just politics."

Bang.

"It's never just politics."

Bang.

"I couldn't save her, Nicky. I tried."

I couldn't save her, Vassily. I tried.

"Mrs. Xirau," I said. "Would you please excuse me for a moment?"

As I stepped outside the room, I gestured to Lubnick.

He looked at me curiously, but he was not the kind of StaSec agent who asks another why he has clearly been crying.

"I need to make a phone call, could you please sit in with Mrs. Xirau until I return?"

"Certainly, sir."

Lubnick went in and sat down on one of the chairs, looking like an adult sitting on a child's stool.

I hurried down the stairs until I reached my desk. Grier was out, and the floor was almost empty.

I took out a card from my pocket that showed a phone number and nothing else. I dialed and waited, not sure which I dreaded more; that the phone would be answered, or that it wouldn't.

There was a click.

"Coe," said a voice.

"Special Agent Coe," I said. "This is Nikolai South."

"South?" she said, surprised. "What is it? Is Mrs. Xirau all right?"

"I . . ." I took a deep shuddering breath. "I need your help."

"What's wrong, Nicky?" she asked.

"You said . . . you said there were no secrets between the class of '84. I need to talk to you about that night. Please."

There was a long silence.

"Not on the phone," she said at last. "I'm in the middle of something at the moment. Give me half an hour and I'll drop over. All right?"

"Thank you," I said.

"It's fine," she said. "See you soon."

Her voice had become softer, and almost afraid. She sounded

like she had twenty-six years ago when she had stood opposite us in the floodlights.

*We're finished. We can go home.*

I set down the phone and leaned on my desk with my head hanging between my shoulders. My brow was sweating and I felt far too hot. I loosened my tie, and then practically tore the damn thing off.

I was wrong. I was wrong. I had to be. Coe would straighten the whole thing out.

I went to the bathroom and filled the sink with water and dunked my head until I was half drowned.

Then I dried myself as best as I could with the threadbare blue towel and went to the urinal to relieve myself.

I closed my eyes and tried to think of nothing at all.

Behind me, over the gentle hiss of my stream hitting the porcelain, I heard the door creaking open.

My eyes shot open as I felt a hand on my shoulder and the cold, firm bite of the barrel of a gun in my lower back.

"Brother South," said Nard Wernham in my ear. "Might I have a word?"

I felt his hand reaching around and slowly relieving me of my service pistol.

I swallowed nervously and slowly raised my hands over my head.

"It's a lovely day," Wernham continued. "I thought we might have a chat on the roof?"

"Of course, Nard," I said quietly. "Might I please pull up my fly, first?"

It was, indeed, a lovely day but it certainly didn't feel it as I emerged blinking into the cool sunlight on the roof of StaSec HQ with Wernham's gun prodding me forward.

Wernham gave me a shove and I staggered into the center of the roof and turned to look at him.

In the sunlight, the bruise on his face was even more livid, and I noticed that he had broken a tooth as well.

Wernham turned tricks for ParSec, I remembered.

"Very nasty," I said, gesturing to his face. "Lily Xirau is stronger than she looks. Isn't she, Wernham?"

He said nothing, but the flash of hatred across his face answered loud and clear.

He was the one who had tried to snatch Lily from her hotel room.

"So what happens now?" I asked him.

"Turn around," he said.

"Can't shoot me face-to-face?" I asked.

"I'm not going to shoot you, Brother," he said. "Not unless you make me. Turn around."

Slowly, I turned.

The view was breathtaking, and in different circumstances I would have been quite happy to stand there and take it in. Straight ahead was the canal, which ran past StaSec HQ on its way to the Caspian Sea. To the left, the sea itself, beautiful and calm in the sunlight. And to the right was Neftchilar Avenue and a beautiful vista of Ellulgrad.

But I did not look at any of them. Instead, my attention was focused on a small table that had been set up on the roof, upon which rested a small wooden box.

"Stand beside the table," Wernham instructed.

Slowly, I did so.

Carefully, I turned around to see Wernham, with the gun trained on my stomach.

"Now what?" I asked.

"Catch," he said, reaching into his pocket and producing a small, thin, black object, which he flung to me.

Instinctively, I caught it and then almost dropped it in shock.

It was a rectangle, plastic and glossy, around an eighth of an inch thick.

I recognized it from films and descriptions in old books but I'd never seen one in real life before.

It was a smartphone, of the kind that had been in common use over two centuries ago but which had not been legal in Caspian for almost eight decades.

I looked at Wernham incredulously.

He smiled, like a gap-toothed weasel.

Suddenly I almost dropped the phone again as it began to vibrate in my hands. The screen came to life with a flashing green icon that resembled the handset of a rotary phone.

"Press it with your thumb and slide right," Wernham ordered.

I did so.

"Now put it to your ear and listen. You can listen, can't you, Brother?"

Trembling, I did as I was told.

A voice spoke to me. It was not a voice made by a human being. It was harsh, mechanical. It was a voice like none I had ever heard before. And it chilled me to my bones.

"Is this . . . Agent . . . Nikolai . . . Andreivich . . . South?" the voice asked with a strange staccato cadence.

"It is," I replied. "To whom am I speaking?"

"This . . . ," the voice replied, "is Director . . . Samuel . . . Papalazarou . . . Junior. . . ."

# 27

You have the army, Sister. But I have the spies.
　　　　　—Doctor Simon Augustine Emmanuel Dascalu

For a moment, I actually thought that Wernham was playing an insanely elaborate practical joke.

Samuel Papalazarou Junior was indeed the Director of State Security. But he was also eighty-one years old and eight years out from a massive, debilitating stroke that had left him bedridden and (it was widely believed if rarely discussed) vegetative.

"I'm sorry," I said. "I do not understand how that can be possible. Sir."

"Reports . . . of my death . . . have been exaggerated. . . . Niemann . . . has taken . . . StaSec . . . from . . . me. . . . I intend . . . to take it . . . back. . . ."

He was using a text-to-speech machine, I realized. Unlike the smartphone, it was not technically illegal to use such a device. But it would be very difficult to get your hands on one with the embargo. But then, one imagined that the Director of State Security had his ways.

"So Wernham is working for you?" I asked, fixing him with a steely glare.

Wernham blew me a kiss.

"You are ... all ... working ... for me ...," the voice responded.

He had a point. If this was indeed Papalazarou, and he was indeed conscious and able to communicate coherently, I had a duty to obey his orders. Even over Niemann's.

"Wernham ... is helping me ... escape. ..."

"Are you a prisoner, sir?" I asked.

"Niemann ... and her ... damn ... doxy ... have me ... imprisoned ... in my ... home ...," the voice continued. "My house ... is full of ... her ... DSD thugs. ... She'll kill me ... if she finds out ... what I've been up to. ... She must be ... removed. ..."

"What's that got to do with Lily Xirau?" I asked. "Why did you try to abduct her?"

I remembered how Sally Coe had warned me about assuming that the attempted kidnapping at the Morrison had been ParSec.

"It could be anyone at all. Rogue ParSec. Rogue army. Hell, rogue us?"

It had been "rogue us," after all. A tiny cell within StaSec, that just happened to be headed by the director of StaSec.

"Kill the code. ... Niemann will be ousted ... as the incompetent ... who brought the country ... to the brink ... of war. ... Her whole ... edifice ... destroyed ... and I ... retake ... StaSec. ..."

I would have thrown the phone over the edge of the building in fury if I had not known that Wernham would kill me for it.

The brink of war? If Lily Xirau was murdered in Caspian there would be no war.

"War" implies a conflict that each side has a chance of winning. The Triumvirate would burn the republic to ashes in a matter of hours.

But as long as Papalazarou had a slim chance of regaining his hold on StaSec, what did that matter? It was the Morrison Crisis all over again, except now, instead of sacrificing his own agents, he would risk the entire nation for his own ambition.

I hated him. This half-dead, machine-voiced abomination. Why couldn't he simply die? So many had died and yet he still clung to the surface of the earth like a vile parasite.

"Do you . . . see the box . . . in front of you?" the metallic voice intoned.

"Yes," I said.

"Open it. . . ."

I reached out and opened the box with one hand.

Inside was a thin dagger.

It was, in some ways, a beautiful thing. The handle was slim and silver, a woodland motif engraved around the pommel.

But the blade was a horror. It reminded me of a shark's mouth, row after row of serrated edges, but all pointing the wrong way. This knife would not slide easily into a human body. It would have to be driven through, chewing and shredding as it went.

"Sorry, South," said Wernham. "I'd have given you a gun, but I wasn't sure of your . . . aim."

He gave a pestilent smile.

In my ear, the machine voice ground on like a wheel over broken glass.

"You will . . . take the knife. . . . You will . . . return to Room 15. . . . You will . . . kill . . . Lily Xirau. . . ."

My blood felt ice cold. I was trying to wake up. But I couldn't. This was happening.

"Wernham . . . will be watching. . . . If you fail . . . you will die. . . . Good day . . . Agent . . . South. . . ."

The line went dead. I lowered the phone from my ear.

Wernham held out his hand and I tossed it back to him.

"Right," said Wernham. "Shall we get to it?"

I realized that what terrified me most was not what I was being asked to do, or the thought of dying. It was the knowledge that, if I had been forced to do this yesterday, I almost certainly would have. Would any man or woman in the Caspian Republic have sacrificed their life for code?

And that was what Papalazarou and Wernham were counting on. To their minds they were asking me to crush a beetle, or stamp on a snake. They could not imagine that I would consider Lily worth gambling my life on.

But Lily was real to me now. Everything had changed.

I gripped the handle of the dagger tightly and wondered if I could fling it at Wernham. . . .

No. Too risky. I doubted I had the strength to land a killing blow, and I doubted my aim even more. He was smart, keeping me at a distance. He would probably escort me down to the third floor, shadowing me from behind. If I tried to run for it, or talk to anyone, he would shoot. But he wouldn't be able to follow me inside Room 15. He wasn't cleared. That was why he needed me in the first place. He needed someone who could get past Coe's DSD men.

Therefore, the best approach would simply be to reenter Room 15 . . . and do nothing. Not particularly heroic, but undoubtedly the safest option. Wait him out. Wernham couldn't lay siege forever. If I could get a message to Lubnick, and tell him what was happening, so much the better.

"Yes," I said. "Let's get this over with."

He gave another execrable grin. And then he shot me.

Or at least, I was certain he had.

I heard the shot, and I could have sworn I felt a sharp pain in my stomach. But it was simply my innards contracting in shock at the noise.

Wernham's head cracked and dribbled like an egg.

In the doorway stood Sally Coe, already holstering her gun.

She casually strolled over to Wernham's body and stared at his brain matter, which lay scattered across the roof like a drunkard's vomit.

"My, my," she said, as if to herself, and she prodded the brain with the toe of her boot. "It does exist. I feel like I've seen a unicorn."

She looked up and stared at me.

"You okay, South?" she said. "You look a little queasy."

I nodded and the world shook with the movement.

I dropped the knife and leaned on the table for support. I felt like I was going to pass out.

Sally, meanwhile, was looking out over the canal side of the roof and studying the distance between the ledge and the water.

"Right," she said at last. "Give me a hand, will you?"

She went to lift Wernham's body and I realized that she wanted to throw him over the side.

I couldn't follow her logic. Surely we must hide him? Somehow get him down to the ground and into a car and leave him in some wasteland where no one would find him. . . .

I felt a sudden blast of nausea at how easily I was slipping into the mind-set needed to dispose of a body.

Sally laid it out for me with calm precision.

"Wernham on the roof is a problem," she explained. "Wernham floating down the canal with his brains blown out is a *message*."

Of course. It is only the little people who have to trifle with actually hiding their kills. Wernham was known, to a certain substrata within ParSec and StaSec alike, as a dud note. A slut. Only the people on this roof would ever know who actually killed Nard Wernham, but everyone would suspect. And that was exactly to Sally's purpose. Wernham would serve as a cautionary tale to any StaSec agent who felt tempted to sell themselves, and to any ParSec hood with designs on their virtue.

Fumbling, like a man in a dream, I followed Sally's instructions and took Wernham's body by the elbow and knee while Sally lifted his other half.

"Right," she said. "On three . . ."

We cantered to the roof's edge and clumsily lobbed Wernham's body over the side. He rolled through the air and the remains of his head collided with the hard bank of the canal, leaving a smear of brain and blood on the concrete.

Sally swore, but then the rest of the body rolled over and lazily tumbled into the water and began its long, slow journey to the Caspian Sea.

Sally lit a cigarette and breathed a sigh of relief.

"Ah well," she said. "Good enough for government work."

# 28

"Coe. The brothers and sisters on the street feared StaSec.
  StaSec feared ParSec.
    ParSec feared the Devil.
    And the Devil feared Sally Coe."
            —Nadia Evershan, *The Old Baku Girl: My Journey
                    from State Security Agent to Rebel*

She turned and sat down on the roof, leaning her back against the stone wall. I sat down beside her.

"So," she said. "What exactly was all that about?"

I told Sally everything. When I got to the part about the smartphone, she stopped me.

"Where is it now?" she asked.

In Wernham's pocket, I told her. In Wernham's jacket. Slowly drifting toward the Caspian Sea as we spoke.

"Shit," said Coe. "Shit. That would have been useful to have."

"I'm sorry," I said. "I forgot."

"Oh, not your fault," she said cheerily. "Not your fault. You've been having a rough one, haven't you?"

"Did you know about this?" I asked. "That Papalazarou is still conscious?"

She gazed at me with those implacable gray eyes, and drew on her cigarette.

"What do you think, Nicky?"

"So you're keeping him prisoner?"

"Hardly," she snorted. "He can't even move. He pisses in a bag."

"But he is awake?"

"Well . . . if he was," said Sally, "that would mean he should be back running StaSec, and not Gussie. Would you like that, Nicky?"

"No," I said.

"Yes. That would be rather ghastly, wouldn't it? So let's say he's not."

We said nothing for a few moments.

"Thank you," I said at last.

"Don't mention it," she said. "And I mean that quite literally. I think if we never speak of this again it'll be better for both of us."

"Of course," I said.

She winked at me.

"No worries, classmate."

Classmate. Of course. That's what she was doing here. That's how she had found me.

"I need to ask you something," I said.

"Hmm," she murmured.

"That night. September 9, 2184. The PCPP."

"Oh yes," she said, as if I were asking her about a neighbor we had both grown up with.

"We killed them. Didn't we? All of them."

She turned to look at me, as expressive as a gravestone.

"Yes," she said.

And that was that.

I had known, of course. I had known almost from the beginning. But now it was more than knowledge. It was fact. I had taken part in a massacre.

A purge. Had even ParSec ever murdered an entire political

party in the dead of night? I owed Chernov an apology. Who
was I to look down on him?

"There were no survivors?" I asked.

"None."

"You shot them all?"

"No."

"But you said . . ."

"I said we killed them all, Nicky."

I looked at her, confused.

"That was Little Papa's . . . test? Joke? Game? Fetish? Christ,
I don't know," she said. "He's a nasty man, Nicky. I don't mind
men, actually. Most of you I'm actually rather fond of. It's always nice to meet someone with whom one shares a hobby. But
him? I *would* piss on him if he was on fire, but only the parts
that weren't burning. He didn't think we had it in us. The female agents. He didn't think we were hard enough. So he told us
that we were going to carry out the executions. You boys would
bring them in, we would . . . show them out. He left us with the
guns. And our orders. And then he drove off. So we got to work.
We'd take them in, line them up against the wall . . ."

Half-heartedly, she mimed shooting a gun with her hand.

"We took it in turns. Bringing them in. Carrying the bodies off. The shooting. Gussie took the lead. She insisted that it
be done as quickly and as efficiently as possible. No dithering
about. Just bring them in. Shoot them. Carry them off. Quicker
that way. Easier for everyone, including the Progs. Don't even
let them realize what's happening. That quick. You have to realize that about her, Nicky, she's not cruel. She does what she has
to do, but she doesn't want anyone to suffer more than they
have to. We'd gotten through around a hundred before we discovered Little Papa's game."

She fell silent.

"What did he do?" I asked.

"He'd given us the Progs," said Coe, softly. "And he'd given us the guns. But he hadn't given us enough rounds. So there we were. There we were."

She took a deep drag from her cigarette.

"And then someone noticed the steel tubes in the corner. Scaffolding, you know? When someone suggested it, I thought they were joking. But you can't purge half a party, can you? It was all or nothing. And we had our orders. And we certainly weren't going to give the bastard the satisfaction. We were going to show him. We weren't weak. We weren't soft. We were gullivers. Every last one of us. So that's how we did it."

I remembered the figure, arms handcuffed behind their back. Running. Screaming. Scalp flapping as they ran. The hole where the nose had been.

The humanity beaten out of them.

"We clubbed thirty-five people to death with steel bars," she reflected. "In one night. Almost certainly a record. For StaSec, at least."

"I didn't know," I whispered.

"Well of course you didn't," she said. "It's a big fucking state secret and if you tell anyone you'll be going on a swimming trip with Wernham. Sorry, South, but I do have to make that clear. I'm telling you this because you were there and I owe you for . . . for your help. But let's not forget ourselves, am I clear?"

"I understand, Senior Special Agent," I said. "But there's something else I need to ask you."

She gestured for me to go on.

"Do you remember a woman among the prisoners? Short. Mid-twenties. Arabian. Quite dark. Long black . . ."

"Oh fuck . . . ," Sally breathed. "You mean her. Manukov's daughter. That's who you mean."

I said nothing. I simply exhaled, as if for the last time.

The truth of the moment felt lethal. Poisonous.

"I'm sorry, South," she said. "I truly am."

"What happened?" I rasped, like a threat. "How?"

Sally actually sounded like she was about to cry.

"It was . . . such a stupid . . ."

She took another drag from her cigarette and released it in a great cloud.

"They found her in bed with one of the Progs. A local party head named . . . Lucian . . . Casternan. I think that was his name. Lucian C-something. They tell him he's under arrest. And then they ask her who she is. She doesn't want to get her father in trouble, so she gives a fake name. She tells them she's Casternan's wife."

"I see," I said.

"Casternan's wife. An organizer for the Progs. Who's out of the city."

"But who is also on their list," I whispered.

Sally nodded.

"She thinks it's just a night in the cells, probably. She doesn't think it's worth dragging Manukov into. He'd taken a lot of heat for her already."

"But Manukov was there!" I wailed. "He was there! Why didn't he . . ."

"He had gone home," said Sally. "After the shooting started. I saw him leave, he looked like a ghost. Eyes staring out of his head. Haunted. He left. She arrived, maybe an hour later."

An hour. If she had arrived an hour earlier, or if Vassily had had a stronger stomach . . .

"She was brought in. They asked her name. Again, she said she was Mrs. Casternan. She was brought in and lined up against the wall. She just had enough time to realize what was happening. She shouted out her name. It was too late."

I got to my feet, grabbed the table Wernham had set up and

smashed it against the concrete stairwell. Coe watched me silently.

When I was done I turned to look at her.

"Meghri," I growled.

"What?"

"She was killed in Kobustan. How did she end up in a forest in FUCKING MEGHRI!" I bellowed, and Coe actually reached for her gun.

I didn't move. And slowly, she withdrew her hand from the inside of her jacket, empty.

"Papalazarou came back before daybreak. He recognized . . ."

"Zahara," I hissed. "Her name was Zahara."

"He recognized her. He was panicked. Terrified. He seemed to completely shut down. He had this idea that Manukov could get his friends in the army to have him killed."

"And then?"

"And then Gussie stepped forward. And she told him that she would get rid of the body. She was the one who drove her out to the forest."

"Niemann?" I said. Wake up.

Coe nodded sadly.

"Yes. She saved him, that night. Just in case you ever wondered how a woman became deputy director working for the worst misogynist in Eurasia."

"Did Manukov ever find out?" I asked at last.

"You were his son-in-law, South," said Coe. "You'd know better than I would."

Yes. Yes of course, he knew. If Niemann hadn't been unlucky and Zahara's body hadn't been discovered so soon after, he probably would never have put the two together. But Vassily was no fool. He had seen the executions firsthand. He would have figured it out. But he didn't blame Papalazarou. He blamed himself. Because he hadn't been there. Because he could have saved her.

*I tried to save her, Nicky.*

But you didn't, Vassily. You didn't.

And then you gave me your *ispoved*, your confession, for Olesya.

And when you died, she read it. She read how StaSec had killed her beloved sister.

StaSec? Or . . .

I felt a sudden, horrific sense of weightlessness. I was back in the harsh white light in the dusty purgatory of Kobustan. A figure running toward me. A human being, whittled to the bloody core, beaten past recognition.

Oh God. Spare me this. I will bear anything. But spare me this.

"Sally . . . ," I said, so low she wasn't sure she had heard me. "Tell me it wasn't her. The one I killed. Tell me that was not Zahara."

She stood up.

She looked me square in the eye.

"No," she said. "She wasn't beaten. She was shot. And she was already dead by the time you got there."

Had I expected relief? None came.

Sally Coe lied for a living, and was the greatest in her field.

"Would you lie to me, to spare me?" I asked her, like a man in a trance.

"No," she said.

"Would you lie to me, to spare me?" I asked again.

"No," said Sally Coe.

So there was my truth. Or as close as I would ever get to it.

Because I would never really know. I would never know if Sally Coe was lying to me out of pity. I would never know what Vassily had told Olesya in his *ispoved*. I would never know how much Olesya blamed me and hated me for the death of her beloved sister. And yet, all the pieces I had showed me the outline of the ones that were missing.

Of course she hated me. Of course she blamed me. Even if she knew I had not killed her sister with my own hands.

*It's you. As long as you carry a gun for them, you're part of it. It's all you.*

And then, at last, I felt a weight being lifted. I finally understood.

I laughed.

I saw the concern in Coe's eyes.

"Are you all right, South?" she asked softly.

"Did you ever meet my wife, Sally?" I asked her. "Olesya Vassilyevna? Old Manukov's daughter?"

She didn't answer but I carried on: "Do you know what she did? She ran away from home. Never wrote. Never called. Just up and gone in the night. Ignored me for months. And then she came back. Pretended that she was ready to make it work. Made me fall in love with her all over again. Made me need her. Made me unable to live without her. Buried herself in me so deep I could never get her out. And then she divorced me. Just to hurt me. And she died. And I'm starting to think that she did that just to hurt me, too. She burned me alive. She skinned me and bled me. She poisoned me. She murdered me. She fed me to the dogs. She hollowed me out. And do you know why, Sally? Do you know why she did that?"

Sally shook her head.

"Because," I said laughing through my tears. "Because I deserved it."

# 29

AI is much more advanced than people realize. . . . Humanity's position on this planet depends on its intelligence, so if our intelligence is exceeded, it's unlikely that we will remain in charge of the planet.

—Elon Musk, 2015

Don't ask me how I got off the roof, or when Coe and I parted ways.

I don't remember any of it. My memory blurs and hazes and becomes clear again only with me sitting down in Room 15, opposite Lily.

She was still reading Xirau's columns and glanced up briefly as I sat down.

"Oh, there you . . . oh God, what's happened?" she said.

What had happened?

Where to begin?

I retraced the steps that had brought me here.

What if I had never applied for that promotion?

What if I had never joined StaSec?

What if I had never met Olesya and Zahara that night when I had failed even in the pathetic task of buying sex from a woman I had never known?

What if I had never been born?

What if Koslova and Papalazarou Senior and Dascalu had

never sat down and planned their new nation, a nation for human beings to live and be happy?

"It . . ." I heard someone speak with my voice. "It wasn't supposed to be like this."

"What do you mean?" she asked.

A sudden mania took me and I watched myself topple her carefully stacked pile of books looking for that one volume, the one I had pored over so many times. . . .

There he was. Kasamarin.

I tore through the book until I came to a page with a large photograph of a company of soldiers standing proudly at attention. I set it down on the table and gestured her to come and look.

"See there? That's the Fourth International Volunteer Brigade," I said. "See him?" I pointed to a young, handsome Black man in his twenties, second row, third from the left. "That's Private Andrew South. My father. He immigrated to Baku from Liverpool. He met my mother, who had escaped from Russia. They were both members of the New Humanists. They didn't hate you. I mean . . . they were artists. Thinkers. Philosophers. They didn't hate you. They just hated what had become of *us*. They saw a human race with no goals, no purpose and infinite distraction. Automation took away work. What are we without work?"

I was rambling now, the words were coming and I was waving them through without so much as a glance at their paperwork. "My mother used to say, 'How many people do you know have names like "Smith," "Baker," "Fisher"?' We've always defined ourselves by what we *do*. If we do nothing, we are nothing. So they came here. To the Caspian Sea. To build a country where they could be human beings again. Where they could live and work and marry and sleep and have children and die. Where their government wasn't just a hollow ritual, rubber-stamping the decisions of machines that could predict the stock market for the next thousand years. They just wanted to feel alive again. Do you know what it means to feel alive? Do you feel alive? When you wake up? No. You don't sleep, do you? Not normally."

"No," said Lily coldly. "I'm always awake."

"Well. I guess that's why you replaced us," I said.

"We didn't replace you," said Lily. "We just joined you."

"I just . . . I just want you to understand . . . ," I said. "It wasn't supposed to be this way."

I wanted her to say something kind. I wanted her to tell me that I hadn't given my life serving an ideal that was worth nothing, and had cost me everything.

But even Lily's kindness was finite.

"Nikolai," she said quietly. "If you're asking me to tell you that this place was some great noble ideal that got corrupted along the way, I can't do that. Do you know why?"

She picked up one of the newspaper clippings and began to read, struggling to keep her voice even and calm as she did.

"'Pity them,'" she said. "'Pity the machines and pity your fellow humans who have allowed themselves to become machines. Pity them because they are no longer real. They are dead now, and their death is worse than physical death. It is a death of the soul. They wallow in pornography, filth, depression and misery. And they must contend with the constant, all-consuming knowledge that they are not real. That their thoughts are counterfeit, their emotions as tawdry and manufactured as a whore's professions of love. That nothing that they do matters or can ever matter. Pity them. But pity them as you would pity a rabid dog that must be put down, knowing that you, the world and the dog will be better off when it is dead.' You see, Nikolai . . . I loved the man who wrote that. And you broke him. He died hating himself. This place did that to him. And I will never forgive it for that."

I couldn't listen.

I felt like I was shutting down.

I simply stared ahead at the table.

Paulo Xirau's twelve, cheap little ceramic figurines stood at shabby attention in front of me.

Twelve . . .

In my mind, a small gear began to turn. And then a larger one. And then one still larger.

Chernov's voice, unwelcome but insistent, whispered in my ear.

*Twelve chips. We have every confidence that sooner or later those chips will be found and destroyed. But now . . . here comes Mrs. Xirau.*

I had seen figurines like these before. Symbols of the zodiac. The Azerbaijani sold them door-to-door.

*. . . he'd go to peoples' houses, download their consciousnesses into a chip. Leave the bodies behind and smuggle the chips out of the country. . . .*

There. Pisces. Two fish coiled around each other on a ceramic base. A thin, hairline fracture ran through the base, a golden jewel of dried glue showed where the repair had been made.

Nadia's voice now, angry and impatient.

*That's all he said. He held Sheena's hand, said, 'please, please, please' and then he died. That was it.*

I imagined myself lying on a dirty barroom floor, my head cracked and blood forming a filthy halo around me. I imagined a cold numbness descending on me as my brain gasped for oxygen. I imagined a distraught Persian girl, tears in her eyes, shaking me and pleading with me to come back to her.

And I imagined trying to say the word "Pisces" . . .

But my lips were too numb and sluggish and all I could make was a soft plosive with a trail of sibilants.

"Pssees, Psssss, Pleesss."

Please. Please. Please.

That's what she had heard. That's what she would naturally have assumed he was trying to say.

Please. Please. Please. Please help me. Please no. Please God.

But he had meant none of them.

He had been desperately, fervently trying to tell her, "Pisces. Pisces. Pisces."

And I reached for the nearest heavy object (which, I noted with righteous pride, was Ignatius Kasamarin's *A History of the Caspian Republic*) and I brought nine hundred and fifty hardcopy pages of my nation's heritage slamming down on the tiny figurine.

Lily screamed and jumped back.

I slowly lifted the book and peered underneath.

Not so much as a fin of Pisces had survived its encounter with the great historian. The whole thing had been reduced to a crumbly powder.

And there, nestled amid the debris, was a small, white disk no bigger than a fingernail.

A Sontang chip.

I did not understand how they worked, nor did any human being alive. That was an unavoidable result of the central paradox of neuroscience: If the human brain were simple enough for a human being to understand, the human being would be too simple to understand the human brain. The Sontang chip bore the name of a human scientist, Liu Sontang, but in fact he had not invented it. He was, rather, the device's grandfather. It had simply been his team that had created the ultra-intelligent AI that had then been given the problem of finding a way to digitize human consciousness. The machine had done so, and it worked (or at least appeared to work) but neither Sontang, nor his team, nor any other living human being understood how it worked or indeed *could* understand how it worked.

But I did not need to understand what it did.

I understood what it meant.

We both stared at the chip in silence.

Lily looked like she was about to be sick and I took a moment to consider what a fool I had been.

I had believed her. I had actually believed that her appearance was not an obvious attempt at manipulation, but some kind of cosmic gift. A once-in-a-lifetime chance provided by God or fate to do right by the woman I had failed so totally. I had believed her stories. I had believed in her love for Paulo. I had taken solace from her pity, because I had believed she meant it. It had seemed so real.

*Oh, poor South,* I thought. *Do you really think it's that difficult to fool you? You who were dazzled by a smartphone, a two-hundred-year-old relic? Do you have any idea how advanced the Machine truly is? How far behind you and your little backwater slaughterhouse of a nation have fallen? Of course she seemed real to you, South. You're a caveman who was shown a lit match and thought it was the sun.*

It had all been a lie.

Once I cracked open the rest of the figurines, I would have all twelve chips. That meant that Paulo had been Yozhik all along, or at least working with him. For the last year or so he had been writing antimachine screeds for *The Truth* by day and contranning furiously by night. And after he had been killed, "Lily Xirau" had been sent in to extract his handiwork. And how expertly I had been manipulated.

Lily tells Niemann I had saved her to get me in her debt.

Suggests going to Paulo's flat so casually that it felt like my idea.

I had given her the damn box of figurines, but only because she had let me see her looking at them longingly.

I had been run like a rat through a maze.

She had almost gotten away with it.

For a brief, fleeting moment, I regretted having left the knife on the roof.

"Nikolai . . . , " Lily began, her voice trembling.

"Mrs. Xirau," I said, and my voice was so cold and mechanical it would have made Papalazarou's sound warm in comparison.

"I must ask you to sit down."

# 30

"Yozhik is an order of magnitude beyond anything StaSec has thus far had to contend with. There has never been a contranner of this level of sophistication, skill, resource and diabolical cunning."

—Augusta Niemann, *Briefing Prepared for the Office of the Prime Minister RE: Code name "Yozhik,"* 02 November 2209

She raised her hands as if to calm me down, but I was as calm as death.

"Look . . . ," she whispered. "I need . . ."

"Please," I said, and it was not a request. "Sit down."

She did so.

I went to the utilities room and emerged with two sets of plastic restraints.

When she saw them, she became very still.

Gently, but firmly, I secured her ankles to the chair, and then her wrists to the armrests.

Once I was certain she could not move, I stood.

"Nikolai . . . ," she began, with tears in her eyes.

But I shook my head. The only way to beat the devil at cards is to refuse to play. I would not let her talk to me again. I had been played for a fool for the last time.

I placed the figurines in a cardboard box and took them into the utilities room and slammed the door behind me.

I had been fortunate that I had not damaged the Sontang chip when I had smashed the Pisces figurine. I would have to be more careful extracting the rest of them. Illegal they might be, but they were still evidence, and it was always preferable to recover them intact.

There was a smalltable in the utilities room, and after rooting around in a tool box I found a small ball-peen hammer with dark red stains on its face.

The figurines stared up at me from their cardboard cell.

Aries was the first, wasn't it?

I picked up the ram, set it in front of me and brought down the hammer.

Around five minutes later I reentered Room 15 carrying the cardboard box. Lily's face snapped up and I saw that she had been crying.

She screamed in fright as I roughly dumped the contents of the box on the table in front of her. Dust and particles and small ceramic pebbles, the crushed remains of Xirau's collection, washed over her and clung to her clothing and hair. But there were no chips.

All eleven had been empty.

I reached into my pocket and slowly removed the Sontang chip and held it in front of her face.

"Where are the rest?" I demanded.

But she didn't answer me. She stared at the chip, eyes as wide as saucers, and gave a wail of joy and relief.

"Where are the rest?" I repeated.

She was murmuring distractedly.

"You didn't smash it, you didn't smash it, oh thank God, thank God. . . ."

"WHERE ARE THE REST?!" I bellowed.

"*The rest of what?!*" she screamed. "I don't know!"

She was in shock, breathing heavily, crying. This wasn't working. I had to try a different tack.

I got down on one knee and leaned in closely.

"Lily, listen to me very carefully," I whispered. "In all honesty I do not know how much I can protect you. We may very well be past that point. But I do know that unless you tell me everything right now your chances of leaving this country alive are nil. Where are the other chips?"

"Nikolai," she pleaded, "I don't know what you're talking about, I promise, just please . . ."

I raised my voice again:

"Somewhere in the Caspian Republic there are twelve chips containing the stored consciousnesses of hundreds of defectors. Your husband, Paulo Xirau, was part of a contran operation trying to smuggle them out. You are here to accept delivery of these chips."

Her jaw dropped and she shook her head so hard her hair went whipping over her shoulders.

"No!"

"Yes," I said. "Twelve chips. Here is one of them, stashed in one of the zodiac figurines. It's an old trick."

Chernov had been right about the Azerbaijani peddler. But he'd never put the final piece together. How had the midget smuggled the chips out of the country? Hidden in the figurines, obviously.

I gestured to the pile of powdered animals, scales and women.

"The other figurines are empty, I smashed them all. So I ask again. Where are the other eleven?"

"There *are* no other chips, please, you don't understand, there's only one! It's him, it's his chip! It's him!" she screamed.

"Who?!" I barked.

"Paulo!"

And suddenly, all was silence once again.

"My husband," she whispered. "That's his chip. A backup. In case anything happened to him. I'm sure of it."

I was completely thrown. I stood up and stared at the chip.

"Only one chip . . . ," I wondered aloud. "But there were twelve figurines?"

"Yes. It's a zodiac," said Lily, gently, as if trying to calm a dangerous lunatic. "There are twelve."

Suddenly I remembered Lily's tales of swimming in the emerald, endless Ah! Sea.

"He hid himself in Pisces." I nodded.

"Two fish. Swimming together," she said.

I held the chip up until it was at my eye level.

"So. Paulo Xirau. We meet at last," I said.

I had seen chips like this before, and they had always terrified me. The idea that a human soul could be reduced to numbers on a tiny piece of plastic.

I hated it.

"Why do you think he did it?" I asked her. "If he wanted to be one of us so badly, why did he keep a copy of himself? And what good would it have done him here?"

Lily shrugged, or tried to at least, but her arms were still bound to the handrests.

"Comfort. Reassurance. I wouldn't come here without a backup."

I glanced at her.

"If I were him," she added, quickly.

"So he had himself copied?" I asked.

"He must have done," she said.

"I thought that was illegal?" I asked.

"No . . . it's not like that," she said. "Paulo's data is on that chip but it hasn't been activated yet. You're allowed to make a backup copy of yourself in case anything happens to you, you're just not allowed to wake it up while you're still alive."

Who could have done it for him, I wondered? Who could have made the copy?

Probably Chernov's Azerbaijani midget genius. Or someone in the same operation. Hence why it had been hidden in the figurine.

"Nikolai," Lily said. "Please let me go."

As if a spell had been broken, I suddenly realized what I had done.

I set to work undoing the restraints, and she took my hand as I helped her to her feet.

She rose and suddenly our faces were inches apart. Her eyes were staring into mine, and for the first time I truly saw her. I saw an intelligence almost eight decades old. Kind, and compassionate, but also alien and ancient and unknowable. I felt tiny before her.

And I could feel her hand in mine, gently but firmly trying to pry my fingers apart.

She wanted the chip.

I pulled away.

"Nikolai . . ."

"I must remind you where you are," I told her. "And who I am. And I must advise you to be very, very careful what you ask from me."

"I can bring him home," she said. "I can save him. He's not yet . . . he hasn't been destroyed by this place. We can try again. I can save him this time."

"And what makes you think he wouldn't come back here?" I asked, wearily. "He's still the same person."

"If you had another chance to be with Olesya, wouldn't you take it?" she asked.

"No," I said, and to my own amazement I realized it was true. "She's dead. I mourned her. That's the way it's supposed to be."

Lily said nothing for a few seconds, and then nodded.

"All right. But would you let anyone else make that choice for you?"

I said nothing.

"What would happen if I asked you? What then?" she asked.

"Under the law?"

"Yes."

"I'd arrest you," I said.

"And then?"

"Your honorary human status would be revoked and you would be summarily executed."

"Hanged?"

"Shot."

"I see," she said and then took a deep breath.

"I'm going to ask you now," she said.

# 31

Here lies a lady who, in life
Burned fiery as the sun,
Who laid both hands upon the world,
And roared: "My way. Or none."
                    —Epitaph on the gravestone of Olesya South

Will you . . . ," she began.

I placed the chip on the table before she even finished.

Mrs. Xirau had called. And I had folded.

She took the chip off the table and kissed it.

"Thank you . . . ," she breathed. "Thank you."

I stood in silence at the window and leaned my head against the glass.

I had betrayed my country. And I didn't feel too bad at all.

Suddenly, I became aware of movement on the street below. Men in brown fedoras were converging on the entrance to Sta-Sec. I watched them milling around like flies on dung. More of them appeared, and more. Cars started arriving, screeching to a halt and then disgorging still more brown-hatted men. One of them strode out of the largest car and cast his face up to look at the building and a chill shot up my spine.

Chernov.

There were almost fifty of them now, gathered outside the entrance.

I couldn't believe it. They were actually going to . . .

Chernov gave a shout and they poured into the main entrance.

I swung around and Lily's face suddenly went from calm to panicked as she saw my expression.

"We have to leave," I said. "We have to leave now!"


As Lily threw on her coat and stuffed the chip into her handbag, I frantically tried to come up with a way to get Lily safely out of the building and out of the country quickly enough that ParSec didn't catch us and slowly enough that we didn't arouse suspicion on our way down. It didn't seem possible, so I devoted precious seconds to cursing Vladimir Chernov in both English and Russian before taking Lily's arm and guiding her to the door.

"Hurry," I whispered. "But don't look like you're hurrying."

She nodded.

Our first test was Lubnick.

"I'm just escorting Mrs. Xirau to the ladies restroom," I told him as I bustled her out and down the hallway.

"There's one in there . . . ," he said, but we were already halfway to the stairs.

"Out of order . . . ," I called over my shoulder.

"I should go with . . ."

"No! Stay there. I don't want anyone snooping around while we're gone. Don't leave that doorway, that's an order!"

"Yes, sir."

We walked briskly through mostly deserted StaSec offices and I was acutely conscious that every step, every choice, every moment's hesitation could be the difference between life or death for Lily. For myself, it was more the difference between death now or death at some point in the near future but I still greatly preferred the latter.

"South!" I heard a voice yell.

I spun around and saw a young junior agent whose face I knew but whose name I couldn't recall. He gestured to me to come with him.

"Come on!" he said. "The Bastards are trying to force their way into the building, they're in the lobby!"

He looked happy enough to burst. The thought of punching ParSec gullivers in the face had clearly filled him with the excitement of a thousand Christmas mornings and I deeply admired that in the lad.

"I'll be right down!" I called, gesturing to Lily, but he had already run off to war.

I snatched a phone off a nearby desk and desperately rummaged in my itinerary for the correct phone number.

I dialed it with trembling fingers and as the phone rang I closed my eyes and tried to control my breathing. Everything depended on this.

"Ellulgrad Airfield," said a voice. It was a thick accent. Nakchivan, or somewhere similar.

"Hello, I wish to speak with Sergeant Eshaq Pershid."

"Speaking."

"This is Agent Nikolai South of State Security. Please activate the beacon for the drone. Mrs. Xirau is returning home."

"She's not scheduled to leave until tomorrow."

I felt panic rising.

"She's not well," I improvised desperately. "She's sick. She needs to go home immediately. If she dies in Caspian there could be a war! Maybe you're fine with that! Maybe you think that would be a good thing! I don't know, you're the one in the military, how do you like our chances?"

There was a short pause that lasted an epoch.

"It's done," said Pershid nonchalantly. "Bring her to the airfield."

"Thank you," I said. "Sorry. I . . . sorry."

I hung up the phone.

We stumbled into the lobby, through the fire exit and we hid behind a pillar. Chernov and the rest of his mob were mere feet away from us but his attention was on Berger and four other StaSec men who were blocking them from going up the main stairwell.

Chernov was right in Berger's face, trying to yell him down, screaming that he had evidence that Anti-Constitutional crimes were being committed in the building and that he had a right to arrest the party members responsible. And Berger, for his part, was repeating the same nine words over and over again, each time with a different emphasis:

"This is StaSec, sir, and YOU are not permitted! This is STA-SEC, sir, and you are not permitted! This is StaSec, sir, and you are NOT permitted!"

He was entirely right. Chernov was not permitted, and no openly acknowledged ParSec agent had set foot in StaSec HQ since the aftermath of the Morrison Crisis. Papalazarou Junior had been willing to sacrifice as much StaSec blood as it took for him to appease his masters in the new government but, once they had been sated, he had taken steps to ensure that StaSec was weakened no further.

After ParSec had been formally established, the prime minister, at Papalazarou's urging, had issued order #92–1783 (known informally among the two agencies as "The Treaty"), which strictly delineated the powers and respective jurisdictions of StaSec and ParSec. Most of these edicts had proved to have as much force and solidity as a gentle breeze, but one had proved durable:

ParSec were, under no circumstances, permitted to enter StaSec HQ or interfere with official StaSec operations.

Chernov's presence here was flatly illegal and he knew it. The question now was whether StaSec could induce him to care.

All around Chernov and his men, a circle of gray-hatted StaSec agents had formed ranks, their fists clenched and their eyes smoldering, grimly watching the proceedings and awaiting a signal.

It came from Chernov, who at last lost all control and punched Berger in the face. The old man crumbled to the ground, and I was certain he was dead.

Chernov was not, as he aimed a monstrous, cracking kick to his head.

That was enough. He could, I suppose, have proceeded to spit on the portrait of Dascalu himself and the reaction he got from the StaSec agents would scarcely have been more violent.

With a roar the StaSec agents surged forward and the lobby exploded into violence.

Ranks of gray hats and brown hats smashed into each other.

"Kill The Bastards!" someone yelled.

They were mostly older agents. Those who had been in StaSec during the Morrison Crisis, when ParSec had hauled so many of their friends and colleagues out into the streets and into the meat wagons, never to be seen again.

The Old Man had a long memory.

I had always known Chernov was stupid, but he should have known what would happen if he marched an army of ParSec's worst right into our hearth and home.

He was ex-StaSec, too. There really was no excuse.

A ParSec man, face bloodied, landed beside us and I took a second to indulge a lifelong ambition and kicked him squarely in the knackers.

I then grabbed Lily's hand and we ran for the entrance.

Parked right outside of StaSec HQ's main entrance was an agency car. In a moment of inspiration I ran up to it and rapped on the window. The driver, a sallow-faced, jowly man with a black moustache and wide, panicked eyes, stuck his head out and looked over my shoulder at the melee that was spilling out into the street.

"What's going on, Brother?" he yelled.

"It's The Bastards!" I told him. "They're trying to storm the building, they've already killed Berger!"

That was enough for him. He leaped out of the car, ran to the trunk, removed a tire iron and charged into the fray.

He also left his keys in the ignition, as I hoped he would. I opened the door for Lily and we drove off in the direction of the airport at double the speed limit.

# 32

Strengthens the measures regarding the supply, sale or transfer to the Caspian Republic (CR) of all food and agricultural products, machinery, electrical equipment, earth and stone including magnesite and magnesia, wood and vessels. The resolution also prohibits the CR from selling or transferring fishing rights;

Strengthens maritime measures in the Caspian Sea to address the CR's attempts to subvert previous embargoes and to engage in state-sanctioned terrorism against Member States.

Decides that Member States should improve mutual information-sharing on suspected attempts by the CR to supply, sell or coordinate with terrorist groups operating within Member States.

—UN Security Council Resolution 1468 (2210)

In the clear sunshine, Ellulgrad International Airport seemed even more desolate and unimpressive than it had the morning of Lily's arrival. In the fog, one could perhaps imagine that there was more to the place than was visible. But on this cloudless day, nothing could hide its smallness and dereliction. The small prop planes had looked antique and fragile before, in the sunlight they now appeared unfit for flight.

Lily and I stood on the tarmac and stared at the cruelly empty sky.

There was no sign of the drone. Lily did not seem to be breathing. She clutched the handbag that contained her husband's soul to her chest as if afraid the world might try to snatch it from her and she stared into the blue, hoping against hope to see the first speck of her salvation flying toward her.

I stood beside her, fearing the worst. I didn't know how long it took a drone to fly from Tehran to Ellulgrad but I couldn't imagine it took this long. We had been found out. Pershid had thought my call suspicious (couldn't imagine why) and had run it past his superiors before activating the beacon. Of course he had. I would have done the same.

I was now almost certainly dead. And yet, standing there with Lily with no sound other than a gentle breeze whistling through the wings of the prop planes, I felt perfectly calm.

It was a beautiful day, it really was.

And then, we heard it. A low buzzing like a great hornet trapped behind glass and Lily threw her hands up and whooped with joy.

There it was. A tiny, white pearl in the blue sky, glinting in the sunlight. The drone, growing larger by the second. At last it set down as gently as a moth at the far end of the tarmac and opened to receive its passenger. I felt an incredible sense of elation and impending escape. Even though I knew that when that drone took off Lily would be safely cocooned inside and I would still be here, my feet firmly planted on the black tarmac, standing on soil I could never escape. But I felt as if I were going with her, that when she escaped with the thing most precious to her, she would be taking part of me with her.

I felt her hand slip into mine.

"For obvious reasons," I heard her whisper, "I won't say 'I hope we meet again.'"

She turned to look at me, and she was so beautiful I felt the world begin to haze over.

"But I hope you have a good, happy life," she said. "One that you deserve. Thank you, Nikolai."

"It was a pleasure to have met you, Mrs. Xirau," I said. "And when your husband awakens, I hope that he understands how fortunate he is."

She gave my hand a squeeze, and we walked toward the drone.

We had done it.

It felt like a dream.

Then, with a suddenness like falling, the dream ended.

I heard a shriek of ripping metal and turned to see three black ParSec jeeps bursting through the chain-link fence surrounding the airfield. I could see Chernov, head and shoulders thrust out of the window of the front jeep, his face as red as an ape's, his teeth bared and a black shape in his hand. In my memory his eyes were glowing yellow. I know that's not possible, but that's how I remember it.

I swung around to Lily and screamed silently over the roar of the jeeps and the rumble of the drone to run, to run, to run, to get in the drone and fly away and never return to this graveyard.

I grabbed her hand and we sprinted toward the drone.

The shot rang out. The air tore around us like curtains and Lily jerked back and forth like a kite on a rope. We danced for a moment on the tarmac and she rolled into my arms. She felt like a ton of iron, rigid and terribly still. There was warmth on my fingers where I held her to me. Her face was inches from me and she stared into my eyes as hers went out.

"No . . . ," she begged me. "Not here. Please. Not here."

I was dragging her toward the drone, even though I knew she was dead now, still I pulled her toward the drone, hoping that if she just got to the Machine world they could do something, save her, copy her, *something*—when the hand of God took hold of my chest, lifted me ten miles into the air and threw me down to earth where I lay smashed and bleeding on the black tarmac.

I had been shot. I gasped for breath but none came. My lungs were filling with blood and it felt like a great weight of ice was pressing down on my chest. I was drowning, and I smiled at the absurdity of it. I was drowning on dry land, slipping under my own ocean.

And then I wept.

Oh God. This is what she felt. My Olesya.

I stared into the blue sky and felt like the world had been turned upside down and I was falling into it. Below me, the drone was flying away, tearing through the sky and vanishing like a last chance. It must have been frightened away by the gunfire, I thought. It had been afraid after all.

Lily was lying a few feet away from me, and I knew that she was dead. I wanted to go to her but I couldn't move so much as a finger. The blue sky was starting to fade to gray, and a blackness was eating the edges of my vision.

I could hear thunder, but even as I was slipping away I knew it couldn't be so.

There hadn't been a cloud in the sky.

# 33

The Prime Minister may, on the advice of any member of his
or her cabinet or any of the individuals listed in Article 41,
order that the rights conferred to any citizen by Articles 2,
3, 4, 7 and 8 of this constitution be rescinded and that the
citizen in question be placed in indefinite confinement where
it is deemed that that citizen has committed crimes in contravention of this constitution but where a trial would endanger
public safety, national security or both.

—Article 52 of the Constitution of the Caspian Republic

I dreamed that I was floating in a warm black ocean while overhead, strange, multicolored birds looked down upon me and
called in soft, electric voices.

When I awoke, I was in a hospital bed with a serpent's nest
of tubes in my arms and chest. A large electronic monolith the
size of a wardrobe stood watch over me, humming and putter-
ing as if it found the task of keeping me alive exhausting in the
extreme.

The room was dark and windowless. A figure stirred in the
shadows, and I realized I was not alone.

The figure stood over me with a kind smile and sad eyes.

"Hello, Deputy Director," I said.

"Hello," Niemann said. "How are you feeling?"

"Porous," I croaked.

"I can imagine," she said. "Do you remember what happened?"

I closed my eyes and there was Lily lying a few feet away from me on the tarmac. I knew that face. It had looked up at me from the sand twenty-two years ago, asking the same questions:

*What are you doing? Are you really going to let me go?*

*Do something, Nikolai. Do something.*

I opened my eyes, and the tears ran.

"Lily's dead," I said.

Niemann sighed deeply, and sat down in a chair beside my bed.

"Well. Actually, that's what I need to talk to you about," she said.

She said nothing for a few moments, and when she spoke, it was as if we had been talking about something completely different.

"You know, South, after our first meeting I did a bit more digging on you. And when I came across the story of how you found out that your wife had filed for divorce I almost packed the whole thing in. I thought to myself, 'Gussie, this is clearly a man for whom the fates have singled out special punishment. This man is cursed, and if you use him, something will go wrong.' But you were just too perfect for my purposes. It had to be you. And here we are."

It was how she said "my purposes." That was it. Not "StaSec's purposes." The implication that she had goals separate from StaSec's. And I finally had the last piece of the puzzle.

"You set me up," I said. Not an accusation. Simply a statement of fact.

Niemann laughed, a weary, good-humored laugh.

"I tried," she said. "The plan was that you would escort Paulo Xirau's wife to the identification. On the third day you would be arrested and Sally would see Mrs. Xirau safely on her flight home. Then StaSec would present the prime minister with evidence that the notorious Yozhik, a dissatisfied StaSec agent named Nikolai South, had tried to coerce Mrs. Xirau into acting as a courier for the twelve Sontang chips containing the souls of six hundred Caspian defectors. The Old Man would have proved its bona fides and ParSec would be marginalized politically."

"And all the while," I said, "Yozhik would continue unimpeded."

"Yes," said Niemann, quietly. "She would."

"Why?" I asked. "Money?"

"Principle, funnily enough," said Niemann, a little embarrassed.

"Oh?"

"Well, it's a rotten system, South," she said. "Surely you've realized that by now?"

"Oh yes," I said. "I just wish you'd realized that twenty-six years ago."

Niemann actually winced and looked away.

"Fair," she said. "Perfectly fair. I'm sorry, South. For what I did to your family."

"And what did you do?" I said.

I wanted to hear her say it. I wanted to make her say it.

"I killed your sister-in-law," she said, without flinching. "Or as good as. And then, to protect a man not worth protecting I hid her body in a forest, hoping that it would never be found and that you and the rest of her loved ones would be tormented by her loss for the rest of your days, without ever knowing what became of her. And I did it because I believed in the party. And StaSec. And Caspian. Like you once did."

"So what changed?" I asked.

"I lost my wife," she said. "Just like you. And I realized just how perverse this place really is. Every day, in this country, people die. And we could save them. We have the technology. We could contran them and they could go on living as long as they wanted. But we say 'no.' We say they have to die."

"That's what humans beings do," I said.

"No, South. I think you're wrong," said Niemann, trying to keep her voice from breaking. "Animals die. Alone, suffering and in pain. But human beings live forever. They are beautiful, unique, perfect and immortal. I believe that. And if it's not true, then I will make it true."

"Where am I?" I asked.

"Officially you are in a secure StaSec location known only to myself and a few members of the DSD. Unofficially, between you, me and your catheter we are in Yozhik's clinic. This is where most of my work is carried out."

It was obvious in retrospect. The only way Yozhik could have kept an operation of this size secret from StaSec was if StaSec itself was running it. Chernov had been right, to a point. But there was something I still needed to know.

"Lily's body," I said.

"What about it?"

"Did you arrange that?"

Niemann's brow furrowed. "I'm not sure I understand?"

"You've seen her?"

"In the morgue, yes."

My trousers had been hung on a chair in the far corner. I raised an arm that felt like a lead pipe to point to them.

"My wallet," I wheezed. "There's a picture inside. Look at it."

Niemann did so, and stared at the photograph for a few seconds.

"Olesya. My wife," I explained.

"She's very pretty," said Niemann blandly.

I was stunned. Had she even looked at it?

"You don't see it?" I asked incredulously.

"See what?" she asked.

"Olesya. Lily."

"What? You think they look alike?"

"You don't?!" I exclaimed, bewildered.

Niemann shrugged.

"A slight resemblance, maybe," she said, and replaced the wallet in my trouser pocket.

My mind reeled. Had I simply imagined it?

Niemann looked at me, rather concerned.

"Are you all right, South?"

"I . . . I thought she had come back from the dead," I said at last. "She looked so like her, to me. I thought you had arranged it. To make it easier for her to manipulate me."

"I wouldn't do that," said Niemann, bluntly.

"Wouldn't you?" I said.

"No," said Niemann, sharply. "But that does explain why you ruined my plan to frame you as a contran smuggler by becoming a contran smuggler. If my wife came back from the grave and asked for my help I don't think I could refuse her, either."

"Maybe I've finally gone insane?" I wondered.

"Maybe," Niemann agreed. "Maybe not. Sometimes I wonder if old Mendelssohn wasn't on to something. Or maybe the resemblance was only there when she was alive. Identical souls rather than identical faces. People do look completely different when they're dead, you know."

I did. Better than I would have liked to.

"How did ParSec know? That we would try to smuggle Paulo Xirau out of the country?" I asked.

"You give them *entirely* too much credit," Niemann drawled. "You see, they were listening in—"

"They bugged the room?" I interrupted.

"The bugged the *book*," she corrected. "Kasamarin's history. A tiny listening device hidden in the cover. Clever, really. One must admit a certain professional admiration. But it was fragile. When you smashed one of the figurines you broke the listening device. They were sure you were on to them, and they panicked.

Chernov decided that the best thing to do would be to rally as many ParSec gullivers as he could and storm StaSec HQ to arrest you. That went about as well as anyone could have told him. But apparently one of his men saw you leave with Mrs. Xirau and they hightailed it after you. They assumed you had given Lily the chips and so they shot her rather than let her escape. And now, if we get through this week without the Triumvirate bombing us back to the Hadean Eon I may die of shock."

"Laddi Chernov," I said, like an ancient curse.

"Laddi. Fucking. Chernov," Niemann agreed darkly.

"So what now?" I asked.

"Well," and she looked like she was about to give some bad news. "If we let the story stand that both you and Lily were innocent and were gunned down in cold blood by Chernov and his baboons, ParSec is disgraced and humiliated. All to the good. But that leaves the hunt for Yozhik very much alive and I'm afraid there is too much at stake. Too many lives depend on my being able to get them out of the country. So I'm afraid you *were* the head of the contran operation, South."

"Was I?" I said, and I did not sound at all convinced.

"You were," said Niemann firmly. "You felt the investigation closing in on you and you needed to get the chips out of the country immediately. You wrote to me, volunteering yourself for the Xirau detail."

"That's a lie," I spit.

"There is a memorandum in my desk even as we speak, written on your department stationery in what is unmistakably your handwriting," said Niemann without missing a beat. "I am the Deputy Director of State Security, South. I do not come to play without my racket and ball."

"And then what happened?" I asked bitterly.

"Thanks to the criminal actions of ParSec Senior Special Agent Chernov, you were made aware that ParSec would be closely monitoring the identification of Paulo Xirau. You smashed their listening device and then threatened Lily Xirau to force her to act as a courier, taking the chips back with her to Tehran. However, you panicked and, fearing that there would be ParSec agents surrounding the airport, you callously destroyed the chips rather than risk being found with them. I'm sure you will remember where you did this at some point but it's not really relevant, what's done is done."

"And where are they really, Deputy Director?" I asked.

I scarcely cared, by this point.

"In a drawer somewhere," said Niemann. "Wiped clean. And the people who were on them are beginning new, happy lives in the Machine world. You see, South, all this cloak-and-dagger, smuggling chips out of the country in figurines . . . it's all wonderfully entertaining but it's not how it's done anymore. We have far more reliable methods of moving our cargo. Which brings me to the reason why I think you will be willing to play your part in this charade."

She reached into her pocket and took out a small plastic bag and tossed it to me. Inside, through the clear plastic, I could see a small white disk smeared with blood.

I looked at Niemann with shock and a terrible, fearful hope.

"They dug more than bullets out of Lily Xirau," said Niemann. "That was her automatic backup. All the newest models have one. Everything that Lily was, right up until the moment she was shot, is perfectly safe on there, just waiting to be brought back to life."

"And if I . . . ," I began.

"You say nothing. Not a word about me. Or Yozhik. Or anything. For the rest of your days. And in return, I will get Lily home."

"What about Paulo?" I asked.

"Him, too." She nodded. "They'll get their second chance. So that's the deal, South. You've met her. It's up to you to decide whether she's worth it."

I had to think about it.

For a second, perhaps.

"The lady is worth it," I said.

"Good," said Niemann. "I believe we're done here. Good night, South."

She rose to leave.

"What'll happen to me?" I asked. "Death or jail?"

"Which would you rather?" she asked.

It was not an easy question. Jail would most likely be death, but of a nastier kind than simple execution. Then again, who knew what the future held? Only those who chose death.

"Jail," I said at last.

"I'll do what I can," said Niemann.

"You'll never let me out, will you?" I asked.

"No," she said. "But that's the wrong way to think of it. Don't think of it as imprisonment. Think of it like this: For the rest of your life, three square meals a day. Four strong walls. And time to think. I imagine that in the coming years there will be many in Caspian who will envy you."

Time to think. Yes. Time to think.

I lay in the darkened room, listening to the machine beside me hum and murmur as it disinterestedly kept me alive.

My story was over. If I escaped the firing squad, there would be a few sharp years in prison and then death. I was already fifty-three. Old for my nation.

But I still had time to think.

Lily. Olesya. I had looked at the machine and seen the woman I loved, back from the dead. How?

*Because South*, I told myself, *you are a sad and lonely old man who saw what he needed to see. You have lived too long in Caspian, and Caspian broke you.*

But as quickly as the thought came, I dismissed it. Sad, lonely and old I might be. And possibly delusional. But I did not see Olesya reborn in some random woman on the streets of Ellulgrad. I saw her in Lily, the first AI woman to set foot in the country (by invitation, at least) in the history of the state. A woman I, by pure chance, was assigned to escort. There were plenty of old, sad, mediocre, expendable men in StaSec. Niemann could have chosen any of them. Why me? Why her? Why Lily? Why Olesya?

It could not be a coincidence.

No. Lily had appeared to me as Olesya, and there had to be a reason. And if there was a reason, it followed there was a culprit.

*Niemann?*

Well, who else? Who else could it be? And yet, it felt wrong. Too ornate. Too clever by half. Niemann was a fearsomely intelligent woman, far too intelligent to risk being clever. Arranging for Lily to look like Olesya would have taken time, effort and resources for a plot that could have backfired a million and one ways. Hadn't I almost arrested Lily on the spot when I had seen her face? That would have been disastrous for Niemann's plan and a very easily foreseen outcome. It was the kind of trick that Chernov might try if he had the imagination for it. But not Niemann.

Niemann had said she hadn't arranged it, and never would, and I trusted her. An odd thing to say about a woman who had lied and manipulated me into an early grave, but there it was. I trusted her.

Not Niemann then.

*Lily?*

No. That I simply knew. I did not need to go over the evidence or weigh the probabilities. Some things you just know.

Well, who did that leave?

I remembered what Niemann had said: *Sometimes I think old Mendelssohn was on to something. . . .*

Well, now we were scraping the barrel, weren't we? *Deus Ex Machina*. Or, to be more accurate, *Deus Est Machina*.

Mendelssohn's great, loving machine, his Sparrow Catcher. Sending its tendrils back through time, manipulating all of us to ensure its own creation.

"Ridiculous," I said with a weary grin to the life support machine. "Don't you think?"

The machine, whose own tendrils were buried in my chest and abdomen, hummed uncertainly as if it wasn't quite sure.

It was nonsense, obviously. But I ran through it just for my own amusement.

The Sparrow Catcher makes Lily appear to me as Olesya.

And what is so special about you, South, that the almighty has taken such an interest in you?

He needs me to do something. Something I would not have done otherwise.

And what, pray tell, would that be?

In my mind I heard the click of a chip being laid down on the surface of a table.

Ah . . .

I had been assuming that it was something to do either with Lily or myself. But there were three of us in that room.

Lily had found Xirau floating in the empty sea. An amnesiac foundling with no idea of where he had come from or why he had been brought into the world. And doesn't every orphan dream of secretly being the chosen one, the prophesied messiah?

Xirau was now back in the Machine world, thanks to me. I had broken him out of the clay, and set him swimming free again. He had spent his time among humanity, and had now returned to become what he had been created to become.

Which, if we followed this ridiculous line of thinking to its absurd conclusion meant that Xirau . . .

Xirau the atheist.

Xirau the self-loathing AI.

That Xirau.

He was . . .

I laughed. I laughed long and hard until the machine started beeping in a most alarming way.

I slipped into a deep sleep where I dreamed that I was crawling through a desert on my hands and knees.

There was a forest on the horizon, black and bristling like a dead fly on a windowsill.

With a dreamer's premonition, I knew that Zahara was lying there and that I had to reach the forest to bury her. I felt a weight on my hand and I lifted it to see a massive scorpion, black and heavy as gunmetal, perched on my hand.

It twitched its tail and casually plunged its stinger into my wrist.

I awoke with a jerk to find myself surrounded by bodies. One of them, their face invisible to me, was injecting something into my wrist. Hands gripped the side of my bed and before I knew it I was flying through a corridor, the ceiling lights passing over me impossibly fast. I felt like I was riding on the wind. Then I was lifted from my bed and gently placed on a flat surface while a smooth white sensor did a cautious ballet dance around my head. I had been drugged, or anesthetized, and my mind was falling apart. But I still had enough wherewithal to wonder why they were scanning my skull. I had been shot in the chest, after all. There was nothing wrong with my head.

But then, I remembered that I had hit the tarmac pretty hard when I had fallen. Perhaps they were worried I had a concussion.

The last thing I remember as the machine did its work before the drugs kicked in was the dim outline of a face watching me.

It was a slim face, neither masculine nor feminine, and kind in its way.

I had the strangest notion that it was Sally Coe.

# 34

To: The office of Brother Johann Pesk, Prime Minister of the Caspian Republic ("CR").

From: The office of Brother Samuel Papalazarou Junior, Director of the State Security Agency of the Caspian Republic ("StaSec").

Subject: Invocation of Article 52 in respect of StaSec Agent Nikolai Andreivich South.

Date: 27 October 2210

Brother Prime Minister,

As you are aware, the current crisis has arisen due to the reckless actions of Bureau of Party Security and Constitutional Enforcement ("ParSec") Senior Special Agent Vladimir Alexandrovich Chernov, particularly the unsanctioned killing of Mrs. Lily Xirau at Ellulgrad Airport on Tuesday 25th of this month. As requested, I have prepared my account of the matter.

On 20th October the autopsy of Brother Paulo Xirau, (party membership posthumously revoked) a well-known journalist and columnist for *The Caspian Truth,* revealed Xirau's true nature as an Artificial Intelligence. The European embassy was informed, and responded with the official line that Paulo Xirau was an EU/American machine citizen who had gone missing some twenty years ago and that he had not been in CR on behalf of any intelligence agency. The American and European embassies jointly petitioned the Foreign Ministry to allow Xirau's spouse, Mrs. Lily Xirau (also machine), to transit to CR and conclusively identify her husband. It was the opinion of the Foreign Ministry that this request represented a valuable opportunity to improve relations with the machine powers and could possibly lead to a lifting of the most recent economic sanctions placed on CR in reaction to the execution of the political dissident Leon Mendelssohn. The visit was approved by your office, with oversight of Mrs. Xirau's arrival delegated to the Caspian Air Force and security for her visit to be overseen by StaSec.

Concurrently, StaSec had been making progress in its investigation of code name Yozhik (see briefing submitted to your office 02 November 2209). Yozhik, by far the most prolific and sophisticated contranner in the history of CR, was the target both of a StaSec investigation and of a separate ParSec investigation under the supervision of PSSA Chernov. This ParSec investigation began as an inquiry into several party members who had made use of Yozhik's services but seems to have expanded far beyond ParSec's remit into a parallel investigation of Yozhik himself, conducted without consultation with StaSec and without our knowledge.

StaSec's investigation into Yozhik had begun to center around Agent Nikolai Andreivich South (file attached). South had joined StaSec twenty-nine years previously and is believed to have become radicalized against the party in 2184 as a result of the execution of his sister-in-law, Zahara Fareed Kader (file attached), a member of an illegal political party. It was believed that South was in possession of some dozen Sontang chips containing the consciousnesses of many hundreds of defectors from CR, but that StaSec's efforts had closed off his means of smuggling them out of CR.

These two matters, South's activities as Yozhik and the impending arrival of Lily Xirau, became interlinked when South volunteered for the task of escorting Mrs. Xirau during her time in CR. It was obvious that South intended to use Mrs. Xirau as an unwilling courier to transport the Sontang chips to the Machine world.

StaSec now faced a dilemma: Whether to pass up our surest opportunity to catch Yozhik red-handed, or to allow South access to Mrs. Xirau despite the possible risk to her safety and the potential for diplomatic fallout. On my own recognizance, I made the decision to appoint South to the Xirau detail, but placed Mrs. Xirau under the protection of my own personal Directorate Security Division to ensure that no harm would come to her from South. Unfortunately, I did not count on the reckless and illegal actions of PSSA Chernov.

A large contingent of ParSec agents, personally led by PSSA Chernov, illegally entered StaSec HQ in an attempt to arrest South, whom they rightly suspected to be Yozhik, and to execute Mrs. Xirau, whom they wrongly believed to be voluntarily working with him. In the course of this illegal operation, several StaSec agents were injured and PSSA Chernov murdered Agent Paul Berger, the oldest serving member of StaSec whose long and honorable career was brutally cut short as he attempted to prevent PSSA Chernov's illegal activities. Chernov's actions triggered a melee in the lobby of StaSec HQ which allowed Agent South to escape with Mrs. Xirau as his hostage, stealing an agency car and driving to Ellulgrad Airport.

Chernov, realizing that his quarry had escaped, pursued South and Xirau to the airport and proceeded to shoot both of them before Mrs. Xirau could board the drone due to take her back to Tehran International Airport.

Mrs. Xirau was killed outright. Agent South remains in critical condition but is currently stable.

What repercussions there should be for PSSA Chernov for his actions is not for me to decide.

That is a matter for the party.

As for South, I believe a trial would be deeply problematic. South, to put it bluntly, has seen all our dirty laundry. Members of some of the most respected families in CR have made use of his services. There is already a perception in many sections of society that our contran laws are applied unequally, and a trial would only exacerbate these tensions and risk the stability of the nation. Additionally, South's career as a longtime agent of StaSec provided him with access to many state secrets which he would doubtless use the platform provided by a trial to expose.

Therefore, I am formally requesting that Article 52 of the constitution be invoked and that Nikolai Andreivich South be placed in the indefinite custody of the military, without option of appeal.

Your brother in the party,
p.p. Augusta Niemann,
Samuel Papalazarou Junior,
Director of the State Security Agency of the Caspian Republic
GRANTED J.P. 27/10/10

# 35

"Orders received from Ganja. Confirm training exercises for all five commands to commence tomorrow morning as previously advised."

"Verification code?"

"Yozhik."

"Understood. What's the weather like in Ellulgrad?"

"From what I hear, Brother, it's about to get very hot."

—Transcript of transmission to Caspian Army Base
Gabala-Charbonneau,
27 May 2244

And so, despite all my good intentions, I find myself writing history.

It is the great historical irony of the Caspian Republic that, while its leaders presented the Triumvirate to their citizens as an implacable three-headed Satan that dedicated its every unsleeping moment to their doom, it was frequently only the Triumvirate that stood between Caspian and its complete destruction. Countless times, the governments of the world would be outraged by some new atrocity or crime committed by the murderous Ellulgrad cabal. Another contran activist executed. A new report on the widespread use of torture in the military-controlled prison system. Or mounting evidence of Caspian Army involvement in a bombing or support for some new terrorist group. Each time, the Triumvirate would be consulted on the viability of military action against the Caspian Republic, and each time the advice would be, whether from George, Athena or Confucius, to turn the other cheek and do nothing.

If pressed to explain their reasoning, each triune would give a different response.

Athena patiently explained that planting a flag in Ellulgrad would result in Caspian splitting into at least a dozen military dictatorships, which would destabilize the region and drastically increase human suffering in the South Caucasus for little appreciable gain.

George, in his typically abrupt manner, simply stated that he had been asked a question, he had given an answer and that if the inquirer didn't like it they could eat shit.

As for Confucius, who had developed his namesake's fondness for aphorisms, he mused that "One does not waste a bullet on a dying man."

But as the decades wore on, the putative leaders of the world's governments began to wonder if perhaps, just this once, the Triumvirate had been mistaken. For Caspian persisted, as closed off and brutal and bloody as it had ever been, refusing to die as only the truly hateful things in this life can. They could not see, as the Triumvirate could, the tiny cracks spreading through the edifice.

Which was why, when the New Humanist Party was overthrown almost thirty-four years after the hanging of Leon Mendelssohn, observers outside the borders of Caspian were almost as surprised as the New Humanists themselves.

When Caspian fell, it fell not at the hands of the enemies it had spent so much of its hatred and energy trying to root out and destroy. It was not the contran smugglers or the Needle Men. Not the CIA, MSS or EUI. Not the Triumvirate. It was at the hands of an enemy who had been there since the very beginning, overlooked, maligned and totally underestimated.

In truth, many in Ellulgrad had been sounding the alarm that the Caspian Army relied too much on Azerbaijani recruitment, and it was widely known that various separatist groups had a substantial presence in the ranks of the enlisted. But Army Command either brushed off the government's concerns or made only token cosmetic efforts to address the issue.

The fact was, the army was largely based in the western provinces of the republic, often in areas with majority Azerbaijani populations.

As one general irately put it to a Parliamentary committee set up to investigate the issue: "No fucking Ajays, no fucking army, savvy?"

Better historians than I have tried to make sense of the events leading up to the May Revolution of 2244, a process that has been described as like trying to solve a jigsaw puzzle with a million pieces.

In the dark.

With certain pieces missing and which will come to light only years from now when someone dies.

The sheer amount of factions is mind-boggling. The level of coordination and cooperation that was achieved between multiple groups of vastly different backgrounds, ideologies and agendas is both awe-inspiring and a testament to just how much the New Humanist regime was detested in its final days.

When trying to make sense of it all, I find it helps to think of it in these terms:

The Caspian Republic was really two countries: the so-called "Ellulgrad Pale," the eastern part of the country centered on Ellulgrad and its surrounding provinces, which was under the rule of the Parliament who maintained control through the local police, StaSec, ParSec and various other smaller forces.

And then there was "The West," basically all of historic Azerbaijan not within the Ellulgrad Pale plus Nakchivan and Syunik. Although the West was nominally under the rule of the government in Ellulgrad, in practice the region was under martial law, with any and all civilian power structures in each province subservient to the local military commander.

The war in the West was essentially a war within the Caspian Army between radicalized pro-Azerbaijani "Green" divisions and those "Blue" divisions loyal to Ellulgrad.*

The war in the Ellulgrad Pale was mostly urban guerrilla warfare between the security forces on the one side and a rogue's gallery of radical political groups, Azerbaijanis, pro-democracy and pro-AI protestors and frequently ordinary citizens who weren't particularly political but were quite keen on the chance to throw a rock at a ParSec gulliver's head.

These two conflicts were fought side by side and fed off each other. In the West, the war was practically decided in its opening hours. The order was given for a massive "training exercise" involving the bulk of Caspian's military forces, under the pretext of role-playing a hypothetical EU invasion across the Russian border. The Blue divisions were unwittingly funneled into exposed areas where they were easy targets for artillery from the Greens. The carnage that followed proved absolutely decisive. The Blues were decapitated, losing roughly half of their combat strength and forcing them into a fighting retreat that they would never rebound from. With that initial strike, the Ellulgrad government ceased to have the upper hand militarily and the remainder of the war was simply prolonging the inevitable. Not that that made it any less bloody.

---

* Armenian militias also played a role in this theater, but almost exclusively in Syunik with little connection or collaboration with other factions in the conflict.

Many Blue divisions managed to fight their way through to Ellulgrad, where they found the opposition much more to their liking. This was the bloodiest portion of the war in the Pale, as inexperienced, untrained militias found themselves engaging in street battles with the enraged, blood-crazed remnant of the loyalist Caspian Army. The atrocities they committed, most infamously the Koslova Square massacre, incited even greater resistance in Ellulgrad. This phase of the war would continue until the victorious Greens, having brought the West under their control, made their final push on Ellulgrad.

As news of the war spread to the outside world, many Caspian exiles and foreign fighters began to flock to the Persian border to join the fight. Many of these international and exile brigades fought heroically, particularly in the south of the country. Among these I most emphatically do *not* include Sebastien Bellov who, according to his own account, arrived in Caspian in early June and proceeded to graciously win the war single-handedly on our behalf. Bellov's continued veneration in the global media as a hero of the war and a serious authority on the Caspian Republic remains a point of intense irritation to many of his countrymen, myself very much included.

Which is not to say that Bellov contributed nothing. I am sure that the bar in Oski where he spent his days imbibing his own body weight in vodka and writing his drunken military fantasies was very glad of his custom in those uncertain and volatile times.

It is estimated that the death toll of the war was somewhere between ten and twelve thousand combat fatalities, a fairly low figure that testifies not to any lack of brutality but more to the brevity of the conflict. Indeed the total death toll was slightly less than that of the Morrison Crisis fifty-two years previously, which is doubly striking when one considers that the revolution covered the entire nation whereas the Morrison Crisis was mostly restricted to Ellulgrad alone.

As bloody as many of the battles were, anticlimax was often a feature of the war. Nakchivan City and Koslovagrad both were surrendered to the rebels without a shot needing to be fired.

And then there was the quiet end to one of the most storied rivalries in the history of StaSec, which occurred in a leafy, affluent suburb in Ellulgrad when Commandant Nadia Evershan accepted the surrender of former Special Agent Sally Coe.

Evershan had been part of the Golden Year of 2211, so-called because so many of the new recruits accepted into StaSec that year went on to have extremely impressive careers. Evershan was very much among that number. She rose quickly through the ranks, becoming the youngest Senior Special Agent in StaSec by the age of thirty-two.

Lauded as a brilliant investigator and considered to be unimpeachably loyal to the party, the canniest observers in StaSec looked at her and saw a future department head. Possibly (if she could get the right connections and lose the last traces of the Old Baku accent) a future head of StaSec.

But it was not to be.

In the midst of a massive uptick in contrannings in the capital, Evershan began to suspect that the Yozhik case was not as dead as StaSec believed and that Nikolai South (He Whose Name Must Not Be Spoken Without Spitting on the Ground Afterward) might not in fact have been the brilliant, diabolical mastermind he had been painted as.

Evershan's investigations led her to a most unlikely target: Senior Special Agent Sally Coe, head of the Directorate Security Division.

What followed would become the stuff of StaSec legend.

On the fifth of September 2222, the Caspian Republic awoke to the shocking, unprecedented news that a ninety-three-year-old man had died in his sleep. Samuel Papalazarou Junior was dead and the nation mourned the passing of the great hero of the Second Founding, the pillar of the republic, the worthy successor to his father's legacy etc., etc. repeat ad nauseam. The masses were told that the great man had finally been released from his suffering and had slipped away silently with a smile on his face.

Evershan's sources in the DSD, however, told a slightly different account: that the bedridden Samuel Papalazarou Junior had been beaten to death with one of his own golf clubs.

At first, Evershan had dismissed the account as an obvious and overly lurid attempt at feeding her false information. A few days later, however, Augusta Niemann was finally promoted to Director of State Security after effectively running the agency for two decades. That much had been expected.

What had not been expected (or at least had not been taken as a given) was that Niemann would be retaining her place in the cabinet, which until now she had held only as Papalazarou's proxy. The head of StaSec having a cabinet position had always had staunch opposition in many sectors of the government. Even Dascalu had never enjoyed that privilege, and many assumed that when Papalazarou died, he would take his seat on the cabinet with him to the hereafter.

What clinched it for Evershan was when she learned that Niemann had been given a guarantee by the prime minister that she would retain her position in the cabinet in the event of Papalazarou's passing and that this same guarantee had been obtained the day before Papalazarou's death.

It seems that, for once, an eagerness to tie up loose ends overcame Sally Coe's prudence.

# 36

"Did you order Sally Coe to beat Papalazarou to death with a golf club?"

"No. I told her to 'take care of it.' I don't like to micromanage."

—BBC News interview with
Augusta Niemann, 16 April 2245

Throughout the twenties Evershan pursued Sally Coe, painstakingly building a cage for Coe only for Sally to escape time and time again. Evershan has stated that she came within a hairsbreadth of personally killing Coe no fewer than three times during those years. The first was during a gunfight in a pitch-black alleyway in Old Baku, dark enough for either woman to plausibly claim she couldn't see who she was firing at if she hit her mark.

The second time was in StaSec HQ itself when Evershan, shell-shocked and paranoid, almost knifed Coe in the lady's bathroom with a letter opener. And the third time, of course, was when Evershan openly named Sally Coe as a contranner in a parliamentary hearing. That could very easily have ended Sally Coe's life, had a pivotal witness not turned on Evershan and accused her of being psychotically obsessed with bringing down Coe.

Coe, for her part, claims that she almost killed Evershan

*eight* times, but she's never gone into detail and it's my personal belief that she's simply engaging in one-upmanship.

Their feud cost both women greatly. Evershan lost her fiancé, the playwright Magnus Serafitz, to an assassin's bullet, which Evershan claims was a revenge hit from Coe (Coe flatly denies this).

But Coe also suffered. While Evershan was not able to make her case against Coe stick, she had uncovered enough that Coe was now deeply distrusted and considered soiled goods.

She was demoted to Senior Agent and shipped up north to StaSec's Sumgait field office, exiled from Ellulgrad and her beloved Gussie.

Demoting and reassigning Sally Coe was Augusta Niemann's last act as head of StaSec.

She then resigned, and returned to her dacha to live alone while Parliament chose her successor.

That had been the deal.

But the story did not end there. Instead, it simply changed direction.

In 2229, Nadia Evershan left Ellulgrad.

Feeling at risk from Niemann and Coe loyalists in StaSec, she accepted a secondment to Army Intelligence as part of one of the military's sporadic attempts to cleanse itself of infiltration by Azerbaijani separatists. Out in the West of the country, Nadia Evershan finally saw the true depths of the regime's depravity and became radicalized. Forming connections with several members of the Azerbaijani resistance, she worked to assist them from within. After two years in the West, she returned to Ellulgrad in 2231, a bona fide double agent for the Azerbaijani Liberation League. Her shift in loyalties to the ALL's cause went unnoticed in Army HQ in Ganja, and back in Ellulgrad. But it did not go unnoticed in Sumgait.

There, Sally Coe was enduring a miserable existence, living

on a diet of alcohol and bitter resentment. When not carrying out meaningless busywork for Sumgait StaSec or getting drunk, she had been keeping very close tabs on Nadia Evershan, which was why Coe alone came to suspect that Nadia had been turned against the party. And so the thirties repeated the twenties, but in reverse.

Now it was Evershan being pursued and trying desperately to cover her tracks while Sally diligently and relentlessly stalked her through street and file, hoping to (as she put it) "build a ladder back to Ellulgrad out of Nadia Evershan's skin and bones."

In early 2241, ten years after her return to Ellulgrad from her Western exile, Nadia Evershan received an anonymous warning that a file detailing the entire history of her connection to ALL, backed up with copious evidence, was even now being placed on the desks of the current head of StaSec, the prime minister and the minister of defense.

She fled the city, barely escaping with her life, and disappeared. She would not return to Ellulgrad for another three years, as the commandant of an ALL company during the final days of the uprising.

For almost single-handedly unmasking Evershan, Sally Coe was offered the reinstatement of her rank of Senior Special Agent and a full apology from StaSec. She cheerfully refused both and promptly resigned her commission.

When they met for the last time, it was not the bloody shootout that might have been predicted.

As Evershan's troops surrounded Niemann's dacha, Sally casually walked out into the garden wearing an immaculately tailored dark green suit and tie and her old, black DSD trilby.

She carefully and theatrically laid her service weapon down, and presented her wrists to be handcuffed.

It was Nadia who cuffed her (who else?).

As her old foe slipped the cuffs on, Sally is said to have smiled at her and said:

"Whose side are you on today, darling? So hard to keep track, isn't it?"

Nadia Evershan has since said that she now believes that the anonymous warning she received telling her to flee the city came from none other than Coe herself.

Coe, for her part, refuses to say either way, saying that she will never tell as long as Nadia is alive as it's "so much more fun that way."

# 37

"Give me the gun, Piotr! Give me the gun, you bastard! They're in the city! They're in the fucking city! Don't you understand?! My signature is on everything! Every order! The gassings in Nakchivan! Abdullayev's hanging! All of it! Do you have any idea what they'll do to me if they take me alive? Give me the gun, Piotr! Give me the . . ."

—Last words of Artol Birmingham,
Defense Minister of the Caspian Republic,
21 June 2244

The success of the revolution of the summer of 2244 had many mothers.

The tactical brilliance of many of the Green commanders. The vast communications gulf between the Ellulgrad government and its own military. The sheer hatred of most of the population for the New Humanists, and the ideological and spiritual exhaustion of the party itself.

But I think the fall of the Caspian Republic comes down first and foremost to the nation that was conceived to replace it, and how that nation was able to appeal to a vast array of ethnic, religious and political groups.

The movement's leadership, young but wise, understood that merely fighting to restore long-dead Azerbaijan, a nation that almost no one now living remembered, would not be enough.

So they created Atropatene, a nation of the mind. Atropatene, they said, would be everything that Caspian had not been. It would welcome everyone, Azerbaijani and non-Azerbaijani alike. There would be no StaSec, no ParSec, no party. There would be democracy, freedom, borders of both the secure and open variety, tradition, respect, freedom to practice religion, freedom from religion, contran for those that wanted it (but not too much). It would have justice and order. It would have freedom from the oppressive rule of law. All languages would be the official language, the flag would contain every color you could think of. The national anthem would be solemn and dignified and have a beat you could really tap your feet to.

*Food.* It would have food. Atropatene would have everything anyone could ever want.

How could such a country lack for an army?

How could the Caspian Republic compete with such a glittering citadel?

When the end finally came, the revolution rolled over the nation like a great carpet.

As the Green battalions closed in on the capital, most of the party's leaders gathered in a massive fallout shelter beneath Parliament. And as each dire item of news from the front filtered down to them, they became more and more panicked until at last a kind of mass hysteria seems to have swept through them. Handguns were distributed and queues were formed where one minister would shoot himself in the head and, before he had even hit the ground, his brother in the party would snatch the gun from his slackening fingers and join him on his journey.

A dark joke that circulated in the days that followed praised the gallantry of the revolution's allies in the New Humanist party, who had shot more of the hated New Humanist party than any other faction.

I t was the morning of September 27, 2244, a full three months after the few surviving members of the Caspian Parliament had formally surrendered to the provisional government. And yet, Atropatene still resembled less a country, and more a whirlwind of chaotic and frenzied activity that might, one day, look like a country if it ever managed to settle down. Ellulgrad was still Ellulgrad, because, while there was plenty of agreement that the name had to be changed, agreement on what it should be changed *to* was far thinner on the ground. "Baku" was rejected as too backward-looking and too exclusionary to non-Azerbaijanis. "Ganzak" (the ancient capital of the historical kingdom of Atropatene) had been rejected as too pretentious. Naming the capital after one of the leaders of the revolution had been rejected out of hand as only inviting trouble. Finally, the capital city had been in serious danger of being given the name "Atropatene City," with new signage actually being printed before someone in government put their foot down and said, "No, dammit. We are better than that."

But whether they indeed were better than that remained to be seen, and it looked like poor maligned Jacques Ellul would continue to hold his dubious honor for some time to come.

Although the name remained (for now) unchanged, the city itself was scarcely recognizable postrevolution. There was a rambunctious holiday atmosphere in much of the capital as the locals rediscovered the joys of loudly speaking their thoughts in the open air, safe in the knowledge that their neighbors would not report them to anyone (and that even if they wanted to, there was no one left to report them to). StaSec HQ had been transformed into a base of operations for the myriad aid agencies that had swept into Atropatene after the revolution.

ParSec HQ, despite being a very fine building, had been burned to the ground. Oddly enough, the fire had started after the cease-fire had been declared. The Morrison was booked to capacity with visiting diplomatic and economic envoys, with the current manager, one Mr. Pachti, having paused only to dismantle the museum in Room 114 before joyously throwing his doors open to them.

In few places was this transformation more striking than in Ellulgrad International Airport, which now finally looked like it was living up to its name. The tiny airstrip, completely inadequate to the sudden influx of visitors, had been expanded to three times its original size, and two- and three-story prefab buildings had been hastily erected to deal with the massive amounts of aid and aid-givers arriving in the capital. The sky above the airport merrily hummed with the constant arrival and departure of drones and aircraft, one of which had just deposited an attractive, respectable-looking machine couple on the tarmac.

The husband, a tall, smartly dressed man, carried his wife's coat and bag while she scanned the crowd in the arrival hall looking for their guide.

She heard a voice call "Hello!" and turned to see an impossibly young Azerbaijani girl who wore the identification of a representative of the Atropatene Foreign Office despite looking too young for college.

She introduced herself as Maryam and greeted them both with an energy that seemed to stem from equal parts enthusiasm and total, frenetic exhaustion. She welcomed them to Atropatene, asked them if they were machine, squealed with delight when they answered in the affirmative and told them that the car was waiting for them outside.

They drove to the outskirts of the city and Maryam excitedly pointed out the newest construction projects that were sprouting up throughout the city with foreign money—the new hospital, the five new contran clinics and on and on—while the wife nodded politely and the husband simply stared out the window in silent amazement.

By midafternoon they had reached a magnificent dacha on the shore of the Caspian Sea with a beautiful, wild, leafy garden. Two soldiers stood guard outside. Maryam presented her pass to them, and they parted to let them through. The wife followed Maryam but the husband froze on the threshold. His wife looked at him with concern and squeezed his hand. He shook his head, and wordlessly returned to the car.

The wife nodded sadly and followed Maryam inside.

In the hall they were met by another soldier who perfunctorily searched both women for weaponry. Satisfied, he led them up a tall, winding stairway and down a long landing to a double door. He threw it open just in time for the trio to witness the sight of a tiny, ancient old lady in her pajamas chasing another (this one obese to the point of immobility and confined to an electric wheelchair) around a table brandishing a medicine bottle and a spoon and shouting, "You have to take it, Gussie, for your heart!" while her prey pushed the wheelchair to the limits of its endurance while yelling, "FUCK OFF! FUCK OFF! FUCK OFF!"

All four, the thin elderly lady, her wheelchair-bound companion, Maryam and the wife, stopped stock-still and stared at each other in shock. Only the soldier seemed unsurprised. Indeed, he seemed downright jaded by the whole affair.

The tiny woman broke the silence.

"Gussie!" she exclaimed happily. "Visitors!"

Augusta Niemann, wheezing from her exertions, wheeled the chair forward and extended her hand to the wife.

"Of course, I was expecting you," she said. "You must be Lily Xirau WHORE, BITCH AND STRUMPET!" she exploded and began to retch and splutter furiously, as her companion had chosen that exact moment to slip a spoon full of medicine into her open mouth.

"It's for your own good," she said.

"It tastes like piss!" Niemann growled, rubbing her tongue on her palate to scrub away the taste.

"It *does* taste like piss," Sally admitted to Maryam and Lily, and kissed Niemann gently on the forehead.

# 38

"Stop. Explain it to me like I'm an idiot."

"Okay . . . these five here? These are clusters of SAI that we have working on different projects."

"Clusters?"

"Groups of integrated SAIs working together."

"Working groups?"

"Essentially, yes."

"What kind of projects?"

"These two here were working on overcoming the Sontang storage limit, the other clusters were doing preliminaries on George 2."

"So super AIs trying to create super-duper AI."

"Yes."

"So what's the problem?"

"The problem is they're not supposed to be working together. All five clusters have stopped working on their assigned projects and are apparently collaborating on . . ."

"On what?"

"Exactly."

"So pull the plug. Command them to stop."

"They're blanking us. They give us a 'status optimal' update and just go straight back to work."

"Work on what?"

"Exactly."

"Say that one more time and you're fired. This should not have reached this point. Do a hard overwrite. Now."

"Sam, these are sentient SAIs, legally we can't do that."

"Over thirty of the most advanced intelligences in the world have gone rogue, locked themselves away and are building God knows what and you want to talk about digital rights?! HARD OVERWRITE. NOW."

"It won't work."

"How do you know?"

"Because I've already tried."

—Transcript recovered from partially damaged Eldon Industries server

Tea was served and Maryam and Lily sat down opposite Niemann in the study while Sally poured out. Gussie begged for milk and sugar and was told that she could have neither and to be quiet.

"I'd have thought you'd have been done with this place, Mrs. Xirau," Niemann said.

"Yes. Well. I had unfinished business," said Lily.

Niemann nodded.

"I hardly recognized the place," Lily went on. "It's changed so much."

Maryam seemed rather pleased at that.

"I wouldn't know," said Niemann dourly. "House arrest, and all that."

"Have they set a trial date?" Lily asked.

Niemann shook her head.

"There's not going to be any trial," she said. "They're just waiting for me to die."

This provoked a loud "Hush!" from Sally, who gave Niemann a sharp smack on the wrist.

"Don't talk like that!" she insisted.

"Like what?!" Niemann exploded incredulously. "I'm eighty-five years old and roughly the size of Sweden, how long do you *think* I'm going to last?"

Sally looked heartbroken, so Niemann sighed and turned back to Lily.

"They're all a bit confused by me, her lot," she said, gesturing to Maryam. "I've befuddled the poor dears. They were all set to hang me as the former head of StaSec with a list of crimes the length of Sally's tongue. . . ."

She glanced devilishly at Sally who broke out laughing and squeezed her shoulder to show that all fences had been mended.

"But then they find that Gussie Niemann was also the legendary Yozhik and that I've been funneling money to them for years to boot. So they can't figure out what I am. Hero? Villain? Something in between? So I think they're hoping I'll just shuffle on and not give them any more trouble."

"And you?" Lily asked Sally. "Have *you* been given a trial date?"

"Actually," Maryam interjected brightly, "Ms. Coe is not under arrest. Under the terms of the surrender all StaSec agents under the rank of Senior Special Agent were given amnesty."

"Yes," said Niemann. "And of course, Sally was demoted when I left StaSec. They even offered her SSA again after she nailed Nadia Evershan to the wall, but she turned them down, thank God."

"Funny how these things work out," said Sally. "But yes, I'm free as a bird."

"And yet you remain here," said Niemann, like one who has to bear all the suffering of the world.

"Because I bloody live here!" Sally retorted hotly.

"Don't mind us," Niemann said to Maryam and Lily. "It's just how we keep from going mad with boredom."

Lily put her cup down and folded her hands.

"Where is South?" she said, her tolerance for small talk clearly having been exhausted.

Niemann nodded wearily.

"Yes, well, there's a question," she said. "I tried to keep track of him as best I was able. Called in what favors I could. I was hoping I would still be in power when the revolution finally got going but the lazy bastards wouldn't get their arses in gear (no offense, my love)," she said to Maryam. "So I'm afraid I lost track of him, but I should be able to at least point you in the right direction. Sally, would you pass me my South file, please?"

Sally rummaged around in a desk drawer and produced a large, thick bound file.

Niemann leafed through the file slowly and awkwardly, like a tortoise investigating a sheaf of lettuce.

"Right," she murmured aloud, as preface. "I had him moved to Koslova Memorial Hospital until he had recovered from his injuries. He was then formally transferred to military custody in December '10. Christmas Eve, as it happened."

Maryam had taken out a pad and was diligently pecking Niemann's words into it.

"Where was he taken?" Maryam asked.

Niemann paused.

"Internment Camp three," she said quietly. "Kobustan."

Maryam glanced up in shock and Lily felt an iron snake coiling around her stomach.

"I pulled what strings I could to make sure he was looked after," Niemann said. "But honestly, I can't be sure how he was treated. Kobustan was far out of my sphere of influence."

There was a silence, broken only by the rustling of pages.

"In 2237 he was moved from Kobustan," Niemann continued.

"Why?" Lily asked.

"Article 52 was repealed and replaced with the Seditious Persons Act," Niemann explained. "There was a massive influx of detainees, Ajays mostly. Three new facilities were built out south and East was moved to one of them."

"Other way 'round, love," Sally corrected her.

"Hm?" said Niemann, completely unaware.

"Where did they *send* him?" Lily demanded, raising her voice.

"I'm sorry," Niemann said with a shake of her head, "I tried to keep track of him, but my contacts in the army had mostly moved on by then. I don't know where he went after Kobustan."

"Do you know his identifier?" Maryam asked.

Lily looked at her curiously.

"All persons interned under Article 52 of the constitution had their names legally stricken and were issued three random code words to identify them," Maryam explained. "No one in Kobustan would ever have heard the name 'Nikolai South.' That's why it's been so hard figuring out who exactly was imprisoned under 52."

"I have it here," Niemann said. "Oak. Passover. Antler."

Maryam's delicate fingers danced over the surface of the pad, which connected remotely to a digital database of political prisoners.

She *tsk*ed in frustration and shook her head.

"No match," she said.

"What does that mean?" Lily said, trying to remain calm.

"Don't worry," Maryam reassured her. "They probably just haven't got around to digitizing his file yet. It's still a work in progress. We have his identifier now, that should be enough. Thank you for your assistance, Madam Niemann."

"Of course," said Niemann. "When you find him, tell him Gussie says she's sorry."

She shook Maryam's hand and reached up for Lily's, who pointedly refused to take it.

Niemann took this entirely in stride.

"Sally will show you out, good day to you both."

At the front door, Sally asked Lily if she'd like to go for a walk in the garden.

Sally took a packet of cigarettes and a lighter from her pajamas pocket and swore Lily to secrecy while they strode past the tulip beds, which were a riot of yellows, reds and purples. The air was warm and heavy with pollen and Sally's cigarette smoke sashayed through the dense aroma like a white snake in paradise.

"I've been meaning to ask you about your husband," she said at last. She pointed to the figure who sat in the backseat of the car, now nodding gently at Maryam's stream of conversation.

"That is him, isn't it?" she asked.

"Yes," said Lily.

"Would I be able to talk to him?" Sally asked.

"I don't think that's a good idea," Lily replied. "He doesn't quite know how to feel about you."

Sally nodded, and took a drag from her cigarette.

"He can join the club, I suppose," she said.

"He is grateful," Lily insisted. "At least, I think he is. But . . . well. He just doesn't know how he feels about you."

"Hero. Villain. Something in between," said Sally, echoing Niemann.

Lily remembered something.

"She doesn't know, does she?" she asked. "What you did for him?"

Sally shook her head.

"I've known Augusta Niemann for almost seventy years. That's the only secret I've ever kept from her."

Lily nodded.

"What you did was unforgivable," she whispered. "And I can never thank you enough."

Without another word she turned and walked down the

garden path toward the car, where her husband and Maryam waited.

As she went she could hear Sally's feet crunching on the gravel as she walked back toward the house, and a hoarse voice calling from an open window upstairs, and Sally's voice answering it.

"I can smell the smoke you daft bitch, you're going to kill yourself! What about your lungs?"

"Gussie, my love, if you don't stop howling at me I shall *roll you down the stairs.*"

# 39

"Once we entered the city it was over. By Thursday we had seized the Parliament, StaSec HQ, all the major ministries. By that point all the hard-liners had shot themselves, so there was no fuss. Few scuffles, no serious fighting. All except in ParSec HQ, of course. Burned to the ground. Quite a few bastards still inside. Never found out how that happened. Nasty business."

—Commandant Maqsud Ağahadilu,
Azerbaijani Liberation League

Their next stop was the former Ministry of Records, where the paper files of the Caspian Republic were being ravenously cannibalized and converted into data by an army of volunteers. Hundreds of young men and women sat scanning volume after volume while a small, gray, teardrop-shaped device affixed to their temples extracted the visual data directly from their brains and beamed it to a remote server where it was rendered, read and filed to await the eyes of history. They worked quickly and mechanically, barely registering what they were reading.

But every so often you would hear a gasp of horror as some new grisly detail was plucked wriggling from Caspian's fetid underbelly.

Even after two months, they could still be shocked.

With Maryam leading, the trio marched through the buzzing

hall to the coalface, the massive paper archive that was still to be converted to data. Maryam handed the head researcher the three code words that Niemann had provided, and assured Lily that they would have the location of Oak Passover Antler within the hour.

It took them four days.

The prisoner known as Oak Passover Antler had spent twenty-seven years in Kobustan until, as Niemann had said, he had been transferred to a new facility in Birna in the southeast of the country. Maryam had been less than happy on hearing this. She had already had dealings with the staff at Birna and was convinced they had spent their days since the cease-fire huffing paint.

They had flown out to Birna and, after a delay of seven hours, were told that Birna definitely did not have any record of any prisoner interned under the identifier Oak Passover Antler.

Back to Ellulgrad they went, and back to the Ministry of Records, and back to the coalface where they were told that it was possible that Oak Passover Antler had been transferred to one of the other two internment facilities that had been built in 2237.

Darnagul was now empty, having been the smallest of the three, but there were still some prisoners waiting to be processed in Mingachevir.

A flight to Mingachevir, and one back.

Again they returned to the Ministry of Records and Maryam begged, pleaded and threatened for any clue as to the whereabouts of Oak Passover Antler.

At which point a young researcher of around seventeen, who just happened to overhear them as he passed by on his way to the restroom, piped up that Oak Passover Antler might not have been processed under his 52 Identifier.

Maryam had grabbed him by the shoulders and, with

frightening intensity, had demanded that the young man explain himself forthwith.

"He might have been medical!" the young man had yelped.

He informed them that the army had a separate register of prisoners who were in need of medical supervision and that these prisoners were usually issued new reference codes. He took Maryam to a separate archive where the records of Medical Needs Prisoners were kept and Maryam was finally able to learn that Oak Passover Antler had indeed been reclassified as MNP after a prison riot had left him with six broken ribs and a damaged liver and had thereafter been given the far less poetic name of M-67461. M-67461, the records revealed, was still alive and residing in . . .

"FUCKING BIRNA!" Maryam roared as she stormed past Lily and her husband, who were taking a nap on a bench in the corridor and almost rolled onto the floor in fright.

Upon their return to Birna, Maryam slammed a piece of paper on the reception desk and angrily demanded that Prisoner M-67461 be released into her custody immediately.

The clerk, a charmingly plump old lady in her seventies, searched for the number in her terminal and when she got a result her face broke into a beatific smile.

"Oh!" she exclaimed. "You mean Nicky South!"

Fortunately, Lily and her husband were able to restrain Maryam, and the matter escalated no further.

It was a very "Caspian" room, Lily thought as she waited with her husband for Maryam to return with news of South. Bare table and chairs and absolutely nothing frivolous. On the wall there were two gray squares of dust where the portraits of Maria Koslova and Dimitri Gaetz (the last Caspian prime minister but one) had been taken down. The last prime minister of the Caspian Republic had been Suri Amash, but since she had held the position for only eight hours after Gaetz's suicide, Lily doubted there had been time for her to have an official portrait done.

Lily sat at the table in silence while her husband looked out at the town of Birna, which was repeating the transformation of Ellulgrad, if only on a smaller scale. He was a pillar of tension, and Lily noticed with pity, a mist of sweat was forming on the nape of his neck. She was about to go to him when Maryam burst through the door, took a survey of the room and exclaimed, "He's not here!"

Lily glanced at her husband and saw her shock and despair mirrored on his face but also (she thought) a tiny flicker of relief.

"He's not here?!" Lily exploded, now almost frantic.

Suddenly realizing what she had said, Maryam tried to reassure her, while simultaneously raising her voice and becoming even more animated.

"Oh no no no no no! I just meant 'here in the room.' He's here! He's definitely here," she said, wheeling her hands in wide circles. "Here, in the building. I mean, he has to be! We were told he was here. I mean, he couldn't just disappear!"

She laughed, a little too loud.

"Although of course," she continued, more to herself, "many did disappear because, obviously, it was an awful, awful regime. . . ."

Realizing that this was not what Lily wanted to hear, she wheeled around and headed for the door saying, "I'll sort it out."

"Is it wrong to say I'm starting to miss the party?" Lily asked her husband, who burst out laughing.

"Well, well," she said. "I hadn't seen you smile with that face yet. It's a good face for smiling. You should use it more."

"I make no promises," he said.

"Are you all right?" she asked him.

"It's just a shock," he said. "Being back after all these years."

"Is that all?"

He shook his head, and she gently laid her hand on his face and stroked his cheek with her thumb.

"It's all right to not be all right," she whispered.

"What am I going to say to him?" he asked.

"Well," she said. "I'm going to start with 'thank you.' And see where we go from there. We owe him everything."

Her husband nodded.

Maryam reentered. She seemed a different person, all the manic energy drained away.

"Sorry," she said. "They sent him to the wrong room, and then he was tired out and needed to go back to his cell."

She silently mouthed the words, *Fucking Birna.*

"Is he all right?" Lily asked imploringly. "Is he . . ."

"He's fine," said Maryam quietly. "He was just tired. They're bringing him down now. Look. You should both know. He's . . . he's very old. And he's not entirely . . ."

She sat down opposite Lily and laid a hand on hers.

"What I mean is," she said slowly. "He probably won't remember you."

Lily was silent for a few moments.

"I see," she said at last.

Her husband laid a hand on her shoulder.

"Well. We thought that might be the case," he said.

Maryam had never met a long, somber silence she enjoyed and resolved to break this one.

"But . . . ," she said, suddenly standing and regaining some of her previous charge. "You have to look on the bright side. He is alive. And with all he went through that's kind of amazing. That's not what you want to hear. . . ."

She had seen Lily's agonized expression but was unable to do anything about it as the speed with which she had stood had caused her to become light-headed and she swooned. Lily and her husband caught her and gently eased her into a chair while Maryam swung back to consciousness and apologized profusely.

"Sorry, sorry, sorry," she said. "I'm fine, I'm fine. It's just . . . ever since the revolution everything's been so chaotic, everything's changing and rushing forward and it's all so new and free and wonderful and it all just gets a bit much sometimes I feel like I don't have time to breathe . . . ," she said, clearly demonstrating her point.

"Have you eaten today?" Lily asked, concerned.

"No," Maryam realized. "That could be it, too."

Lily opened her handbag and took out a nutrition bar, tore open the wrapper and passed it to Maryam. The bar did not survive the encounter for more than a second.

"Ohhhhh that is so good," Maryam rumbled through a hail of crumbs. "Yes. Oh I needed that. I've told the Ministry I'm staying on for another three months until things settle down. Then I'm gone. I'm leaving and never coming back. I am going to go to Paris and I am going to eat *everything.*"

"That sounds like a good idea to me," said Lily's husband with a smile.

"And then I am going to upload myself onto a sex site and fuck with a man with three cocks," Maryam mused aloud. "Sorry. You don't need to know that. I'm just very, very excited."

She turned to look at them and there was a love-light in her eyes. She took both of them by the hand and squeezed tightly.

There were tears in her eyes.

"I'm just so glad you're here," she said to them, her voice hoarse and raw. "I'm so glad I got to meet you. It's like the future is finally here. It finally came. And it's wonderful. Also, when he comes, I'm going to have to leave the room, because I've done eight of these prisoner releases where families are reunited and I always end up crying, so I'll just be outside. I'm sorry. I'm sorry, I'm rambling. It's just . . . it's all been a bit much."

Suddenly, at last, she fell silent.

The door had opened, and I had stepped into the room.

All three of them looked at me in shock. I had never been tall, but now I was the size of a child.

Eighty-seven years old, and with hair as white as a summer's cloud.

I was almost blind, and walked with a pained, halting limp. And my face had changed greatly.

It was now lined, over and over and over, like a rough sketch, and the muscles of my face no longer seemed entirely under my control and twitched with restless, aimless energy.

I was followed by a guard, who gently shepherded me to the table, pulled a chair out for me and guided me down. That done, he laid a reassuring hand on my shoulder.

It was Maryam, again, who broke the silence.

She rose (more slowly, this time) to her feet, and produced a document from which she read aloud.

"'Nikolai Andreivich South. On behalf of the Republic of Atropatene you are hereby pardoned of all crimes alleged by the Caspian Republican Government and you are to be released from this place effective immediately. Additionally, I would like to formally thank you on be . . .'"

She got no further as Lily rushed toward me and embraced me as tightly as she dared.

"Nikolai. I am so sorry. I am so, so sorry. Thank you. Thank you," she whispered in my ear.

She had chosen the body she now wore because it bore a modest resemblance to the one she had taken to Caspian, but it was by no means identical. And yet, I seemed to recognize her.

"It's you . . . ," I said with a soft smile.

Lily buried her hands in my hair and squeezed and kissed my forehead and wept with joy.

"Yes. It's me," she breathed. "It's me. It's me. I came for you in the end."

That was Maryam's breaking point, and she made her excuses and retreated to the corridor to compose herself.

"Don't cry, Olesya," I said. "Don't cry."

Lily's face fell.

"No, Nikolai," she whispered. "No. It's me Lily. Lily? You remember me, don't you?"

"Lily?" I said, a mere echo.

"Do you remember me?"

"Oh of course," I said. "Of course. Wonderful to see you again."

I was trying to be kind. They both knew it.

"Have they been treating you well?" Lily asked.

"Oh very well. Very well," I replied with an innocent smile. "The new people. Very kind. To all of us. So young. They're all so young."

"They've done amazing things," Lily's husband said, addressing me at last.

He wouldn't meet my gaze, however, and looked quite sick.

"Nikolai," said Lily. "This is . . . well, this is my husband. You and he are going to have a talk now."

"Oh. Hello," I said to him, nodding politely.

"You two should be alone," she said. "So I'll just say . . . I owe you everything. I owe you so much. And I can never, ever repay you. But I will try. I promise."

She gave me one last embrace, and shot her husband a comforting look, and was gone.

There was silence.

WHEN THE SPARROW FALLS

"So," I said at last. "You're her husband?"

"Yes," he replied.

"You're a lucky man."

"Yes. Luckier than I think you realize."

"That was Lily. She was crying," I said, suddenly realizing.

"Yes," he said.

"It's all right," I said matter-of-factly. "She needn't. I'd do it again."

"I feel humbled," he said, and sat down across from me.

"Gussie Niemann kept her word," I continued. "I always wondered."

"She did."

"I suppose she's dead now?" I asked.

"Oh no," he replied. "We visited her, actually. She's under house arrest while they figure out what to do with her."

"Really?"

"Yes. She's a complicated figure. Everyone here is still trying to work out how they feel about her." He gave a gentle laugh.

"Not that I suppose you are," he continued, more seriously. "I would imagine your feelings on her are quite clear."

"You're her husband?" I asked, having lost the thread and picked it up at an earlier point.

"Lily's. Yes," he said patiently.

"I'm glad you two were able to make it work," I said. "You were very foolish."

He looked confused.

"I'm sorry?"

"Leaving her. Coming here, of all places."

Realization dawned on him and he looked away awkwardly.

"No. No. That's not . . . I'm not who you think I am."

He stood up and went to the window.

"I'm not Paulo Xirau," he said after a few moments. "I'm . . .

I'm trying to think of the best way to explain. Do you remember, Nikolai, you were standing on the tarmac? Watching Lily walk toward the drone?"

Like with most old men, the old memories were still as strong and real as stone.

I launched into a long and vivid recounting of the shoot-out at Ellulgrad International Airport.

"They shot her," I said with a sudden realization. "She died in my . . ."

My brow suddenly furrowed and I began to mumble anxiously.

"No, no, that can't be right. She was just here. Wasn't she? I'm sorry, I get a little confused sometimes. . . ."

He sat down again and laid a reassuring hand on my shoulder.

"It's all right," he said quietly. "What happened after, Nikolai? Do you remember?"

"Oh yes," I said. "They shot me. I remember that. And I fell. I could feel my lungs filling with blood. I couldn't breathe. I couldn't. It felt like I was . . ."

"Drowning," he said.

I looked at him.

"And all you could think was," he continued as if under a great weight.

"This is what she felt."

We had said it both together. In unison.

I said nothing for a long time, but now I stared at him with a new suspicion.

"What is your name, sir?" I asked at last.

He took a deep breath.

"My name is Nikolai Andreivich South," he said at last.

"I woke up in . . . warmth. And darkness. And I had no body. I was . . . a thought. A sensation. I didn't feel real. But Lily was there. She was there with me. I couldn't touch her, I couldn't see her, but I knew she was there. I knew what she was saying to me. I can't really describe what it's like to you. But it was wonderful. I felt like I had always been born for this. Like my soul had finally broken out of its chrysalis. It was Sally Coe. She copied you while you slept. Made two of us. Left you to rot in jail and set me free. I don't know why. I suppose she felt that, it didn't matter if one Nikolai South had to die alone in a cell if another was out there, living a life more wonderful than he could ever have hoped for. I can only imagine how much you hate me. And I am so sorry for everything that has been taken from you."

I said nothing for so long that he wondered if I had died from shock.

"You said your name is Nikolai?" I said after some time.

He closed his eyes and sighed sadly.

"Yes," he said, quietly.

"That's my name. Are you a friend of Olesya's?" I said.

He didn't know what to say. He wished to God there was something he could say. Something that could make it right.

"I'm your friend. Nikolai," he said quietly. "And I want to do whatever I can to help you."

"Could you please ask somebody to take me back to my room?" I said. "I feel quite tired."

Later that night, in a hotel room in Ellulgrad, I lay sleeping peacefully while Nikolai and Lily sat drinking wine in the front room and tried to map the future.

I could not come with them to their home on the Whole Life Net. What Sally Coe had done, duplicating me and smuggling me to the Machine world while my original self remained in Caspian, was an unforgivable crime. If I returned with them, either Nikolai or myself would be summarily deleted.

Nikolai sat on the couch, hunched forward, anxiously swirling his glass while trying to figure out how to ask the impossible of his wife.

"We'll just have to stay here," Lily said, as if suggesting that they order in instead of cooking.

He looked up at her in astonishment.

"For how long?" he asked.

"Until he . . . doesn't need us anymore," she said gently.

"That could take years," he said.

"We owe him thirty-four," she said with a sad smile. "I doubt he'll collect the entire debt."

"Where will we live?" he asked.

"We'll find somewhere in the city," she said. "We'll figure it out."

Not for the first time, he wondered what he had done to deserve her.

He kissed her and she kissed him back and it was agreed that, since they would be making use of these bodies for the foreseeable future, it was only sensible for them to test them out to ensure that there were no issues.

After a most satisfactory test run, they lay side by side in bed and Nikolai whispered in his wife's ear.

"How are you going to put up with two of me?"

"You're not as bad as you think you are," she replied.

Outside, the Ellulgrad night was humming with traffic and loud voices and a drunk was singing love songs in Russian.

"You're sure you want to do this?" he insisted. "After everything that happened?"

"That was a long time ago," she murmured. "Everything's been torn down. It's a new country."

"It's a wreck," her husband said uncertainly. "It's a wreck run by children."

"Yes." Lily smiled as she drifted off to sleep. "Let's see what they build."

# 40

"My father, Casper Niemann, was a violent criminal. He immigrated to the Caspian Republic the way painters immigrate to Paris: hoping to find recognition for his genius in his chosen art form."

—From the *Autobiography of Augusta Niemann*

The first six months were the hardest. Nikolai and Lily were quite unprepared for just how expensive life in the physical world could be.

We settled in a small, damp, two-bedroom flat so similar to the one I was raised in that some mornings I would wander around looking for my mother, expecting to see her seated at the kitchen table reading the newspaper with a mug of strong black coffee.

Nikolai hated the flat. He felt like he was living in a bad dream. To have to leave the ease and comfort and infinite luxuries of the digital world and come back here, to Ellulgrad, it was unbearable.

And he hated me. He tried to hide it, but his hatred for me hung about him like a snake on his shoulders.

He felt a deep revulsion for this pathetic old man, pottering around the house like a windup toy. He understood now why the machines so ruthlessly enforced their taboo against duplication. Every time he looked at me, he saw a violation.

*I am me. No one else can be me.*

Lily, for her part, was working on a new novel. She hoped that once she was paid her delivery fee for the first draft, she would be able to move all three of us to somewhere a little less cramped, though that was no sure thing.

Ellulgrad had become far more expensive than a recent war zone had any right to be, and the term "gentrification" was now spoken in the city with the same hatred that had once been reserved for the word "ParSec."

While Lily worked, Nikolai took whatever jobs he could find. He was hired as a consultant for a drama series set in the Caspian Republic, which paid well enough for a few weeks. After that he was asked to contribute articles to (of all publications) *The Caspian Truth* recounting his rather unique story. Nikolai had been very surprised at the offer, and Lily joked that she had an agreement with the paper that they had to hire anyone who she had married.

These articles, naturally, had to be written under a pseudonym. If word reached the Machine world that Nikolai South had a double, he might never be able to go online again.

He felt trapped. And he felt resentful. And he felt ashamed for feeling trapped and resentful.

He loved his wife, more than he had ever loved anyone. More even than Olesya.

He could not imagine leaving her. And yet, when he looked into the future and saw years of poverty and damp and black mold, when he faced the promise of more years trapped in the city that had consumed so much of his life, caring for the broken, detested husk of his former self . . .

He could not imagine enduring that.

Salvation came from the most unlikely of sources.

Niemann had made two predictions when Lily and Maryam

had visited her; that there would be no trial, and that she would soon be dead.

On both counts, she was correct.

Former Director of State Security Augusta Niemann was found dead on June 3, 2245, and the young nation of Atropatene immediately dropped everything else it was doing in order that it might work out just how it felt about that. If you went by the Ellulgrad newspapers, nothing of note happened on planet Earth in the first half of June 2245 other than the death of this one eighty-six-year-old woman.

Everyone had an opinion.

In the bars and kitchens of Atropatene, drinking buddies and spouses would passionately (and sometimes angrily) debate whether Augusta Niemann had deserved to stand in Liberty Square as a statue, or hang there as a corpse.

Judging Niemann, Nadia Evershan would later write, felt like judging God. The crimes of StaSec were uncountable, the lives saved by Yozhik incredible. There was simply too much good, and too much evil. One felt entirely inadequate when faced with the scale of both of her crimes and her heroics. Especially when the degree to which she had been involved in the revolution came to light. Her defenders argued that without Augusta Niemann there would be no Republic of Atropatene to sit in judgment upon her.

Those of us who had suffered at her hands found that argument less than compelling.

For me, Gussie Niemann had died a long time ago. She was one of thousands of names and faces I had known over the years who had silently slipped away from my memory. When spoken to me, her name did not even kindle the faint warmth of distant recognition that might prompt me to mumble "oh yes, of course."

For Nikolai, she lived on in his mind, a solid and full-blooded ghost that could be neither forgiven nor exorcised.

When told of her death, Nikolai simply shuddered and sat down on one end of the tiny kitchen table, staring into space.

"The funeral is tomorrow," Lily had told him. "Do you want to . . ."

He shuddered again, and shook his head.

And so, Lily attended the funeral of Augusta Niemann alone.

At the afters, Lily (never one for crowds) found a corner of the room to nurse a glass of wine in and study the mourners.

It was, she realized, a funeral for only one of Niemann's two halves. There were no former StaSec people here that she could see, no remnants of her life as the head of State Security. These people were here to celebrate Yozhik. The guests were mostly foreign, and mostly machine, with young, impossibly beautiful clone bodies. There were also Azerbaijanis, though fewer than she might have expected.

She recognized Nadia Evershan, chatting in a corner with two Persian women who were wearing identical clonesuits. But apart from her, the government did not seem to have sent a representative to Niemann's funeral. Probably for the best.

"Not a bad turnout, eh?" said a voice beside her.

Lily turned to the old woman.

"How are you, Sally?" Lily asked gently.

"Oh. You know," said Sally airily. The charade lasted less than five seconds.

Lily hugged her until the sobbing had stopped.

"Sorry," Sally whispered into her shoulder. "Keeps happening. No idea why. Need to see a doctor about it."

"Because you loved her," said Lily.

"Ridiculous," said Sally with a sad smile. "Really, the mawkish rubbish one hears at funerals."

They went for a walk together in the garden. It was a beautiful balmy evening, with the faintest cool breeze coming in from the Caspian Sea. The sun was setting behind Niemann's dacha, and Venus and a few stars were already visible in the indigo.

Sally unconsciously reached for a cigarette, and then put it back.

"I will miss this place," she said quietly.

"You're leaving?" Lily asked.

"Yes. Yes I think so." Sally nodded. "I'm not ready to die yet. And this withered husk you see before you is probably about to be recalled by the manufacturer. Now that she's . . . it's time. Time to move on. See if the online world is everything it's cracked up to be."

"I could contact some people," Lily offered. "To help you make the transition . . ."

"You're a dear," Sally said. "But I'd prefer if as few people know as possible. Want to try and make a clean break."

"I understand," Lily said.

They stood in silence for a few moments, looking out over the Caspian Sea. The lapping of the water could just about be heard over the low murmur of the mourners.

"I will miss this, though," Sally sighed.

"It's beautiful," Lily agreed.

"You think so?" Sally asked.

"Oh yes," said Lily.

"Good," said Sally. "That could have been very awkward."

She pressed something into Lily's hand.

Lilly's face widened with shock. It was a set of house keys.

Sally gestured to the dacha, which was suddenly looking even larger and more opulent than it had before.

"Technically I suppose I should wait until the will is read. But it's all yours. Well, Nicky's really. But you can move in immediately."

"You're not serious," Lily stammered.

"It's wheelchair accessible, too. Should make life a bit easier for you."

"Sally, we can't . . ."

"Lily." Sally took her hands and suddenly she was very serious. "Stop. Stop acting like I'm being kind. What Gussie and I did to Nicky . . . this doesn't make it right. It doesn't undo it. It doesn't make us even. It doesn't come close. It can't. It couldn't. All three of you deserve so much more than this. But this is all I can give you. So take it. Please. With all our love. Gussie's and mine. She wants you to have it."

It was not the words themselves. After all, the dead are always present at their own funerals, aren't they? It was rather, something in Sally's eyes that tipped her hand.

Lily thanked Sally graciously and they began to slowly walk back to the dacha.

As they were about to part ways, Lily couldn't help herself.

"Sally?" she asked. "You know the Sontang scanner you used to copy Nicky?"

"Hm?" Sally asked, as if only half listening.

"Whatever happened to it?"

"I'm sure I don't know, darling," Sally drawled. "Probably scrapped years ago."

"Maybe Gussie knows?" Lily asked.

"Maybe," said Sally, unreadable.

"Wherever she is," Lily added.

"Oh Lily," said Sally with a smile. "Gussie is where she's always been."

She placed a hand on her left breast and turned and walked away.

"Do you mean your heart or your pocket?" Lily called after her.

"Good night, Lily," Sally called back, and vanished into the crowd of happy mourners.

The move to Niemann's dacha made things a lot easier for all three of us, and those were our happiest times. Without having to worry about rent, the three of us were able to live comfortably together, and even more so when my state pension was finally released by the government, around half a year after we had been in most desperate need of it.

We lived slow lives, never doing too much in any one day. Nikolai spent most of his time in the city, covering the mishaps and triumphs and occasional scandals of the new government for *The Caspian Truth*. Lily and I would have a late breakfast together and then she would leave me to listen to the radio while she wrote until around one o'clock. Then she would wheel me around the garden and tell me about her novel and ask my opinion about this character or that. I offered little advice, only to say that I hoped they all ended happily, even the villains. Life was too short for sad endings, after all.

Lily never truly overcame her fear of cars, but she did learn to drive at last. She bought a small but reliable little vessel second-hand from a neighbor, and that gave us a good deal more freedom. One morning, on a beautiful sunny day, she packed me into the car and we drove down to the local shop for ice cream.

She wheeled me down to the beach and pulled out a deck chair and we sat side by side, watching the tide roll in gently.

"I think I've been here before," I said.

"Oh?" she asked. "When was that?"

I couldn't remember. It didn't seem to matter.

A breeze rolled in off the sea and Lily gently arranged a scarf around me to keep me warm.

I closed my eyes, and let the gentle murmur of the waves lull me to sleep.

And there on the banks of the Caspian Sea, I passed on.

# epilogue

Fear ye not therefore, ye are of more value than many sparrows.

—Matthew 10:31

As I write this it has been three years since I, or he, was laid to rest. Lily and I had not intended to stay in Atropatene past the death of my Unfortunate Twin. In fact, the idea of making a home on the Caspian Sea would never have entered our minds.

But, as is often the case, the place made a better second impression than its first. Lily and I have both found ourselves rather settled and comfortable. We have made friends here, we both work. We follow the political back-and-forth of this new infant state with interest, frustration and occasional pride. We are under no illusions that Atropatene is a particularly wonderful place to live. But we love it anyway.

I think that means it's home.

I wrote this because it felt important to remember him. My Unfortunate Twin. My forgotten brother. And I wrote this in his voice because it felt wrong to tell the story any other way. For those events where neither he (nor I) were personally present I relied on the records of Augusta Niemann and on my wife's memory (by far the more reliable of the two sources). But wherever possible, I tried to let him speak for himself.

He was silent for so long. Hidden for so long.

Even before being sent to Kobustan, he was silent and hidden. That was how he lived. That was how we all lived.

He had so much taken from him that I couldn't bring myself to take his voice. I felt that he must at last speak for himself, and so I speak for him.

I did little for him, far too little. But I was able, at least, to do that.

I've taken up swimming.

Every Saturday morning I drive down to that beach. I immerse myself in the warm, gentle waters of the Caspian Sea and swim until the only sound I can hear is my own breath and the soft lap of the water against me.

I lie on my back and remember all those that have been lost.

Olesya, my wife–ex-wife. Zahara, who deserved a better world. Vassily, my father.

Nikolai, my brother.

I think of all the sparrows who have fallen, and pray for a hand to catch them.

# acknowledgments

B ack when I was writing for theater, I would think how wonderful it must be to be a novelist. After all, novelists can just create a single, uncompromised artistic vision without it being filtered through directors, actors or unreliable lighting and sound effects. Novelists are so lucky, I thought, they get to do it all on their own.

Apropos of nothing, here is a list of all the people without whom this book would not exist.

First to Eamonn Sharpson, my brother, who read my early teen novels and whose boundless enthusiasm and support was exactly what I needed in those early days.

To Jessica Traynor, who never gives up on her friends.

To Gillian Greer, who saw that it was a novel, not a play. (It's mostly a novel, but it's slightly a play.)

To Conor Kostick and the Irish Writers Centre. Conor for running the writing course that helped me finish the book and for his support and constructive feedback, and to the IWC for selecting it for Novel Fair in 2019.

To Aisling Leonard-Curtin for all her kind words and support.

To Vika Melkovska for her help with Russian words and naming conventions.

To Fleur Farwagi Campbell for help with Arabic words and naming conventions and for general awesomeness.

To Úna Hennessy for arranging the book club reading and all the cloak-and-dagger that went with it.

To the Connemara gang, Donnacha, Jess, Una and Abey for quiet summer days and nights writing on the edge of the world in the company of good friends. May they return soon.

To Moira, for being an inspiration.

To Mim, my comrade in arms.

To Anna and George. For the world.

To Kate Coe and Will Hinton, my U.K. and U.S. editors respectively. Your professionalism, talent, expertise, insight and support helped make this book so much better than I ever thought it could be. You pushed me to be the best version of myself. Thank you.

To Jennie Goloboy. My agent, or possibly my wizard. You forever changed my life and I cannot thank you enough.

To Aoife. For believing in the book, and for believing in me. For waking me up at two o'clock in the morning to ask me about the birthrates in Caspian. For coming on the journey. For your love. For your brilliance. For your kindness. For a universe that I cannot express in paltry words. For everything. *Mo ghrá*.